Noel Primrose was born in Glasgow and lived there until moving south in 1961 to further his career. He now lives in an East Sussex village with his wife, Lynda. He has three children and eight grandchildren. Noel began work as an apprentice with British Railways in 1954, before joining the NHS in 1966, where he became a chartered engineer and rose to board level in 1982, before retiring in 2000. His main interest is his family and being outdoors where walking and gardening are his main pursuits. In the past, he was passionate about running, especially marathons and half marathons. Noel is a keen football fan and follows *Rangers, Liverpool,* and *Brighton.*

This book is dedicated to my darling wife, Lynda, without whose encouragement and assistance it wouldn't have happened.

Noel Primrose

A FALL TO THE TOP

AUSTIN MACAULEY PUBLISHERS™

LONDON ★ CAMBRIDGE ★ NEW YORK ★ SHARJAH

A CIP catalogue record for this title is available from the British Library.

ISBN 9781398440241 (Paperback)
ISBN 9781398440258 (ePub e-book)

www.austinmacauley.com

First Published 2022
Austin Macauley Publishers Ltd®
1 Canada Square
Canary Wharf
London
E14 5AA

To everyone who took time to read early versions of this book, said nice things, or offered constructive criticism; thank you.

Prologue

Central African Republic: 1993

A small SAS group, six in total, under the command of Captain Colin MacKinnon, had been dispatched at short notice to deal with a well-organised rebel group operating in the Central African Republic. Based on what they knew about the operation, the Brits regarded the mission as little more than a good training opportunity with a bit of bridge-building with the local military junta thrown in for political reasons. It was a covert operation, known only to a few of the Republic's high-ranking officers and back in the UK, no-one was saying much about the politics involved. His orders were blurred around the edges, but it seemed to MacKinnon that eliminating the rebels rather than their capture was the preferred option. When he had sought clarification, he had been tersely advised to *use as many bullets as you need to, Captain*.

Supporting MacKinnon was the up-and-coming Lieutenant Jack Somerton, who some considered was a touch cavalier, but he was a proven winner, however questionable his methods.

Local intelligence had identified the general area where the rebels were operating but it took four long, hot, sweaty days through jungle terrain to track them down to the small settlement that they had forcibly occupied and now served as their base. It was highly likely that most of the locals had run away or been driven out and their homes commandeered. The villagers that remained were mostly women, no doubt held captive to serve the needs of the rebels.

MacKinnon's team kept the settlement under observation for a few hours, concluding that the rebel force was around fifteen in number, the locals numbering about eight.

The Brits waited patiently until the rebels were gathered around a campfire for their evening meal, their last meal as it turned out. Somerton called on them to lay down their weapons—not that they were holding any whilst they ate—

then, with minimal delay, instructed his men to open fire. Why give them any opportunity to ready themselves for a fight was his argument.

Eight rebels were killed in the initial salvo, the others scattering away into the huts. A brief fire fight ensued, but the rebels were covered on all sides and lost four more of their number in just a few minutes. At that point, they accepted they were no match for the SAS and a white shirt tied to the end of a rifle was waved from one of the huts. MacKinnon raised his arm aloft. 'Cease fire, men, but remain on guard; open fire if you come under threat.'

Figures were emerging from the huts, the few remaining rebels mixing with the locals; all were looking apprehensively at the bloody corpses strewn around, no doubt wondering what would happen next.

'Looks like we have them all, Jack, no weapons on view that I can see.'

Somerton grunted, 'Well, they wouldn't, would they, not if they want to survive.'

MacKinnon and Somerton had stationed themselves about a hundred yards from the huts. 'Get MacLintock to move forward and check them out.'

Somerton nodded. 'Will do, Colin.' He moved forward to pass the order on to Sergeant Douglas MacLintock, 'Mad Duggie' as he was known in the Regiment, a nickname borne of his heroic efforts over the years. His bravery, his willingness to put his life on the line for his comrades was legendary. There wasn't a man present, including the two officers, who hadn't been rescued from a tricky situation by Mad Duggie. He was well into his forties but showed no signs of slowing down, though in his darker moments, he did wonder for how much longer he could meet the demands of his beloved SAS.

'Sergeant, take Anderson and make sure that lot aren't armed. We'll cover you but be careful, we don't know who we can trust.'

MacLintock nodded. 'Yes, sir. Come on, Willie, let's sort out these bastards.' Willie Anderson was a relative newcomer to the SAS ranks, just 23 when he had joined two years ago. Both he and MacLintock had bonded instantly; the older man had become a father figure to the young recruit.

The two men moved forward, guns at the ready, eyes fixed on the group ahead of them; there was no way of telling friend from foe, villager from rebel, not even the women could be trusted with any certainty. One of the few men started to walk towards them, hands above his head, jabbering in broken English, 'I have information, I can help.' He glanced over his shoulder. 'They kill me if I talk to you.'

Mad Duggie wasn't sure what to do; he was wary of the guy, but enemy intelligence was hard to come by. 'Go get him, Willie, but watch him like a hawk. I'll cover you.'

Corporal Anderson stepped forward quickly. 'On my way, Sarge.' He moved forward a further five metres or so and beckoned the man to approach him. The man smiled and did as he was told, all the time chattering on about "secrets". He was getting too close. 'Stop there and lie down.' The man had ignored the instruction and suddenly rushed towards him.

'Watch out, Willie!' The sergeant's warning was of no avail; the man triggered a concealed explosive device, killing himself and the young corporal. MacLintock looked on aghast as his protégé was caught by the full force of the blast. He had ordered his friend forward; it was his fault the lad was dead. He looked down at the ravaged body—an arm missing, blood gushing everywhere from a crushed torso, the face, what was left of it, was unrecognisable. He had given the order, it was all his fault; hate and revenge surged through him; his friend's assassination could not go unanswered.

'Bastards, terrorist bastards.' He strode towards the onlooking group; whether they were rebels or innocent locals didn't matter, they were all guilty. The group realised instantly what was happening and turned to run away but the distraught sergeant opened fire, gunning them all down before they could reach the safety of the huts. One by one they fell to the ground but it made no difference to the distressed sergeant whether they were dead or dying; he continued firing, riddling them with bullets. Mad Duggie was oblivious to the shouts of his officers and colleagues; the need to avenge Willie Anderson was all that mattered.

The incensed Duggie MacLintock emptied his magazine, reloaded and continued firing; all reason had deserted him. In his mind, they were all terrorists, they were all to blame for his friend's death, he wouldn't stop until they were all dead.

Somerton and MacKinnon rushed forward from their position of safety, horrified by what they were witnessing, shouting as they ran. 'Sergeant, cease fire immediately, that's an order. Cease fire immediately, cease fire.'

At last, the commands penetrated the sergeant's vengeful rage and he stopped firing, turning with vacant eyes, rifle hanging at his side, to face his officers.

'Christ, Duggie, what have you done, man?' Somerton turned to MacKinnon, pausing when he saw the look of anguish on his commanding officer's face. Big trouble lay ahead if news of this massacre got out; MacKinnon was the officer in command, a court martial, a dishonourable discharge, they would throw the book at him. The traumatised sergeant gazed around at the carnage, his staring eyes taking in the fourteen blood-soaked corpses, shaking his head from side to side, totally bewildered. 'The bastards killed Willie, captain. I couldn't help myself. I'll be in big trouble for this, won't I, captain?'

'We'll work something out, Duggie.' MacKinnon reached forwards and squeezed his distraught sergeant's shoulder, taking the rifle out of his hands. 'I understand how you feel; I know you and Anderson were close.'

MacLintock shook his head. 'I'll carry the can, it's down to me; I'll take what's coming to me. I saw Willie go up and I lost it, but those bastards got what they deserved. He was the son I never had. The boy had just gotten engaged; he was going to get wed when he got home; he'd asked me to be his best man. Oh God, who's going to break the news to Cathy?'

'Leave that to me, I'll tell Cathy. Now you go and stand with the rest of the men, sergeant.'

MacKinnon turned to face Somerton and the other four men in his unit. The sergeant was facing a prison sentence, but he knew that it could end his own career if the incident became public. 'What Sergeant MacLintock has done was wrong, very wrong.' He paused, looking at each man in turn. 'Effectively, this incident would be classified as a war crime. We'll be crucified if news of this incident gets out; Duggie would end up in prison, have no doubt about that.' Again, he looked slowly along the line. 'But it's not going to get out. Sergeant MacLintock is one of us, one of the SAS brotherhood; in the heat of the moment, he took revenge for the killing of a colleague under the protection of a white flag. Ask yourselves, who amongst us hasn't felt the same way at times?'

He waited a few seconds to let his words sink in. 'I'll tell you what I'm going to do; I'm going to walk away from here and never mention this incident again and hope I can rely on you to do the same. To do otherwise will condemn Duggie to a lifetime behind bars; believe me, that's what will result from a court martial. I don't want that to happen to a brave and honest soldier and I hope you all feel the same?'

His words sounded sincere and perhaps were sincere, but he was motivated as much by self-interest as he was by MacLintock's plight.

His eyes travelled around the four men, settling on each in turn, getting the response he expected. To a man, they all nodded their agreement, brothers all; in the heat of the moment, who knows what they might have done.

The crisis seemed to have passed but one of the men motioned with his rifle. 'We have a problem, Captain.'

Somerton and MacKinnon swung around to find that a young woman had appeared from somewhere, wailing and crying as she knelt next to one of the bodies.

'What the fuck do we do now, Colin? She probably witnessed everything that happened. Sooner or later, she'll tell some war correspondent and get well paid for it; we'll all face a court martial.' Somerton knew there was only one solution but didn't voice it; he would have no qualms about taking her life. The SAS was his chosen career, it was his life; he wasn't in command, but he was an officer and his service record would be tarnished by the incident if this news got out.

MacKinnon could feel the men staring at him, wondering what would happen next. The men heard Somerton's question and waited for MacKinnon to respond. 'Nothing has changed, I'll talk to her; I'm not going to see Duggie end up in prison. Lieutenant, get packed up, we'll set out as soon as you're ready.'

Somerton held MacKinnon's gaze for a second, then shrugged and turned his attention to the men. 'Two of you search the huts; if you find anyone alive, bring them to me. One of you gather up all the rebel weaponry; MacLintock, you look after Anderson's body, wrap it up in something, we'll be taking him with us when we leave.'

He turned around to see MacKinnon walking towards the distraught woman, momentarily thought about following but his inner voice told him not to; MacKinnon was in command, it was his problem.

As MacKinnon neared the woman, she rose to her feet and ran towards him, her eyes blazing with fury. 'You've killed my father, my mother, my sister, all my family gone. I hate you. I hate you. They were all innocent, British bastards.' Her English was heavily accented but perfectly understandable. She reached him and began to swing punches at his chest and face; he avoided the latter but let her land blows on his body; she needed to vent her anger. He let her continue until finally she tired and sunk to her knees, her energy exhausted. 'You will pay for this, I promise you. I swear.'

MacKinnon reached down and took her hands, pulling her to her feet. 'This should never have happened, I'm truly sorry. The sergeant saw his friend blown to pieces, but he should never have reacted in the way he did. I'm very, very sorry; he will be severely punished for his actions, I promise you. Take me to

13

your hut and we'll talk about how this outrage will be dealt with. Do you understand what I'm saying?'

The woman stared at him. 'There is nothing you can say or do that will help, my family is gone from this world, I am alone.'

'I know, I'm sorry. My sergeant will be punished, I promise. Take me to your hut and I'll bring you some food.'

The woman studied MacKinnon briefly; he sounded sincere, but she didn't trust him; how could she after what had happened. But heartbroken as she was, and with her heart full of vengeance, she was starving and the thought of food brought a moment of calmness. Revenge could wait, she would see that the authorities got to know what had happened. She nodded and turned away, beckoning MacKinnon to follow.

Reaching the small log-built hut that served as her home, she walked through the doorway closely followed by MacKinnon who swung the door closed behind him. His hands were around her neck before she had a chance to turn; she struggled and kicked but was no match for him and her life ebbed away.

MacKinnon was shocked and shaken by his actions; his heart was racing, he had killed an innocent woman in cold blood; it was murder, but self-preservation was what mattered most. He wasn't prepared to sacrifice his career or Duggie MacLintock at any price. She wouldn't have had much of a future, he told himself and who knows, she might have been a rebel and deserved what she got.

He lowered her onto one of the bunks, turning her onto her side to face the wall and was bent forward pulling a blanket over her when the door was pushed open by Somerton.

MacKinnon thought quickly and raised a finger to his lips and stood up, blocking the Lieutenant's view, ushering him back outside. 'Ssssh, she's sleeping, I've calmed her down and told her MacLintock will be punished. I've given what cash I had. There's nothing else I can do. Are we ready to leave?'

Somerton shook his head. 'You can't be serious, we can't leave her here; sooner or later, she'll tell the world what's happened.'

'She won't tell anyone about what's happened. Prepare to depart, Lieutenant.'

MacKinnon's blunt formality told Somerton what had taken place; he wasn't asking any questions, he knew his career was safe.

'What about the bodies, shouldn't we bury them?'

MacKinnon shook his head. 'We leave them where they lie, the rebels wouldn't bury them. If they're found before the animals get them, the Junta will be happy to blame it on the rebels. There's no reason to point the finger at us, we Brits don't do that sort of thing. We'll be in the clear if we all keep our mouths firmly shut and never speak of this incident.'

Somerton shook his head. 'I'm not happy, Colin, the military command know we are in the area and you've just proved that we Brits are as unscrupulous as the rebels. It's a bad business, all our heads on the chopping block, but I'll go along with you.'

'I feel as bad about this incident as you do, Jack, believe me, but I'm not prepared to sacrifice Duggie after all he's done for the regiment over the years. He's saved my bacon a time or two, I owe him and so do you. All for one and one for all, it's a code we rely on.'

Somerton nodded resignedly. 'I guess you're right, Colin; in my heart, I know you're right but it's hard to believe we would do this kind of thing. What about Anderson, or what's left of him? I've assumed we'll take him with us.'

'Yes, we take him with us and bury him well away from here.'

'And you're sure the woman can be trusted to keep her mouth shut?' He just couldn't resist playing with MacKinnon.

'I've told you it's all OK, now don't mention the woman again.'

Somerton shrugged. 'Just wanted to be sure; if the men ask about her, I'll tell them you've, what can I say, sorted it.'

MacKinnon inwardly flinched, *Somerton knew what he had done.*

Duggie MacLintock had insisted on carrying what was left of his friend to his final resting place, a shallow grave marked by a small pile of rocks. The weapons retrieved from the rebels were buried in a deep trench a mile further on. That done, they had tramped on a further three miles before setting up their overnight camp. Next morning, the group marched on a further twelve miles to a suitable clearing before radioing the military, to confirm the rebels had been permanently dealt with and to request an airlift to Bangui Airport.

Two hours later, a helicopter duly touched down and the squad was flown to the airport where they were ushered to a waiting plane and flown home to the UK. Soon afterwards, one of the junta's generals wrote to the Foreign Office expressing the Republic's appreciation of the SAS operation; no reference was made to the massacre that had taken place and the file on the Operation was closed.

As MacKinnon had predicted, the bodies of the slaughtered villagers were found eventually but birds, creatures and general decay ensured that very little could be done to reconstruct whatever had taken place, not that anyone was interested.

During the flight back to the UK, a contrite MacKinnon expressed his deep regrets to Somerton about what had taken place and added that he would give some thought to resigning from the regiment in the not too distant future.

Jack Somerton continued to serve in the SAS and achieved the rank of Major and numerous medals in the course of a dazzling career before he too resigned. He went on to set up a mercenary agency, operating mainly in the Middle East and African trouble spots. He recruited the four soldiers from that fateful Massakori day to join him on a series of lucrative operations.

One of them was subsequently killed when he stepped on a landmine and another died during a fire fight. The two survivors, Mike Davies and Eddie Black, became close friends and were employed by him in a security company he set up to operate predominately in the oil-rich states. Whatever needed done, they would do it. Ever on the alert for business opportunities, Somerton developed his computer skills and knowledge of electronic technology and established a successful company advising on both internet and physical security. His reputation grew apace; if you wanted a problem solved or removed, Jack Somerton was your man.

MacKinnon went on to serve another eighteen months in the SAS alongside Alan Croudace, a mixed-race lieutenant with whom he had many discussions about ethics, morals and politics. Alan went strictly by the book. 'We're here to do a job, Colin; in a nutshell, politicians decide direction, generals give orders, judges hand down justice and we do as we're told within the bounds of the law.'

The pair had formed an unbreakable friendship and it had been Alan who had pointed him in the direction of a career in politics. Listening to the radio, he had reacted strongly to an announcement on the BBC World Service about a treaty between the UK and a notorious African leader. 'Our politicians are a duplicitous shower, one minute they have us fighting those bastards, next minute, we're licking their arses, I hate politicians, sod them all.'

'Calm down, Colin, they have a difficult job to do, they have to do what's best for our country at any moment in time. They have to consider the big picture, peace in the region, trading interests, all that kind of stuff, our focus was much tighter, a straightforward mission.'

'Yeah, yeah, I hear you, but that doesn't make it right.'

Croudace sighed, his friend was on his hobby horse again. 'Colin, listen up, if you think you could do better, why don't you go into politics when you leave the SAS? Your father is a bigwig in the Conservative Party, I'm sure he could find you a safe constituency that would jump at the chance to be represented by someone with your background.'

MacKinnon nodded, a thoughtful look on his face. 'I might just do that. Tell you what, if I do, would you consider joining me, we'd make a good team?'

Croudace had laughed. 'Yeah sure, you go ahead and blaze a trail and I'll await your call. Just remember, Colin, who dares wins.'

Chapter 1
The Beginnings

Croudace's remarks had sown the seeds of his future and shortly after leaving the Army in 1995, MacKinnon pulled the family strings and sought nomination for a constituency. His father's political contacts, coupled with a distinguished military career, ensured his selection as a parliamentary candidate in the Surrey heartlands. He went on to stand for election in a rock-solid Conservative seat in 1996; predictably, he had been returned with a sizeable majority. He hadn't dared to reveal his innermost feelings about politicians to the local Selection Committee; he'd simply told them what he thought they wanted to hear. His personal crusade to reform his Party, and politics in general, would begin after he had taken his seat in the Commons.

Along the way, he pulled strings and called in favours to find a safe seat for Alan Croudace. His friend was understandably sceptical, but he cited their long-ago conversation whilst in the SAS and persuaded Croudace that he needed his sound values and strong ethical beliefs to help him rebuild their nation's standing in the world.

'Pie in the sky, Colin, do you really think we can make that much of a difference?'

'Remember what you said at the time, Alan—"who dares wins". Please, I'm begging you, give it a go; I want you at my side.'

'OK Colin, let's do it.'

MacKinnon desperately wanted a staunch ally to stand with him, to watch his back, and there was no-one better suited to the role than Alan. Together, they bulldozed a path through the political landscape and what a roller coaster of a journey it was. MacKinnon did whatever was necessary to impress the Tory grandees, and along with his father's influence in the background, they ensured that he won the 1999 contest for leadership of the Party. Important achievement as it was, it was just the start of a campaign to reform his Party and win the forthcoming general election.

The country was ready for change, the economy was in the doldrums and sinking fast, unemployment had gone past three million and was rising, relationships with Europe were strained to breaking point, immigration was out of control, the nation was losing belief in itself; the Great in Great Britain was fading away. The UK was crying out for a messiah to lead it out of the political wilderness and Colin MacKinnon, not long past his 43rd birthday, was determined to be that man.

He presented himself as a crusading figure ready to dismantle the established order, willing to challenge political heavyweights at home and abroad, and, ever dear to the hearts of many, lead the UK out of the clutches of the European Union at the earliest opportunity.

People admired his seemingly inexhaustible energies, his plain speaking and his enthusiasm for change. More importantly, the electorate came to believe what he was telling them, no mean feat in an era when regard for politicians was at an all-time low. But the reality was that the Labour Government had a huge parliamentary majority and the prospect of overturning this, and gaining a working majority for his Party, seemed unlikely. His upper-class origins and schooling at Eton followed by Oxford weren't attributes designed to endear him to voters in the industrial heartlands or the Celtic regions.

His detractors and political foes universally referred to him as being another one of the posh boy fraternity and out of touch with the man in the street; to them he was just another Tory destined to favour his own kind, the rich, the bankers, the brokers. But against all the odds, he struck a chord with the electorate and steadily won over hearts and minds; he toured the Labour heartlands tirelessly, nibbling away relentlessly at Labour's lead in the polls. Such was his success, with only a few days to go to election day, some polls put his Party ahead by a few points. The political pundits started to predict a hung parliament. His Party's vote seemed to have plateaued when, out of the blue, came a game-changer.

With Alan Croudace at his side, he was about to go into an important campaign meeting with some of the Party's faithful when his personal mobile buzzed; a number known only to his family and a handful of very close friends outside the world of politics, or so he thought. He pulled his phone out of his pocket and checked the caller display, concerned when he saw it was his wife.

'Hold a sec, Alan, it's Chloe, must be urgent, she knows I've got this meeting. Hello darling, nothing wrong, is there?'

His anxiety was replaced by anger when he heard a male voice; he went ballistic. 'Who the hell is this? How did you get this number? This call is ending now.'

But in that split second, as he was about to press the button, his anger was silenced when the caller said just one word, 'Massakori.'

His thoughts went into overdrive, his stomach churned, he felt like throwing up. Some damn investigative journalist had found out about his Achilles heel, all his hard work, his campaign was about to unravel. 'Who are you?' His voice croaked as he asked the question.

The voice ignored the question, instead revealing details of MacKinnon's life he had long since chosen to forget; it was as though the deepest recesses of his mind had been accessed. If what the caller was saying was made public, his reputation—the one he had painstakingly built—was headed for the shredder.

'What do you want? I won't submit to blackmail.' The words came easy; he would pay anything to keep what the caller knew about him out of the public domain.

He listened carefully as the voice issued its instructions, 'Go to your laptop and switch it on, key in 1993.' The call ended abruptly, no explanation, no goodbyes.

The ever-thoughtful Croudace had drifted away to afford him privacy whilst he was dealing with the caller. *Bless you, Alan.* He beckoned him to his side, his expression revealing the anxiety in anticipation of the conversation to follow.

'Alan, sorry but I can't go in just yet, I have to go back to my office; I'll be as quick as I can. Make my excuses, tell them I'm dealing with a family matter or whatever you think is best.'

'What's happened, Chloe's OK, I hope?'

'She's fine, I can't explain now, we'll speak later.' He was brusque, almost rude but there was nothing he could do in the circumstances.

'Christ, what am I supposed to tell them, Colin? We need these people 100% behind us, you know that. We have an election in a few days in case you've forgotten, and these are the very people who will be out on the doorsteps canvassing for us. Tell me, just what is more important than building their enthusiasm and commitment? Tell me...'

He brushed away his friend's protests and started to walk away, talking over his shoulder as he went, 'I'll explain later, I won't be long, I promise, this can't wait.'

Croudace shook his fist in exasperation, then turned on his heel and made his way into the meeting.

MacKinnon's thoughts were racing as he made his way back to his constituency office, a short walk, less than ten minutes away. Once there, he fumbled with his key as he pushed it into the lock, his hands shaking, fuelled by the apprehension that had taken hold of him.

His laptop was there on his desk, seeming to take longer than usual to fire up. *Please God, not another update.* Suddenly, the home screen was there, he keyed in the four-digit code the caller had given him, his stomach wrenching again with the realisation it was the year of the Massakori incident.

He didn't know what to expect but it hadn't been the grey shadowy male form that filled the screen.

'Good evening, Mr MacKinnon, thank you for making contact.'

MacKinnon was fearful but seething and almost snarled, 'We're alone now, who the hell are you, what do you want?'

'Calm down, Mr MacKinnon, I have a proposition for you.'

'I have to know who you are, you could be a blackmailer, a journalist, any Tom, Dick or Harry.'

'I'm none of those things, Mr MacKinnon, and I'm not going to reveal my identity so let's move on; we both know why you're here.'

'What is it you want of me? This mustn't take long; I have a meeting to address.'

'I don't want anything from you at this time; I want to make you an offer, one I hope you'll accept.'

MacKinnon hesitated, wary but curious. 'Go ahead, I'm listening.'

The mystery man spoke for just five minutes then disappeared from the screen, leaving MacKinnon bewildered, wanting to believe what he had been told but fearful that he was being manipulated in some way by an investigative journalist or some hacker acting for his opponents. Meanwhile, a meeting was waiting to hear what its aspiring leader had to say; he had to get back to the venue; he had an election to win.

Back at the hall, he put a smile on his face as he walked down the aisle through the audience to the vacant seat at the front, apologising for his late arrival as he went. His confidence was returning, his speech was well received, subsequent questions were undemanding and even the still-disgruntled Croudace patted him on the back.

'That went well, Colin, despite your late arrival, I hasten to add. I'm still looking for answers.'

'I'll explain everything after the election, I promise, but for now I need some space to think through an unexpected development.'

'Why is it such a fucking mystery? It had better be good, Colin; I hope to hell you're not in any trouble?'

'No, of course not.' The words came with more conviction than he felt. 'I just need some time to think. Let's leave it for now, please, we both have work to do.'

He had never told Croudace about Massakori and didn't want to, silence was the best option for now. Besides, the conversation with the Mystery Man had opened up a future of unbelievable opportunities, unless, of course, it was just a gigantic hoax.

Chapter 2
Election Night, 2000

The day of the general election arrived at the end of a bitter hard-fought campaign with the main Parties neck and neck in the polls. A hung parliament was widely predicted; the minor parties were rubbing their hands and having internal discussions as to they could work with and their demands for cooperation.

When evening came, MacKinnon's party held the narrowest of leads in the exit polls but with no overall majority in prospect. The projections had the New Conservatives, so named by MacKinnon's marketing people, ending up with most seats but, crucially, without the overall majority necessary to govern effectively. The betting fraternity were offering short odds on a coalition government.

Thankfully, there would be no long, drawn-out teasing announcement of results and changing-by-the-minute forecasts; most would become available shortly after midnight courtesy of the new computerised voting system covering all but a handful of UK's constituencies.

MacKinnon and his wife, Chloe, cast their votes late afternoon, smiling and trying to exude confidence as they stood together posing at the ballot box for the media—a confidence that was paper thin. Immediately after the photo shot, they set out on the journey back to Party HQ in London, to mingle with the faithful and follow events as they unfolded.

When they walked into what was called the control room, there was a ripple of applause, which he gauged as polite, not the rousing welcome he had hoped for. As he stood with his arm around Chloe, he looked around at the gathered throng wondering what they were thinking. Had they concluded he was a winner or were they preparing the last rites for him; he knew that if he lost, there wouldn't be a second chance. A smile flickered across his lips as he pondered what lay ahead; they would have thought he was out of his mind if they'd known he was hoping for a substantial overall majority.

'A penny for them, darling.' Chloe stepped in front of him, staring into his eyes.

She was his rock, his soulmate; with Chloe at his side, he could cope with whatever came his way. He smiled at her, *if only she knew* 'Oh nothing, darling, just wondering what it will be like when we move into No. 10.'

She laughed. 'It'll be an honour, of course, but it won't be like our real home; anyway, you shouldn't be tempting fate, darling.'

'I guess not, but I've got a feeling we're going to win.'

He still hadn't given Alan Croudace an explanation for his departure following the mystery telephone call; it would have been totally devoid of credibility. But he knew as soon as the election was over, he would have to tell his friend everything. He couldn't help wondering if Alan would believe him; he would take a lot of convincing. If the positions were reversed, he doubted he would. But he'd had a brilliant idea and had given Croudace a sealed envelope, making him promise not to open it until they met after the results were declared and verified.

The computerised voting system had been introduced by the previous government and had been a controversial proposal at the time. The voices of doom had had a field day as they always did when any new technological venture of such magnitude was muted. But common sense had prevailed, and after countless debates and numerous amendments, both in the Commons and the Lords, the legislation had passed. To safeguard democracy and ensure the integrity of the system, a stringent verification process was put in place; this would be undertaken by a team of respected expert systems analysts nominated by the three leading political parties.

Croudace had been puzzled by the envelope but had gone along with it. *What are you up to now, Colin? I'm guessing that it has something to do with the explanation you owe me regarding your somewhat irrational behaviour of late, I certainly hope so.*

The Party's makers and shakers had gathered; its chairman, big Tam as he was known, Thomas Ross on his birth certificate, was in whispered conference with Linda Jones, the campaign manager. Big Tam, an irascible Scot, though his constituency was in Yorkshire, owed his nickname as much to his girth as to his near two metres height.

Linda, also a Yorkshire MP, 1.5 metres tall and on the skinny side, was dwarfed by comparison. She was a natural blonde with a camera-loving smile and welcoming manner who said what she had to say in no nonsense terms. The voters had loved her seemingly honest, easy going, but enthusiastic approach to politics. Little did they know that underneath the public persona was a real toughie who dealt ferociously with anybody who didn't toe the party line. She had been the brains behind a superb campaign and would be rewarded when Cabinet posts were being handed out, assuming results went his way.

'Now I wonder what those two are plotting, darling?' Chloe interrupted his thoughts; she had lost none of her Baltimore accent although she had lived in England since their marriage, twenty years previously. Chloe Delmar, as she had been then, had connections to the Kennedy dynasty through her mother's side of the family. She had gained an honours degree in economics at Oxford and had somehow managed to get married and bear two children in the process.

Her transatlantic connections would have ensured that a glittering career in the US lay ahead, but she had fallen instantly in love with the man who was to become her husband. Importantly, her economics credentials had served him well over the years and he was devoted to her. He bent his head and kissed her; whatever happened at the ballot box, she would make it bearable.

Attractive and classy, at just over 1.6 metres, Chloe MacKinnon was petite; a lady of impeccable manners until riled, on which occasions she had a spiteful tongue and wasn't afraid to vent her feelings.

'Lord knows, darling, probably deciding who our next leader will be if we don't pull this off; or else, deciding between them the membership of my Cabinet assuming we get to form the next government.' She kissed him again and broke into a smile. 'You'll win, Colin, the country loves you.'

'The country might well love me, Chloe, but it might not want me to govern it; history is littered with lovable might-have-beens.'

'You're going to win, darling, I can feel it.'

He smiled at her appreciatively. 'I can always rely on you to boost my confidence, sweetheart, I don't know what I'd do without you, of course, we're going to win, there's no doubt about it.'

At that moment, Ross caught his eye and moved towards him, fellow Party members standing aside, like the parting of the Red Sea, to let him through.

'How's it going, Tam?' MacKinnon asked, bracing himself for the reply, good or bad.

'No change, Colin. Based on what we've gleaned from our exit polls, I think we'll win but no sign of clear water so far. There's no need to write your victory speech just yet.'

'Thank you for that reassuring titbit, Thomas; you're such an encouraging chairman when you put your mind to it,' Chloe MacKinnon interjected icily, shooting Ross a hard glare out of her husband's line of vision.

'Just being realistic, Chloe,' Ross replied testily, 'mustn't raise false hopes; I'm sure we'll come out on top, but it's looking like we'll need partners to form a government.'

Chloe MacKinnon summoned a false smile and nodded. 'Of course, I've obviously got it wrong, Thomas.' She knew he hated being called Thomas. 'Here I was thinking it was part of your remit to keep spirits up, rouse the Party faithful and all that kind of thing.' She didn't care much for Ross and their encounters generally had a frosty tone.

Ross's eyes narrowed but he said nothing and turned directly to face his Party leader. 'Just telling you how it is, Colin; I'll keep you informed if there is any change in the current trend.'

As he walked away, MacKinnon frowned at his wife. 'Don't needle him, darling; I have to work with him, and all credit to him, he's good at his job.'

'He's a bumptious sod, I can't stand the man. I do hope you aren't going to find a place for him on the Cabinet?'

MacKinnon raised an eyebrow. 'You know better than that, Chloe, he's too important a figure in the constituencies; I'd ignore him at my peril. Besides, it's best to have him close at hand where I can keep an eye on him and apply the muzzle of collective Cabinet responsibility.'

His thoughts had inevitably turned to the make-up of his Cabinet, though he had tried hard to avoid doing so, not wanting to tempt Fate or annoy Lady Luck; his deep-seated Celtic superstitions did tend to surface from time to time. And it was also the case that some of those he favoured were standing in traditionally safe Labour constituencies and might not win a seat.

Kevin Ogilvie would be his Chancellor of the Exchequer; he'd been a sizeable wheel in the City, an investment banker of some note and one who had repeatedly warned of the financial crash a few years ago. Laura Taylor would be a surprise choice for Home Secretary, an appointment he hadn't discussed with anyone, other than Alan Croudace who had agreed to be his Foreign Secretary. As a trio, they worked together harmoniously and, more importantly, they all had his total trust; they would form the backbone of his Cabinet. A role would be found for Linda Jones as a reward for her campaign efforts; Chief Whip or Leader of the House, the choice would be hers.

Ross would have to be rewarded and would be offered the Local Government Minister post. He would enjoy firing-up those councils sympathetic to his views and riding roughshod over those that weren't. The man in question was pacing up and down in front of the TV screen, grinning like a toothpaste advert and punching the air at regular intervals. Something was happening, something big; MacKinnon eased his way through the onlookers until he was alongside Ross. The computer had done its work, the results were beginning to run across the large TV screen together with a summary of Party gains and losses.

'Good news, Tam? You look excited. Either results are going our way or you've won the lottery.'

'We're on a roll, it looks like we're going to win. In fact, I'm sure of it. I can't believe it but we're taking seats we shouldn't have had a sniff of. Get your acceptance speech ready, you're going to need it. Noddy will be on the blower any minute now to concede defeat.'

MacKinnon frowned. 'Try to be magnanimous, Tam, if it's not totally beyond you. Show the man some respect, he's Prime Minister until the Queen accepts his resignation.'

Ross sniffed. 'Yeah, yeah, load of crap but whatever you say, Colin; going on the results so far, he's a dead man walking and good riddance I say.'

Noddy was how the Press had come to refer to Labour Party's Norman Clarke. In the early days, he had been referred to as Norman the Conqueror, but those days were long gone. A bit of MacKinnon felt sorry for his opposite number; one day he could well suffer the same fate. Conservatives had a history of all too readily thrusting the knife into a loser's back, just as they had done to Margaret Thatcher.

'Let's not forget how quickly political fortunes can change, Tam.'

'Bollocks! To the victor the spoils, that's what I say. You can start thinking about your Cabinet and don't forget about yours truly; I've worked my arse off to win this election for you.'

MacKinnon nodded, giving the Ross physique a pointed once-over. 'It doesn't show, Tam, believe me.'

'Ha, ha, very funny, I must say; I'm glad I make you laugh. Just don't forget the effort I've put into this campaign; our Party constituency stalwarts will expect me to be recognised.'

'Relax; I'll announce my Cabinet, if and when, Her Majesty asks me to form Her government.' *I'm going to keep you dangling and guessing until I'm good and ready.* 'What's your assessment of our likely majority?'

'Fifty as of now, bloody unbelievable, but if this keeps up, maybe even as many as sixty.'

'OK, keep me posted.'

'You didn't answer my question, Colin.'

MacKinnon's eyes glinted. 'No, I didn't and at this moment in time, I'm not going to. Let's get tonight over and done with. I appreciate all you've done, Tam, but you're not the only one who has worked their socks off to win this election.'

Just then Chloe nudged him, her face wreathed with excitement. 'Look darling, look at the screen. Isn't it wonderful?'

He glanced up at the screen just in time to catch the BBC headline flash 'New Conservatives projected to have an overall majority of 70.' He nodded. 'Looks good but it's only a projection, let's not start counting our chickens just yet.'

In truth he was elated, he knew he was going to be Britain's next Prime Minister and with a sizeable working majority; he gave Chloe's hand a squeeze. Over her shoulder, his attention was drawn by the sight of his personal assistant, Jessica Tate, threading her way through the screen watchers, her expression animated.

She was almost breathless with excitement when she reached his side. 'He's on the phone, Colin, Norman Clarke; congratulations are in order, you're our new Prime Minister.'

'Thanks, Jess, I'll come straight away.'

Jessica Tate exercised the quiet command expected of a leader's secretary and led the way, moving people aside to ease his passage, nodding at voices offering congratulations as Party members sensed what was going on. MacKinnon made his way into the Party leader's private office, pausing briefly at its door to look at how bare and simply furnished it was compared to what awaited him in Downing Street. His heartbeat had stepped up a gear and he found himself, for the first time, wondering seriously how well, and how quickly, he would adapt to the responsibilities of being Prime Minister.

Lifting the telephone handset, he suddenly realised that he wasn't sure what to say, but the words came from somewhere. 'Norman, you have my sympathies, it's not been a good night for you.' *Christ, what a tame ingenuous thing to say, he didn't feel in the least sorry.* The conversation was brief, polite and predictable; defeat was acknowledged along with an offer made to meet for a briefing if wanted. Clarke would go to the Queen at the earliest opportunity to tender his resignation. He wished MacKinnon luck. 'You're going to need it, Colin, the country's finances are in the shit; see you at the Opening.' And that was it, handover of leadership of the country was complete.

MacKinnon sat for a few minutes gathering his thoughts before returning to the main room. His appearance brought prolonged applause, applause that was noticeably more enthusiastic than that he'd received earlier. Frequent back slapping and shoulder squeezing punctuated his journey to where Chloe was standing. A chorus of "For he's a jolly good fellow" broke out followed by "Hip, hip, hip, hooray".

He raised his hands for silence and looked around at the sea of smiling faces; the Party faithful waiting for its pat on the head and a victory speech. He grasped Chloe's hand and exchanged smiles, squeezing and holding on to it as he began, 'We've won and won well, our success is down to the efforts of each and every one of you, I thank you all. And I do mean *everybody*, especially those who toiled hard every day of our campaign canvassing for votes, promoting our Party on the doorstep, on the phone and online knowing that most of you never get to share the limelight.

'A general is only as good as his troops, and I've got the best army a leader could have. This is your victory, savour it, but get ready for the hard work and tough decisions that lie ahead. Together, we are going to change this country, make it stronger and better than it has ever been. We're going to make our country one that all its citizens can be proud of; one that offers opportunity for everyone irrespective of colour, class or creed. A country in which all our citizens will enjoy a good, and I emphasise good, standard of living.

'I promise to deliver change quickly; I want this to be a government that history will remember as the one that returned prosperity to all our people, not just the rich and famous. I want our people to stand tall in the world. Most of all, I want us to put the Great back into Great Britain. I'll be trying to have a few words with as many of you as possible over the next hour or so but for now, break out the champagne.'

Chloe hugged her husband as the applause died away. 'I love you, Colin MacKinnon, and I'm very proud of you.'

He nodded, suddenly feeling drained and emotional. 'I couldn't have done it without you, darling, the good times are easy to deal with, but you got me through the bad times.' The words weren't empty platitudes, she had been his mainstay as well as his comforter, she meant the world to him. The public loved her too, admiring the tireless way in which she worked for a range of charities.

She gasped, 'Oh my goodness, look at the screen.' *Clarke concedes defeat. Shocks all around the country as the New Conservatives head for a majority of over 80.* She gave a little skip and hugged him again, excited as a schoolgirl getting ready for her first dance. 'Oh look,' she pointed to the door, 'Abigail and David are here to share your success.'

MacKinnon turned to greet them, arms outstretched, a broad smile relieving the tension he'd felt all night. Abbi was the image of her mother though she hadn't inherited her academic abilities.

'Congratulations Dad, you'll be the best Prime Minister ever, I'd bet on it.'

'Thank you for that totally unbiased vote of confidence, darling; it has indeed been a wonderful night. The results are way beyond my most optimistic expectations. You've heard that Clarke has conceded?'

She nodded. 'Good riddance.' Father and daughter stood looking at each other with mutual pride.

David Singleton extended a hand. 'Congratulations Colin, or perhaps I should say Sir, or Prime Minister; technically, you're my boss now.'

'I'm still Colin to you, except when you're in uniform; on those occasions, you'll have to be impeccably respectful.' Singleton was already a chief inspector with the Metropolitan, a rising star, a chief constable in the making. He was a striking figure, standing 1.86 metres tall with a muscular athletic frame topped out by a handsome open face; his blue eyes and blond hair, which he kept short, suggested Scandinavian origins. Nature had been doubly kind to him and had blessed him with a brain good enough to earn him a first in computer science at Brunel University.

His daughter pulled at her father's sleeve. 'Dad, David and I have got an announcement to make, and this is too wonderful an occasion to miss the opportunity.'

MacKinnon glanced at his wife and winked; it was obvious what was coming next. 'I'm all ears, I can't begin to guess what you're about to say.'

'David has asked me to marry him and I've said yes, and we want yours and Mummy's blessing.'

He summoned up a serious expression and pursed his lips, a thoughtful frown crossing his brow. 'You're barely twenty and I suppose I *should* say that you're far too young; but knowing you, you'll go ahead with or without our blessing.'

She feigned a pout and said, 'True, I am only twenty, but I seem to recall that Mummy was only nineteen when she married you and, more to the point, you were both still at university.'

He turned to his wife. 'Well, what do you think, darling? Shall we give them our blessing?' Chloe MacKinnon beamed a smile and hugged her daughter then kissed her newly acquired fiancé.

Britain's Prime Minister in waiting shrugged his shoulders. 'I guess you have your answer, congratulations to you both.' The two men exchanged handshakes and MacKinnon hugged his daughter. 'There is just one condition; make sure your wedding date doesn't coincide with some vital Parliamentary debate.'

He hardened his expression. 'I warn you, if you don't, I'll ensure David's leave is cancelled and he's put on night duties for a year. Welcome to the family, David, we'll celebrate tomorrow evening; dinner at our place unless you have other plans.' He looked around the room; most faces were pointed in his direction wondering when he would move amongst them. 'Look, I'm sorry but I'm afraid I must break off, duty calls. I've got this lot to wind up and some decisions to make about my Cabinet.'

Singleton nodded. 'Of course, understood, Colin; come on Abbi, let's make ourselves scarce, our next Prime Minister has work to do.'

Chloe put her arms around her husband's neck and kissed him. 'I'll go too, darling, I'll only be a distraction, don't be too late. Forgive me if I'm asleep when you get home, I'm absolutely shattered.'

Chapter 3
The Day After the 2000 Election

He slept fitfully the night of the election, but the adrenaline of newly acquired power was coursing through his veins and he didn't feel a shred of tiredness when he set out for his early meeting with Alan Croudace. Chloe was still sleeping soundly when he left their Surrey home and set out for Downing Street. During the drive, he rehearsed what he was going to tell his friend; he knew it wasn't going to be a relaxed conversation, Cabinet appointments first then his revelations if he felt up to it.

It was going to be the biggest day in his life; he was due to meet with the Queen at 11 am when, in accordance with the Constitution, she would formally ask him to form her government. Outgoing Prime Minister, Norman Clarke, would meet her earlier that morning to tender his resignation.

Alan and he had sneaked into Downing Street using the rear entrance at around 8 am to avoid the media army camping opposite the door to No. 10. Clarke had graciously agreed that they could meet there, but nevertheless, he felt something of an intruder, particularly since the Clarkes were in the process of packing up to move out. He and Chloe were due to move in the following day provided his predecessor had managed to clear the decks.

'That's about it, Alan, we have ourselves a Cabinet, or should I say, Foreign Secretary?'

Croudace smiled. 'I reckon you've got a good balance in the Cabinet, lots of energy and ideas amongst that team, streets ahead of the last lot.'

'Obviously, I agree with you, Alan, but virtually no experience of government. The media is bound to pick up on that.'

'We'll just have to learn quickly and don't forget this is the *New* Conservative Party; we don't want the baggage of old ideas and care-worn experience. In any case, in Opposition we had to do our homework if we wanted to score points off the Front Bench; we've built up a lot of knowledge over the last five years, we'll be fine, I'm sure of it.'

MacKinnon's brow furrowed. 'We can't afford to be too gung-ho, Alan, this isn't a military exercise; we have a whole nation to consider. Millions of people rely on us to make the right decision, many of whom won't have supported our Party.'

Croudace wagged his head mockingly. 'Oh my lord, the gravitas of a Prime Minister. Lighten up, Colin, we have the vision, that's why we won the election. Why do you think we ended up with such a whopping majority?'

MacKinnon drew breath; now was the time to tell the strangest story he would ever tell. He had to trust someone and other than Chloe, he had no closer friend than the man sitting opposite. He hesitated, doubts flooded in, perhaps not now; he would need a goodly amount of time to tell his story and formation of the government team was the overriding priority. They had agreed all the main posts but there were many other ministerial appointments to be dealt with. Any delay would be pounced on by the press and deemed to be dithering or indecisiveness; his revelations would have to wait.

MacKinnon spread his hands on his desk. 'Alan, I'm going to break off now; I have to be at the Palace by eleven and I've got the other appointments to deal with. I know I promised to explain my recent behaviour but now's not the time. How about we meet up tomorrow morning after the inaugural Cabinet meeting? I reckon we'll need about an hour, if you're free.'

Croudace pursed his lips. 'I'm glad you raised it, it's been uppermost on my mind. Don't keep me on tenterhooks, tell me now, out with it.'

'Not now, Alan, tomorrow; all will be revealed tomorrow, I promise.'

The meeting with Her Majesty lasted about twenty minutes and he told himself it had gone well. He was now officially Britain's Prime Minister and the business of government could begin in earnest.

Later that Day

The process of appointing the Cabinet and the array of other posts took much longer than he anticipated; the hellos, the congratulations and the setting of initial objectives and directions had devoured time. Individuals had revealed expectations he hadn't anticipated, and he'd been persuaded to go along with a few relatively minor, but time-consuming changes. But finally, his team was complete, and he breathed a loud sigh of relief as his last disciple left his office; objective achieved, his new government was in place.

He was packing his briefcase in readiness for departure when his mobile buzzed. *Damn.* 'MacKinnon speaking.'

His stomach knotted when he recognised the voice. 'You know who this is, Prime Minister. Be at Clawhanger Colliery at seven tomorrow morning.'

The phone went dead. 'Bastard,' he thumped his desk in anger, 'who the fuck do you think you are.' It was bravado speaking; for the moment at least, Mr Unknown was holding the trump cards.

It was nearing 11 pm by the time he got home, absolutely drained at the end of what had been a long gruelling day. Chloe had left a note, 'Gone to bed, supper under the grill.' He smiled as a thought came to him. *Even Prime Ministers had to deal with domestic realities.*

His spirits lifted and he broke into a smile when it transpired that Chloe was still awake reading when he went upstairs. He felt weary when he slid into bed beside her. 'God, I'm tired, what a tough day it's been, I thought it would never end. Still, it's all done and dusted, and I think we have the makings of an effective government.'

'I'm sure you have, darling, I'm sorry I couldn't wait up, felt the need to stretch out and get myself refreshed for tomorrow's move. I'm so proud of you; I never dreamed that I, an American citizen, would end up being married to the Prime Minister of the United Kingdom.' She drew her breath sharply. 'Does it change anything? I mean, should I become a British citizen? The public might think I should, now that you're its leader.'

'No darling, I'm very happy being married to one of Uncle Sam's daughters; Winston Churchill's mother was an American, so I reckon I've gone one better. I'm afraid I've got an early start tomorrow; I'll try not to disturb you.'

She shrugged. 'You always go out early, darling, what's new? If you ask me, you deserve a lie-in after all you've gone through in the last six weeks. Don't be overdoing it; more than ever, you've got to be on top of your game. When you get to the top, the only way is down; everything you say and do from now on will be put under the microscope. The media has built you up, now it'll want to pull you down; you know the British tabloid press as well as I do.' She let out a deep sigh of resignation. 'So what time do you have to leave?'

'I have to be away no later than six.'

'Goodness, what's so important it can't wait another hour? You deserve a decent night's sleep.'

He hesitated, wondering what reason to give; he had never kept secrets in all the time they had been married and had in fact seldom told her a lie. Without thinking, he said the first thing that came into his head. 'I'm having an early meeting with Alan at his place, away from the spotlight. We need to exchange views on how the Cabinet announcements have gone down. He's my eyes and ears outside No. 10, I rely on him to give it to me straight, not something got up to please me.'

'My God, Colin, you're being paranoid. Alan will be in and out of Downing Street on a regular basis, it's perfectly normal for him to see you here.'

'I know, but it will be more relaxed, no interruptions guaranteed and anyway he's got a tight schedule; an early meeting with his constituency office.' It was always the same in life, tell one lie and another followed. He kissed her, their lips lingering together. 'You worry about me too much. Now I really must get some sleep, darling, I'm exhausted.'

She nodded understandingly. 'I'm not surprised, it's been a jam-packed day for you. I'll leave you in peace but I'm going to snuggle in. You've set the alarm?'

'Yes, I'll be as quiet as I can when I go out. After seeing Alan, there's the first Cabinet meeting and a pile of papers awaiting my attention; it's unlikely I'll see you till late on. I'm afraid I won't be able to help much with the move but, if you do end up with any free time, you can spend it planning Abbi's wedding.'

She grunted, 'Fat chance of that! You know Abbi; she has a mind of her own.' The tone of her voice changed. 'Colin, about Abbi's wedding.'

He held his breath, knowing that she only used that tone when she knew he wouldn't be pleased with the topic. 'Yes darling,' he said warily, 'why do I get the feeling I'm not going to like what you're about to say?'

'I guess because you know me so well. I won't mince about; Abbi wants Lachie to come to the wedding.'

Anger instantly welled up in him. 'Well, he can't and that's the end of it,' his voice blunt, almost vicious.

'Colin please, I beg you, Lachie is her brother, they were always close. You know her as well as I do, she won't let it go.'

'I don't want to discuss this, Chloe, it's a simple choice, him or me.'

'Colin, listen to yourself, please tell me you don't mean that.'

'Try me,' he snapped fiercely. 'I can easily come up with a last-minute excuse for not being there on the day; a sudden major diplomatic incident of one kind or another that only the Prime Minister can resolve with one of his opposite numbers. The Middle East is always good for a crisis. And you never, know it might win me some sympathy votes.'

'You don't mean it, Colin, that's not the real you saying those things.'

'You're wrong on this, Chloe, if Lachlan's there, count me out; end of story. Now let's both get some sleep.'

She knew that further discussion was pointless. Knew too that she should never have raised the subject; it would have been better to leave it to Abbi. 'OK darling, I'm sorry, sleep well, I'll see you tomorrow when you get home. I promise not to raise the subject again, but I can't speak for Abbi.' She kissed him gently and stroked his cheek then turned over and sought the comfort of sleep.

He had a night of broken sleep, his thoughts consumed by his forthcoming meeting at Clawhanger. *Why had his mysterious caller insisted on such a strange venue?* Added to that, he had the inaugural meeting of his Cabinet and the session with Alan Croudace. And, if that wasn't enough, there was potential conflict looming over Abbi's wedding.

It was happening again; his failure of a son, Lachlan, was coming back to haunt him. His good-for-nothing alcoholic, drug abusing, dropout of a son was being resurrected. God knows how many times he'd rescued him from gaol, or literally picked him up out of the gutter before the final major bust up when he'd kicked him out. And not just out of his home, but out of his family and out of his life. It had been the final straw when he'd caught him red-handed stealing from Chloe and subsequently discovered he had been fraudulently writing cheques. His tolerance had been breached irrevocably; he'd consigned his son to the rubbish heap and hadn't set eyes on him since.

It took him ages to fall asleep only to wake at regular intervals and watch the clock tick around until finally, it was time to rise. He disengaged the alarm before it rang and slid carefully out of bed, pausing momentarily to look fondly at his wife; he thought he could see a trace of a smile in the early dawn light showing through the curtains. *I'm sorry, my darling; you're caught in a dreadful tug-of-war of family allegiances.* He pondered on kissing her forehead but didn't want to risk waking her, settling instead for blowing a kiss as he made his way to the bathroom to dress.

Come six o'clock, he was on his way, leaving behind a note for Chloe, 'Hope the move to No. 10 goes well, love you, Colin.' At that time in the morning, it should take less than an hour to drive to the colliery where his clandestine meeting was due to take place. Clawhanger was a disused coal mine in Kent having ceased to operate many years previously; one of the casualties of the Thatcher-Scargill conflict. It was now just a derelict ruin, a sad shadow of its glory years.

Why on earth had he agreed to meet in such a strange setting? Truth to tell, he hadn't been offered an option. Thanks to the wonders of internet mapping, he knew exactly what route he was going to take, and just in case he got lost, his Satnav was programmed ready as backup.

His pulse quickened when he turned down a quiet lane and saw the colliery come into view; he felt like pinching himself to see if he was dreaming. It was as though he had entered some strange fantasy from which he would awaken at any moment.

He parked his car and strode quickly to the main entrance, surprised when he found the high metal gate unlocked. The silence that engulfed the colliery was eerie, he felt like he'd entered a ghost town. Fortunately, the old signposting, though faded, was still in place and as instructed, he headed for the entrance to mineshaft 8. He had only just arrived at the mine entrance when his mobile buzzed. *Bastard must be watching me.*

'Mr MacKinnon, thank you for getting here promptly, time is important to me. You've brought your laptop as I asked?'

'Where are you? I thought you would be here to meet me?'

'We can't meet on this occasion, if indeed we ever do. Activate your laptop and we'll discuss the way forward.'

He did as he was asked and almost immediately, the screen filled with the same shadowy backlit figure he'd seen before, this time sitting at a desk or control console of some kind. Behind the figure, he could make out an array of screens; there must have been at least twelve, all lifeless. As his eyes accustomed to the lighting, in front of the figure, he could just discern a line of consoles, each with a myriad of switches and buttons presumably serving the screens above.

'Why have you brought me here? I could have activated my laptop anywhere; Clawhanger Colliery is not at all convenient for me.'

'Quite simply, I wanted you to be familiar with this site. If we enter into the partnership I proposed, this will be my base. As to your other question, let us just say that there are technical difficulties limiting the distance over which I can transmit vision. This will be resolved in due course. I'm sorry, but could we get down to business, my time is limited.'

MacKinnon's jaw clenched but he didn't protest and for the second time found himself conversing with a grey featureless form that remained seated and made no attempt to introduce itself in any conventional manner. The male voice was the only evidence he was talking to a human. He felt ill at ease and had a sense of being watched. At one point, he gave way to his frustration, 'This is intolerable, I must know who you are, where you are from, why you are doing this and what exactly are you expecting to get out of a partnership?'

His mysterious caller firmly but politely refused to answer any of his questions. 'I meant what I said, Mr MacKinnon, all your questions might be answered in the fullness of time, provided trust is established between us and we can work together amicably and constructively.'

It was a crazy situation; here he was, Prime Minister of the United Kingdom, allowing himself to be pigeonholed by an unknown. There were moments when he felt like walking away but he hadn't, and although he didn't realise it, his future, his family's future and that of the world would be changed.

The meeting lasted forty minutes. The shadowy figure called a halt and within minutes he was back in his car heading back to Downing Street, almost oblivious to the rush hour traffic surrounding him. So deep were his thoughts, he almost put himself into a kind of self-induced trance, his thoughts consumed by the encounter and the future that beckoned. What he had been shown on his laptop, what had been described to him, were miracles of science; the opportunities that had been presented and the undertakings he had been given had almost numbed his brain. And amidst all the mental turmoil, a persistent little voice was never far away. *Why are you risking all on some character you know nothing about, MacKinnon? Is it really for your country or are you mindful of your own personal ambitions?*

The dashboard clock showed 08.25 and the traffic was appalling, five minutes to get to the meeting, impossible. *Shit, I'm going to be late; bugger it, I'll have to phone Downing Street and make my excuses. Alan's going to blow a fuse.*

'Hello, 10 Downing Street, who's calling, please?'

'Alan Croudace, please.'

'I'm sorry but the Foreign Secretary is attending a meeting of the Cabinet, he can't be disturbed. I can—'

MacKinnon interrupted impatiently, 'It's the Prime Minister, get him to the phone ASAP.'

'Sorry Prime Minister, I didn't recognise your voice. Hold please and I'll get him.'

'Colin! Where the hell are you? You're supposed to be chairing a Cabinet meeting, the inaugural meeting of the Cabinet, no less.' Croudace was annoyed and anger laced his voice. 'We're all assembled and waiting for you to grace us with your presence. I was about to phone Chloe.'

Oh my God, that would have been awkward. 'I'll be with you in fifteen minutes, make a start without me; tell them the President phoned me at home.'

'Fuck it, Colin, this isn't good enough, it's the second time you've let me down on the verge of a key meeting. What the hell is going on? When we meet up, you had better have a bloody good explanation.'

'Thanks Alan, I'm sorry, truly. I'll explain everything after Cabinet, I promise.'

'It had better be good, Colin, that's all I can say.'

Following the Cabinet Meeting

Croudace sat opposite MacKinnon, making no effort to conceal his irritation. 'OK Colin, forget the niceties and the whisky for now and come straight to the point. It's not like you to miss meetings or be late for them but you've done it twice now, it's just not acceptable. What in God's name has gotten into you? If you've got a bit on the side, tell me about her and stop seeing her now before it's too late, assuming it's not already too late. Excuses will wear thin and people will start to recognise that your old mate, yours truly, is covering up for you. I don't want that to happen; I've got my own career and reputation to think about, not just yours.

'And while I'm on about your behaviour, you can't just go driving yourself around now, nor can you go anywhere without your personal guard. For God's sake, get it into your head, you're the Prime Minister. So now that I've got that lot off my chest, tell me in words of one syllable what's going on.'

'Calm down, Alan, and I'll tell you everything, but before I go on, let me say up front that everything I will tell you is entirely true. I haven't lost my marbles.'

Croudace slumped back in his chair, eyes wide open and fixed on his colleague. 'Now I am very concerned, please don't tell me you're in a relationship with the Speaker.'

'No, it's much bigger than a mere relationship issue, believe me. We're at the beginning of a new era, a golden era, for this dear old country of ours.'

Scepticism showed in Croudace's expression as he shook his head in disbelief. 'You have my undivided, I'm well and truly intrigued, fire away, I'm all ears.'

'Before I say anything, you must promise me that this won't go any further, it's between you and me only. I haven't even told Chloe. Understood?'

'Scout's honour, I won't breath a word to anyone.' Croudace dropped his voice to a conspiratorial whisper. 'You haven't by chance stumbled across the elixir of eternal life? Bags I some if you have.' His voice was thick with sarcasm, a smirk hung on his lips.

The moment of truth had arrived; once he started, there could be no going back. He told his friend everything…well, nearly everything. There were some things he couldn't reveal, Massakori being one of them.

When he finished, his friend sat in silence for a few moments, unsure how to respond; Croudace couldn't bring himself to believe what he had just heard. 'Colin, old chap, you're right; I do think you've lost your marbles and lost them big time. If I gave any credence to what you've just told me, we would both be consigned to the loony bin. The pressure of the last few months has taken its toll; you've had some sort of a breakdown, old friend.'

MacKinnon's fist thumped angrily on to his desk. 'Fuck it, Alan, there's no if about it, everything I've told you is true, every damned word.' He spat out the words. 'Got it? Got it?' Then he remembered the envelope. 'Have you still got that envelope I gave you before the election? Open it before you say anything else.'

Croudace shrugged dismissively. 'Forgot all about it.' He took his wallet from his jacket pocket and retrieved the small white envelope from within, tore it open and removed the folded piece of paper it held. The message written on it was short: *overall majority 84*. Amazement took over, his eyes visibly widened; his head shook slowly from side to side and his mouth fell open. Bewilderment increased as he read and re-read the message, even his hand was trembling. 'Oh my God, Colin, you don't think your man could have hacked the computerised voting system? Surely that's just not possible? Tell me that's not what happened.'

That possibility hadn't occurred to him and MacKinnon felt his stomach knot. 'I'm not going down that path, Alan; we are where we are and that's an end to it. At least you believe in his existence, that's a step forward.'

Croudace began to protest, 'Colin, we can't just dismiss that possibility, it's illegal, it's undemocratic. We must—'

MacKinnon silenced him waving a clenched fist. 'We don't know the system was hacked, let the monitors do their job, see what they come up with when they've carried out their review. He might just be an expert at analysing public opinion and worked out how the vote would go. We can be good for this country and I'm not letting this chance pass me by.'

Croudace shook his head sadly. 'I don't like it, Colin, don't like it one little bit.'

MacKinnon squeezed his colleague's shoulder. 'Let's give it a try, we can pull out at any time if needs be.'

Croudace thought for a moment, then shrugged. 'On that basis, reluctantly, I'll give it a go.'

The revelations and discussion that followed lasted a full hour. Croudace had been stunned but the note was the clincher; it couldn't be argued with. Still, there were some big questions that required answers, and Croudace had them. 'I'll go along with you for now, Colin, but we're in completely unknown territory; we know virtually nothing about this character or where he's from. All that stuff he demonstrated could be straightforward computer graphics, this could all be one gigantic hoax. Who is he? Where did he spring from? And why choose you, Prime Minister MacKinnon? How did he miraculously set up in a disused Kent coalfield and no-one noticed? Just what is the extent of his capabilities and what is his motivation? If the guy is the real McCoy, he's a genius; so why does he need us?'

'Thank you for all that, Alan. You know I don't have the answers. You're the only one I can talk to about this and although I share your reservations and trust your wise counsel, I intend to go along with him for now. We can pull out of the partnership at any time if it takes a turn in the wrong direction. Alan, I'm sorry to call a halt, but that's all I've got time for; I've got other business I must get on with. We'll meet back here tomorrow morning to agree next steps. We need to be clear what UK Ltd wants out of this partnership. I need ideas please, big ideas.'

Croudace nodded. 'Just bear in mind one thing; we can come up with what we want, but what will your mysterious partner want in return? I must warn you now, Colin, that I won't go along with anything unethical or illegal no matter what he puts on the table and I still have reservations about the integrity of the election results.'

MacKinnon shook his head. 'Fair enough, he's asked for nothing so far, but for sure he's not doing this out of the goodness of his heart.'

His friend nodded. 'You'll have to be on your guard when you meet this guy, you can bet your life that sooner or later he'll want something in return. Whatever happens, be sure we get what we want up front.'

Downing Street, Next Morning

'Coffee's on its way, let's get right down to business. What have you come up with for our friend?'

Croudace shrugged. 'The obvious really; I've focussed on fame and fortune and not necessarily in that order. Seriously, this country of ours needs money, shed loads of it if we're going to balance the books over the next five years; fame has its attractions, but it won't line the nation's pockets.'

MacKinnon nodded but didn't display great enthusiasm. 'Don't undervalue what you refer to as fame, Alan; I want us to be highly regarded in the world, only then can we be truly influential. It seems to me that whatever we come up with must be seen to benefit all of mankind, that way we might get the best of both worlds.'

Croudace grimaced. 'Straighten up your halo, Colin, you're sounding a bit like Mother Theresa; I'm supposed to be the one that's strong on ethics. Let's look after our own people before looking further afield. I know you harbour a wish to establish the UK as a world power again but that can wait, has to wait, leave that to the big players.'

'I'm not disagreeing, I just want us to think big, grab this once in a lifetime opportunity and try to achieve all our goals in one fell swoop. Just because mankind benefits, doesn't mean we can't fill our coffers and eliminate the nation's balance of payments deficit in the process. Between us, we must come up with a short list of ideas to create that golden scenario. So, what have you got that can put UK Ltd on the top of the pile? What will have the world coming to us cap in hand? Something that has the potential to change the course of history?'

Croudace laughed. 'Oh yeah and in the process, just maybe make you, Colin MacKinnon, the most influential leader in the world. Let's keep getting this country out of the financial mire as our top priority, that's why we were elected.'

MacKinnon nodded. 'You can be sure that's my priority but I'm not averse to fame and recognition and I don't suppose you are either.'

'I wouldn't want it to take us over, Colin. I want to be remembered for the right things.'

'Jolly noble of you, my whiter than white chum, voice of my conscience; now let's cut the bullshit and get down to the detail.'

'I'm serious, Colin, the line has to be drawn somewhere.' The grim expression on his face made his feelings clear.

Their deliberations continued for the next hour and concluded with a list of four priorities—energy, security, travel and medicine. All of them had the potential to benefit the whole of mankind and bring suitors, and of course their wallets, to UK's doorstep. MacKinnon eased back in his chair; he now had a clear vision of the way forward.

'Thanks for that, Alan, a really useful session. I think we've taken this as far as we can. The ball's in my court now; it's up to me to negotiate the best deal I can.'

'When are you due to see him?'

MacKinnon frowned. 'I don't know, I have to wait on him contacting me.'

Croudace was visibly surprised. 'Haven't you got some way of getting in touch?'

'Nope, he refused point blank. Just said he would contact me when he was ready.'

'You'll have to insist, Colin, phone, text, email, whatever. He can't have you at his beck and call; start as you mean to go on, it's supposed to be a partnership.'

'I know, but until I know how strong my cards are and find out what he wants, he's calling the shots. When the time comes, I'll fight our corner, believe me.'

At that moment, his private mobile phone rang. 'That must be Chloe, something to do with the move probably or maybe it's our man. Who's calling please?'

The hollow accent-free voice didn't need to introduce itself. 'Are you having a good meeting with your friend Croudace? I suppose you've told him all about me?'

'How did you know I was meeting Alan? Are you spying on me? If you are, I don't like it.'

'Your secretary maintains a computerised diary, I simply accessed it. But you have told Croudace, haven't you? I specifically asked you not to tell anyone of my existence, I'm very disappointed, Colin; it's not a good way to build trust.'

'You're damned right I've told Alan, he's my right-hand man, I'd trust him with my life. I'm sorry I didn't keep my word, but I need someone to confide in, I can't do this alone. I promise you can rely both of us, it won't happen again. No-one else needs to know but I have to have a confidant and there is no-one I trust more than Alan.'

'Just another promise to be kept or broken as you choose, not a good start to our relationship. However, I was sure you would want to involve Mr Croudace, and I understand your reasons for doing so, but it leaves me wondering whether I can rely on you to keep a confidence. You should have asked me before you told him.'

'I've said I'm sorry, but I refuse to take this forward without Alan. I recognise that it is in my interests to keep your existence secret and, as far as possible I will, but who knows what situations will arise in the future. And I have to point out that I had no means of getting in touch with you even if I'd wanted to.'

'I'll grant you that point, and I will provide a channel of communication in due course. Let's leave this business for now, Prime Minister, but always remember, I can be a good friend to you and your country, or I can take my offer elsewhere.'

'That sounds like a threat.'

'Not a threat, Prime Minister, it is the reality of the situation. I want you to meet me tomorrow, same time and same place as before.'

'I'll have to check my diary; I can't just cancel meetings to suit you.'

'You will find that you are free.'

The call ended abruptly.

Croudace looked at him expectantly. 'Well?'

'He's not at all happy that I've told you of his existence, but I think he's gone along with it. He wants to meet me tomorrow, same time, same place; I had no say in the arrangement. Worryingly, he seems to be able to access my computer and no doubt yours as well. We shall have to be careful.'

'Doesn't surprise me in the least, Colin. If he's as clever as he claims to be, hacking our computer systems is probably child's play. Anyway, what choice do we have? We don't know who he is, where he came from or whether he's the genuine article or just some mad computer boffin. For all we know, he could be working for Russia or China. But he's in the driving seat for now and I don't think you have any option but to go along with him until we find out what he wants and if he can deliver on his promises.

'I just hope we end up with some leverage. Be careful, old friend, if this is a put-up job, our heads could already be on the proverbial chopping block. I look forward to hearing how you get on at your meeting but be on your guard; if what you've told me is true, this guy has got more brainpower than an entire regiment. And let's hope and pray that this business doesn't blow up in our faces; we might end up being the shortest government in history.'

Chapter 4
Clawhanger Colliery, the Following Day

MacKinnon's mouth was dry, his pulse racing as he stood at the entrance to mineshaft 8. Nothing had changed since his last visit; the preliminaries were the same, his new partner still wasn't making himself known. Yet again, he found himself engaging in dialogue with a shadowy, shapeless, nameless figure via his laptop screen.

'Thank you for coming at such short notice, Prime Minister; it is necessary, I assure you. Opportunities for us to converse are limited and necessarily of short duration for the time being.'

It may have been his imagination, but the voice sounded weaker than it had at their previous meeting. 'Why is that?' A trace of concern filtered its way into MacKinnon's voice. 'You're not ill, are you?'

'Nothing like that, I won't offer explanations at this time; just accept that I have my reasons and leave it at that.' The voice sounded tired, almost laboured.

'You're sure? I'll help if I can?'

'Please Colin, may I address you as Colin? It's quicker and less formal. Let's get down to business. What are our priorities, what are we setting out to achieve? Have you and your friend Croudace come up with some proposals for us to move forward?'

'I'm happy to be on first-name terms and for the same reasons it would be nice to have a name for you but since you won't provide one, I shall refer to you as Jupiter. I do have some ideas I want to put to you but before that, I must make one thing clear.' MacKinnon took a deep breath. 'It troubles me when you refer to *our* priorities, there can be no question of you meddling with my political decisions or directions; they are exclusively mine to make and mine alone.' At the back of his mind, he'd had a niggling feeling over the last few days that there was a danger of losing any semblance of control if he didn't lay down some sort of marker; it was now or never.

Jupiter sighed loudly. 'I thought we were partners, Colin, working together to help mankind and of course, there is the incidental matter of furthering the United Kingdom's influence in the world, not to mention your own personal ambitions. Maybe I'm wrong about the latter assertions but you'll surely agree that your chances of achieving any of the foregoing are most certainly negligible without my help.'

How the hell do I play this? Do I bow the knee or hold my ground? A change of tone but not direction; be more conciliatory. 'I've obviously offended you, I'm sorry. I know very well that I need your help but, as Prime Minister, I'm answerable to the British people and political decisions must be left entirely to me. Surely you understand that? I very much want a partnership, but it can only be a business relationship, pure and simple, nothing else. You help me, I help you, that's as far as it goes. I can't allow you to be involved in political or governmental decisions. I want to be crystal clear that I'll be running the United Kingdom for the next five years, as far as politics are concerned, it simply cannot be a joint venture.'

His legs were trembling like those of a schoolboy up before the headmaster; he felt like he was standing on the brink of a chasm. An ominous silence filled the air; it felt like a guillotine was paused, ready to fall. The few seconds that passed seemed like an eternity before the reply came.

'*Can't allow me to be involved,*' Jupiter echoed MacKinnon's remark and spat out, 'except, that is, when elections are in progress. Have it your way, Colin, but let me be equally frank. It seems that you envisage a partnership where I am not your equal. Instead, I'll be a junior partner, regardless of what I have to offer. So be it, but to me you are a politician and like all politicians, you seek power and through that power, you desire influence and fame. You assert that what you do is for your country, not for self-aggrandisement; I wonder if that is entirely true. Over time, assuming we continue to work together amicably, we shall see how you deal with what lies ahead. The days, months and years to come will reveal the truth of the matter. I suggest we let this issue rest for the moment; tell me how I can be of help to you.'

MacKinnon breathed a sigh of relief. 'Thank you. I have no doubt that over time we will form an alliance of equals. Before we go further, could I ask that we meet face to face next time? As things are, you are just a voice and it's not helpful to conversation. I'd like to see your reactions, your expressions and have a better idea of how you are receiving what I have to say, it would help to avoid misunderstandings. And, as I mentioned at our previous meeting, in absence of a proper name for you, I shall address you as Jupiter.'

'We cannot meet in the foreseeable future, Colin, accept my word that it has to be this way. In any case, I'm not given to emotions and I rarely display my reactions. As to how you address me, the choice is entirely yours.'

MacKinnon shrugged. 'I don't understand why you won't tell me your name; it looks as though you have something to hide. But have it your way, Jupiter it is for the moment.'

'As you wish.' Somewhat out of character, Jupiter chuckled. 'On reflection, knowing what I do of Jupiter, it might well transpire to be entirely appropriate. Now we really must move on to more serious matters, what you want from me. Please try to be succinct, I can't be with you for much longer.'

What did he mean by Jupiter might be appropriate? 'Why not, where are you going?' MacKinnon barely concealed his anxiety.

Jupiter pointedly ignored his question. 'Come to the point, Colin, what do you want from me? Let's not waste what time we have left on this occasion with unimportant details.'

'Very well, there are four areas of interest to me. Low cost sustainable energy, advanced medicine, ultra-fast travel and global security.'

Jupiter's response came instantly, 'I will not assist you with global security in whatever guise you have in mind, weaponry of any kind is not on the agenda. There is no question of me providing you with a means to kill others. Perhaps at some future date, I'll consider your travel aspirations. You may choose between medicine and energy.'

MacKinnon reacted angrily. 'You're making entirely the wrong assumption. I'm not looking for a means to kill on some grand scale. I really do mean security, the means to make people feel safe and—'

Jupiter interrupted, his voice laced with scorn, 'But of course, what you want is an advanced deterrent that only you could unleash if you or you allies felt threatened, or perhaps if some unfortunate country didn't comply with your policies. The answer is an emphatic no.'

MacKinnon gulped, there was a lot of truth in what Jupiter had said. He had mulled over such possibilities with Alan. *God, I wonder if he can listen in on our conversations wherever they take place.* 'Understood and point taken, it was simply an area of interest. My main priority, if you are willing, is a low-cost, non-polluting, sustainable means of producing energy.'

Jupiter's response came swiftly, 'I'm sure I can help with that, Colin. I suggest we refer to this project as SEG—sustainable energy generation.'

MacKinnon could scarcely contain his joy; it was happening, fame and influence was on its way. A pang of guilt asserted itself as he realised his first thoughts had been for himself not mankind. 'Thank you, Jupiter. Might I ask how quickly you could make such a device available?'

There was a noticeable pause before Jupiter responded, 'I wonder if you have thought this through, Colin, not that I would want to interfere with your prime ministerial decision-making processes.'

'Of course I have,' MacKinnon blurted out the words. 'It's patently obvious that the world needs energy; it's essential to mankind's survival. Current generation methods are either expensive, hazardous or pollute the atmosphere and are irrefutably a major contributor to global warming.'

'Thank you for enlightening me, Colin, I didn't know all that.' Jupiter made no effort to conceal his sarcasm. 'And no doubt the United Kingdom will profit financially from this pseudo-altruistic priority of yours. Let's say that I could make SEG available within months, what then?'

MacKinnon sensed he was being drawn into some sort of trap, his words were hesitant and lacked confidence. 'Well,' he paused, searching for words, 'we would move into full-scale production and market the product as quickly as possible. The sooner SEG is available to the world, the better. What else would you expect?'

'You really haven't thought it through, have you, Prime Minister?' *He had been referred to as Prime Minister, not Colin; Jupiter was making a point of some kind.*

'I'm sorry. I've clearly overlooked something, perhaps you could explain.'

Jupiter didn't hesitate. 'Let's take it step by step, shall we? At some stage you will announce to the world that the UK has invented SEG; a reasonable first step but—'

MacKinnon interjected, 'Of course, that goes without saying.'

'Please let me finish what I was saying, Colin. To whom are you going to attribute this invention of mine? If you involve some compliant scientist, can he or she be relied upon to keep the truth secret? And for that matter, would he or she have the knowledge to explain the science behind this ground-breaking invention. Just how would you explain second-generation helium plasma-based thermal fusion to the world?'

MacKinnon's stomach knotted, as inwardly he conceded the point being made; there was nothing he could say.

Disdain continued to sound in Jupiter's voice. 'And just how do *you* envisage the device being manufactured? Are *you* sure there is a company with the capability, given the hitherto unknown technology it will involve? And even more important, a company that can be relied upon to keep the design secret? Finally, when SEG is eventually sold to the world at large, how will you prevent the device being copied with resultant financial loss to your country? Then of course, as you alluded to earlier, there is the question of what I will want in return.'

MacKinnon was utterly deflated; he hadn't thought the process through. 'You're absolutely right, I've behaved like a bull in a china shop. I'm sorry, you're way ahead of me. What do you suggest?'

A note of triumph sounded in Jupiter's reply. 'I can in fact provide the answers to all these problems.' He paused briefly before scornfully adding, 'Although I wouldn't want to do anything that remotely interfered with *your* political decisions.' Jupiter paused to let his words sink in and having made his point, all too painfully for MacKinnon's liking, continued, 'Firstly, before we can proceed, you will have to build a new facility on this site, one which will incorporate my living quarters, my laboratory and a small production capability.

'Secondly, on the same site a laboratory area will be required to house a team of research scientists. They will work together to invent and discover the innovations necessary to meet your aspirations; the technologies that I make available will be ascribed to this team. My area, of course, will be self-contained and accessible only by me and its purpose known only to yourself and no doubt your confidant, Mr Croudace.'

Relief surged through MacKinnon that it was all going to be OK, but then the thought struck him. 'How will these researchers gain the knowledge necessary to invent SEG? And how can I ensure that they don't expose your involvement?'

'You must leave that to me, Colin; let me assure you that I have the means to enhance their intelligence and direct their thought patterns via their subconscious. They must not, and will not, be aware of my existence.'

MacKinnon was alarmed. 'How will you do that? They mustn't come to any harm, Jupiter.'

'They will come to no harm, I assure you; on the contrary, they will enjoy the fame and respect that will follow in the wake of these discoveries. Their cerebral function must be enhanced if they are to produce the scientific discoveries and breakthroughs necessary to achieve the future you want. Surely you realise this simple truth? How else could they acquire the skills and knowledge required? But you are getting ahead of yourself; before anything can take place, you must bring about the construction and equipping of a research establishment to my specification and put in place the researchers. That done, I will do the rest. I will embed the necessary designs and specifications for the facility within your personal computer. You will require fifteen researchers to fulfil your ambitions; a list of thirty possible candidates will be embedded within your computer for your consideration.'

'My God, how long have you been working on this? You've known all along that I would accept your proposals, how, how…' MacKinnon was absolutely dumbfounded, rendered almost speechless by what he had just heard.

'You sound shocked, Colin, I've simply done what is necessary to meet your aspirations. If you are unhappy with anything I propose, you are at liberty to walk away at any time.'

MacKinnon instinctively felt very uneasy, but he wasn't going to turn down the offer. 'I guess I've got to trust you, but the idea of altering an individual's brain causes me concern. I can appreciate that enhancing their knowledge base is necessary, but I would not wish their well-being to be impaired in any way. I insist that they must suffer no harm.'

'I can assure you that nothing I do will be detrimental to any of the researchers involved. Just consider, for the moment, the possibility that memory capacity can be expanded, that intelligence and understanding can be enhanced within an individual's chosen field of interest. The technicalities of the process are eons ahead of your understanding but can be likened to downloading the best knowledge available at any moment in time from a computer directly into the billions of neural pathways that make up the human brain. It is a process that I personally have benefitted from.

'In simple terms, evolution is being speeded up. The work of such luminaries as Newton, Faraday, Maxwell, Edison, Einstein, Crick, Higgs, Hawkins and hundreds of others condensed into a few minutes and downloaded. I can tell you that there are scientists in the United States, China and the Russian Federation researching this capability even as I speak.'

MacKinnon gasped, 'I'm astounded, I had never dreamt of such a possibility. How have you been able to find a way of doing this?'

'That's my secret, Colin, and one I shall never reveal.'

'Fair enough; there is one problem though, and it's a major problem in the country's current economic circumstances. Getting Parliament to sanction this very expensive facility will be difficult, exceedingly difficult.'

Jupiter all but sneered, 'A political problem, Colin, and, as *you* so emphatically explained to me earlier, political matters are *your* sole responsibility. It's the first real test of our business partnership—you provide the facility and I provide the sustainable energy device. And now I must take your leave, this has taken longer than I expected.' Jupiter's voice was noticeably strained and weary.

'You really don't sound well, are you sure you're alright?' MacKinnon was genuinely anxious.

Jupiter sighed loudly. 'It's nothing you can help with, I'll be OK.'

MacKinnon shrugged. 'Very well but before you go, please tell me how I can get in touch with you if I need to.?'

'Next time you access your personal computer, you will find a password which will provide a channel of communication for urgent matters only.'

'How will you know it's me?' MacKinnon waited but there was no reply; Jupiter had gone.

He didn't know how to feel as he drove back to London, a golden future beckoned but how the hell was he going to persuade Parliament to fund what was certain to be a horrendously costly facility at a time when he was preaching austerity? How was he going to explain to Parliament such a project arriving out of the blue? And of course, assuming it got the green light, its construction would take time, and then there would be a lengthy period of equipping and commissioning. And on top of that, recruiting researchers couldn't happen overnight; thankfully, Jupiter had come up with a shortlist. How had he managed to do that?

He groaned inwardly, difficult times lay ahead but he was determined not to let anything, anything at all, get in the way of SEG. It was a problem he and Croudace would have to solve and solve quickly.

Chapter 5
Prime Minister's Office, Next Day

He met up with Alan Croudace at the end of Prime Minister's Questions, a session made tiring and querulous by an opposition determined to rebuild its credentials following a painful election experience.

'Well? Don't keep me on tenterhooks; I'm gasping to know what went on between you and our mysterious new-found friend. Have you got a name for him yet? Any news on where he's from? I still can't figure out why he's chosen you out of all the world's leaders.' Croudace's eyes were gleaming.

MacKinnon had to laugh at Alan's almost boyish excitement. 'No to all those questions. He's very secretive and refuses to say anything about his background, I've christened him Jupiter to be going on with.' He had pondered all day about how much to tell Alan; the very fact that Jupiter could somehow interfere with the human brain and manipulate an individual's neural pathways still concerned him. As for Alan, with his ethical and moral beliefs, who knows how he might react; the party could be over before it got started. Deep down he knew that he shouldn't sanction such an act, but his concerns were paper thin, he allowed ambition to drive him on. *It's all for the greater good*, he told himself.

He just couldn't be sure that Alan wouldn't adopt a self-righteous stance and veto the proposal. And if he didn't go along with it, what then? In a war situation, it was different; no matter what the folks back home liked to believe, there weren't any limits to what you would do to survive and succeed. But in the here and now...?

'It went well, Alan; we're going to get what we want but there are problems we hadn't anticipated. It's going to take some time to explain and I'm peckish. How about you pop out and ask Jess to arrange some sandwiches?'

'Sure thing, and might I suggest a bottle of bubbly? I think a small celebration is in order, though I have to say you don't seem to be overjoyed.'

MacKinnon shook his head vigorously. 'No, no, I'm fine, really; go ahead and fetch the bubbly. I'm tired and my thoughts are engaged with how we move forward; it's going to be costly and we have virtually no fiscal headroom. Our worthy Chancellor says we're broke, but we must come up with a solution and I mean must. Let's hope the bubbly and the grub fuels the generation of some radical ideas.'

In the outer office, Croudace passed the request onto Jess, bringing a raised eyebrow. 'Celebrating! Might I ask what we are celebrating?'

'Sorry Jess, my lips are sealed, all very hush-hush, my darling. Tell you what, bring an extra glass and I'll pour you some bubbles to compensate. I think a longish session lies ahead, it's best if you can avoid us being interrupted.'

Back in the PM's office, the two men faced each other glass in hand. 'OK Colin, my curiosity is at fever pitch, what transpired? Out with it.'

'First the headlines—we can have our Sustainable Energy Generator, SEG as our friend refers to it. In return, he wants his own secure laboratory area. We'll also need a research facility, equipped with all the latest gear and fifteen researchers. This invention and hopefully others to follow will have to be ascribed to someone, hence the need for a research team and its laboratory. I've got to hand it to the man, he really has covered every angle, I just didn't think through the implications of announcing our new mankind-saving invention to the world.'

Croudace slapped his forehead. 'Of course, why didn't we think through the process, we really should have done. But wait a minute, how are these researchers going to come up with the ground-breaking inventions we're hoping for?'

MacKinnon had reasoned that Alan would ask the obvious and he replied with a well-rehearsed lie, 'Jupiter claims he can implant pathways to a discovery on their computer hard drives. It's all beyond my understanding but he seems to know what he's doing.'

Alan's expression revealed his scepticism, but he went along with the concept. 'Sounds dubious to me, Colin, things don't appear on your hard drive and not get noticed, but if he delivers, who are we to question the science behind it. On reflection, I guess it's a bit like subliminal advertising.'

An hour later, the champagne bottle stood empty alongside an equally empty sandwich tray, but a possible way forward had emerged that might just persuade Parliament to come up with the funds for a new all-singing, all-dancing research centre. But it was problematic; the country had entered a period of austerity, the funds available were limited and earmarked for emergencies; the opposition were certain to object to the proposal. Thankfully, Croudace, good old practical Alan, had a eureka moment and shone a light in the darkness with a single word.

'Security, Colin, that's what we can hang this on.'

'Security?' MacKinnon echoed. 'I'm puzzled, enlighten me, what's the link between security and our multi-million pounds research establishment?'

'National security, Colin, Parliament and the nation's Achilles heel. We can hang virtually anything on security or defence, we've been doing it ever since the Cold War. When we want something of this order, all we have to do is create a major security scare based on internet intelligence.'

MacKinnon pursed his lips. 'Sounds plausible, but what kind of security problem do you have in mind? And I still can't see how it would link to the research centre. We're supposed to be running a tight fiscal economy, Parliament won't go for just any old grandiose scheme.'

'I haven't got all the answers, Colin, but there's plenty of choice. For example, terrorism, espionage, missile threat, cyberspace computer hacking are all possibilities. The list is endless, remember the scare when the Pentagon was hacked? Top of the list is terrorism; Joe Public understands terrorism all too well and I reckon hacking into our defence computer systems would ring all sorts of alarm bells.'

'I can see that,' MacKinnon said tentatively, 'but we can't just summon up these risks at the drop of a hat.'

Croudace nodded. 'I agree, *we can't*, but I know a man who can; an old friend of ours and an expert on security. Someone we both know who'll do what he's told and be guaranteed to keep it to himself.'

'Forgive me, Alan, I'm too tired for guessing games; I haven't the faintest idea who you're alluding to.'

'I had in mind Jack Somerton.'

'Jack Somerton?' With eyebrows raised, MacKinnon's voice held more than a trace of incredulity. 'He was always a bit too cavalier for my liking. I remember him well though we weren't what you would call close friends. He was under my command for a few tours of duty.' *Somerton knew all about the Massakori incident, did he really want Somerton on his doorstep after all this time? Still, the situation demanded action and if Alan was putting Somerton in the frame, he would have good reason for doing so.*

'Forget the past, Colin, we need someone who can think out of the box. Someone who operates in the terrorist environment and knows security systems inside out. Jack fits the bill; he got to be Major before he left the Regiment, ended up outranking both of us. He has a Military Cross and an assortment of gongs awarded by grateful countries around the world; his exploits have achieved legendary status. Back in civvy street, he went on to set up a security company specialising in the provision of both systems and personnel. He very successfully advises all sorts of governments and businesses in the Middle East and Africa, and, does a lot of his dealings beneath the radar. He'd be the ideal man to have on our team.'

'You seem to know a lot about him, Alan, and yet I would put him at the opposite end of the ethical spectrum to your good self. I can't risk any shit ending up on my doorstep.'

'I've kept in touch with a number of our old SAS mates and he often gets a mention; many of them are still involved in both overt and covert security. In fact, I meet up with Jack from time to time, the last occasion a couple of weeks ago. We get on quite well; I rather like the guy though I agree he does sail close to the wind when the occasion demands it. We've chatted about our respective careers and I think he's looking for a new challenge and might even be a bit envious of the direction we've taken. I got the impression he'd like to be doing something for this old country of ours. I think, if you had a role for him, he'd jump at the chance. He's made his pile; money isn't his main motivation now and he's a true Brit through and through.'

MacKinnon shook his head, still puzzled. 'I have to confess I'm somewhat surprised at you two getting along, given that *you* always seek the moral high ground. I would have thought you would steer clear of someone like Jack. As a matter of interest, how come you've never mentioned him in conversation?'

'Well, for one thing, I know you're not that keen on him and you must admit you've never shown any interest in our old SAS colleagues. I do have high standards of moral rectitude but they're not absolute and sometimes compromise is demanded, like now, for instance.'

'True enough. I'm not proud of everything I did, Alan, but Somerton's methods didn't always sit well with me.'

'Come off it, Colin, don't be so righteous from the safety of an armchair. He got results under fire; we all did what we had to do if the occasion demanded it.'

'Maybe, but he seemed to enjoy the brutality of it more than the rest of us.'

'Get real, Colin, he did what was necessary to achieve the objective, no more, no less; we all did, including yours truly, despite my moral rectitude as you call it. He's the man for this job, the more I think about it, the surer I get. We need someone we can trust implicitly, and he gets my vote. Anyway, enough of this pontificating, time isn't on our side and I don't hear you coming up with any better ideas.'

MacKinnon sighed deeply and dwelt on the issue for a few moments. 'You're right, I don't have a better suggestion and we need to move this on. Are you absolutely sure we can control him? I don't want a loose cannon on the payroll.'

'I reckon I can keep him on a tight rein, but we don't want a yes-man in this kind of role; we'll have to trust him if we want to get the best out of him. Look, we've talked enough; it's decision time, what do you think?'

MacKinnon was still wary. 'There's nothing shady is there, Alan? Nothing hidden away in the recent past that could come back to bite us? I can't afford to take this guy on in an advisory role only to see him exposed for some unsavoury dealings by an investigative television documentary.'

Alan answered without hesitation, 'I'm not aware of anything that would be likely to surface but why don't you ask him that question face to face. I'll vouch for his honesty and his loyalty; he'll be straight with us, of that I have no doubt. If you do take him on, he'll need a title and an office base; and I reckon it would be best if he was accountable to me, albeit you'll be pulling his strings.'

MacKinnon was still nervy with the idea of having Somerton on board but couldn't think of a better alternative, and Alan was stepping forward to be the guy's boss—he had nothing to lose. If it went wrong along the way, Alan would have to carry the can. 'OK, I can't come up with a better option as we speak but I'll give it further thought. In the meantime, sound him out but make no promises. Set up a meeting for the three of us and check out his shadowy activities as best you can. There can't be any comebacks if we go ahead, it would finish your career for sure and maybe take me down as well. If we end up convinced that he's the right man for the job, he can name his own salary within reason. I'm totally reliant on you for this one, old friend. One other thing; normally, this post would report to the Home Secretary, so you'll have to clear it with Laura Taylor.'

'I'll ask around to see if there are any skeletons in the closet, though I reckon he would be too clever to leave any evidence of wrongdoing behind, no more than you would. I'm certain he'll come on board if we ask him. Cash won't be an issue; he'll be more interested in the challenge than the rewards. I'll come up with something to keep Laura happy.'

'OK, go to it. We'll have to give some thought to just how much we tell him about what's driving his engagement; I don't want to say anything about Jupiter. And we still need to address Jupiter's request for his own purpose-built environment.'

Croudace nodded. 'I have a glimmer of an idea; our new Head of Security, or whatever we call him, will need a headquarters stuffed full of surveillance systems. It could be attached to the research facility with some linkage made just to make the proposal plausible. Jupiter's base could also be incorporated in one way or another.'

MacKinnon's face lit up. 'Sounds feasible, I like that idea though God know what MI5, MI6 and Cheltenham are going to say about how they relate to this kind of development.'

Croudace waved a hand dismissively. 'They'll huff and puff like they always do but you're in charge and they know it. In any case, they're always claiming that they can't cope with their current workload. By the way, do we know precisely what sort of setup Jupiter requires?'

'Christ, I almost forgot, Jupiter says he's embedded the designs on my computer, God knows how. That's something to watch out for by the way; he claims to be able to access any system anywhere in the world. We'll have to be very careful what we put on record; it wouldn't surprise me if he was listening in on our conversation this very minute.'

'He probably is, so we just have to be sure we say the right things.' He cupped his hand around an ear. 'Are you listening, Jupiter, old boy?' He smiled. 'Seriously, don't get paranoid, Colin, or you'll become a nervous wreck. Get the information downloaded into drawing form and have it available when we meet Jack.'

'Will do, I'd like to study them before our meeting. I'm still not completely sold on recruiting Jack, I still feel we're taking quite a risk.'

'Look at it this way. If you take him on, he'll be based in the new facility and well placed to advise us on its security. He'll keep a lid on what goes on there, preventing any leaks will be one of his major responsibilities. Also, if you appoint him, he becomes our fixer; he arranges construction and equipping through sources he knows to be reliable. Added to that, we might not want full transparency in everything we sanction, our usual route, the Civil Service can be leaky at times.'

Not for the first time, MacKinnon felt his stomach knot. 'I'm beginning to get the shivers about our new Security Chief; he sounds like another J Edgar Hoover.'

'Christ, you are edgy today, Colin. Relax, talk with him before passing any judgements. My guess is you'll like what he has to say. I don't think we can take this any further and I must be going, got things to attend to.'

Prime Minister's Office, 8 Days Later

MacKinnon rose as Croudace and Somerton entered his office, extending a welcoming hand and breaking into a smile that conveyed a warmth he didn't really feel. 'Jack, you look great. Not an extra pound or grey hair to be seen since we last crossed paths. In fact, you look as good now as you did when you were in the Regiment.'

At 37, Somerton both looked and was fit, a testament to his arduous daily workout. A lean, tanned and muscled 1.9 metres, he looked like an athlete in peak condition and he exuded the confidence of a man who was used to getting what he wanted.

'You look pretty good yourself, Colin, for a politician that is, though I doubt you could go ten times around the circuit like the old days.'

'Doubt if I could get halfway around one circuit nowadays, Jack. The odd game of tennis, a bit of cycling, the odd jogging session and that's about it. Anyway, let's leave that for now, take a pew and we'll get down to business.'

Somerton nodded and sat down. 'Pleased to see politics hasn't changed you, Colin, straight to the point. You didn't waffle on in the old days, not like I've seen you do on television of late. I'll take the job. Is that sufficiently direct for you?' He smiled and leaned back in the chair.

'Same cocky bastard as ever, Jack; let's not cut too many corners. I think it merits more discussion than that. You must have questions about the job's parameters?'

Somerton shrugged. 'Alan has explained the situation to me; you want a National Security Advisor and I'm as good as you'll get, probably the best this side of the pond. You want a guardian of the nation's security, someone who can fix and facilitate, overtly and covertly. Someone you can rely on and, more importantly trust, someone who can keep his mouth shut. I'm your man if you want me.'

'That's a very succinct summary, Jack. Now tell me why you want the job; you could probably earn double anything you'll get from me doing what you're doing now.'

Somerton's expression hardened. 'Money isn't the be all and end all, Colin; I've got all the loot I need. I like the idea of being the nation's security supremo and I like the sound of the challenges the job will present. I'll be paid handsomely as a matter of principle, but money is secondary and I'm hoping that I might just end up with a knighthood, like lots of useless civil servants I could name.'

Croudace spoke up, 'I've suggested £180,000 a year plus expenses, Colin, I thought that was fair. You know what the chief executives of public bodies are being paid, this is small beer by comparison. We want the best and I think 180K is a reasonable pay cheque. It's your decision, of course.'

Somerton raised a finger. 'If I might cut in; don't pay me anything for twelve months. Then, if you like what I've done, you can pay me a year's salary retrospectively. If you don't think I'm worth it, tell me to piss off. I shan't take offence, I promise.'

MacKinnon had to smile. 'You certainly haven't changed, just the same confident bugger you always were, Jack. OK, we have a deal, you're hired. Let's shake on it.' He extended his hand. 'Welcome on board, I assume you can start as of now?'

Somerton showed no emotion and simply nodded.

'Right then, let's discuss what's on the agenda and get you started. We're working to a tight time schedule; in fact, there is no deadline other than we just want things done as quickly as possible. The big question is how you can pull it off.'

Somerton shook his head. 'Alan has already briefed me; it's better from your point of view that you only brief me in person when it's absolutely necessary. You need a barrier of deniability between you and me, just like it always was between politicians and the Regiment. Some of the things you'll want done, and how I'll have to carry them out won't always sit well with the Archbishop of Canterbury or your political opponents.

'It's like it always was, Colin, the higher up the ladder you go, the cleaner your hands need to be. I'll take my directions through Alan, then you can sack both of us if an incident becomes too hot to handle. You'll get the credit for the good outcomes, of course.'

That gnawing feeling in MacKinnon's gut started up again. 'You're beginning to worry me, Jack, this isn't a war we're in; we have to draw the line somewhere.'

Alan joined in, 'I second that, Jack, you'll have to operate within the law, give or take a smidgeon.'

Somerton smiled wryly. 'First of all, Colin, it is a war, a war between us and them, whoever them might be. Secondly, *you* may have to draw a line somewhere, whereas little old me can draw it wherever it needs to be drawn to achieve what you want. If you want results, I might just have to ignore the Human Rights Act from time to time. Now, if that's settled, Alan mentioned that you would bring along some plans of my setup. I understand that it's on the site of an old Kent coal mine; I won't ask why it has to be there, that's your decision, end of story.'

MacKinnon's anxiety racked up another notch. 'Please Jack, be careful, don't be too gung-ho; I can't afford too much flak this early in my prime ministerial tenure. I'm still very much the new boy without a track record of any kind.'

'Do me a favour, Colin, I'm always careful, believe me. I don't want to end up in the shit any more than you do. Let's see this plan.'

MacKinnon spread the drawing out on the table. 'That's the footprint we're working to, you can add another floor if you need to. Take this plan with you and have a play; the internal layout and specification are for you to decide along with any security measures you require. Subject to what you come up with, area A on the first floor of the plan is your domain.'

Somerton scanned the layout and scowled, puzzlement furrowing his brow. 'What's going on here?' He pointed at a subterranean area and one at ground floor level annexed to the main building.

'Area B is a top-secret research facility housing fifteen or so of our best young scientists. It will have the capability to manufacture and test experimental devices.'

It was Somerton's turn to display anxiety. 'This isn't germ warfare stuff, is it? I won't have anything to do with it if that's the case.'

MacKinnon was flabbergasted. 'Christ no! This isn't another Porton Down, its function will be to look at how to apply cutting edge science and technology to security, medicine and energy.'

Somerton was puzzled. 'I don't get it, what's on the current agenda that can't be undertaken in our existing research facilities? Universities are stuffed full of professors and experts.'

MacKinnon knew this question would be thrown at him by all and sundry as time went on and had his answer at the ready. 'Area B is going to bring together the cream of young British talent, hopefully unfettered by old university thinking and bureaucracy. That's all you need to know at this stage. It's your job to make sure it's totally secure from cyber or physical attack of any kind from any source.'

Somerton expression hardened in reaction to the annoyance he felt at being excluded. 'A very pat answer, Colin, but I sense I'm not being told the whole story. A State Secret, is it?' His tone was laden with sarcasm.

'You've hit the nail on the head, Jack, a State Secret it is.'

Somerton shrugged and pointed to the drawing. 'And might I know to what use Area C will be put?'

'Area C is to be accessible only by me and the very few others I authorise; as we speak, that doesn't include you.'

Somerton was irritated and showed it. 'You're rapidly pissing me off, there's nothing like making a guy feel part of the team, is there? Are there any other State Secrets of which I should be made aware of, Prime Minister?'

'Not at this time, Jack; with your service background, you should be well acquainted with the "need to know" principle. If you're not happy with my ground rules, best walk away now.'

Croudace grimaced at this blatant bout of arm wrestling, but in the event, he needn't have worried. Somerton smiled broadly. 'Fair enough, Colin, you're the boss, I'll stay on board. In fact, I'm more intrigued than ever.'

'Great. Now what else needs discussion at this time?'

'For one thing, Colin, I need to know what time scale you envisage and what the resource limitations are, both capital and revenue. What support staff do you envisage I'll have, in fact, all the usual kind of things associated with a major project.'

MacKinnon puffed his cheeks and sighed; the truth was he didn't know. The whole venture still had to go through the Parliamentary mill at a time when public expenditure was being cut to the bone. 'Those are questions for you to answer, Jack. When you're ready, come back to me with your accommodation layout and equipping requirements along with your initial thoughts on support staff. I'll need an idea of the costs involved; do bear in mind that times are hard and don't go overboard. I'll have to find the resources and that will be problematic in the current financial climate. I told you earlier about the time-scale, any time after today.'

'I hope I'm not hearing any weasel words, Colin. I wouldn't want to find I'd wasted my time; I don't like the sound of *problematic resources*. But I will come up with the building and equipping specification; it won't be the first security setup I've designed. Staffing is a different kettle of fish though; I don't believe in these tidy pyramid structures beloved of the civil servant fraternity. I go for ad hoc arrangements to meet the needs of the moment and, you must admit, it's not crystal clear what you'll expect of me as time goes by. It would be best if you could build in some flexibility as far as the budget is concerned.'

'Now who's using weasel words, Jack, come up with your best guess. Whitehall budgets can be flexible if we want them to be. Your thoughts on staffing cause me concern; if you don't have a right-hand man, who takes over if you're incapacitated?'

Somerton smirked. 'Thanks for your concerns about my health, Colin, I'm touched. I'll give the matter further thought and come back to you, but just bear in mind, every link in the chain is a potential security breach and much of my know-how is up here.' He tapped his head. 'That's how I work and I'm reluctant to change.'

Alan lent his support. 'He's right, Colin, best if we get this lot operational and then look at top tier staffing in light of experience.'

Somerton leaned back in his chair. 'Based on the scenario Alan described to me, would I be right in saying that Parliamentary support is more likely to be forthcoming if, say the country was in a state of high security alert, perhaps following a significant incident of some kind?'

MacKinnon rolled his eyes. 'Almost certainly, but I can't sit back and wait for an act of terrorism to occur or a nebulous threat to come along; I need to move ahead quickly.'

Somerton looked puzzled. 'I can understand you wanting to make progress but there's a greater air of urgency about this than the scenario as told to me would seem to demand. Add to that the mysterious Area C and I get the feeling I've only been told the absolute minimum. However, I'll drop everything and deal with this project as a matter of urgency. My reading of the situation is that you want me to do whatever it takes to set the wheels in motion.'

MacKinnon glanced warily at Croudace, relieved when he nodded his acquiescence. 'Within the confines of the law, Jack.'

MacKinnon stared momentarily at his Foreign Secretary waiting for a cautionary note to emerge, disappointed when none came. He shifted his gaze to Somerton, waiting for further explanation. Neither man spoke, their faces expressionless.

'Have you two got something in mind? Is there something you're not telling me?'

Alan shrugged. 'I think we have to leave it to Jack to progress this, Colin, we've made our expectations quite clear.'

MacKinnon looked back to Somerton who tapped the side of his nose with his finger. 'Not your concern, Colin, don't forget your deniability shield.'

MacKinnon wagged his finger. 'Be careful, Jack, we're not in some Third World backwater.'

'There, there, dear boy, of course I'll be fucking careful, Colin, I'm not an idiot,' Somerton said soothingly. 'Leave it with me, it'll all work out, I promise. And of course, if the shit hits the fan, take comfort from the fact that my head will be first to end up on the chopping block. That hasn't happened to me this far and I intend to keep it that way.'

That gnawing feeling kicked in again and MacKinnon made to reply, 'But—'

Somerton cut him off. 'Leave it, Colin, please. Terrorism is a dirty business, you know that. Now it's best if I push along and get this baby on the road; I think I'll begin by having a look at the colliery site.' He rose and extended his hand. 'Trust me, I know my business.'

Croudace followed suit and rose to his feet. 'I'll leave you in peace, Colin, duty calls, another meeting.'

'Alan, can I have few minutes of your time before you go? Come back to me when you're ready, Jack.'

Somerton was already moving towards the door; he didn't turn, just waved a backward hand over his shoulder in acknowledgement and closed the door behind him.

Croudace regarded his friend. 'I can almost feel the tension in you, Colin, what's troubling you?'

'Are we doing the right thing? Jack was always an adventurer, a bloody pirate if ever there was one.'

Croudace expressed his exasperation. 'Make your mind up, Colin, his track record is impeccable, we've been through all this. This role doesn't call for a shrinking violet; Jack's SAS record is littered with spectacular results and no failures. He will deliver on this, I promise. I'll see to it that he keeps within acceptable bounds, though I wouldn't expect him to tell me everything.'

'Now you're worrying me, Alan, it's one thing operating on foreign soil but operating on your home turf is a different matter altogether.'

'For Christ's sake, now's not the time to get cold feet; think of what's at stake. This is the biggest prize we've ever played for; it's worth taking bigger risks than we've ever taken before. I'll keep an eye on Jack, believe me; you know my views on where the line gets drawn.'

'I guess so; I'm just not sure Somerton knows where to draw the line.'

Croudace spread his hands and shrugged his shoulders. 'Let's deal with that line of yours in light of emerging circumstances; even for me, the ends can justify the means on occasion, as long as there's no risk to life involved. I really must wander off now; at the end of the day it's your decision to make, Colin. You can call a halt any time you want; just keep in mind what the prize is.'

'Do you have any knowledge of what Jack has in mind, Alan?'

'No idea, he's playing it close to his chest. Leave him to it, Colin, bear in mind what's at stake here.'

When he'd gone, MacKinnon poured himself a large malt whisky, sipping it slowly as he reflected on the meeting. Alan was right, the prize was stellar but what price was he prepared to pay for it? The phone rang, rousing him from his thoughts.

'It's your daughter, Prime Minister.'

He felt his mouth go dry. He knew exactly why she was calling; it wasn't going to be a pleasant call. 'Put her through please.' He drew a deep breath and mustered up false enthusiasm. 'Hello sweetheart, to what do I owe this pleasure?'

'I hope I'm not interrupting anything important, Dad; we can talk another time if it's difficult?' She sounded tense, reluctant even.

'I'm on my own, darling, just winding down so you couldn't have timed it better. Is all well with you?'

'Not really, I'm sure you can guess why I'm phoning. I spoke to Mummy today and she told me how you felt about Lachie coming to my wedding.'

'I'm sorry, darling, I really am, but that's how it is.'

'But it needn't be that way, Dad, I beg you to reconsider. It's my big day and I so much want it to be perfect. Lachie **should** be there and I want him there, he's my brother, he has a right to be there.'

'I know how you feel, Abbi, and I hate to hurt you, but my mind is made up. I'm sorry. You *can* have Lachie there but without me. As far as I'm concerned, he gave up any rights he had with this family a long time ago.'

'Please Dad, please, I'm begging you one last time; you're spoiling everything for me.'

He could hear that she was near to tears. He'd never knowingly hurt her; he felt his eyes moisten at the sadness he was creating but there was no turning back. 'Sorry, I just can't.'

That was it. Without another word, she terminated the call, leaving him holding a dead phone to his ear. *Oh my God, what am I doing, I kicked my only son out of the family and now I'm breaking my daughter's heart.* 'Damn you, Lachie, damn you.'

MacKinnon spent the next hour buried in work and would have carried on but slowly began to realise that his angry mood was influencing his decisions and responses to correspondence to the point of rudeness. He was subconsciously being unfair and uncompromising, pouring cold water on promising proposals and being generally negative. 'Fuck it, this is hopeless, I give up; I'll have to go over everything again in the morning. Curse you, Lachie.'

Chapter 6
Prime Minister's Office

The SAS troika, MacKinnon, Croudace and Somerton, gathered in the PM's office, coffee and biscuits at the ready. On this occasion, decent-sized mugs had been provided for the trio, rather than the customary genteel fine bone china teacups which seemed to empty with a couple of mouthfuls. They sat together around a table where the who's who of British politics had gathered over the ages to mould the nation's future. All eyes focussed on the plans Somerton was pulling from his briefcase and spreading out on the table.

MacKinnon nodded appreciatively. 'I've got to hand it to you, Jack; you don't let the grass grow under your feet.'

'I'm not one of your Whitehall minions, Colin, time is money in my world. In my book, if a job needs doing, it needs doing now, not following countless committee meetings and corridor chin-wags.'

'Yeah, yeah, Jack and I expect the sun shines out of your arse whilst you're working. Let's cut the bullshit and look at these drawings.'

Somerton chuckled, smoothed out the drawings and sat back in his chair. 'There it is, Colin, though with your limited knowledge of security and computer systems, I doubt if it'll draw much constructive comment from you. Obviously, I can't produce any details for the research setup or the mysterious Area C.'

'You weren't required to; I've got the details for those.'

Somerton raised his eyebrows. 'Really Colin, do you mind if I take a look them?'

'Not at all, though I doubt if they'll reveal too much to you at this stage; the room designations aren't shown, and the equipment is just a series of numbered boxes which tie into an equipment schedule.'

Somerton nodded in appreciation. 'My turn to be impressed. I don't suppose you've got a specification for the build; it would be very useful if you have? Might I enquire as to who produced these for you?'

'The answer to your first question is yes, I do have the build specification for Areas B and C, and I've got details of their security requirement. Regards your second question, you don't need to know who produced them.'

Somerton shrugged and sighed loudly. 'I suppose I have to get used to not being told the whole story, but I insist on vetting the security systems, Colin; that's my area of expertise.'

'Your views will be welcome for Area B, the research facility, but Area C is for my eyes only.'

'Bollocks Colin, you can carry this secrecy thing too far. I think that I should have an input into the security system for Area C at the very least; I needn't remind you that security is why you engaged my services.'

'We've been through this, Jack; I thought I made it clear that Area C is off limits to everyone except me and its occupant. It's not negotiable, got the message? I can't stress how sensitive his identity is at this time. Now, do you have a specification for your area and an equipping cost? I need to get a handle on how much the taxpayer is going to have to stump up for this lot. At this stage, the combined estimate for Areas B and C is of the order of £40 to £50 million.'

Somerton grunted, 'Of course, yes to both questions but it's a rough costing, given the time available. I'm still not happy about being kept in the dark; if it goes on like this, I might just jump ship.'

Croudace suppressed a smile; he was enjoying watching his two friends trying to best each other but enough was enough. 'Come on guys, cut the caterwauling.'

Somerton managed a wan smile and relaxed. 'I reckon, including the cost of a high security perimeter fence, improved access and site road works, together with landscaping the whole area, you're unlikely to get any change out of £20 million. Adding that to your estimate for areas B and C, it looks like we're going to hit £60-£70 million for the whole project. And if previous government-run contracts are anything to go by, we could well go beyond that figure. I wouldn't be surprised if we ended up with a price tag nearer to £100 million. Let me manage the project and I'll deliver within the estimate; let's budget for £80 million. I doubt very much if your Whitehall mandarins could match that.'

MacKinnon looked over to Croudace in dismay. 'How the hell am I going to get the House to support a proposal of this magnitude appearing out of thin air?'

Somerton didn't conceal his glee. 'Pleased to say that's your problem, Colin. You're the boss, the cost is the cost, hi-tech equipment is mega-bucks, especially if you want the best. Anyway, you have a healthy majority; issue a three-line whip or whatever and vote it through.'

'It's not as simple as that, Jack; you might be a security whiz but when it comes to politics, you're a novice. I've promised the public an era of open government, added to which, we're going through a period of financial stringency, in case you hadn't noticed.'

'Yeah, yeah, my heart bleeds for you, Colin. It's still your problem; you either want this facility or you don't.'

Croudace butted in, 'Cut the bickering, guys, it's not constructive. I've taken discreet soundings in the House, Colin, and the mood isn't conducive to unplanned expenditure on security, or anything else for that matter. I've spread word around to the effect that GCHQ is overloaded with internet traffic including an abundance of terrorist-generated messages, the majority of which are intended to get us chasing moonbeams.

'I've stressed the risk of our systems being hacked by hostile governments and freelancers and I've laid it on thick that it's only a matter of time before we miss something serious. I've also let it be known that we're worried about current terrorist activity, particularly with a new IRA faction that's appeared on the scene lately. It doesn't exist; it's a figment of my imagination. If I get the right opportunity, I'm going to issue a Red Alert sometime soon.

'You can be sure that searching questions will be asked by both sides of the House when this proposal surfaces; it'll meet with opposition every step of the way. I get the impression that there's an air of complacency around regards security, and in fairness, I can understand their attitude, we haven't had a major event for a quite a while.'

MacKinnon sighed. 'And I guess very few will accept that it's been that way because our security services are on the ball. Damn it, Alan, surely that's recognised?'

'Calm down, Colin, don't shoot the messenger. It's perfectly reasonable for expenditure of this magnitude to be challenged at the best of times, never mind it appearing out of the blue, in the midst of an austerity programme. That is why we live in a democracy and have a Parliament.'

Somerton leaned forward. 'If it's helpful, I've picked up on my network that Middle Eastern groups are in touch with Irish Republican dissidents about attacks on the mainland, so your wishes might be answered sooner than you think.'

MacKinnon had been shocked by the very thought of those two evil factions getting anywhere near each other. 'Where did you hear this? Have you picked up anything on your networks, Alan? This could be the breakthrough we need.'

Croudace was puzzled. 'Not a dickie bird, but I'll check it out as soon as I get back to the office.'

Somerton chuckled. 'Don't bother, Alan, I just made it up. But it's the kind of disinformation we need to put around to create a bit of unease. We need to heighten the general public's anxiety level.'

Croudace laughed. 'You're a bugger, Jack; still, it's not a bad idea, Colin.'

MacKinnon shook his head. 'It's not an idea that's come to my ears, Alan, it's entirely a matter for you and Jack to pursue. I don't think we can take this matter any further for the moment; I'll have to give it some thought as to how we play this. If the House did turn it down, as appears likely, it would be a long time before I could raise the proposal again. Jack, go over your estimates and see if you can achieve any savings; I'll do the same for my areas.'

Somerton shook his head. 'I won't cut corners, Colin, and nor should you; I will have a looksee but the bottom line is, I need what I need, just as you do. There's no sense going forward on this without the right tools to do the job.' He rose to his feet and nodded at Croudace. 'I'll walk you out, Alan; I think we need to discuss how we move forward.' He turned back and winked at MacKinnon. 'Mustn't compromise the Prime Minister, can't have Colin getting his hands dirty.'

Croudace stood and glanced at his watch. 'OK Jack, I can give you ten minutes max before my next meeting.'

MacKinnon watched them leave, his stomach churning. 'Keep me briefed on anything you come up with.'

Somerton halted and turned. 'Deniability, Colin, remember? You don't want to know and don't need to know.'

MacKinnon slumped back in his chair. Somerton was right, of course; he couldn't get too involved. *I just don't trust you, Jack; fuck it, where is this all going to end up? Stop worrying, Colin, Alan will keep Somerton within bounds.*

Somerton accompanied Croudace back to the Foreign and Commonwealth Office building in King Charles Street, confining their conversation to purely social issues. 'Don't discuss any business in the car, Jack, best if my driver doesn't hear anything untoward.'

Croudace's secretary looked up as he and Somerton walked into the outer office, fixing her attention on the latter and liking what she saw. *Hmm, you're a bit of all right, better than most of the Downing Street crew.*

'Jack Somerton, meet Jane Martin, my irreplaceable PA; Jack's helping me with a security issue.'

She extended her hand to Somerton and held his eyes for a fraction longer than necessary. 'Pleased to meet you, Mr Somerton.'

'And I you, Jane. I'm sure we'll meet again; I certainly hope so.'

She smiled broadly and eased her hand away. *I hope so too.* 'You have a meeting shortly, Foreign Secretary.'

Croudace nodded. 'It's logged in, Jane; I'll be as quick as I can. This shouldn't take long, should it, Jack?'

Somerton shook his head. 'Only a few minutes if we're on the same wavelength, Alan.'

Inside Croudace's office, the two men regarded each other; their expressions suggesting that each knew where the conversation was going.

'Just how high are the stakes, Alan, be straight with me?'

'They're as high as they can be, Jack; they may never be higher.'

Somerton raised his eyebrows. 'That bad? I'll start scattering my terrorist threat seeds this afternoon, but run-of-the-mill scare tactics may not be enough. Our Intelligences Services do a superb job dealing with these threats, very little has gotten through the net. We may have to come up with something more dramatic.'

'You've been briefed, Jack, you know the score. Keep it legal; you know my general outlook on how we should conduct ourselves.'

'I do, Alan, and with due respect, I don't think it's an attitude that would get us very far with this situation. Leave it with me; I'll do whatever it takes, all within reasonable bounds of course. Anything else you want to discuss? Is there anything you want to tell me about what's going on behind the scenes for instance?'

Croudace shook his head. 'There's nothing I can tell you, Jack. Good luck with whatever course of action you decide on. I'll see you at the next meeting.'

Somerton shrugged. 'Thank you for that underwhelming vote of confidence, Alan. Enjoy your meeting.'

Britain's Foreign Secretary grimaced. 'Not much chance of that; it's another session of bonhomie and bullshit. Mind how you go.'

'Goodbye Mr Somerton.' Croudace's secretary began to rise to show him to the door.

'As you were, Jane, I reckon I can open that door all by myself, not that your company would be unwelcome in any circumstances. I'm Jack to my friends by the way and I'd like to think of you as a friend.' He winked at her and made his way out.

She watched as he departed, pleased that he had remembered her name. *Hmm, you're a bit different and dishy with it; I wonder if you're spoken for? I'll be more than happy to get to know you better if the opportunity arises.*

Prime Minister's Question Time

The Speaker called on Liz Anderson to open the proceedings, MP for Hounslow, one of MacKinnon's 83 women members. At 28, she was the Party's youngest member and had been one of its poster girls during the election campaign. She really was a looker; her thick fair hair was cut in an attractive short bob with a fringe, but it was her Wedgwood-blue eyes that really grabbed attention. She always dressed smartly, this time wearing a plain black slim-line dress over which she wore a tailored yellow jacket. She wanted to be noticed and was succeeding.

MacKinnon knew what was coming, the Whips had done their job. Not that it had proved difficult; Liz Anderson was ambitious and all too ready to please the leadership.

'Can the Prime Minister advise the House what he knows about the current rumours circulating regarding an imminent terrorist attack? Representing a London constituency, I am all too aware of the devastation caused by previous cowardly and despicable terrorist attacks.'

MacKinnon rose and stepped forward to the dispatch box, his expression serious, his voice grave.

'I thank my honourable friend for raising this issue though I have no details to offer the House at this time. Word has come to us about a rumour, and it's no more than a rumour, suggesting that a Middle East terrorist organisation and an unnamed Irish terrorist group are planning an attack on the mainland. As the

House is aware, it is all too easy for terrorist groups to start these rumours in the full knowledge that they can't be ignored. I can assure the House that our security services are doing everything possible to ascertain the source and authenticity of this rumour.

'Either I or the Home Secretary will report back to the House as soon as more reliable information is received. Our hard-working security services have been put on red alert. I would take this opportunity to confirm that I regularly hold discussions with the Foreign Secretary and the Home Secretary to discuss homeland security issues. We are in fact currently investigating what else might be done to ensure the safety of this nation and its people.'

Alan Croudace nodded vigorously. *Well done, Colin, sow the seeds.*

Will Cotton, Norman Clarke's successor and leader of the opposition, rose quickly to his feet. 'Madam Speaker, the Prime Minister has warned of a possible threat and I'm sure he's right when he says, and I quote, "our security services are doing everything possible". But can he assure the House that what they are doing is enough to prevent an attack and, more importantly, that they have the resources to do so.'

Croudace displayed no emotion, but inwardly he was smiling, the leader of the opposition had asked the question he had hoped for.

MacKinnon was elated; it was all going exactly as planned. 'The Right Honourable gentleman well knows that I can offer no such guarantee, but I can say that we have some of the finest security services in the world and they have my full confidence. Of course, if the Party opposite hadn't left the nation's finances in such a mess, we would have more money to invest to ensure the safety of the United Kingdom. The Chancellor will, of course, keep the resource situation under review and do all he can to provide the security services the necessary resources.'

Will Cotton sprang to his feet again, his mouth open in exaggerated shock. An imposing 1.9 metres tall, he turned to face the Speaker. 'Madam Speaker, I have to point out that it is the Right Honourable gentleman's duty to ensure the safety of this country and, if he is acknowledging that he's under-investing in the nation's security, why doesn't he do something about it?'

MacKinnon leapt to his feet, his face livid with anger, a look he had rehearsed for such occasions. 'Madam Speaker, we can always invest more in security, and in defence, and in education, and in health, but unlike the Party opposite, we seek to balance our priorities within, I repeat, *within*, the resources available. The

Party opposite took the country to near bankruptcy and I have no wish to return to the days when the then government freely spent money the nation didn't have. I will not push the country deeper into debt unless I have no alternative.

'There is very little scope for investment in public services thanks to the profligacy of the Party opposite. If he thinks we should divert resources from the NHS, defence, education or the police services, he should say so. I say to him, live in the real world, the world of austerity that the opposition bequeathed to our hard-working families.'

The House erupted into an uproar of cheers on the government side, boos and catcalls on the other.

'Order, Order.' The Speaker, Theresa Davies, rose to her feet. 'Order, order. Questions and answers must be heard. Will members on both sides stop behaving like unruly schoolboys and conduct themselves in a proper manner? This is my final warning. This session has been particularly noisy and ill-tempered; if this behaviour continues, I will suspend business for the rest of the day.'

Will Cotton bustled forward, a look of feigned exasperation on his face. 'Madam Speaker, the Prime Minister is a master of excuses, how many more is he going to come up with? He can't escape the simple fact that the security of this country and the safety of its citizens is his overriding responsibility. Keep the nation safe, Prime Minister, more action, fewer excuses.'

MacKinnon made no move to reply, he would respond to Cotton when the time was right.

Croudace leaned back in his seat, smiling. *The seeds were well and truly sown, but would they bear fruit? Let's hope Jack can pull a rabbit out of the hat.*

Chapter 7
Prime Minister's Office

Big Ben was striking nine and MacKinnon was going through his mail when the intercom on his desk buzzed. 'What is it, Jess?'

'Eric Fenton is here; he wants to speak to you regarding a personal matter. He says it's urgent.'

Personal and urgent. A tiny alarm bell rang in his head. *Now then Eric, I wonder what you've been getting up to?* 'Show him in, Jess.' He operated an open-door policy and was happy to give members of any Party his time whenever possible.

Eric Fenton, MP for one of the London suburbs, small of stature, with sandy coloured hair and almost angelic features, looked anxious, almost apologetic. He motioned for him to take a seat and he made his way across the room and sat down.

'Eric,' he endeavoured to sound welcoming though sensing from his demeanour that something troubling was afoot, 'nice to see you. What can I do for you?'

'Sorry to disturb you, Colin, something has happened that directly affects you, I'll come straight to the point. I'm not sure if you're aware of the reporting system we operate in relation to the Exceptional Care Protocols?'

MacKinnon almost groaned, ECP was one of the most controversial pieces of legislation introduced by the previous government. Effectively, a patient who had a serious criminal background, or had a history of substance abuse either drugs or alcohol, and had failed to participate in, or respond to, rehabilitation, could be refused exceptional care. They would always receive basic care but not the extremely costly intensive therapy or an organ transplant, if one were needed, that could be used by another patient on the waiting list.

In cases where ECP was going to be invoked, invariably resulting in a reduced chance of the patient's survival, the Department of Health had to be informed. As a safeguard, the Health Minister had the authority to grant an exemption to the protocol where it was thought appropriate.

The proposal had received widespread public support following a series of headline grabbing examples of how the healthcare system was apparently being abused; MacKinnon recalled a tabloid headline that had posed the question— *Should priceless donated organs be given to drug abusers?*

Ex-Prime Minister Norman Clarke had forced the legislation through just before the general election in a belated effort to win votes. He had laughingly told MacKinnon, '*It's a win-win situation for me, Colin; I might pick up some votes and if I don't, you'll have to live with the consequences.*'

'*You're a bastard, Norman.*'

'*Anything goes in politics, Colin, you would do the same. And in any case, the legislation has a lot of public support.*'

When MacKinnon took up office, he had pondered on repealing the legislation but didn't want to look soft and had decided instead to let it run on a trial basis for two years, then carry out a formal review.

'I'm reasonably familiar with it, but Jess said it was a *private* matter you wanted to discuss with me.'

'It is, Colin, very private. I personally review any candidates for ECP as one of my first daily chores, just to make sure there are no names on the list that might produce adverse headlines for the Party. I don't feel confident that my staff will always pick up on the political angle. There were four names on today's list, one of them raised my concerns. I investigated further and what I've found brings me here. I'm not quite sure how I should proceed, and I'd welcome your guidance.'

'You have my full attention, Eric, but really, if you are in any doubt, shouldn't you speak to Laura Denton? She is the Secretary of State and I don't want to tread on her toes. If all the criteria are fulfilled, the protocols prescribed by the Act should be applied.'

'And normally they would be, Colin, I assure you, but the name I'm referring to is Lachlan MacKinnon, who I believe to be your son. As I speak, he's in Guy's Intensive Care Unit, condition critical, a liver and kidney transplant are essential if he's to live. I've covertly ascertained that he could be kept alive long enough to receive a donor organ, provided, of course, he isn't ruled out by the Exceptional Care Protocols.'

MacKinnon's brain cells started whirring, this was a potential minefield. 'I see. In effect you're asking me if I should exempt my son from the protocols?'

'That's about it, Colin; I'm sorry to say it, but Lachlan has an abysmal history of drug and alcohol abuse and under the terms of the protocols wouldn't qualify for further treatment. But I can intervene if I choose to.' He sat back in the chair and stared into MacKinnon's eyes. 'It would all be handled very discretely; no-one need know of his relationship to you. We do let a few cases go through for monitoring purposes, a final chance for those selected; we record the outcomes and will refer to them when we come to review the legislation. I do have to make it clear that, given his deplorable record, Lachlan would not come anywhere near qualifying for a transplant.'

MacKinnon tried not to show it, but he was struggling with the dilemma presented to him. *He's my son! I should intervene to save him but what would the media make of it? If my intervention came to light, I'd be crucified but if I don't intervene, the same fate awaits me. I'll be damned if I do and damned if I don't. But there was a bright side to my dilemma; Fate was handing me an opportunity to get rid of a recurring thorn in my flesh. Lachie had damaged my public standing in the past; fingers of blame for his wrongdoings had been pointed at me, as his father, for reasons I never understood. Lachie had always been a divisive force in the family, he deserved all the misfortunes that had befallen him. And now, it seemed, Fate was giving me an opportunity to eliminate him from my family once and for all.*

MacKinnon summoned up a pained expression. 'I don't see how I can make him an exception, Eric. If word got out, there would be a public outcry and the opposition would crucify us.'

'But he's your son!' Fenton sounded incredulous. 'I promise you no-one need ever know you intervened. It's possible that I might be questioned but I would firmly deny knowing that he was your son. This conversation never took place, you can rely on my utmost discretion.'

Of course, unless, that is, it suited your career to do otherwise. MacKinnon put on his best holier-than-thou voice, shaking his head with due solemnity. 'I'm Prime Minister, Eric, I can't just favour my own kin when I feel like it. I would know, even if nobody else did, it's morally indefensible; everyone caught by ECP is someone's son or daughter.'

Fenton made no effort to hide his surprise. 'Come off it, Colin, we all do favours when it suits us. Your predecessors certainly did, as well you know. This is your son we're talking about; you will be sentencing him to death if you don't intervene.'

MacKinnon mustered his self-righteous tone. 'You don't need to rub it in, Eric; I'd just remind you that we promised to put an end to politicians feathering their own nests. I got elected promising to clean up politics. If it came out that I was favouring my own son, every promise I made would be devalued. Thank you though, I appreciate you coming to see me, I really mean that. You've given me something to think about; can I have the weekend to mull it over, it's the least I can do. I assume he'll last that long?'

Fenton shrugged; he was clearly having difficulty coming to terms with MacKinnon's position. 'Should do, but it's not really for me to say; I'll ask the clinicians involved if you wish?'

'No, don't do that, it might raise suspicion. Are you absolutely sure no-one else is on to this?'

'As certain as I can be, Colin, the name MacKinnon isn't uncommon; I was just being super-cautious when I checked it out.'

'Keep it to yourself, Eric, strictly between you and me. Come and see me on Monday at 8 am if you're free. Your discretion really is appreciated, I shan't forget it.'

'No problem, Colin. I'll see you on Monday.'

MacKinnon poured himself a malt whisky and began to think about how he should manage the situation. *In his heart of hearts, he knew he wasn't going to change his mind; he was going to let his son die and get him out of his hair once and for all. Damn you, Lachie, for putting me in this position, why couldn't you just crawl off and die in an alley somewhere?* Then suddenly, out of the blue, he knew exactly how he was going to take advantage of this stroke of good fortune.

Later that Day

MacKinnon poured a malt, savoured every sip, then picked up the phone and dialled Chloe. 'Darling, how goes the day?'

78

'It goes well, Colin.' She was hesitant; social calls from her husband were not the norm when he was at work. 'Now I'm sure you haven't called just to ask me how my day's been, tell me why you've really phoned.'

'This situation with Abbi weighs heavy on me, I'd like to resolve it if possible. I'd like you to ask her and David to lunch on Sunday, it's time to mend fences.'

Chloe sighed deeply. 'I'll try but she's not in the most receptive of moods these days. There's only one thing she wants to hear from you.'

'I know, but please do your best, darling. See you tonight, I promise I won't be late.'

A short time later, his private mobile vibrated, his spirits lifted. *Good, that must be Chloe about Sunday.* 'Hello darling, that was quick.'

'You're mistaken, Prime Minister, it's not Mrs MacKinnon.' There was no mistaking Jupiter.

'Sorry, I was expecting a call from my wife; I didn't think we were due to talk, I haven't been able to put the matter of the facility to the House yet; the circumstances aren't right.'

'That's not why I'm in contact. I just thought that I should let you know that when you access your computer, you'll find a list of thirty names.'

'Names, what names?'

'The names of candidates I'm putting forward for your research facility. All of them are technically qualified to deal with what lies ahead.'

'That's a lot more than I envisaged.'

'Look upon it as a long shortlist, you'll need at least three from each of the five academic categories we require.'

'But we haven't talked this through, it's not just a straightforward matter of recruitment; there are security issues to be considered and the confidential nature of the situation.'

'I have to remind you that it was me who first alerted you to the security risks associated with the SEG project. Do some background research, Prime Minister, then we'll talk further. By the way, I would just mention that there are no records of our telephone calls or retention of our communications on your computer hard drive. There is nothing whatsoever to show that I exist. I'll contact you in a week or so when you've made progress. Goodbye.'

As ever, MacKinnon was impressed at Jupiter's scientific prowess. He moved over to his computer and typed in the code. There were indeed thirty names along with their place of residence, eighteen men and twelve women.

They were all at university and were either about to graduate or had done so and were studying for a doctorate. MacKinnon printed out the list and locked it away in his desk drawer. The researchers selected would have to be above reproach, there could be no loose tongues where SEG was involved or other future inventions for that matter. Confidentiality would be essential, the candidates would all have to be vetted. *A task for Somerton, methinks.* Jack would have to run background checks on everybody on Jupiter's list and come up with his recommendations.

MacKinnon Family Home

Chloe met him at the front door and hugged him. 'I heard the car. It's good to be in our real home, I'm so pleased you agreed we should try to get away from Number 10 at the weekend.'

'Me too, darling, though I don't think everybody on my staff thinks it's a good idea and we have to accept that it won't always be possible.'

'Just as well you're the boss then, sweetheart; go and freshen up, dinner is nearly ready.'

Later

MacKinnon pushed his plate away. 'That was superb, Chloe, a perfect start to the weekend. Tell me, what's the news on Abbi? Is she coming to lunch on Sunday or not?'

She rose and moved around the table and kissed him. 'She and David are coming though I wouldn't say she was enthusiastic. I do hope you have good news for her.'

He smiled at her and winked. 'Let's just say I think she'll go home a very happy girl. Now I vote for an early night; let's go see if we can make a perfect end to the day.'

She raised an eyebrow. 'Can I take it that your suggestion of an early night isn't because you're feeling tired?'

'Tell me what you think in the morning.'

Sunday Afternoon

'They're here, Colin.' Chloe MacKinnon called her husband in from the garden.

Abbi and David were seated in the lounge when he entered. He smiled and stepped forward to greet his daughter. There was no smile, her usual embrace and warmth were absent, her customary full kiss and hug replaced by a cool peck on the cheek and an even cooler, 'Hello Dad, how are you?'

'Fine thanks. And you?'

'Oh, everything is just dandy, thank you. You know how we girls just love arranging our wedding, the most important day in our lives.' The undisguised animosity on her face exposed her inner anger.

An ill at ease David reached a hand forward, allowing MacKinnon to turn away from his daughter's scowling countenance. 'And what about you, David? How are things at the Met? Enough crime going on to keep you busy, I hope?'

'The crime I can cope with, Colin; it's the paperwork that weighs me down, but I suppose that comes with the territory.'

MacKinnon pulled a face. 'Everybody complains about paperwork; we'll have a talk about it sometime and see if we politicians can reduce it. Could be that it's self-inflicted by the Association of Chief Constables or other such august body. But let that be our last bit of business; I have an announcement to make that affects us all.'

Three faces turned in unison to give him their full attention. He looked directly at Abbi. 'It's about your wedding; I've given it a lot of thought and it's wrong of me to try to exclude your brother. It's your big day and he has every right to be there. Who knows, maybe it will mark a new beginning for him. I'm sorry I've acted like a brute, forgive me. I hope we can put this rift behind us and all look forward to your big day.'

The future bride could barely contain her relief and excitement. 'Oh Dad, do you really mean it? Thank you, thank you, thank you.' She jumped up, threw her arms around her father and hugged him tightly, tears filling her eyes. 'I know how hard it is for you, Dad, I really do, but it means so very much to me.'

Chloe's face was wreathed in smiles. She mouthed 'I love you' to her husband. David looked on fondly at Abbi's elation, briefly nodding his gratitude at his future father-in-law.

'I'm hoping that you know where to send Lachie's invitation; we don't have an address for him. Still,' he nodded at Singleton, 'I'm sure the man standing beside you will be able to track him down. Isn't that right, David?'

'I'll do my best,' Singleton gulped. 'But I can't just use the Met as my private detective agency. Don't forget, I'm the new kid on the block.'

MacKinnon shrugged. 'We all have to make the best of our positions from time to time.' *Inwardly, he shuddered as he thought of how he was currently using and abusing his position in equal measure.*

'I have his last address,' Chloe and Abbi spoke almost simultaneously.

'Leave it to me, Mum. I'll get onto it first thing tomorrow morning.'

'Well,' MacKinnon spoke hesitantly, 'you know Lachie's lifestyle as well as I do, he might have moved on. He hasn't had what I'd call a fixed address for some years now.'

'I know, Dad, but I can give it a try; I won't give up till I've found him.'

Chloe intervened, 'Let's leave that for now, Colin. The occasion calls for champagne; you attend to that whilst I put the finishing touches to lunch. It's such a relief to be a family again.'

Monday Morning

Fenton arrived punctually at eight and was shown into the Prime Minister's office. 'Sit yourself down, Eric, tell me what's happening in health. Is there anything you think I should know about from your standpoint?'

Fenton eyed him warily, ever mindful of political pitfalls. 'I shouldn't think that there is anything you aren't aware of, Colin. Let's see, the previous lot's reforms are still bedding down, staff are struggling to keep the ship afloat and there are grumbles about pay but that's nothing new. Overall, there is an acceptance that the NHS settlement is better than the rest of the public sector. But you know all that, Colin; that's not why you asked me here. What do you want me to do about your son? I haven't checked on his condition this morning; showing too much interest might prompt awkward questions.'

MacKinnon sat back and chose his words carefully. 'Let me say again, Eric, that I really appreciate your discretion, I really do. I need your personal assurance that no-one will ever learn about our conversations concerning my son; I can't be seen to have been involved. If you can keep this business under wraps, I won't forget the favour when the next Cabinet reshuffle comes around. It might be some time away but the first opportunity that comes along, I'll ensure that you get a promotion. At worst it might not happen until after the next election but let's hope we don't have to wait that long.'

Fenton responded eagerly, almost bouncing in his seat. He could almost smell career advancement. 'You have my word, and there's no obligation attached, my loyalty comes as a matter of course. I understand the position you find yourself in; we would all want to do the best we can for our families. I'll see to it that Lachlan is made an exemption from the Exceptional Care Protocols as one of those to be monitored for statistical purposes.'

'Thank you for that, Eric, I shan't forget your loyalty, believe me. But I'm afraid you've misunderstood me. I don't want him to be made an exception. I want you to leave matters as they stand.'

Fenton jaw dropped, aghast at what he was hearing. 'But, but…what on earth has gotten into you, Colin? He's your son, your only son; do nothing and you condemn him to certain death.'

'Do you think I don't realise the implications, Eric? If I make Lachie an exception and it got out, I'd have to resign. I don't want to have to do that; I believe this country needs me at this juncture in time. He's been an unhappy soul for most of his life; a slave to drugs and alcohol and sex of any kind that came along. Psychiatrists and psychologists have done their best for him on numerous occasions; the family has spent a small fortune on Lachie and bent over backwards time and time again to try to persuade him to change his ways but to no avail. It's reached the point where I'm happy for the Almighty to decide his fate. I'm grateful for your concerns but I've made my mind up.'

Fenton shook his head in disbelief. 'It's got nothing to do with the Almighty, Colin, it's in your hands and your hands alone. I couldn't do what you're doing. Is your wife in agreement?'

'When you sit in this chair, life-changing decisions are a daily occurrence; I haven't shared the decision with the family, it would cause untold distress and tension. It's a most painful decision and one I haven't taken lightly. I haven't had a good night's sleep since you sprung this on me; it's been the subject of much soul searching, I assure you. Now, if you don't mind, I'd like to let the matter drop; this is a very traumatic moment for me. Thank you again, Eric, and please, not a word to anyone. I promise you I won't forget this favour; you'll be offered the next Secretary of State post that comes up, provided, of course, it's suited to your skills and experience.'

Fenton rose quickly to his feet, trying not to show his feeling of triumph. *I have you firmly by the balls, Colin, old chap.* 'Rest assured, you can rely on me, Colin.'

MacKinnon breathed a sigh of relief as Fenton walked across the room and left, closing the door behind him. *Thank God that's over. Why couldn't you have been a decent son, Lachie, you've brought this on yourself. I hope I can trust you,*

Eric. The number of confidants who now have leverage over me is growing, Croudace, Somerton and now Fenton. Oh well, in my game, I guess three isn't such a bad number.

Chapter 8
MacKinnon Family Home
Sunday, Late Evening

'Sorry, we have to leave that story.' Huw Thomas was looking closely at his desktop monitor, his expression one of concern. 'News is just coming in of a large explosion in Canary Wharf.' He fingered his earpiece and paused. 'The explosion took place only minutes ago; there is widespread damage but no reports of casualties at this time. Emergency services are on the way and we'll have a reporter at the scene before the end of the programme. We'll keep you informed of developments as and when we learn of them; for the moment I'll return to the previous story.'

MacKinnon sat numbed, his eyes transfixed on the screen. The newspaper he had been reading lay discarded on the floor. Chloe bit on her lip and turned to her husband. 'How awful, I pray to God that no-one has been killed or injured.'

The red telephone, with its distinctive insistent buzz, sounded in the hall and he moved quickly across to answer it. 'That'll be for me, it's probably Alan.'

'Colin, it's Alan, there's been an explosion in Canary Wharf. I'm headed there as soon as we finish this call. Laura has gone back to her constituency this weekend and I'm covering Home Office emergencies. I'll keep her in the picture.'

'I've just watched the announcement on television. I'm about to set off for Downing Street. Have any casualties been reported?'

'Not yet but it's early days, I'll keep you posted as soon as anything useful emerges, bye.'

Chloe joined him in the hall and he put his arms around her. 'Sorry darling. I must return to No 10, not that I can do anything but it's best that I'm there. Whatever else, the press will expect a statement from me standing in front of No 10.'

'Of course, darling, I understand, that's how it should be; people will want to know that the PM is sharing their concerns and is close to the situation. Let me know how things are when you get a chance, and what your movements are likely to be. I'll join you in the morning. Try to get some sleep, you'll need to be at your best over the next few days. If there's anything I can do, anything at all, let me know.'

'Thanks darling, I know you'll always be there for me. When something like this happens, it does make me wonder if we should reduce the number of weekends we spend here.'

His wife pulled a face. 'Oh Colin, don't say that, please. This is our home, our real home. I really don't want to rent it out or put it into mothballs for that matter; Downing Street just doesn't have the family feel that it does here.'

He gave her a hug and kissed her. 'Neither do I, but I have to do what's expected of me. We'll talk about it another time.'

10 Downing Street

Back in his office, whilst he waited anxiously for feedback from Canary Wharf, he used the time to catch up with correspondence and Cabinet papers. The on-duty staff knew the ropes and would fend off all but the most important calls. Other world leaders would no doubt phone to offer support, sympathy and condemnation in equal measure, most would be deflected with an apology and an excuse. *The PM is dealing with the aftermath and can't come to the phone, be assured he appreciates your concerns, blah, blah, blah.* Only the most important individuals would be put through. The press would be given regular statements in his name and a Downing Street spokesman would ensure that the public were given the impression that he was in constant contact with the Emergency Services.

In the event, an eternity-long twenty minutes elapsed before he heard from Alan Croudace. 'Tis I, Colin, hardly an unbroken window below six floors; appears to have been a single explosion emanating from a parked van. Police, fire brigade, bomb disposal and a few ambulances are at the scene.' There was no waffle with Croudace, no unnecessary garnish, just a straightforward account of the facts.

'Are there any reports of fatalities or casualties?' MacKinnon asked anxiously.

'None reported but the search is ongoing, so far so good. Thankfully, the timing was such that the area was virtually deserted when the bomb went off; it's a bit of a backwater at that time of night. Pretty sure that no passers-by have been involved, so it's security staff we're checking out. If it turns out to be a terrorist incident, it seems certain they weren't targeting people.'

'Has anyone, any group, claimed responsibility?'

'Not yet.'

'OK, keep me in the picture; I'll spend the night here at Downing Street. Be ready to give a full report to Cabinet tomorrow morning; I've arranged for an 8 am start. We'll probably have to convene a meeting of COBRA later in the day.'

'Will do, Colin, bye.'

It was shortly after 2 am when MacKinnon slid into bed, voicing his final thoughts aloud. 'Looks like the old saying holds true, this particular cloud might well have a silver lining; good old Providence might just have come to my rescue, the research and security facility might just have taken a massive step closer.' Then a thought struck him. *Oh my God, what if Providence goes by the name of Jack Somerton? Oh my God, this is too much of a coincidence for my liking. One thing for sure, I'm not going to ask any questions in that direction. Christ, surely Alan isn't involved in this. Please God, don't let anyone be injured.*

The thought relentlessly emerged and re-emerged throughout a night of broken sleep but what was done was done; there was no turning back the clock. *Prepare to do a Pontius Pilate, Colin, old son, wash your hands any blame and use the situation to your advantage.*

Cabinet Meeting, Next Morning

Croudace reported that there had been two developments overnight. Sadly, a security guard standing adjacent to a ground floor window at the time of the blast had been killed in the explosion. Secondly, a group calling itself Green Freedom had claimed responsibility and had issued a chilling warning: *This* time our target was buildings, next time, it will be people. Let Ireland unite.

Nothing was known about Green Freedom, but it was almost certainly a newly formed dissident Irish Republican splinter group. It wasn't known if it was a breakaway element of the Provos, the INLA or a newly formed collective of the residual hard-core extremists from the old days of violent protest, the Troubles as they were known.

MacKinnon looked on admiringly as Croudace fielded questions, weaving in the need to improve intelligence gathering and security provision, stressing that GCHQ was working to full capacity and beyond. 'As we all know, terrorist groups are increasingly using the Internet and airwaves to communicate and disseminate misinformation. In my view, the infrastructure necessary to follow up intelligence leads needs to be strengthened and extended; investment in the latest surveillance technology was essential and overdue. There had been a single reference last week to the possibility of an imminent terrorist attack in London, but there just hadn't been the resources available to investigate this in depth. We must bear in mind that terrorists are masters of disinformation, regularly planting red herrings to keep the security services chasing their tails.'

MacKinnon nodded his support throughout Croudace's statement. *Well done, Alan, lay it on thick.*

Croudace paused and looked around the table. 'We were fortunate to escape with only one casualty, a married man with three children. His widow is understandably in a state of shock; we're doing all we can to ensure she gets the support she needs. Building damage and interruption to business is estimated at £5-£10 million. The Met is retrieving all CCTV footage from the area for examination as a matter of urgency. That's all I have for now, I'll keep Cabinet informed and will be making a statement in the House this afternoon.'

'Thanks for that Alan.' MacKinnon nodded at his friend and looked around the table at his colleagues, pausing for effect. 'I've given this outrage a great deal of thought and I'm determined that this mustn't happen again. It seems that we picked up that terrorists might be planning an attack but didn't have the resources to track down the perpetrators and nip the threat in the bud. These threats, real and false, are becoming all too frequent, something has to be done and done quickly. I've decided that I shall inform the House of my intention to proceed with a new high security facility here in the South-East. It will, of course, work closely with GCHQ and the other security forces.

'Moreover, although not directly related, I'm going to announce that I will be bringing forward a proposal I've had in mind for some time. I want to establish a high-tech facility where the best young brains in the country will have the opportunity to pursue cutting edge research and development. I want to usher in a new era of British inventiveness which will put us back at the forefront of science and technological innovation.'

There were murmurs of approval around the table with only Ken Ogilvie, the Chancellor of the Exchequer, dissenting. 'And where is the money coming from, Colin? I'm not happy with this, we're supposed to be balancing the books and cutting back on expenditure, not adding to it. Not too long ago, you accused your opposite number, our friend Will Cotton, of not living in the real world and you risk being accused of joining him.'

MacKinnon sighed. 'I appreciate that, Ken, but there are times when we have to invest, and this is one of them. We're talking about the security and future of our nation; there's nothing more important. You're a whiz at manipulating budgets; I want you to find whatever it takes to make this happen over the term of this Parliament, let's say £100 million. I believe that this is essential to our security and, if the research centre delivers what I think it will, it could well become the engine room of our economic recovery. Raid the contingency reserve, dip into overseas aid, empty your back pocket, do whatever is necessary but find it.'

Ogilvie shook his head. 'Give over, Colin, sounds like a big bit of blue sky planning just fell onto the table; the opposition will have a field day. Perhaps we can discuss this outside the meeting?'

MacKinnon nodded, smiling icily. 'I hear what you say, Ken, set up a meeting, but I want you to produce proposals for sourcing up to £100 million before we meet. In the meantime, I'll get our PR people working on the headlines and the press release.'

As the Cabinet filed out of the meeting room a few minutes after 10.00, MacKinnon caught Croudace by the elbow. 'Arrange a meeting with Jack in my office as soon as, preferably early morning. I'll mention it to Jess.'

Croudace nodded. 'Sure, what's on the agenda?'

'The Canary Wharf business, the new facility and some covert investigations I want him to carry out. You didn't have any prior knowledge of this Canary Wharf business, did you, Alan? Please tell me you didn't.'

Croudace's jaw dropped. 'Of course not, you know me better than that; I would never put civilian lives at risk. What are these investigations about?'

'Learn all about it on the day, Alan. I just hope our friend Somerton isn't involved with Canary Wharf either; it's the sort of stunt he would come up with. Sorry I have to go. I've got another meeting lined up.'

Parliamentary Session: Prime Minister's statement

The Canary Wharf incident ensured that the Commons was full; the buzz of conversation dying away when the Speaker called on the prime minister Prime Minister to make his statement to the House.

MacKinnon rose, his face showing no emotion, his voice solemn as he reported on what had taken place the previous evening and current progress with the aftermath and police investigations.

Then his tone changed. 'These are difficult times financially, but nevertheless we must do more to combat the increasing threat of terrorism and internet malpractice, and that is why I'll be bringing detailed proposals before the House in the near future for the provision of a new security facility on a brown field site to be found somewhere in the Southeast, within easy access of London. This will house the best counter-terrorist surveillance systems money can buy.

'I acknowledge that this will involve significant cost but even in the current restrained economic climate, I am determined that our nation will be adequately safeguarded against terrorist action such as that which took place in Canary Wharf last night. I hope that I will have the full support of the House.' His speech completed, MacKinnon resumed his seat and fixed a challenging stare on his opposite number.

Will Cotton rose to his feet, knowing he had no option other than to offer his support; the public would expect no less, but he wasn't going to miss the opportunity to score a few points. 'Madam Speaker, if the Prime Minister is able to find additional resources for security, why didn't he find them months ago? If he had done, we might have avoided £10 million pounds of damage to one of the city's major financial centres and, most regretful of all, loss of life. This Party will always seek to support what is best for the country, but I'm not going to commit to a pig in a poke when our hard-working people are being required to sacrifice so much to meet the government's unnecessarily stringent spending cuts. I'm sure that the House will want full details of what is being proposed, and I hope that the expenditure involved will be contained within the government's current spending plan.'

MacKinnon stepped forward to the dispatch box. 'I deeply regret the loss of life and I know the whole House will want to join with me in sending its deepest condolences to the security guard's widow. I'll ensure that we do what we can to help Mrs Baker cope with her loss.

'The House will be provided with details of the cost, but the centre's capabilities will be classified as Top Secret and will not be made public. As the Right Honourable gentleman opposite suggests, the Chancellor of the Exchequer will be seeking to contain expenditure within the existing budget envelope. I will, of course, be happy to meet with him in private to brief him on the more sensitive details.

'And now Madam Speaker, I would like to take this opportunity to turn to another issue, that of science and technology. Throughout history, the United Kingdom has achieved worldwide acclaim for its innovation in the fields of scientific research and development, a reputation it has held since the very birth of the Industrial Revolution. I believe that we are no longer the force we were; many of our best young graduates are being lured overseas where facilities are often better. I want to reverse this trend by establishing a new facility here in the United Kingdom, one to rival any in the world.

'Under its roof, I want to assemble a team of our brightest young graduates who will be encouraged to carry out cutting-edge scientific and engineering research. Subject to a detailed study, a possible option would be for this facility to share a site with the security centre alluded to in my previous announcement. It seems to me that there would be opportunities for cost savings if these two facilities could share certain aspects of the infrastructure. And of course, in anticipation of the Right Honourable gentleman opposite asking, we'll also be seeking to contain the costs involved within existing budgets.'

Will Cotton stepped briskly forward to the dispatch box and stood there briefly, looking around the Chamber, his lips set in a sneer. 'My, my, the Prime Minister has been a busy boy; where *has* austerity gone? I congratulate him on finding so much slack in existing budgets; budgets that were supposed to be squeezed to the limit. Or is it that he didn't get his sums right first-time round? Maybe he should invest some of these new-found monies in an up-to-date calculator for the Chancellor?' The opposition benches roared with laughter and order papers were waved enthusiastically, smiles disappeared from the government members.

Cotton waited for the laughter to die away then continued, 'However, I will say how pleased I am to see the Prime Minister investing in the public sector rather than the private sector. Are we witnessing the beginning of a U-turn? We on this side of the House will certainly try to support the proposal when we've had the opportunity to consider the detail. Let's hope the Right Honourable gentleman's backbenchers will lend their support.'

MacKinnon rose instantly. 'I welcome the Right Honourable gentleman's support; it's clear he recognises a good investment when he sees one. With respect to his comments on public sector investment, I would just say that this new proposal will not in any way affect the overall level of investment in public services laid out in the Chancellor's budget statement.'

Later in the MacKinnons' Downing Street Apartment

'Looks like you've had a good day, darling.'

'What makes you say that, Chloe?'

'I've been watching the six o'clock news and every member of the public interviewed was singing your praises; your crackdown on terrorism has been well received, of course, but business and education gurus are enthusing about the new research facility. The idea of getting the country's best young brains together under one roof is seen as a wonderful initiative, though one professor was a bit concerned about its relationship with the universities. Whose brainchild was that?'

'All mine, darling,' he said unashamedly. 'Let's hope I can make it happen; there are major hurdles ahead, not the least of which is funding. I'll tell you more over dinner; I missed lunch today and I'm absolutely ravenous. In truth, I can't claim all the credit for everything we're proposing, some ideas evolved in discussion with Alan. Thankfully, the whole Cabinet was supportive, except for Ken Ogilvie, needless to say.'

'Well, that's hardly surprising, is it? After all, he has to find the money, money you've told everybody we don't have. Isn't that so?'

'I suppose so, but Ken will find the cash one way or another. Have you heard anything from Abbi?'

Chloe nodded. 'We had a brief chat on the phone not long before you came in.'

'How was she?'

'What makes you ask, Colin? She's as well as she was when you saw her yesterday.'

'I was just wondering if she had managed to contact Lachie, that's all.'

'Give her a chance, Colin; it's been less than twenty-four hours, so no real news. She has spoken to some of his friends, but they claim they haven't seen him for ages. Her plan is to check out all places where he used to bed down, hostels and the like.'

MacKinnon rolled his eyes. 'Does that include shop doorways and pavements?'

'Don't be sarcastic, darling, it's not helpful.'

'I just hope she doesn't do that on her own; Lachie lived in an unsavoury world, his associates were all addicts of one kind or another, some of them are potentially dangerous. Goodness knows what they might do to a woman on her own; hopefully, David will go with her.'

'I expect he'll help if he can, but he can't just walk away from his desk at the Met when he feels like it.'

'I guess not but I hope he finds the time nevertheless, I don't want Abbi to get hurt.'

Prime Minister's Office, Wednesday, 8.30 am

As directed, Croudace arranged for Somerton to brief MacKinnon on the current position re Canary Wharf and the trio duly assembled in Downing Street in a sombre mood. MacKinnon was in two minds as to whether he should directly question Somerton about his possible involvement, he really didn't want to stir him up but felt he had to; it would have looked odd if he hadn't.

'Have you heard anything about this Canary Wharf business on your network, Jack? It seems a bit of a coincidence coming along so soon after our meeting. I sincerely hope you had nothing to do with it.' MacKinnon looked Somerton in the eye searching for any signs of guilt.

Somerton for his part put on his best look of hurt innocence. 'Christ, Colin! What do you take me for? The idea of blowing up a building in London appals me but, and it's a big but, even if I had something to do with it, you should know better than ask questions. Deniability, remember what we agreed? But rest assured, you have my word, the bombing was not of my making. At the risk of repeating myself yet again, it's time you made your mind up whether you trust me or not. If you don't, then *you* should be asking *yourself* why you hired me. And bear in mind, I'm not in this for the money nor am I stuck for a job.'

MacKinnon's eyes narrowed; Somerton was issuing a thinly veiled challenge, but he had to swallow it. 'OK Jack, my apologies if I've offended you but keep in mind, we have to draw the line somewhere.'

Somerton relaxed; the moment of confrontation had passed. 'Of course, Colin, the line will always be drawn where you decide.' He grinned widely. 'But you've got to admit, Fate has certainly dealt you a good card. Your statement went down well in the House and from what I've heard and read, Joe Public thinks you're a superstar. It looks like you'll get this project through Parliament, so maybe you should just thank your lucky stars and get on with it.'

MacKinnon turned to Croudace who had watched the exchange with some doubts of his own; by any standards, it was quite a coincidence. 'What's the latest from the security services, Alan?'

'The bomb disposal people are just describing it as a very large explosive device almost certainly triggered by a telephone call. They've found one or two bits of evidence to suggest that our old friends from across the Irish Sea were probably the culprits. To date though, we haven't turned up anything on this group calling itself Green Freedom, and there has been no contact from them since. All we've got to go on as I speak is the Reuters report saying Green Freedom carried out the attack in pursuit of a united Ireland. There was definitely no warning given in advance although, as I said, the timing of the explosion suggests they weren't looking to inflict casualties.'

MacKinnon looked pensive. 'Not this time it seems, but who knows what they'll attempt next time? Is there anything from the Met?'

Croudace's eyes lit up. 'News is better on that front. They're following up two leads, one of which is very promising. The van used by the terrorists was stolen recently and they are working on that. But the big breakthrough is CCTV footage showing the van being parked at the scene of the explosion. It shows that two men were involved; we know what they were wearing, their height, build etc. and, wait for it, we've got a near perfect facial image of one of them. It's being enhanced as we speak, so by the end of the day, we might be able to identify the individual and get something out on TV if the Met agrees.'

Somerton made a clenched fist gesture. 'Great, we should be able to track the bastards down; if I can help, let me know. If we can identify them and don't have evidence to bring them to Court, let me know and I'll see they take early retirement.'

MacKinnon shot him an angry look. 'Forget that line, Jack, let justice take its course. Leave it to the Met and the security services to deal with; I've got another job for you.' He passed Jupiter's list to Somerton. 'I want you to check out every name on this list, find out all there is to know about these individuals.'

Somerton studied the list. 'Am I to be told anything of the background?'

'There's not a lot I can tell you, other than they are all candidates nominated by those in the know for the new research facility. I'd like your report as soon as possible.'

'Christ Colin! There's a lot of work here if you want a thorough job, I reckon three months.'

'You can have two months and I still want a thorough job.'

'Thanks a bundle, Prime Minister, you certainly know how to motivate a guy. On that note, I shan't hang around gassing, I'll need to move quickly on this.'

He stood to leave and was joined by Croudace. 'I'll come with you, Jack, I want a quick word.' He turned to MacKinnon. 'Do you need me for anything, Colin?'

'Not at this moment, just keep me informed of any developments.'

On their way along the corridor, Croudace guided Somerton into a small waiting room and took his colleague by the shoulders, almost as though he was going to shake him. 'Tell me again, Jack, swear to me you had nothing to do with this Canary Wharf explosion.'

Somerton didn't blink. 'You have my word that I had nothing to do with it, I swear. We really do have to start trusting each other, I can't see the point going on if we don't. Those fucking Irish paddies were responsible, the real fanatics have never accepted the Peace Accord, you know that.'

Croudace let out a resigned sigh. 'Sorry Jack, I just had to be sure. I won't raise the subject again.'

Somerton kept a smile off his face, he'd pulled it off, the bomb seemed to have done the trick and he'd covered his tracks well. His men had been disguised and it had been no accident that one had been caught on CCTV. The full-face mask the so-called terrorist was filmed wearing was the best money could buy and undetectable at anything more than a couple of metres. Maybe not even that if you didn't know what to look for. Added to that, his men had been bulked out and wearing shoe lifts, so descriptions of their physiques were substantially inaccurate.

'That's all for now, Jack. Be a good boy and steer clear of trouble, we'll all sleep easier..'

Somerton smiled and nodded. 'Guaranteed Alan, now please, once and for all, start trusting me.'

'You're right, Jack, forgive me; I guess working in political circles day after day has lowered my capacity for trust. No matter what Colin said use your resources to come up with the identity of that guy caught on CCTV; I can hardly believe he wasn't wearing the traditional black hood.'

Somerton nodded. 'A big mistake even terrorists can be complacent; we'll come up with his identity sooner or later.'

Chapter 9
Prime Minister's Office

It had brought a sense of relief when the call finally came, one he had known would arrive sooner or later. It was one he had wanted to come, one he wanted to face up to and get through the fallout as quickly as possible.

'Hello darling, how are you?'

'Oh Colin, come upstairs right away.' She broke down and sobbed uncontrollably and he knew then that it had happened. 'I've just had the most dreadful news, Guy's Hospital has just rung about Lachie…' The words wouldn't come, her voice drowned in emotion. 'He's dead, Colin, he's dead! Our poor son is dead.'

'My God, Chloe! When? How? Oh my God, this is terrible.' Her news stirred no feelings of sadness or regret, nor even a modicum of shame. MacKinnon felt no guilt as he feigned the shock and despair he knew she would want to hear.

'It's just awful, Colin, he died three days ago; they've only just found out who he is. He died alone, unloved, uncared for, in a hospital bed. How could this have happened? I feel so ashamed.' Her words came in a flood of grief punctuated by sobs and although MacKinnon couldn't share her emotions, he felt her pain.

'It's not your fault, darling. You've always loved him and Lachie knew that; if anyone is to blame, it's me. But we can't talk about this on the phone, I'm going to drop everything and come up right away. I'm sure the NHS would have been at his side comforting him in his final moments.'

'Thank you, darling, please hurry. They're expecting us at the hospital; they want us to formally identify him.'

'Are the police involved, the request for identification, I mean?'

Chloe hesitated. 'I don't think so, there's been no mention. Why should there be?'

'I just wondered, that's all, have you told Abbi?'

'No, I phoned you as soon as I heard. She'll be heartbroken, they used to be very close.'

'Give her a ring and ask her to come here or meet us at the hospital. If you don't feel up to it, I'll call her.'

'No, leave it to me, Colin, it's best if I do it; just come up as soon as you can, I need you with me.'

'I'll just finish up what I'm doing and tell Jess to cancel all today's meetings. I won't be long, darling; this really is the most dreadful news.'

MacKinnon moved over to the drinks cabinet and poured himself a whisky, his thoughts travelling through what lay ahead; the funeral, of course, that would be routine and manageable but how would Abbi take the news? He wasn't worried about her feelings; he was concerned for himself in case she blamed him. And the media would be like vultures when the news got out.

Lachie's past would be dragged up. His drunken escapades, his drug abuse and his sexual trysts with male and female partners would make lurid headlines. Christ, where had those genes come from? Why had he and Chloe not been able to deal with it, nip it in the bud before it grew beyond control? Lachie had even stolen from his family; money, jewellery and other precious sentimental possessions, whatever he needed to feed his habit.

His despicable behaviour could have resurfaced at any time, even at Abbi's wedding; heaven forbid had he been able to attend. With a bit of luck, it would no longer be newsworthy by the time the big event came along. He smiled and raised his glass. 'Here's to death; we're well rid of you, Lachie.'

Even the slightest tinge of sadness eluded him. He felt only relief that his errant son was out of his hair forever. He just prayed that Abbi wouldn't blame him for her brother's death and would understand that it was the inevitable outcome of Lachie's lifestyle. But for the moment, he had to comfort Chloe, free up the rest of the day and brief his PA. Jess looked up at him expectantly, her concern registering as the expression on his face told her something was amiss. She said nothing, her look of concern asked the question for her.

'Jess, I've just had the most devastating news; Guy's has just rung Chloe to inform us our son has died. We didn't even know he was in hospital, sad to say it but we had lost touch.'

She smiled sympathetically; she knew the history. 'I'm so sorry, Colin, I know you were estranged but he was still your son. I'll clear your diary for the next couple of days.' She rarely used his first name, but it seemed right to do so in the circumstances.

'Just clear it for the rest of today please; this is so painful I think best if I keep myself busy. You know, try to take my mind off it.'

'I understand. Do you want me to tell anyone or do you want to break the news yourself?'

'Thanks Jess, I'm not thinking clearly. I guess we'll have to inform Cabinet colleagues, the Cabinet office, the Speaker, the Leader of the House and the Leader of the Opposition. Could you do the necessary for me?'

'Will do. What about a statement for the press?'

'No announcement from me at this stage; get someone from PR to do the necessary. If the press try to get in touch with me personally, just say I'll make a formal statement shortly, family in shock, grief-stricken, that sort of thing.'

He made his way upstairs, settling a look of despair on his face and readying himself for Chloe. He found her talking to someone on the phone and hung back waiting for her to finish. As soon as she caught sight of him, she ended the call and rushed across the room, throwing her arms around his neck and burying her face in his chest. She wept uncontrollably and he held her close for a few minutes before gently easing her away to make eye contact.

'I'm sorry, darling.' He tried to summon tears to his eyes. 'I'm absolutely numbed by the news; Lachie and I were estranged but I didn't want it to end this way. I had hoped the wedding would bring a new beginning.' *How easy those false sentiments fell from his lips.* 'Did you manage to get a hold of Abbi?'

She nodded, wiping away her tears and dabbing at her nose. 'She didn't say much really; she's terribly upset as you can imagine. She'll make her own way to the hospital. We should leave now. I'd like us to be there for her when she arrives.'

'Of course, I'll ask Jess to have the car sent around.' He moved away and made the call, also asking that Guy's be alerted to his imminent arrival. 'Make sure they keep it low-key, Jess, no leaks to the press or I'll take a very dim view of it. While you're on, tell them that Abbi will be arriving separately and to look after her.'

Guy's Hospital

Jess had done her job well; their arrival was a low-key affair and MacKinnon was relieved to see that there was no press presence. The hospital's chief executive offered his condolences and led the two of them along a series of corridors to the door to the mortuary viewing room then took his leave. 'I'll make sure someone is on hand to meet your daughter, Prime Minister.'

The room was small, barely large enough for its purpose. There were no chairs; presumably mourners weren't expected to stay long. Inside, they were greeted by a nurse who offered a few kind words in a suitably sombre tone, then moved forward and pulled the white sheet down to reveal the face of their late son. 'I'll leave you now, I'll be outside if you require anything.'

'Did he suffer?' Chloe's voice was little more than a whisper, as though afraid she might somehow waken her son from a deep sleep.

The nurse shook her head sympathetically. 'Not while he was with us; in fact, he never regained consciousness from the moment he arrived. That's what made it so difficult to determine who he was; we had no idea he was the Prime Minister's son. All we had to go on was an old student identity card we found in his pocket.' With that, she turned and left the room, closing the door silently behind her.

A few minutes passed; Chloe squeezed his hand. 'I wonder if Abbi will want to see him like this, cold. lifeless, I can hardly bear it.'

Before he could reply, the door opened and Abbi was shown into the room by the chief executive. She looked drained, a picture of misery, her face stained with tears. MacKinnon could see relief in her eyes when she saw both her parents were there. His apprehension faded instantly when she moved towards him, arms open wide; he hugged her and felt her tremors of grief as she sobbed into his chest. He stroked her head, as he used to do when she was a little girl. 'I'm so very sorry, darling; if it's any comfort, the nurse told us he didn't suffer. His liver and kidneys just failed; nothing could be done.' The words were out before he realised his mistake. He saw Chloe's searching gaze; no mention had been made of how Lachie had died. He raised a finger to his lips to silence any question. She nodded, assuming—as he hoped she would—that his words were intended to bring some comfort to Abbi.

Minutes later, the three of them stood together in silence looking down at the still pale waxen form that was Lachlan MacKinnon. For the first time, the thought occurred to MacKinnon that there would be no-one to carry on his name; his own tiny branch of the MacKinnon clan would end when his time came to join his forebears. Lachie's face was haggard and lined, ravished by years of abuse, it had the appearance of a man twenty years older. *You poor fool, Lachie, life could have been so good for you.*

Abbi was slowly regaining her composure and he steeled himself in readiness for her recriminations, but she simply turned to him, tears streaming down her cheeks and asked, 'Please can we go? I can't bear seeing him like this.'

He put his arms around her and held her close again. 'I know, darling. I feel the same, such a waste of a young life. I deeply regret not trying to reconcile our differences months ago; it will haunt me for the rest of my life.' *How easily the lies flowed, how easy to deceive.*

It was all he could to refrain from smiling when she pulled back from him, wiping away her tears. 'We're all to blame in one way or another, Dad; Lachie led a life we weren't part of, a life he didn't want us to be part of. It's a comfort to me to know that you would have invited him to my wedding; sadly, it just wasn't meant to be. At least he's spared now from further pain and distress. Let's go home, and I mean our real home, not Downing Street.'

'I think that would be best for all of us.' MacKinnon felt ecstatic, it was all he could do to keep a smile off his face; he was free from his accursed son and his daughter was truly returned to him. *I pray you or your mother never find out the truth.*

MacKinnon Family Home

That evening, he asked Chloe and Abbi if they knew whether Lachie wanted to be buried or cremated. 'I'd want to respect his wishes if only I knew what they were.'

Abbi spoke up, 'He wanted to be cremated. No fuss, minimum ceremony and as low cost as possible; he always regarded funerals and burials as a waste of money. He didn't believe in God, so no church involvement. He wanted his ashes to be scattered in a forest. I recall he once said that in bygone days, he would have had a Viking funeral, just laid out in a burning boat and pushed out into a lake or the sea but I don't suppose that would be legal.'

MacKinnon was surprised. 'You actually spoke to him about his funeral? He was so young to be thinking about death.'

'He touched on the subject when I last saw him, a year or so ago, Dad; he knew that his lifestyle wouldn't bring him a long life.' Her eyes filled with tears and she faltered. 'He said I was the only one he could trust to see that he got what he wanted.'

He glanced across to Chloe, inviting her comment but she just lowered her head. 'Alas we can't have a Viking funeral but we'll honour his wishes and keep it simple, darling; you understood him better than anyone. As a family, we'll be there, of course, but I've no idea who his friends were.'

'Leave it with me, Dad.' Abbi's voice was firm. 'I'll make the arrangements. When I've got a place and a date for his funeral, I'll go around his London haunts and put the word out; maybe somebody will turn up to say a last goodbye. I don't think he retained any contacts from his school days or from his short time at university.'

'Thank you, Abbi, I know you'll do all you can for him; we'll go along with whatever you decide. Pass any bills on to me and I'll deal with them; it's the least I can do. Please take David with you when you visit Lachie's old haunts, he mixed with very unsavoury characters.'

He slept soundly that night, a smile on his lips as his eyes closed.

Five Days Later

Following the cremation, Lachlan MacKinnon's ashes were scattered in a designated area of a forest near Epsom, a strong breeze helping to disperse them. As expected, attendance was small; the three remaining members of the MacKinnon family, Abbi's husband and four scruffily dressed individuals, three male and one female. Introductions were neither sought nor offered and after a few moments of silent contemplation, the unknown mourners shuffled away.

The media hadn't been briefed about the funeral arrangements and thankfully weren't in attendance; another hurdle had been cleared. It meant that MacKinnon had been spared any awkward questions or photo shots. He couldn't believe his luck; the whole business had gone more smoothly than he could ever have wished for.

But inevitably, news did get out and a few tabloids ran front page stories about Lachie's murky past and the circumstances of his death; what wasn't known about him was fabricated in lurid terms. And, as expected, questions were asked about the family's role in his life and how they had failed their son so dismally. Downing Street's Press Office did a sterling job handling enquiries, the *PM is too upset to answer questions, the PM is consoling his wife over the loss of their son, the family is devastated…etc.* Ultimately, Lachie's demise had been little more than a one-day wonder and tabloid interest disappeared as quickly as it had emerged.

On his return to Parliamentary business, the Speaker offered condolences on behalf of the House. MPs, friend and foe alike, expressed their sympathies and letters poured in from the world of politics, far and wide. The ever-faithful British public spent a fortune on condolence cards and tributes, every one of them read and treasured by Chloe and Abbi.

But there had been a few embarrassing moments, such as when he had found himself in the presence of Eric Fenton, particularly when their eyes had met during his heart-rending speech in the Commons. But finally, the whole episode ended, the last word spoken, the final chapter written and it was back to business as usual.

In an opportunistic, calculated act of timing, Alan Croudace submitted detailed proposals for the new research and security facility during MacKinnon's absence from the House, ending his speech with some well-chosen words. 'The Prime Minister desperately wanted to attend this debate but I'm sure the House understands that his family bereavement must take precedence. However, he was insistent that his personal circumstances mustn't cause the country's security to be put at risk for a day longer than necessary. He particularly wanted to thank the Chancellor of the Exchequer for identifying the finance necessary for this facility to go ahead during a very difficult period of austerity.'

His job done, Croudace sat down, his face deadpan but inwardly satisfied with his performance and confident that when the vote was taken, it would be approved with a substantial majority.

Meanwhile, efforts to track down those responsible for the Canary Wharf attack continued, but in the end, enquiries dried up and the investigation ran out of steam. CCTV footage of the incident had been given wide publicity but to no avail. Just as Somerton had predicted, no-one came forward to identify the perpetrators.

Prime Minister's Office, Two Months Later

'Grab a pew, Jack, can I offer you coffee, tea or something stronger perhaps?'

Somerton shook his head. 'No thanks, Colin, I'd rather get down to business if you don't mind.'

'Suits me, go to it, tell me what you've found out about our young graduates.'

'It's all here in the report,' he handed MacKinnon a bundle of folders. 'Read this lot at your leisure; you'll find a photograph of each subject with their detailed history and a run-down on immediate family and close friends. As far as possible,

I've ascertained their political leanings. They're young so, unsurprisingly, there's a tendency to idealism, mostly of the liberal or left-wing variety. There's no potential extremists or activists as far as I can tell. Not too much on their health, but I've retrieved what I could and there's no problem in that regard. Where possible, I've included a pen picture of what others think of them, friends, lecturers and the like.'

Somerton never ceased to amaze MacKinnon with what he was able to achieve. 'To say I'm impressed is an understatement, Jack, I'm truly grateful and appreciate the effort you've put in. It's frightening really, how you and your counterparts can access so much personal material.'

'All part of the service Colin. One more thing, with security in mind I've indicated my opinion as to who might not be totally reliable. I stress this is just my opinion based on best judgement, nothing more.'

'I understand that, Jack, but yours is the best opinion I've got. I just can't afford any security breaches on this project.'

'Well, that's about it; I've given you the only hard copy of the security report that exists and there's a copy on this flash drive. I have the only other copy and it's on an encrypted memory stick.'

'The only copies you know of, Jack, or is everyone on your team of impeccable character?' MacKinnon was teasing him, of course.

Somerton guffawed. 'You're right to be cautious, Colin, but I have one big joker in my pack that you and your ilk don't have.'

MacKinnon's curiosity was roused. 'How so? Enlighten me, Jack.'

'You don't really want to know. All I'll say is that anyone who betrays me doesn't get his wrist slapped, or get suspended on full pay, or retired on a generous pension. Punishment is somewhat more final in my game; the only form of suspension in my organisation is likely to be on the end of a rope.'

MacKinnon shook his head in disbelief. 'I hope you're kidding, Jack! Best if we leave it there. I'll study the report and if needs be, will get in touch. By the way, those contractors you recommended are really pushing on with the facility.'

Somerton nodded. 'I'm keeping a close watch on them and giving them a kick up the arse when it's needed; they'll do a good job, I promise. With my contacts in Africa and the Middle East, I can open doors for them; they owe me and they'll deliver if they know what's good for them. Now, if that's it, I'll be on my way.' He rose, waving goodbye over his shoulder as he went. When he reached the door, he turned back briefly. 'I'm still curious about what's going on,

Colin. My instinct tells me that this project isn't all that it appears to be. Just bear in mind that you really can trust me if, or should I say when, the going gets tough.'

'I'll remember that, Jack, I promise.'

Clawhanger Colliery

MacKinnon looked closely at the shadowy figure on his laptop, not for the first time trying in vain to make out some identifying features, wondering still why it was that they couldn't meet face to face. 'I'm still unhappy at having to stand here conversing with a screen; this situation really does have to change.'

'Perhaps at some future date we will meet, Colin, but not yet, there are technical difficulties.' Jupiter's voice lacked its usual authority and seemed listless.

'Are you OK?' MacKinnon asked anxiously. 'You just don't sound well to me.'

'I'm not at my best, shall we say. I'll recover when I move into the new facility. Construction progress is better than I anticipated, it appears to be coming on rather well.'

MacKinnon's anxiety persisted. 'Is there anything I can do to help you in the meantime, anything at all?'

'How long before my facility is available for use?'

'Best guess is nine to twelve months.'

'I had hoped for something more specific than a guess, Colin. Do whatever you can to speed up completion.' There was an edge of irritation in Jupiter's voice. 'I need you to expedite completion, try to ensure that it takes no more than nine months, six would be better. The earlier I'm in residence, the sooner you will benefit from what I have to offer.'

MacKinnon tensed; he wasn't happy being told what to do but now wasn't the time to be difficult. 'I'm doing everything I can, I assure you that the contractors are being closely supervised.'

Jupiter's voice level rose, the tone insistent. 'I must also stress that it is vitally important that the specification for my area is complied with in full, there must be no compromises or substandard materials employed.'

'There won't be any departures from the specification, I promise. Have you any comments to make on the report I forwarded about the researchers? Which of them will best suit your purposes?'

'Not *my* purposes, Colin, *your* purposes. There will be a reply waiting for you when you return to Downing Street, now I really must take my leave.'

'A moment please, just one question; how soon after you are settled in the new facility can you provide a prototype of SEG?'

'First things first, Colin; I will forward a final list of requirements and provided the facility is equipped as I directed, I would expect the first SEG to be completed within twelve weeks. But aren't you forgetting that it is your researchers who will have to produce the first prototype, not me; I will simply complete the activation stage electronically overnight whilst the Centre's staff is asleep. I warn you now that there must be no attempt to access the device to determine how it operates; the final assembly and circuitry must remain a secret. There will be massive consequences if SEG is tampered with by unauthorised personnel.'

'Twelve weeks! Is that all? Twelve weeks?' MacKinnon couldn't contain his excitement. *In less than a year, his climb to greatness would begin.*

'Yes, twelve weeks, and you will have your hands on the most effective energy producing device ever assembled. But Colin, don't forget that I will demand something in return.'

'I hadn't forgotten, though now that you've raised the matter, I'm curious to know what you want from me, given that you apparently have the skills and knowledge to create anything you desire.'

Unusually, Jupiter chuckled before answering, 'I told you that the name you gave me was appropriate; the mythical God Jupiter and I share a rather unfortunate failing. Do some research, Colin, and you'll find out what my price is.'

Before MacKinnon could respond, the screen went blank, leaving him puzzled and irritated. *Why the fuck can't you give a straight answer to a question?*

Downing Street

MacKinnon drove back as quickly as traffic allowed, so keen was he to find out what Jupiter was alluding to. On arrival, he hurried along the corridor to his office, pausing only for Jess to update him. 'I've left various notes on your desk. There's nothing urgent but you do have a meeting in fifteen minutes; a small delegation from the CBI, seeking to give its view of the economy.'

MacKinnon groaned, 'Armed with all the usual requests, I bet; reduce interest and business rates, reduce regulations and provide greater stimulus for the economy. I don't think their script has changed all the time I've been in politics. Give me twenty minutes, Jess, tell them I'll be as quick as I can.'

He fired up his desktop and entered his password to access what Jupiter had to say about the proposed researchers and their employment, his eyes widening as he read the report. *Christ, I don't know if I can go along with this! The UK isn't a police state.*

Next, he googled "Jupiter" and trawled through the main references related to the ancient god, aghast when he finally realised what Jupiter had been referring to. *Oh no! Surely not?* His thoughts were interrupted when Jess buzzed through. 'The CBI lot are still waiting; do you want me to make excuses?'

'Just two more minutes to make a phone call then show them in.'

There was only one person who could help him. 'Hello, Jack. I need to see you tomorrow morning, as early as possible.'

'Sorry Colin, I've already got something on.'

'Change it, Jack, I want to see you tomorrow without fail. Shall we say 8.00?'

'That serious, is it?'

'Yes, it's that serious, Jack, and this is strictly between you and me, and I really do mean just you and me. Not a word to Alan.'

'Sounds serious. I'm convinced, I'll be there at eight.' *I wonder what you've been up to, Colin, something under the radar, I'll bet.*

Chapter 10
Downing Street, Next Morning

MacKinnon woke early the following morning, his night's sleep punctuated by what he'd googled about the ancient God, Jupiter. *I hope I'm wrong about this, I'll have to confront my shadowy partner, tell him straight it's not on.*

It was just approaching 7 am when he went down to his office and sent a brief message to Jupiter. 'Please contact me immediately; I need to clarify your requirement in respect of our agreement. I may have misunderstood what you want; I am very concerned that I will not be able to fulfil my side of our agreement.'

Ten minutes passed before his mobile rang.

'Contact as requested, Colin. How can I be of help?'

'I've read up on your namesake and I'm not sure I can deliver what you might be asking for.'

'You're speaking in riddles, Colin, please come to the point. This contact is inconvenient, I don't want it to last any longer than it needs to.'

MacKinnon hesitated, not sure how to proceed, not wanting to be insulting or provocative but he had to be clear as to what was involved. 'It's just that I've ascertained that Jupiter had a particular interest, one I might not be able to accommodate. It could be that I've gotten the wrong end of the stick. I mean, I wouldn't want to be...' he paused, searching for a word, '...offensive. It's just that...how can I put it...I hope that you don't share your namesake's practices.'

Jupiter interjected, making no attempt to disguise his annoyance. 'Let me help you, Colin; let's not beat about the bush. My interest is precisely as you surmise.'

MacKinnon's worst fears had been realised. 'Then I'm afraid I won't be able to honour my side of our agreement. I'm sorry but I just can't.'

Jupiter gave a sigh of impatience. 'Then I too am sorry, I'm very disappointed in you, Colin. What I ask is such a small price to pay for the unlimited benefits on offer. However, the choice is yours; refuse and our partnership is ended as of this moment, as, of course, is any prospect of SEG.'

MacKinnon felt his resolve crumble, saw his vision of the future fade away in an instant. UK's chance of pre-eminence in the world and the political power it promised would be lost forever, and with it, his chance to wield that power and claim a place in history's hall of fame. Without Jupiter's scientific genius, he'd be just another run-of-the-mill British Prime Minister, meriting a meagre sentence or two in the annals of the yesterday's people; the future he dreamt of irretrievably lost. The price demanded was too great, or was it? In the great scheme of things, perhaps the price to be paid wasn't too high after all.

The implications came in a millisecond, like a volcano exploding in his head, he would have to bow the knee. He offered no resistance; he was beaten. 'You're right, Jupiter, I can't deny my country, the whole of mankind in fact, what you have to offer but—'

'No buts, Colin, our agreement remains unchanged; you ask for what you want, I do likewise. The choice will always be yours, decline or accept, there will be no bargaining. I hope I'm making myself clear?'

MacKinnon nodded glumly; the die was cast; Jupiter had won. He felt sick. 'Yes, I understand completely.' *What kind of man am I becoming? Just how low will I stoop to get what I want?*

Jupiter's tone softened, the atmosphere of threat gone. 'Thank you, Colin. Let us say no more about this moment of disharmony and look to the future. I have to go.'

The call ended abruptly, leaving MacKinnon to consider anew the magnitude of what he had agreed. He slumped over his desk, head in hands; the enormity of what lay ahead knifing into his very soul, self-doubt ravaging his thoughts. *Where is all this going to end up?* He began to wonder if there were any limits to what he would do to achieve his ambitions. He hadn't just crossed the line; he was in danger of rubbing it out.

Minutes passed as he sought the sanctuary of justification; new, comforting thoughts slowly began to surface. *What's done is done, there's no turning back now. It's all for the good of the country and for that matter the entire planet; an unpalatable decision but one he was man enough to make. Relax, Jack will provide a solution.* He ignored the nagging little voice of his conscience reminding him that he, Colin MacKinnon, would also be a major beneficiary of the decision he had just taken.

Somerton was punctual, his air of expectation obvious as he settled comfortably into an armchair opposite MacKinnon.

'Thanks for coming at such short notice, Jack.'

'Spare me the thanks, Colin, you made me an offer I couldn't refuse. I have to confess though; you have me wondering what can be so urgent as to merit a three-line whip.'

MacKinnon bridged his hands, gently tapping his lips; his thoughts still coming to terms with what lay ahead. Somerton would have to be told everything. *He would become another link in the chain of secrecy, another source of leakage or even blackmail. And what would he want in return?* No matter, he had no choice.

'Pin your ears back, Jack, and prepare to be astounded. What I'm about to tell you is known only to myself and Alan; you're about to join a very elite group and I want it kept that way. This is a State Secret like no other, one that will never be recorded or see light of day. Understood?'

Somerton nodded without any real sign of conviction; in his experience, circumstances always arose, sooner or later, when secrets came to be passed on. 'OK, I've got the message loud and clear, so what dirty business needs my area of expertise?'

MacKinnon had to smile. 'No weasel words, straight to the jugular as always, Jack.'

Thirty minutes passed at the end of which Somerton knew everything from beginning to end. MacKinnon painted a golden future for the whole of humankind, describing at length the special position the UK would hold in the new world; a gold mine of scientific advancement to which Jupiter held the key. 'So that's the background, Jack, now you know why I've been so secretive. You've joined a very exclusive club of three, a membership that hopefully will never have to increase. You do understand that, don't you? I hope I can rely on you.'

Inwardly, Somerton was astonished but he just grunted. *Play it cool, Jack.* 'The way I see it, you have no option but to trust me, Colin, although I confess, you've all but blown me away.' He shook his head in amazement. 'Nothing I can say could possibly do justice to your revelation. Who is this guy? Where does he hail from? Is he some brilliant dissident scientist on the run from his political masters? And why has he chosen you? I don't suppose I'll ever get to meet this person, Jupiter or whatever you're calling him?'

'Not a chance, he won't even meet me face to face; he doesn't even like me telling anyone about his existence. I've told you all I know about him and that's not much. I'd just add that he might well be listening in on this conversation.'

Somerton frowned. 'He can listen in all he wants. I don't give a fuck. Tell him bollocks, you can't let the guy dictate everything. At the risk of repeating myself ad nauseum, let's get one thing straight once and for all. Watch my lips. You can trust me implicitly in any matter, including this latest breath-taking announcement. My employer, you in this case, will always have my loyalty and complete discretion. On top of that, I'll do anything for this nation of ours. If the rest of the world benefits, so be it; personally, I don't give a shit about places outside this island of ours. I assume you'll tell Alan that I've joined this privileged little circle of yours?'

'Thanks, Jack, I really was never in any doubt about trusting you. I just had to be reassured. There's no problem with Alan knowing that I've briefed you about Jupiter.'

Somerton sighed. 'I think you're a fucking liar, Colin, I remain sceptical as to whether or not you trust me. But now that this soul-baring moment has finally seen light of day, I'll make a couple of observations so there are no lingering shadows between us. Don't think that I can be fobbed off with some nice words or that I'm totally naïve. First off, I can see that you, Colin MacKinnon Esquire, will do very well in the fame and fortune stakes, so let's not pretend that you are being entirely altruistic.'

MacKinnon bit back a retort but he felt his eyes glint and narrow momentarily; deep down, he knew Somerton was right on the button. 'Fair point, Jack, but you're going to do very well out of this when it all comes to fruition.'

Somerton smiled icily. 'Rest assured I know I will, the difference between you and me is that I admit it. In fact, I'm now certain that you'll recommend me to Her Majesty for a knighthood when *I* think the time is right. Now that we've cleared that up, I can make my second observation.

'It occurs to me that nothing has changed since we last met, yet here you are letting me in on this mighty secret you've been at great pains to conceal up to now. That being the case, I'm pretty sure that you want something from me, something murky, something distasteful that you don't want to soil your hands with. So out with it, tell me what you want Jack Somerton to arrange.'

The moment had arrived, MacKinnon's mouth was bone dry, he licked his lips searching for the right words. 'Before I go on, I have to ask that this bit of business goes no further.'

'For crissake, Colin,' Somerton snarled. 'How many times do I—'

'Give me a chance, I mean that I don't even want Alan to know of this arrangement.'

Somerton let out a whistle. 'Why not, for fuck sake? You can trust Alan with your life, we've both had to in the past.'

'I unreservedly trust Alan, but in this one instance, I don't want him to have to struggle with his conscience. There's just a chance he might not concur with the path we're about to embark on, you know how righteous he can be.'

Somerton raised his eyebrows in a show of scepticism. 'OK Colin, I'll buy it, but only just. Go on, hit me with it.' He leaned back in the chair arms spread invitingly.

When MacKinnon finished explaining what he wanted, what Jupiter wanted, Somerton thought carefully before replying, 'I don't like it much, but it won't be the first time I've been involved in such arrangements, visiting Arab Princes and African dictators, and some notable aristocrats nearer to home. It is distasteful but sadly, it happens.'

'Perhaps I should be clear, Jack, there's a bit of a twist in the tale. I want you to handle this personally, it's got to be security proof, untraceable; I'm not sure what the future will hold once we start this business.'

Somerton's eyes opened wide. 'I hope you're not implying what I think you are?'

MacKinnon grimaced. 'I genuinely don't know, Jack. It's just that the stakes are astronomically high, or I wouldn't even consider going down this route.'

'I accept that and as I said, I don't like it one little bit, but good old Jack here will deliver the goods for you. Let me know when the first consignment is due, we'll talk through the details at that point. If you need to talk in code, just refer to Operation Nightjar and I'll know what you mean. Now, if you've completed your dirty business, I'll be on my way. I have another commitment.'

MacKinnon raised his hand, hesitating before he spoke, 'At the risk of incurring your wrath, Jack, one further thought occurs to me. I'm convinced that I have your loyalty, truly, but what happens if you're ever faced with a conflict of loyalties? Who wins in the final analysis?'

Somerton stared at him, lips making a taut narrow smile. 'Surprised you can't figure that out, you're a politician; I'd fucking win, of course. Think about it, it can't be any other way. Let's hope for your sake that situation never arises.'

MacKinnon felt relieved as he watched Somerton go, the deal was done.

You've got a big hold over me now, Jack, it couldn't be avoided. I wonder if you'll become a risk that needs to be eliminated someday? My God, listen to yourself, Colin, how duplicitous will you become before this all ends!

It was a question that would return to haunt him many times in the years that lay ahead.

Chapter 11
Official Opening of the National
Research and Security Centre, 2003

At last it arrived, the big day, the opening of the NRSC, another step nearer the destiny MacKinnon dreamt of; Her Majesty wasn't available but the heir to the throne, with his keen environmental interests, was the ideal deputy.

'...and I now declare this truly wonderful facility, open.'

The Prince stepped forward, pulled the gold tasselled cord and the short purple velvet drapes slid apart to reveal a black granite plaque engraved with all the usual attributes in gold lettering.

When the great and the good finished their warm dutiful applause, a smiling Prince turned to MacKinnon. 'I'd like to be invited back in six months or so for a low-key informal visit, when I can see this place in operation, talk to the research staff and of course, the security people. If it lives up to your political hype, it really will be a showcase for British scientists and engineers.' A thoughtful frown briefly crossed his face. 'Well, at least I hope they will be British or at the very least graduates from our universities?' He looked at MacKinnon pointedly, seeking a confirmatory response.

'That's precisely the plan, Sir.'

The Prince grunted. 'My long experience makes me wary of plans and good intentions. Let's make it more than a plan, let's make it a promise, shall we?'

His Highness had put MacKinnon on the spot, he couldn't recall the nationality or ethnicity of every candidate on Somerton's list. *Could I make such a promise?*

He scanned the list of graduates in his mind's eye; as far as MacKinnon could recollect, the current recruits all appeared to be British, but would that always be the case?

Tell him what he wants to hear, Colin. Damn it, of course, I can promise; with Jupiter's and Somerton's help anything was possible. Besides, it would be a popular undertaking when the media and the public get to hear about it. And I will make sure they do.

MacKinnon looked the Prince in the eye. 'Of course, Sir, it's a promise.'

The Prince chortled, almost gleefully. 'I shall hold you to it, Prime Minister.'

MacKinnon dutifully smiled and nodded, making a mental note to brief his PR guru to stress the inaugural all-British nature of the NRSC. The Prince undoubtedly meant what he said and had shown in the past that he could be a formidable opponent when he chose to be. Walking around the outside of the facility, the heir to the throne remarked on how much he admired the architecture comparing it with other public edifices, carbuncles as he referred to some of them. MacKinnon caught his breath when he stopped at the door leading to Jupiter's area and took a tentative step towards it.

'Where does this lead?'

MacKinnon said the first thing that came into his head, 'I'm pretty sure it's just a store.'

Alan Croudace, who was in the party taking part in the guided tour, nodded in agreement, adding that it was, of course, securely locked. To MacKinnon's relief, the Prince just shrugged and carried on. His Royal Highness didn't stay much longer; one of his aides stepped forward, whispered a brief message which was duly acknowledged with a nod and a wave of the hand with departure following shortly afterwards.

Downing Street, later that day

Mindful of his undertaking to the Prince, back in the office, MacKinnon hurriedly dug out Somerton's report on the prospective graduate researchers and scanned it feverishly, breathing a sigh of relief when he found that all the preferred candidates were indeed British citizens. *Was this by chance or had Somerton, with his fervently patriotic outlook, engineered it? No matter, it was the result I had hoped for.*

He buzzed the outer office. 'Jess, could you take a letter please?'

The letter was short and to the point, an invitation to the selected graduates to attend a meeting at Chequers just over two weeks hence. They were advised to bring night attire and toiletries since an overnight stay would be necessary in

115

the event they were offered, and accepted, a position at the NRSC. The graduates were required to make their way to any mainline London station for 9 am from whence they would be transported to Chequers for an introductory briefing. Later, they would be taken to the NRSC for a tour of the establishment and an explanation as to what would be expected of them.

Chequers

July 2003

All graduates had accepted the invitation and were in attendance; as expected, the prospect of employment in UK's newly built prestigious research centre just couldn't be refused. They were ushered into the meeting room just five minutes before 11 am and directed to sit where indicated by the place-setting bearing their name.

Eight males and seven females, all young and all reasonably dressed, there were only a few instances of gaudy attire. Thankfully, they all looked the part; there were no weirdos and no unsightly tattoos or undue body piercing in evidence. MacKinnon knew that his view was highly prejudiced, but an unflattering photo and a lurid headline could be damaging. *You've done your research well, Jack.*

Croudace and he made their entrance at eleven precisely; about half of the assembly immediately got to their feet, the others following with various degrees of hesitancy. MacKinnon took his place at the head of the table with Alan on the right. Smiling, he cast his eyes around the assembled group and opened the proceedings. 'I'm going to flatter myself and assume that you all know who I am, anyone who doesn't, can leave now.' He looked around the group. 'I was being serious when I said that. Not that he should require introduction, but on my right is the Foreign Secretary, Alan Croudace, a friend and colleague of long standing. Now, before we get down to business, I want each of you in turn to stand and introduce yourself, stating your age, your university and the degree or degrees you've attained. So, without further delay, I'll ask the graduate on my left to start the ball rolling and then we'll go clockwise around the table.'

The young man in question, sprawled back in his chair, smiled, and stated his name but before he could go on, MacKinnon interrupted, 'Sorry, but I did ask that you stand when making your statement. I want, we want, a good look at you.'

The graduate gave a half shrug and raised an apologetic hand then continued in a soft Ulster accent. 'Hi, I'm Denis Moore. I'm 23 and I attended Belfast

University gaining a degree in molecular biology,' he concluded with a smile and a small bow to his fellow graduates.

Fourteen others followed in similar vein, the last to rise a slim brunette. 'Hi, I'm Kate Forbes, I'm 25, I attended Oxford and my degree is in nuclear science.' She then turned directly to MacKinnon, bowed and smiled. 'Here ended the first lesson.'

MacKinnon chuckled and rose to his feet. 'Thank you everybody, an impressive assembly, undoubtedly a cross-section of Britain's best. All you need to do now is prove me right by going on to show that the education you've received and the degrees you've attained can produce tangible results. You'll have the opportunity to get to know each other a bit better later, but for now, let's get down to the main business of the day.

'Those of you who read the publicity following my statement to the House will know that my hope, my aim, is that the NRSC will become the finest research establishment in the world. It has the best equipment money can buy backed up by a state-of-the-art computer installation. It will have a generous budget for its first two years; after which, I'll be looking for those tangible results I referred to earlier, before authorising further investment; airy-fairy ideas and pie-in-the-sky thinking will not gain support.

'The in-house team of researchers will have access to other research facilities around the UK. Your overriding objective will be to place this country at the forefront of scientific discovery and invention.

'I believe you can fulfil that dream. You're young and you're inexperienced but I believe you have the ability and intellectual potential to deliver my objective. With that in mind, I am offering all of you a post at the NRSC.'

There were gasps all around the table, jaws dropped, eyes widened as the graduates absorbed what had been said. 'I would add that we didn't draw your names out of a hat; extensive enquiries were made to identify the finest young brains in the country. In effect, you have been head-hunted.'

MacKinnon paused, waiting for the murmurs to die away, giving everyone a few moments to fully digest the offer. 'I'm now going to go around the table, anti-clockwise this time, and ask each of you if you are interested in taking up a post at the NRSC. Those of you who accept my offer will be transported to the facility for a tour, after which, if you remain interested, you will be given a copy of the model Contract of Employment and the Official Secrets Act to examine.

You will all receive the same salary for an initial term of employment of three years and invited to dinner and an overnight stay on site.

'In the morning, if you are happy to sign the terms of the contract, we'll complete the formal processes and the NRSC will have its research team. That's all I want to say at this stage, if any of you have already decided, for any reason, that you don't want to join us, you are free to drop out now without explanation.'

MacKinnon looked around the table, catching the eye of each graduate in turn, but no-one indicated a wish to opt out. 'Good, the opportunity to leave will be made again after the visit to the facility. I recognise that this must all come as a bit of a shock and I'm conscious that I'm pushing things along at breakneck speed but that's how it is; I make no apology for the urgency. Now, are there any questions?'

Julie Powell raised her hand. 'Who'll be heading up the NRSC and who'll be steering the research programme?'

'Good question and one that I anticipated. Alan Croudace here will have full accountability for the facility and will brief you on the general areas of research the government wishes you to pursue. However, it's your responsibility to come up with specific research proposals. You will be expected individually and collectively to determine the detail of the programme. There will be no professors breathing down your neck, unless of course you fail to make progress in which case, the whole project will be reviewed.'

Concern crossed the young woman's face. 'I'm sure none of us have ever heard of a research programme proceeding on that basis, it's customary practice for a professor to head up the team.'

'That's not how the Centre is intended to operate, I want you lot to take the initiative and do the steering and the driving.'

MacKinnon looked around the table for more questions, but there weren't any. 'Right, that appears to be the only question for now, let's move on to the next stage. You are all invited to a tour of the NRSC. You will be driven to the facility and will have a couple of hours to walk around, get a feel for the place, inspect the laboratories, and view the equipment installed to date.

'You will also be given the opportunity to view the residential accommodation which, by the way, will be provided free of charge. That reminds me of an important requirement that I should have mentioned earlier, it will be a condition of employment that you reside on site for the first two years. There will be no exceptions to this rule, though you will, of course, be free to go home for weekends, holidays, etc.

'At this point, should you need to make yourself comfortable, the toilets are back out through the door you came in, girls on the right, boys on the left. After that head for the entrance and take a seat in one of the cars; five to a car, first come first served. Each car will leave as soon as it has five passengers.'

Somerton, who had followed the proceedings on CCTV, travelled with MacKinnon to the NRSC. 'First impressions, Jack?'

Somerton grinned. 'There's a couple of the girls I wouldn't mind shagging.'

'For God's sake, Jack! I'm asking for your professional opinion.'

'Lighten up, Colin, I've been analysing this crew for months and I've observed them all at some time or other, they wouldn't be here if I hadn't been happy with them. This is your show now, I might ask *you* what your first impressions are?'

'Fair enough; from what I've seen, they seem a good bunch though I haven't spotted any natural leaders yet.'

'Too soon for that, you should know that from your days in the Regiment, the moment bringeth the man, or the woman for that matter.'

National Research and Security Centre

The tour of the facility took just over two and a half hours; the graduates were clearly impressed, the walk around regularly punctuated by whistles and gasps of astonishment.

Afterwards, the graduates gathered in the facility's common room, breaking down into smaller groups and starting up animated conversations. All around the room, there was an undeniable buzz of excitement. The chatter faded away as MacKinnon made his way into the room and stationed himself facing all the graduates. 'OK, first thoughts please?' He looked around inviting their responses. The replies didn't disappoint…*unbelievable…top class…impressive…out of this world…world-beating…years ahead of anything I've worked with.*

'I knew you would be impressed; I won't tell you how much it all cost, the Chancellor will throw a wobbly when he studies the accounts. So, can I take it you're all still on board?' There were no dissenters. He glanced at his watch. 'OK, it's nearly six-thirty, time to break up; the notice board on the wall to my left has a list showing which room each of you has been allocated. If you accept a post here, the room you occupy tonight will be yours on a permanent basis. I suggest that you retire to your rooms now, freshen up and report back here for dinner at 8 pm sharp.

'On this occasion, alcohol will be available, but this is an exception. In future, alcohol will only be permissible on special occasions. This rule is not negotiable, any transgressions will result in instant dismissal…instant. You'll find that each room has a telephone and you can make such national calls as you wish. International calls are barred and can only be made through the switchboard and may not be authorised.

'You'll find a computer in your room with a secure ultra-fast broadband connection; use will be monitored. You might not like that but that's how it is and how it will be in the future. Laptops and other devices capable of downloading information can be used for data searches but they must not be used to hold research data. At no time must NRSC data be removed from the site in any form. You'll find that all the foregoing is covered in your Contract of Employment.

'Finally, tomorrow morning after breakfast, each of you will be required to give me your final decision regarding employment here at the Centre. Understood?'

Fifteen heads nodded in unison.

'Right, I'll see you at eight for dinner, hopefully the caterers have arrived. Any questions before we split up?'

Two hands were raised. MacKinnon pointed at Lizzie King. 'The labs are equipped to an unbelievable standard, they must be amongst the best in the world; clearly a lot is expected from us and I retain concerns that there is no-one heading up the research effort.'

'That question was raised this morning and dealt with this morning, I've nothing to add to my earlier reply. You will receive a brief setting out general directions, after that it's up to you to come up with ideas. If you can't work in such circumstances, then it's probably best you don't take up a post.' Lizzie King made to protest but thought better of it and just shrugged her shoulders.

The other question was raised by Alan Glen. 'I'd just say that there are a number of us who share Lizzie's concerns, but my question relates to what happens after breakfast tomorrow, assuming most of us decide to stay?'

'You'll be given a Contract of Employment and invited to sign; all are identical in content. You can hold group discussions if you wish and seek such clarifications as necessary. I can tell you now that changes to the contract will be

120

resisted and most likely refused. You'll also be required to sign the Official Secrets Act, no negotiation on that one. Breeches of the Act would most likely result in a substantial prison sentence. When that business is completed, you'll be free to return home with a requirement to report back here in three weeks. And just so it's crystal clear, I have a reserve list of equally well-qualified candidates to call upon if needs be.'

There were a few gasps and gulps; Julie Powell spoke up. 'That's pretty quick, some of us might have difficulties disengaging from our current commitments.'

MacKinnon shrugged. 'I appreciate I'm pushing things along, but that's how it is. We'll be in touch with your current, or prospective, employers tomorrow morning; I'm sure they'll cooperate, but if they are obstructive, feel free to refer them to me personally. That's it for now, see you back here at eight; I don't know about you but speaking for myself, I'm starting to get hungry. By the way, your overnight bags have been brought in and you'll find them outside in the corridor.'

After Dinner

Pre-dinner drinks came and went, a decent three-course meal followed, wine flowed and as time passed, voices grew noticeably louder. Like-minded graduates were forming groups, bonding was in progress. At 11 pm, MacKinnon moved to a central position and sought attention. 'That's it, everybody, I'm off, no doubt you youngsters could while away the night, but I have a pile of Cabinet paperwork to wade through. I would hope though that this room was empty by midnight.'

A voice issued forth from one of the groups. 'Will there be a curfew every night?'

MacKinnon pursed his lips. 'I hadn't thought of that one; let's say midnight for the first week or so and see how it goes. It's one of those rules you can sort out amongst yourselves, but I don't want a bunch of tired researchers on my hands. You are all being generously remunerated, I want 100% from all of you 24/7.' He looked around trying to judge reactions; young people, particularly graduates, were notorious nighthawks but they were here to work, not party. To his relief, there were no challenges and after a few moments, MacKinnon bowed out, feeling it had been a successful day.

Back in his room, MacKinnon went directly to his laptop and punched in the Jupiter code. His message was brief, any lingering doubts set aside once and for all; a group of young people's lives were on the threshold of being changed forever. *They're all in the process of retiring to bed for the night, do whatever you have to do when you're ready.*

Chapter 12
NRSC Later that Night

02.00, it was time to make a start. Jupiter sighed contentedly, he could at last begin to put his plan into action; the graduates should all be sleeping soundly by now. Just to be certain though, he called up a monitor display of each of the fifteen rooms in turn. He smiled to himself, only he knew that every room in the NRSC was under the surveillance of the concealed microscopic wireless operated cameras he had personally installed towards the end of the equipping contract.

The fact that all the graduates were sleeping soundly hadn't been left to chance, he had taken care of that too; a miniature capsule inserted within each pillow would release an odourless sleep-inducing gas when the occupant got into bed. A minute of exposure to the gas would result in the victim's virtual unconsciousness for several hours. He hadn't informed MacKinnon of the existence of the cameras or the gas; they weren't optional so why risk a confrontation. If everything went to plan, he reckoned that the task he was about to begin would take about three hours.

Jupiter crossed to a console and entered the code controlling the access from his living quarters to the lounge, which had been a hive of activity just a few hours ago. The room stood quiet and empty but anyone watching would have seen the large floor-to-ceiling tropical fish tank slide slowly and silently downwards into a void beneath the floor. The door behind the tank could only be discerned by close inspection, the decorative wall panels had been chosen carefully to provide very effective concealment.

The console registered that the lowering of the tank had completed successfully; the work of the night could begin. Jupiter gathered up his equipment, placed his hand on a wall-mounted scanner and looked on as the door from the lounge swung slowly open. He stepped forwards briskly, full of energy;

the few weeks spent in the controlled environment of his new laboratory had restored him to full health and he was eager to get on with his task. He felt a tremor of excitement as he contemplated the future that lay ahead. As a precaution, he closed the laboratory door but left the tank in its lowered position. There was no chance of it being discovered, the Research area's sole security guard, like the graduates, was in a drug-induced sleep.

Room 15 was nearest to the lounge and he made his way there, then used his master swipe card to gain entry. Light from the corridor spilled into the room and onto the bed directly opposite the door; on it lay Jess Reid, atomics physics graduate, fast asleep, totally oblivious to the world around him. He barely stirred when Jupiter eased the earphone-like unit over the graduate's head and onto his temples. Reid had an honours degree, but his abilities barely registered on the device.

Jupiter smiled. *You have such a long way to go in your intellectual development, young man.* The analysis took a few minutes, after which Jupiter programmed the device to deliver the neural transfer of knowledge necessary to give Reid the advanced scientific capability required in the years of research that lay ahead. Other subtle changes were made to ensure that Jess Reid's persona would be forever susceptible to Jupiter's wishes. The process completed, he left the graduate as he had found him, sleeping deeply and blissfully unaware of the astounding transformation his brain had undergone.

Lizzie King was next, brighter than some with two first class honour degrees but still intellectually short of what was required to deliver the future he and MacKinnon sought. Jupiter eyed her appreciatively; she presented a very attractive sight with her blonde shoulder-length tresses spilling over the pillow. She looked so peaceful, her breathing light and steady, her lips slightly parted.

He placed the neural transfer headpiece in position and initiated the process necessary to enhance her abilities; she was destined to become one of the brightest stars in the NRSC. On impulse, he eased down the duvet, disappointed when he found she was wearing a plain white cotton nightdress with a high ruffled collar.

Nearly two and a half hours went by before he entered the last bedroom, smiling contentedly when he saw Maggie Hurst. *You are very beautiful, Maggie, I think you are my favourite graduate.* He stroked her cheek gently as he put the neural transfer device into place and initiated the transfer process.

As he had done with all the female graduates, he lowered the duvet, catching his breath when he saw she was naked. His eyes travelled slowly over her body, admiring every curve, his heartbeat registering his excitement. Much as he wanted to, he made no attempt to touch her. When the transfer completed, he stroked her cheek fondly, took one final longing look at her unclad form then pulled the duvet back into place and left the room.

His work was done. Henceforth, when he needed to, he could control their thought processes, their inventiveness, their creativity, even their emotions if he wished. The future had begun. He hurried back to his sanctuary and emailed MacKinnon. *The process is complete.*

Next Morning

Breakfast was in progress, sounds of chatter and the occasional outbreak of laughter filled the room; there was nothing to suggest that fifteen young people had gone through a life-changing experience. Everything was as it should be, perfectly normal, or so it seemed. At a table for two near the door, Maggie Hurst and Alan Glen sat opposite each other, making small talk.

'I'm sorry but I can't recall your name.'

'Maggie Hurst, thermodynamics and hydromechanics; and you?'

'Alan Glen, physics and mathematics. Did you get a good night's sleep? I often have difficulties first night in a new bed but last night I slept like a log, a long, jam-packed day, I guess.'

'Me too, although over-indulging in champagne and that delicious Bordeaux might have had something to do with it. I don't know about you, but all this talk of research and invention must have sent my subconscious into overdrive, I woke up this morning with all sorts of ideas buzzing around in my head.'

Glen's interest was immediately roused. 'What sort of things exactly?'

Maggie Hurst grimaced and shook her head. 'Nothing I can describe in detail, but it related to energy generation and thermal fusion; it's all a bit hazy but there's something there. I can't wait to move in here and get started on it.'

Glen chuckled. 'You're certainly coming to the right place, sounds like you'll get off to a flying start; the PM will be delighted. I'm interested in that area of work, by the way; if you need someone to bounce ideas off, I'm your man.'

MacKinnon elected to eat in his room, all the while pondering the future he had helped set in motion. *It all seems too good to be true, am I really standing on the brink of fame, greatness perhaps? Will I really be taking the UK into a golden era? I still wonder why Jupiter has chosen me. Who is this man? Just what is his motivation? Is he a defector from China, Russia or even USA? Those were the countries where the science involved, and the resources to support them, were most likely to exist.*

He might even be an alien, maybe that's why he's happy to be called Jupiter; no, that's too fanciful, the preserve of science fiction. I must insist on meeting him, he can't go on just being a shadowy outline. Could Jupiter really access and engineer the very workings of the brain? He had certainly been convincing.

The worry bugs surfaced and planted the thought that this could all still be a giant hoax.

Please God, make it real but don't let those kids get damaged. And what would happen if I were to upset Jupiter and the guy walked away? But why would he if he's getting what he wants? And believe me, I'll see that you get whatever you want, Jupiter, nothing is going to get in the way. Oh my God, Colin, what happened to that line you're always telling Somerton not to cross? And Alan, what would be his reaction if he found out about Jupiter's neural manipulations?

MacKinnon groaned out loud. 'Fuck it! Somebody has got to make the big decisions.' He glanced at his watch, 9.10; time to get dressed, he was due to address the graduates at 9.30. *Formal dress, I think, it is a business meeting after all.* It was time to go, he gathered up the fifteen graduate folders, each contained two copies of a contract of employment and two copies of the Official Secrets Act. Just to put the frighteners on, he had attached a list of the penalties that could result from breaching the Act.

At 9.25 there was a quiet knock on the door; he knew who it would be and called out. 'Come in, Jack, the door isn't locked. Thanks for being on time, I want to set a good example for this lot.'

'Good morning, Colin. Like you, I try to be on time, our old SAS habits die hard.'

'That's for sure, let's go and address the troops. Alan went back last night so it's just you and I today.'

The buzz of conversation died away quickly when the two men strode purposefully into the dining room.

'Good morning, everyone, I trust you slept well. Before I begin, let me introduce Jack Somerton, my National Security Advisor. Alan Croudace has gone back to Downing Street to mind the shop. Jack reports directly to Alan and has responsibility for the security of all the functions carried out within this facility. More importantly, he has responsibility, along with the other Intelligence Services, for the security of our country. It was Jack who personally researched your background in depth; if he hadn't been satisfied with what he found you wouldn't have been invited to join us. I can assure you that if you step out of line, he'll know.'

'Sounds like Big Brother is watching us,' voiced John MacCleod.

MacKinnon frowned. 'You can see it that way if you want but that's how it is. The research taking place in this facility will be far too precious to put at risk, either by something you do, or by an unauthorised external source.'

Somerton chipped in, 'The Prime Minister has told it like it's going to be; obey the rules and you won't know I'm around. Step out of line and I'll be the first to know, followed in close order by you. I can promise you that you won't enjoy the experience.'

MacKinnon flinched inwardly at Somerton's unveiled threat but nodded his support. 'Moving swiftly on, I'll come straight to the point. Any of you who don't want a job here should raise your hand now, call out your name and then leave.' At that point, the door was pushed open and a graduate entered, quickly making his way to the nearest empty chair. MacKinnon was angry and showed his disapproval in his expression and in his voice. 'Wilson, isn't it?'

'Yes, Matt Wilson, my apologies.'

'Have you got a problem with punctuality, Matt?'

'Not really, I just overslept, that's all, sorry.'

MacKinnon's eyes flashed their annoyance. 'Don't let it happen again.'

Thus far it had been a cosy affair, but it was time to introduce the aspiring researchers to the real world. 'As of today, you are all being well paid, I expect you to work hard and be on time for appointments. I can fill your place ten times over, believe me; don't have me resort to the reserve list this early in our relationship. Now, returning to where I left off, those of you who don't want a post, call out your name and head back to your room and pack your gear. There will be no questions asked, no attempt made to get you to change your mind.'

He looked studiously around the room, the mood had changed; his and Somerton's change of tone had hit home, the atmosphere was noticeably more subdued, but no-one elected to leave. 'Good, now for the paperwork. As I said yesterday, there is a Contract of Employment, a copy for you and a copy for me; same goes for the Official Secrets Act. You'll retain a copy of both documents along with a summary of the penalties if you breach the Act; essentially, we could lock you up and throw away the key.'

MacKinnon continued, 'As previously advised, you will all be on the same salary and conditions of service, money isn't negotiable. I will listen to comments on the contract terms but I'm extremely unlikely to change them. I want you to come forward now and collect your paperwork for signing. I've split the files into two, Mr Somerton has the girls, I have the boys. You have twenty minutes to read and sign both copies and bring them back to me; I'll countersign and return one copy. If you have any queries, attract my attention and I'll invite you to address your concerns in open forum. I'll do my best to answer to your satisfaction. That's it, when twenty minutes have passed, Mr Somerton and I will be ready to sign the contracts to complete the process.'

MacKinnon and Somerton retired to a corner of the room, out of earshot of the graduates. 'I'm glad you dropped the cuddly uncle persona towards the end, Colin, we mustn't have our young friends thinking that you're a teddy bear.'

They sat watching as little groups formed here and there, presumably to exchange views on content or interpretation. A few sought a quiet corner and were happy to read through the documents on their own.

Thirty minutes later, the whole process had been completed, no matters had been raised for clarification, every graduate had signed up and was now an employee of the NRSC. MacKinnon called for order and when the room was quiet, made his closing remarks, 'Thank you, everyone, I'm delighted that you have all decided to stay with us, and that includes you, Wilson.

'If you live up to your credentials, a golden future lies ahead for you and for your country. I believe that this facility, you in effect, have the qualifications and skills to propel this great nation of ours to its rightful place at the forefront of scientific and technological development. Don't let me down; set the world on fire. Good luck to all of you.' He smiled broadly and added, 'Let's aim for at least one Nobel Prize. You are now free to return home; travel warrants are available in Reception and there are cars waiting to take you back into the city. Enjoy some time out with your family and friends then come back in 3 weeks ready for business. There will be an official on site to answer questions and provide administrative guidance for the first few weeks. But remember, this is your ship; it's up to you to decide on the nature of the permanent administrative support you require.'

'Will we see anything of you after today?' someone called out.

MacKinnon smiled. 'I hope so; if for no other reason, it'll mean you've come up with something special.'

Chapter 13
Downing Street, 2003

Just before 1 pm, MacKinnon asked for a TV to be wheeled into his office, tuned into BBC and waited for the news to begin. He knew what the lead item would be, UK's ground-breaking Sustainable Energy Generator, SEG, was about to become public knowledge. The summer of 2003 was drawing to its close when Jupiter had delivered on his promise, MacKinnon's long wait was over.

Selected representatives of the British media had been invited to attend a deliberately low-key event. Attendance would be thrown open to the world when the first production model made its debut. He had chosen not to be present; he wanted the focus to be on the invention and the NRSC, wanted the public and parliament to see that their investment had been worthwhile.

He watched with pride as Maggie Hurst and Alan Glen jointly released the news and answered the journalist's questions, acknowledging that the low-cost, non-polluting, non-hazardous generating process was theoretical at this stage, but insisting that a prototype would be in operation within months. MacKinnon nodded his approval when the duo terminated the question and answer session after fifteen minutes, as briefed by Alan Croudace.

Discoveries all too often didn't live up to early promise and the scientific world, for its part, received the news with a degree of scepticism, in some instances verging on scorn. *How could these two young inexperienced researchers possibly come up with one of science's holy grails?* In some quarters, scorn had been poured on the undertaking to unveil a working prototype within three months. Perhaps understandable, given that there had been similar claims made through the years, all of which had been consigned to the scrapheap. But a couple of the tabloids hailed the discovery as the beginning of a golden future and history would prove them right.

True to his word, Jupiter guided the researchers to the production of a prototype within the original three months forecast.

For his part, MacKinnon had planned his strategy carefully; the entire SEG production output in the first year would be installed in the United Kingdom, giving British companies the huge advantage of virtually nil cost energy. Projections showed that manufacturing costs would fall quickly, and the level of oil and gas imports progressively reduce, fossil fuels would be phased out. Exports would benefit from falling energy costs and increase rapidly. The promised golden era, his golden era, really had begun; he knew the projections would become realities.

There were practical issues to be overcome; to prevent any chance of industrial espionage, SEG production would take place in an old Ministry of Defence factory with advanced security regimes and surveillance systems put in place by Jack Somerton. All staff employed in the manufacturing process would be vetted and covered by the Official Secrets Act and, ever cautious, Jupiter had insisted that he would personally activate the internal security system within each unit.

A SEG unit had the capacity to produce 100 megawatts and was unbelievably compact; just sixty centimetres deep and two metres square in cross section. In the early months, the units were transported to Jupiter's secure area at the NRSC where he checked the integrity of the circuitry and activated the internal security system. The fully operational units were then shipped out to their destination the following morning. A unique signal-omitting identifier was built into every unit and monitored by Jupiter to ensure that any attempt to access its secrets would be detected. Once the alarm was triggered, a unit was programmed to self-destruct unless Jupiter intervened.

The first year's target of one thousand units was achieved but barely satisfied demand in the UK. A second larger factory was constructed, quadrupling output to serve the export market. Every nation in the world was now clamouring for SEG and demanding that in the interest of ecology, UK share the details of the science involved. MacKinnon rejected the demands politely but firmly.

But SEG hadn't been the whole story; without prompting, Jupiter had steered another pair of NRSC researchers to design a compact ultra-high capacity electricity storage unit to provide motive power for road vehicles. This resulted in a ten-year programme being instituted to phase out petrol and diesel vehicles.

GB Ltd moved another notch higher in the world's esteem, the NRSC moved centre-stage and MacKinnon's power and influence began to be recognised.

His refusal to share the science with the world led to an outcry with retaliatory action threatened by friend and foe alike but he had held his nerve, his answer had been blunt and public. *If you apply sanctions of any kind on the UK, you won't get SEG; take it or leave it.* The threats had faded away; the world was learning that when he said "no", he meant "no". Allies and friendly trading blocs were given priority and, ever alert to his image, he had made a limited quantity available at minimal cost to disadvantaged underdeveloped nations.

All buyers were issued with a warning that on no account should any attempt be made to open the unit and every nation complied, until one day he received an unexpected call from Jupiter. 'Sorry to disturb you, Colin, but our Chinese friends are currently attempting to access one of the SEG units. I've shut it down pending this call. Do you want me to take any action?'

'Thank you for getting in touch, I'll deal with it.'

MacKinnon immediately contacted President Chang to inform him that they were aware of what was taking place. The President denied all knowledge of the attempt and promised to investigate and deal severely with those responsible. A short time later, he contacted MacKinnon with an apology of sorts, claiming that it had been a misunderstanding. Disciplinary action had been taken; it wouldn't happen again…blah, blah, blah. But it had given MacKinnon the opportunity to flex his muscles and set an example; he suspended the supply of SEG to China for three months.

Meeting world demands for the unit became problematic, impossible in fact; Jupiter's insistence on activating each unit was effectively a serious bottleneck, limiting output to 4,000 units per annum. Colleagues and allies began to question why production capacity wasn't increased. The issue had to be resolved and after a lengthy conversation, MacKinnon persuaded Jupiter to acknowledge the problem and challenged him to resolve it. He had taken up the challenge and found a way to remotely activate the units, resulting in a further doubling of production, which Jupiter had insisted was the maximum he could accommodate.

There was one other major event in 2003, one MacKinnon would never forget; Jupiter summoned him, that was what it felt like, to an online "meeting". He was required to present himself, as soon as possible, in a secure room in the NRSC, one that was only accessible from Somerton's office. Jupiter insisted this was necessary for security reasons; apparently, the room was soundproofed and screened *to his standards* and would ensure absolute privacy, implying in fact that Downing Street wasn't. MacKinnon had no option but to comply and was chauffeured to the NRSC later that day.

Jack Somerton shook his head and rubbed his eyes in disbelief when MacKinnon turned up unannounced at his office. 'What brings you here, Colin, a nuclear missile threat or has one of the Downing Street crew been kidnapped?'

'Ha, ha, very funny, Jack, but sorry to disappoint you, I've been asked to contact Jupiter online and he thinks it's best if I do it from next door,' he pointed across the room, 'he reckons it's more secure.'

Somerton wrinkled his nose and shook his head. 'Not as far as I'm concerned, be my guest. I store a few bits and pieces in there but never use the terminal; he must know something I don't.'

'Rest assured, Jack, he knows a lot you don't.'

MacKinnon made his way over and pushed the door open, surprised by how heavy it felt, guessing it must be the soundproofing. The room was small and furnished with a small table and office chair plus a few boxes that he presumed belonged to Jack. He sat down and switched on the desktop that sat on the table and entered the Jupiter code when the screen livened up.

MacKinnon felt his jaw drop when Jupiter appeared on screen, but this time not in his customary shadowy form; instead, there he was, in full view, standing behind his console setup. MacKinnon was so shocked he couldn't speak and just stood there in silence, gaping at the figure on the screen.

Jupiter was indeed male, white, around forty with a thick crop of short dark hair above an unremarkable countenance. He had a square face, piercing unblinking dark eyes, an aquiline nose and a thin-lipped unsmiling mouth. His form of dress, a one-piece silver-grey outfit zipped up the front, was unusual to say the least. *Oh no, please don't tell me you are from space; no, you look too ordinary.* He had a lean physique and appeared to be of average height, though on screen it was difficult to tell. At a guess, he was of Russian or Slavic descent. The high forehead traditionally associated with those having intelligence of genius level was not in evidence. Jupiter moved forwards and took a seat behind the console as usual.

Still taken aback, words didn't come to MacKinnon. He said nothing and continued to stare.

'Have you nothing to say, Colin, a greeting perhaps?'

'I'm too shocked to say anything; to what do I owe this honour?'

133

'A level of trust has been established and our interdependence has reached a level where I felt it was fair to reveal myself. As you can see, I'm perfectly ordinary.'

'I'm truly grateful, Jupiter, and now that you've come this far, perhaps you will tell me more about yourself: where you were born, where you were educated and which research establishment you worked in, all the usual biographical details partners normally share.'

Jupiter gave what resembled a smile. 'Curious as ever, Colin, always wanting to know more about me, though it would change nothing. Perhaps someday, I might tell you of my origins, but not now.'

MacKinnon shrugged. 'I know better than to try to persuade you. Why did you ask to see me?'

'Quite simply, the time has come for you to deliver on your side of our agreement.'

'I thought I'd done that; you have a laboratory built and equipped exactly to your requirements.'

Jupiter nodded. 'Yes, and I'm grateful for that, but don't play games, Colin, you know full well that our agreement has not been completely fulfilled. You know precisely what I'm referring to.'

MacKinnon's stomach was churning, the moment he had dreaded had arrived. 'I was hoping you'd had a change of heart.'

'I'm not given to changing my mind, Colin, I will be forwarding full details of my wishes in the usual way; by the time you return to your office, these will be accessible via your computer.'

'Please reconsider, please, is there nothing else I can do for you, anything?'

'Let's not waste time, Colin, don't disappoint me. Bear in mind I can disable every SEG unit in the world if I choose to; it's best if you honour our agreement, believe me. Now I must leave you, we both have work to do. Your young researchers have to be monitored and guided if they are to meet your aspirations and of course, you have to give Mr Somerton his instructions.'

MacKinnon nodded glumly, he had to comply, but maybe, just maybe, he could get something out of the meeting. 'With regard to the researchers, I was wondering if you could enable another major discovery.'

A flicker of a smile crossed Jupiter's lips. 'I think that might be arranged, Colin, but only after you've delivered your side of the bargain. Give it some thought and let me know then what you have in mind.'

The screen went blank, he was summarily dismissed as usual; MacKinnon felt sick inside as he made his way into Somerton's office, numbed by what he was about to instigate.

Somerton looked up from his desk. 'You're looking a bit pale. Are you OK?'

His pulse was racing, heart thumping. 'Our man has revealed himself to me for the first time.'

Somerton blinked. 'No! Well, don't keep me on tenterhooks, out with it. What does he look like?'

'Very ordinary really; white male, short dark hair, in his forties and there's something Slavic or Russian about his appearance. But that's not what is troubling me, I'm afraid we have to action Operation Nightjar. I'll let you have details as soon as I have them.'

'Details, what details?' Somerton spat out the words.

MacKinnon understood his anger and didn't react. 'Details, that's what the man said, Jack. I'll be in touch with you when I know more.'

He was about to exit the office when Somerton shouted 'Colin, I suppose he is the real McCoy?'

MacKinnon stopped mid-stride and turned, puzzled. 'What are you getting at, Jack?'

'Well, it strikes me that our man, with his abilities, could project any image he wanted onto the screen. It could be a computer-generated android, for all you know.'

'Oh God, don't go there, Jack. Please don't muddy the waters, for fuck sake, it's difficult enough dealing with Jupiter as it is.'

In the course of the journey back to Downing Street, Jupiter's words hit MacKinnon like a bombshell—*Bear in mind that I can disable every SEG in the world if I choose to.* He shuddered and felt his stomach knot; not only was he in his power, so was much of the developed world. Fear flooded through MacKinnon, he could stop production but what reason could he give, anyway, it wasn't something he was going to do. Maybe over time, he could persuade Jupiter to pass responsibility for SEG security to the NRSC, but now wasn't the time.

Chapter 14
Downing Street Friday

MacKinnon's thoughts were in turmoil as he entered Downing Street and headed for his office. He barely grunted at Jess and waved a declination of any messages as he passed her desk. During the drive back from the NRSC, his guilty innards had reminded him that he would be going to Abbi and David's at the weekend to celebrate their anniversary. He was looking forward to the day with them and their two children, Maggie and Murray; time seemed to have flown; married in 2001, Maggie born in 2002 followed by Murray in 2003, an idyllic family. He had everything life could offer but here he was, proud father and grandfather, countenancing a heinous crime.

His conscience was playing with his emotions, he wanted to picture Maggie with her blue eyes and golden curls so like Abbi when she was little, but dark thoughts of Operation Nightjar replaced the image. He fought them away and a picture of Murray filled his inner screen; he had inherited David's characteristics though some of his expressions reminded him of his late son. *Trust you to find a way of haunting me to the very end, Lachie.* He shook his head violently, hoping to somehow banish his conflicted thoughts. He had to move on, had to build a barrier between his political and private life.

He turned on his computer, logged in to Jupiter and there they were, Jupiter's requirements. He wanted a young white woman, no more than 25 years old with blonde hair and what he termed a shapely physique. She mustn't be a "street-walker" as he referred to prostitutes. It was a description that would apply to many young women. *Including your own daughter*, the voice of his conscience whispered to him. Shame flooded through him relentlessly, but what had to be had to be. There were times when tough decisions couldn't be avoided, this was one of them. *You shouldn't have a problem meeting the specifications, Jack. God! What am I saying? "Specification". This is a young innocent life I'm talking about. A young innocent woman that you, Colin MacKinnon, are arranging to be removed from her everyday life and consigned to slavery. And for how long?* He didn't know and in truth wondered if he really cared; as ever his inner voice offered comfort—*It's for the greater good, Colin, a small sacrifice.* Easy to say; he wasn't the one making the sacrifice.

He reached for the phone and dialled, relieved when it was answered immediately, he was desperate to set the wheels in motion and wash his hands of the whole sordid business. Once he'd dumped it on Jack, his feelings of guilt would fade away.

'Jack, he's been in touch; Nightjar has started. Have you got pen and paper handy?'

'Fire away. I'm sure I'll remember the details.' Somerton listened but made no notes. 'Got it, Colin; you want a white, young, blonde girl with big tits and not on the game; how very fucking predictable.'

'Under 25, Jack; and please try not to be so crude. Try to show a modicum of respect.'

'Piss off, Colin. I shan't be asking to see her fucking birth certificate, shall I? And don't talk about *respect*; it's in short supply and you're certainly not earning any this time round.'

MacKinnon winced. 'One more thing, Jack; he says as soon as possible.'

'Is that fucking right?' Somerton snarled. 'Hold on, I'll see if I've got a candidate in my fucking stationery cupboard. I won't linger around on this dirty business, Colin, but I'll do it when I'm ready, not before.' Somerton was angry and was making no attempt to hide it.

He was right, MacKinnon knew it; it was time to be conciliatory. 'I understand your feelings, Jack, I really do, I share them. But at the end of the day, we must go along with this, there's no alternative. Do your best, I can ask no more.'

'Leave it with me; I'll deliver this weekend, most likely Saturday night.' Somerton slammed the phone down. 'Fuck it, fuck it, fuck it!' He knew it had to be done and he wasn't squeamish, but kidnapping innocent kids, that was something else. Acting on behalf of a client to pick up a hooker or a call-girl for the night was something he had done many times, but not this; this was human trafficking and, worse still, it was something he would have to do personally. The risks were too high to pass the job on, MacKinnon was right about that.

Needlessly, he glanced at the calendar though he knew full well it was Friday. He'd do the job tomorrow. Saturday nights were always awash with young people drinking themselves into oblivion and there were always some who walked home alone, isolated and vulnerable. *Damn, damn, damn. Where? That was the question. Not London or its suburbs; that would be too close to home, the elite of Scotland Yard and security cameras on every corner. Maidstone, Ashford or Tunbridge Wells would be ideal, all readily accessible from a motorway.*

Saturday

Next night, Somerton set out in a nondescript Ford Focus, timing his journey so that he would arrive in Tunbridge Wells around 11 pm; that would allow time enough to reconnoitre the area. The younger fraternity would be on the move between hotspots; some would be calling it a night and making their way home, the rest draped over a bar waiting last orders.

He slowed as he drove into Southborough, keeping below the speed limit just in case there were any eager cops around. From there, he went on a reconnaissance trip through Tunbridge Wells before making a sweep around and heading back towards Tonbridge. On route, he made a mental note of lively pubs and pavement gatherings of young revellers then finally settled on the area he would carry out the abduction.

It was just after midnight when he drove back into Tunbridge Wells, this time keeping to the area at the lower end of the town near the railway station and the Pantiles. He knew his car would be picked up on CCTV somewhere along his route. Not that it mattered; the plates wouldn't show up on the Vehicle Licencing System; they were false and the vehicle itself belonged to Her Majesty's government.

Shortly before 1 am, he spotted his target, a duo of young lovelies, both blondes, giggling and chatting noisily as they made their way up Major York's Road towards Mount Ephraim. It was a pity there were two of them but on the other hand, the location, with its absence of houses, was ideal for what he had to do, and as far as he could see, there was no-one else in the immediate vicinity. Somerton drove past them and stopped about 50 metres ahead in the middle of a line of parked cars, got out and fiddled with his keys apparently in the process of locking the car door.

The girls were alert to his presence and sensibly, were watching him but probably felt safe since there were two of them and the man ahead didn't appear to be showing them any interest. Somerton deliberately walked away from them, smiling when he heard them resume their chatter, having decided he didn't present a threat. Then, trying to make it look as though he had left something behind in the car, he stepped onto the road and turned back. His timing was good; they drew level with him as he reached the car and pulled open the rear door.

Caution returned, their girly chatter died; sensibly they moved to the opposite side of the pavement, eyeing the man discreetly. He looked harmless enough and wasn't paying them any attention, but he was a man and they weren't taking any chances.

Somerton made a point of ignoring them as they passed; his attention devoted to scanning the area ensuring that there were no cars approaching or other late-nighters stumbling up the road. The girls weren't aware of his movement when he stepped swiftly to the rear of the car and silently doubled back behind them. They yelled out with pain simultaneously as the tasers hit them in the back. Somerton dropped the weapons and grabbed the girl nearest to him, preventing her slump to the ground. The other girl buckled at the knees and crashed unconscious onto the pavement. 'Ouch, sorry darling; it's not your lucky night, or on second thoughts, you are the lucky one.'

He wasted no time in bundling his captive onto the backseat of the car where he taped her mouth, wrists and ankles before covering her with a blanket. All that was left now was to retrieve the tasers and make his getaway. He took a few seconds to scan the area to make certain there were no witnesses, smiling when there were none to be seen. There was one parked car, but it was some distance away and there was no sign of its driver. The girl lay motionless as he got back behind the wheel and drove away. 'God, I hope you're OK, darling; don't peg out on me.'

As soon as he was out of the town, he pulled over into a deserted layby to blindfold the still unconscious girl and check her pulse, relieved to find it was strong and steady. He took a moment to transfer the tasers to the car boot, then he was back on the road. With luck, the journey back to the NRSC would be uneventful.

The unfortunate girl recovered consciousness and guilt stabbed at him when he heard her muffled cries of fear and anguish. Occasionally, he caught sight of her in his rear-view mirror, writhing and bucking as she tried to release herself.

Why the fuck am I doing this? After a while she went quiet, probably realising that her efforts were futile, either that or she had tired herself out. Somerton turned on the radio and selected Radio 2, setting the volume high, not wanting to hear any further sounds of distress. *Who are you, I wonder? Poor little bugger, what's the story of your life this far?*

He tried to stop himself dwelling on her plight and attempted instead to convince himself that she was just another consignment being delivered to a client; the other half of a bargain, blood money being paid.

Two miles short of the NRSC, Somerton pulled over in front of a field gate entrance and got out of the car; he knew nothing of the girl's terror when she felt the car come to a halt. She thought the time had come when she would be raped, or worse. Why else had she been abducted? *Please God, don't let him kill me!* Her fear subsided momentarily when she realised her captor had gone to the rear of the car but gripped her again as the thought occurred to her that he might just be relieving himself in readiness for what he was about to do. She heard the boot open and close almost immediately. *What was happening? Oh God, please help me!*

She had no way of knowing that Somerton was swapping the number plates in readiness for the scanning system and CCTV installed at the NRSC. If the plates weren't recognised, awkward questions would be asked and although he could come up with a plausible excuse, the incident would be logged. It was a task that he had carried out on countless occasions and took only a few minutes.

The girl's terror returned as the rear door was pulled open and the man reached across her body. Oh God, his hands were on her throat, she was about to be strangled; her darkest fears were about to become reality, she was going to die. She struggled, the pressure on her neck was increasing; she felt herself losing consciousness and thought her end had come. But Somerton knew exactly what he was doing, her unconsciousness wouldn't last for long if he'd applied pressure properly. He couldn't risk her calling out, or her movements being detected by the NRSC security guard. The job done, he pulled the blanket over her and continued his journey.

The last couple of miles to the NRSC seemed to take longer than usual, probably because he wanted the whole sordid business over and done with. Time was dragging its feet and he could do nothing to hurry it along, but at last he was at the barrier and lowering his window to look directly at the security camera and wait to be recognised. The car number plate would have already been checked out on the Centre's database. The loudspeaker blared into life and filled the quietness of the night. 'Another one of your late nights, Mr Somerton?'

He recognised the voice as that of Tom Martin, a guard he had become quite friendly with. 'Afraid so, Tom, the world never sleeps in my business.'

Martin chuckled. 'Serves you right for being so well paid.'

The barrier rose, Somerton drove through and headed for a parking bay adjacent to his private entrance at the rear of the building. This area was in a CCTV blind zone; he'd seen to that at the design stage. Once there, he punched in his security code and pushed the door open, leaving it ajar whilst he returned to the car for the girl. Thankfully, the weather had been kind, it was cold but there wasn't a breath of wind and more importantly, it wasn't raining.

He paused a second to glance up at the sky, admiring the full moon, or was it a new moon, he never could tell the difference. Whichever it was, it shone down amidst a myriad of stars. Not for the first time, he asked himself how despicable deeds, such as this, could take place in his country under such a beautiful sky. The girl stirred as he pulled open the car door but offered no resistance as he slid her off the backseat and took her under her shoulders to drag her into the corridor. Kicking the door closed behind him, he breathed a sigh of relief; he was safe, the job was nearly done.

He moved forward to the door at the end of the corridor, which afforded access to his office. Easing the girl gently onto the floor, he placed his palm on the sensor pad and waited for it to turn green, enabling the door to swing open into a short passage. Halfway along, another door gave access to a staircase leading to the sanctuary of his office suite. But that wasn't where he was headed, he had to get rid of the girl first. She was still groggy and squirmed in protest as he dragged her along to the wall at the end of the passage where he left her to her fate. *You must be terrified, poor little bugger.*

A concealed entrance to Jupiter's area was built into the wall and Somerton's instructions were to deposit her there and leave immediately. He was tempted to lie in wait for Jupiter and confront him, but he was sure that somewhere, a concealed camera would be observing his presence.

He didn't climb the staircase to his office, instead returning to his car and driving around to the front of the building as would have been his normal practice. The security staff on duty showed no surprise when he strode purposefully into the control room; late night visits were part of his routine.

'Just keeping you bastards on your toes,' he said loudly as he made his entrance. As he always did, he wandered from console to console exchanging pleasantries with the security team before retiring for the night. The overnight room attached to his office was literally a home from home, equipped with everything necessary for his comfort. Ten minutes later, he was in bed and sleeping soundly.

Sunday

Next morning, Somerton rose at 7 am, showered, dressed and made ready for his journey back to his London home. He resisted the temptation to check that the girl was gone; he knew she would be. *Poor wee soul, what did the night have in store for you? Sometimes I hate you, Jack Somerton, fuck it.*

Hunger was tightening its grip by the time he pulled off the motorway into a service plaza for breakfast. *A full English breakfast for you, Jack, you've earned it.* Newspaper headlines blazoned the previous night's abduction with photographs of the unfortunate girl, one Becky Swift, aged 19, from Tunbridge Wells who had been attacked and taken away in a car just after 1 am on her way home from a night out. Her companion believed they had seen their attacker but couldn't provide a detailed description, although she did allude to a man in a black car. Police were asking for witnesses and pursuing various leads. No mention was made of the use of a taser.

Somerton watched as a news item flashed up on the TV screen; a police superintendent was trying to tread the fine line between warning girls to be cautious whilst saying that such attacks were rare.

I wonder what's happening to you now, Becky? Are you sitting down to a nice breakfast? No fucking chance of that, Jack. Christ, I don't want to know! The girl was no longer an anonymous victim, she had a name and a family; he felt the pangs of guilt return. *Forget it, Jack, what's done is done; it serves no purpose to feel sorry now.*

MacKinnon learned of the incident via Radio 4 whilst having breakfast. He too was gripped with guilt; he too had his own escape route of justification. *It's all in the national interest,* he told himself. His wife, still in her dressing gown, shook her head sadly. 'Poor girl, I do hope she'll be found soon; imagine if it was Abbi. Her family must be distraught; left to me, I'd castrate any man involved in that kind of thing.'

MacKinnon nodded vigorously. 'I totally agree, darling, but it's not going to happen. Civilised societies are far too tolerant when it comes to handing out retribution.'

Chloe grunted. 'Maybe, but I bet the public would vote for it; not that public opinion counts for much, except in the run-up to an election, of course.'

Her husband grimaced but didn't argue; there was a lot of truth in what she said.

Downing Street

Back in his office, MacKinnon phoned Somerton on his secure line. 'Mission accomplished, Jack, well done. No trouble or anything untoward, I hope? It doesn't appear that anybody got a good look at you.'

Somerton's inner anger erupted on MacKinnon, the only one he could vent it on. 'I don't want fucking praise! I'm not fucking proud of what I've done; it was all a piece of cake. I just donned my invisibility cloak and she walked straight into my arms. We'll speak another time.' The line went dead; their conversation was over.

MacKinnon shrugged. 'Touchy as ever, Jack; some things never change.'

Leaning back in his chair, he pondered on his next meeting with Jupiter and what he might get out of it. Jupiter had got what he wanted and so would Colin MacKinnon. Life was good, very good. On the political front, government business was under control; his comfortable majority in the House ensured that. And, if the polls and newspapers were to be believed, his popularity was sky high with Joe Public. But that wasn't enough; he wanted to continue his climb up the ladder of international standing.

Chapter 15
Downing Street

MacKinnon was on his way back to his office following a routine Cabinet meeting when his mobile vibrated. 'MacKinnon.'

'Sorry to disturb you, Colin, I know you have a Cabinet meeting, but please contact me urgently on your laptop, it's regarding China.' There was no need to ask who the caller was; Jupiter terminated the call abruptly as was his usual custom.

MacKinnon scurried along to his office and keyed into his laptop; Jupiter filled the screen immediately.

'Thank you, Colin, the matter is urgent; our Chinese colleagues are seeking to access one of the SEG units again. I wanted to let you know before I disabled it; if I don't act soon, the unit will explode with resultant loss of life.'

'I can understand the urgency; take no action, I want to teach them a lesson; it will serve to put the rest of the world on alert.'

'I warn you that it will be a large explosion, there will be multiple deaths and injuries. Are you certain you don't want me to intervene?'

'Absolutely certain. How long before it explodes?'

'That will depend on how quickly they progress; probably within the next ten minutes. I repeat that the explosion has the potential to kill and injure many people.'

'I think we've completed our business, thank you for contacting me.'

That evening, he kept tuned into the television waiting for news about the China situation; the administration was secretive in that great country but sooner or later, there would be a leak. Sure enough, Reuters broke the news. *A massive explosion had destroyed one of China's most prestigious research facilities killing fifteen of their leading scientists and injuring scores of others. No information was available as to the cause of the explosion.*

MacKinnon smiled wickedly; the world would soon know what had happened. *Talk your way out of this one, President Chang.* He made his way to the red phone.

'Yes, Prime Minister?'

'Get me President Chang on the line as soon as possible.'

Minutes later, the phone buzzed. 'Sorry Prime Minister, President Chang is ill and unable to take your call.'

MacKinnon grunted. 'I'll bet he is. Get onto the Ambassador and tell him to be in my office at 10 am tomorrow morning.'

Downing Street

The Ambassador duly reported the next morning. He barely let the poor man speak.

'Ambassador, let me say from the outset that there is no point denying what I'm about to relate; the facts speak for themselves. Yesterday morning, at a location on the outskirts of Beijing, your scientists attempted to open SEG No. 26217. We know this to be a research facility. We know there was a huge explosion, we know there were many deaths and casualties. Our sympathies are with the families of those who lost their lives.' *Lives you could have saved, Colin,* his conscience whispered. 'This is in clear breach of the agreement between our countries and I require an explanation.'

The Ambassador nodded his head gravely and apologised profusely, blaming the incident on an inexperienced technician and gave his assurances that it would never happen again.

MacKinnon summoned up a look of exaggerated incredulity, shaking his head from side to side slowly. 'A similar excuse was given on the previous occasion an attempt was made to access a unit. Please convey to President Chang my extreme annoyance that this incident has occurred. Tell him that China has been forthwith removed from our supply programme and will not be eligible to re-join for at least twelve months. During this period, no further units will be supplied. Further, if President Chang wishes to apply for re-admission to the programme, China will be required to donate £50 million pounds sterling to the Disaster Emergency Committee. That's all I have to say, Ambassador.'

'But—'

'No buts, Ambassador; this meeting is concluded.'

He knew he was being extremely rude and felt sorry for the poor man who he knew to be a decent sort, but an example had to be made. And truth to tell, he rather enjoyed figuratively kicking China in the balls.

Within the hour, President Chang sufficiently recovered from his illness to pick up the phone, ranted on about MacKinnon's behaviour and threatened the United Kingdom with a range of trade sanctions. He told him to go ahead and advised that in such circumstances, the United Kingdom would impose a permanent ban on the supply of SEG units. MacKinnon was enjoying the exchange and regretted that it was taking place via interpreters. He smiled at the President's explosive reaction of what he presumed were a series of expletives. At which point, he terminated the call and made a note to brief the Cabinet on the incident and the aftermath.

In the event, the UK had not been subjected to sanctions and ultimately £50 million had been paid to the DEC. The supply of SEG units to China resumed twelve months later. President Chang and MacKinnon never conversed directly again, albeit their paths crossed on occasions, such as G20, when world leaders assembled to make the planet a better place for humanity. Poor old Alan Croudace was left with the task of rebuilding diplomatic relationships; MacKinnon never dared tell him that he could have prevented the explosion.

Downing Street, 2004

Towards the middle of 2004, Jupiter dropped a bombshell of a demand. 'I want another girl.'

MacKinnon was unable to control his anger. 'No, I will not do it. Why two girls? Isn't one enough for you? They are human beings, not a commodity to be traded at will.'

Jupiter reacted calmly. 'Make it happen, Colin, treat it as a demand, not a request.'

'And if I don't?' It was sheer bravado and he knew it.

'Quite simply, you will lose my cooperation for future inventions and of course, there is the question of existing and future SEG units.'

It was no contest, Jupiter held his future in his hands, but he couldn't give up without a fight. 'So, you're resorting to blackmail, the lowest of the low. Why can't you be satisfied with one girl? Have you no sense of humanity?'

'Don't lecture me, Colin; your words are somewhat hollow given your actions in the short time I've known you. Setting aside Massakori, you have, this far, sacrificed an innocent young woman for my pleasure, allowed fifteen Chinese researchers to be blown to pieces and perhaps most unforgivable of all, condemned your son to death when you could have saved him. Hardly a humanist outlook, I would suggest?'

Oh my God, he knows about Lachie! MacKinnon stammered out his words. 'I-I-I have done what I had to do for the good of my country, for the good of mankind.'

'Of course, Colin, of course you did. And now, for all the same reasons, you're going to sacrifice another young woman.' Jupiter was almost sneering.

'I tell you, I did it for the good of mankind. Unlike you who are just satisfying your own personal needs.'

'Don't treat me like a fool, Colin; you are motivated by power and the prestige that follows in its wake. Be honest with yourself, if you haven't forgotten how. This discussion is over, my request is not negotiable, and I shall take this opportunity to inform you that I shall require a new girl to be provided every six months or so.'

His heart sank, he felt despondent, yet again he was having to bow the knee. In his heart, he knew he would comply but felt he had to put up some resistance. 'I can't bring myself to sacrifice an unending stream of young girls, I can't. My conscience just won't allow it.' The words were said with little conviction and Jupiter knew it.

Jupiter's tone softened. 'Colin, you have my assurance that the girls will be returned to society with no trace of physical harm. And as you know, someone is murdered every week in the United Kingdom. Thousands are killed in wars all over the world every month; compare that with a few girls.' What Jupiter had said was true; sacrificing a few for the benefit of many could be justified; at least that's what MacKinnon told himself. It was a tough decision and one he was prepared to make, but his emerging compliance sank away as quickly as it had arrived.

'But you can't just release the girls; they will be questioned and reveal everything that has happened to them.'

'Not at all, Colin, I can take care of that eventuality.' Jupiter's voice was almost soothing. 'I will simply erase their memory; they will have no recall of events, I assure you. The current girl will be returned to society fit and well as soon as I have a replacement.'

147

He opened his mouth without thinking. 'Are you mad? I can't agree to that, experts will question her, she'll reveal everything!'

Jupiter's eyes blazed with anger. 'I am neither mad nor stupid as you appear to suggest. Listen to what I'm saying, I will repeat myself, she will have no memory of past events whatsoever. In fact, she won't even know what her name is.'

His mind was in a whirl; Jupiter had reassured him to a large extent, but he wanted something concrete out of the stand-off. He just couldn't think what to ask for on the spur of the moment. 'What can you offer me in return, a breakthrough in the health field perhaps? If our partnership is to continue, I want something tangible out of this situation and that's not negotiable either.' It was a bluff, but MacKinnon had to try. 'In fact, I'll go further; if we go down this route, each time a new girl is provided, you must give me a new major invention in return, and I mean, major.' He tried to sound defiant but surely Jupiter knew he was bluffing.

To his relief and surprise however, Jupiter nodded. 'I knew you would have a price, Colin, everyone does in this world. Can you be more specific about what it is you want? The health field is wide, what precisely do you have in mind? Prosthetics, medicines, vaccines, diagnostics? The choice is yours.'

He had one of those inexplicable flashes of inspiration. 'What about a diagnostic scanner that an individual can lie on and have his or her health status analysed, with any current illness and potential illnesses diagnosed, like one of those machines out of science fiction, like they have in Star Trek.'

Jupiter pursed his lips. 'A highly complex device and one beyond even my capabilities; I'm afraid we are yet to enter the fictional world of Star Trek. The best I could possibly offer is an enhanced MRI scanner perhaps with integral DNA analysis capability. Bear in mind though that when illnesses are diagnosed, they will require treatment and the individual will have to live with the diagnosis for better or for worse. The implications for your NHS could be very costly.'

MacKinnon nodded. 'Hmm, yes, I can see that, but I'd still like you to proceed.'

Jupiter shrugged. 'Very well, your decision, I'll do my best to set your researchers on the right track. For your part, you will arrange for your friend Somerton to henceforth meet my requirements during the first weeks of April and September each year. Commit to that and I'll instigate any scientific development you request. In fact, I suggest that you prepare a list of aspirations for my consideration; that will make it easier for me to programme the researchers.'

His angst evaporated, gone were any concerns about the girls; all that mattered now was that he could have whatever he demanded. 'I'm taking that to mean that you'll start the invention process immediately and will continue at all speed until the scanner is produced?'

'Precisely that, provided you keep your side of the bargain.'

'And,' MacKinnon insisted, 'to be absolutely clear, on every occasion your requirement is met, you will initiate a new discovery of my choice?'

A flicker of a smile crossed Jupiter's lips. 'You drive a good bargain, Colin. I was confident that we could reach an agreement that would assuage your guilt and overcome your professed moral outrage.'

Waves of elation flowed through MacKinnon, any reservations he had had about the girls were gone; the future was shining more brightly than ever. 'Could you give me an indication of the timetable for the scanner?'

'Your researchers should be able to produce designs within six months. A prototype could emerge three months after that. I would suggest a team comprising Moore, Powell, Wilson and Hamilton would be ideal for this venture.'

'The choice of personnel to take this forward is always yours to make. Thank you, I'm sorry if I was unreasonable. As time goes by, the whole world will be in your debt; mankind will be the great beneficiary of this agreement.'

'Of course,' Jupiter sounded almost patronising, 'and not forgetting your good self.'

He stifled a protest; denying the truth was futile. He shifted the conversation to an easier topic. 'I wonder, could you give some thought to the research group as a whole; I want them all to be usefully engaged. Ultimately, every one of them should be given the opportunity to head up a discovery and share the limelight.'

Jupiter shrugged. 'You bring forward a list of proposals and I'll ensure every researcher has his or her moment of fame, but I must remind you that the question of weaponry must not arise.'

'Of course not.' MacKinnon was eager to please, eager to cement this re-launch of their partnership. 'I had in mind health, food production, security, travel; any suggestions from you will always be welcome.'

'We shall see as time goes on, Colin, now I must go, I think our business is concluded.' As usual, Jupiter didn't wait for a reply and MacKinnon was left looking at a blank screen.

'Charming, thank you, Jupiter, and goodbye to you too.'

When he met with Somerton the following day and told him of the new arrangement, he went ballistic.

'What the fuck do you think you're doing, Colin? A girl to be stolen from her family every six months! I won't do it! I can't do it.'

'I know how you feel, Jack, honestly I do. But think of the benefits the UK is securing from SEG and the electricity storage units, now and long into the future; our balance of payments has gone through the roof. The new diagnostic scanner is an unbelievable concept and has the potential to save millions of lives; it's possibly a hundred years ahead of its time. Jupiter will ensure the girls will be released with no physical harm and no memory of what has happened to them; surely the memory loss of a few beings is worth it however sad it might be for those involved? Christ, Jack! We killed dozens in our SAS days, wars result in the deaths of thousands every year that passes. Does adding a few girls into the mix really make that much difference?'

'Stop trying to put a gloss on these evil acts, Colin, for fuck sake; these are young innocent lives you're talking about. Don't you care about what happens to them? Are you happy for us to join the scum of the world?'

'Of course, I care, Jack, I have a daughter of my own.'

'Yes, but you're not asking me to kidnap her and pack her off into slavery, are you?' snarled Somerton.

He slumped back in his chair, his head in hands. 'I appreciate what you're saying, Jack, I really do, but Jupiter says that they will be fit and well when they're released. The only downside is that they will have no memory of what took place; effectively, he'll wipe their memory clean. They won't even have to bear the psychological burden of recalling whatever happened to them. That's not so bad, is it?'

'Bollocks! Listen to yourself, Colin, he's not teaching them to bake fucking cakes! We can guess what's he's doing to them. At least try to be honest with yourself, for fuck sake, the poor little bitches will have no memory of their childhood, their family or their friends. That makes it all fine and dandy in your book, does it?'

He felt sick in his stomach, Somerton was calling it as it was, denial was pointless. 'I know you're right, Jack, and I don't like it any more than you do but I've got to look at the big picture. The benefits to the UK and its people, the whole of the world for that matter, will be enormous. I'm not going to throw it all away if I can help it.'

Somerton gazed at the man opposite. 'Bravo Colin, like all politicians, you know how to put a gloss on bad news. Enter Colin MacKinnon, Britain's very own Messiah, the new savour of mankind. You're an even bigger bastard than I gave you credit for; Massakori must have been all in a day's work for you.'

'That was different, Jack, and you know it; that was war.'

'War, my arse.'

'I'm not proud of what happened back then, Jack; we did what we had to do and that's all there was to it. Anyway, we gave our word not to speak of the incident after we got home.'

Somerton made to reply, but in the end just shook his head silently. 'What are we becoming, Colin? How far will we sink into the swamp before this is over? I'll do what you want but I don't fucking like it.'

'Thanks, Jack. I have my sleepless nights, lots of them, but I have to go along with what Jupiter requires; the stakes are too high not to.'

The abduction of girls continued thereafter at six monthly intervals, Becky Swift, Elsie Wood, Michelle Hislop, Toni Clarke, Sally Calder—every one of them a badge of shame. But they were badges MacKinnon was prepared to wear as long as Jupiter gave him what he wanted.

He had to hand it to Somerton, the guy had been clever; he'd gone far and wide to conceal the fact that the abductions were linked in any way. His strategy was successful for several years, helped in great measure by the fact that Jupiter, true to his word, ensured that the girls had no recollection of what had happened to them. The kidnappings and subsequent return of the girls to society continued to be meticulously planned and executed; luck must have played its part, it's there whether you recognise it or not, but one way or another, he avoided detection by police forces throughout the country.

But MacKinnon knew that luck wasn't infinite and sooner or later, it would run out, then what? *Tomorrow's problem, Colin, forget it.*

Chapter 16
Downing Street, 2007

'Thank you, everybody, a good meeting, keep up the good work.' MacKinnon wound up another Cabinet meeting, gathered up his papers and was about to go back to his office when Laura Denton approached him.

'Could I have a few minutes of your time, Colin, a personal matter?'

'Of course, I'm free now if that suits?'

They waited until the others cleared the room and MacKinnon invited her to sit down.

'I'll come right to the point, Colin, I'm offering my resignation as of now, though I'll stay on until you name my replacement.'

'Gosh, that's a real shock, Laura, I don't want to lose you. But what's brought you to this decision? You're doing a superb job; the NHS and public love you in equal measure; you're likely to go down in history as our best ever Secretary of State for Health.' MacKinnon was laying the praise on thick, he really didn't want her to go.

She smiled broadly. 'Thanks Colin, that's kind of you, but I'm no fool, it's easy to do good things when resources are flowing.'

'Granted, but you haven't just done good things; you've done the right things and got rid of a lot of bureaucratic deadwood in the process. You obviously enjoy the job so how come you want to resign?'

She patted her tummy. 'One very good reason; my biological clock has been ticking for some time and I'm happy to say that at last I'm pregnant. Mike and I have been trying for over two years and there have been a few false alarms along the way. I won't bore you with the details, but my obstetrician has strongly advised me to reduce my workload and live as normal an existence as possible. As you'll know all too well, we can't give any less than 24/7 in our job so sadly, I'm standing down as Secretary of State for Health.'

'Congratulations, that's wonderful news, I'm thrilled for you; having a child will open up a new world. I hope it doesn't mean we'll be losing you as an MP as well?'

She grimaced. 'To be honest, I don't know, Colin; that's a decision I'll make after the baby is born and I've experienced life as a mother. If an election gets near and I'm not going to stand, I'll give you plenty of notice. Although by that time, I'll be nothing more than a low-profile backbencher.'

'Knowing you, Laura, that just won't happen; I suspect you'll be in the thick of it when the need arises. Have you told anyone else?'

'It hasn't gone any further than close family, but I'd like to make it public as soon as possible after this meeting. And if it's all right with you, I'd like to inform my close colleagues and constituency party today. I don't want the news to come out via the public relations people or the Cabinet secretary or even yourself.'

MacKinnon nodded his understanding. 'Go ahead, play it as you see fit. In the meantime, I'll give some thought to your replacement. It might provide an opportunity for a bit of a reshuffle.'

She pursed her lips. 'Eric will be looking for a step up, that's for sure.'

'Ah yes, Eric. What's he like?' Alarm bells were ringing, memories of the Lachie scenario came flooding back. Fenton would expect to be promoted and he'd have no alternative but to appoint him Secretary of State for Health.

'Well, he's competent; I can say that. He works hard but lacks vision; a good Party man though and won't let you down.' It seemed to MacKinnon that her voice lacked enthusiasm. His instincts told him she was holding something back. 'I sense a touch of reluctance in your voice, Laura, out with it.'

'Nothing major, Colin, there's nothing I know of to justify blighting his career. I guess I just don't warm to him. He can be a touch arrogant and a bit of a bully at times; he lacks sensitivity, shall we say. But it's not just that; there's something there I can't put my finger on. I really don't want to do him down but there are better candidates around such as Linda Jones and George Andrews.'

'Thanks for that insight, Laura, I'll give it some thought. Fenton does have one advantage though—he knows the department. He's been involved in the reform process from the beginning; he probably merits a chance even if he might not be the best candidate.'

'Your decision, Colin, you're the PM. Good luck.'

'Thanks for everything you've done for the Party and the government over the years, Laura; I'll give more fulsome praise on a formal occasion. Pass my regards on to Mike and all the best with your pregnancy; it'll be worth it, I assure you.'

She made her announcement that very evening on her local BBC television news programme. After that, the media got on to Downing Street and MacKinnon paid her the glowing tribute she deserved. When pressed, he declined to give any indication as to her successor. With the news in the public domain, he sat in his office waiting for a call, hoping against all odds it wouldn't come. But come it had.

'Eric Fenton is on the line for you, Prime Minister.'

'Thanks Jess, put him through. What can I do for you, Eric?'

Fenton laughed out loud. 'Have a wild guess, Colin. I'm sure you'll get it right first time. It's payback time, I've come to collect my reward. It's sad that Laura is standing down but as I see it, the wind of good fortune has blown in my direction. I don't think you'll find a better candidate than yours truly.'

'Self-praise is no honour, Eric, you'll dislocate a shoulder patting yourself on the back so enthusiastically. I'll be in touch when I've completed my deliberations.'

'Sure,' confidence exuded from his voice, 'deliberate all you need to, Colin, but I want Health and I'll be absolutely gutted if I don't get it. In fact, if you pass me over, I'll probably resign and publish my memoirs; who knows what muck I might dredge up to boost the book sales. I'll wait to hear from you, Prime Minister,' he paused before adding with more than a trace of sarcasm, 'when your deliberations are complete, of course. Have a nice day.'

Cocky bastard! He didn't like it, but Fenton had the upper hand, there was no other option, he had to offer him the post. Still, it meant there would be stability and continuity within the Department of Health and Social Services, and he doubted if he would have any difficulty persuading Cabinet colleagues that Fenton was the man for the job. He just didn't like being blackmailed and if he did appoint Fenton, what would he demand in the future? *You've got me over a barrel, haven't you, Fenton? Fuck it.*

Coincidentally, the SAS Troika or Military Mafia, as Croudace, Somerton and MacKinnon had come to be known by colleagues, met later that same day for their routine monthly meeting. National and global security issues were always top of the agenda, with Somerton taking the lead, reporting on terrorist threats, relevant newspaper articles and, occasionally, large-scale criminal issues. Jack's input was invaluable, especially so when it was beneficial to direct

154

attention away from potentially awkward press for the government; he could always be relied on to find a way of generating a cyber security threat or dig up a terrorist plot of one kind or another.

'Thanks for that, Jack, I do appreciate all you do behind the scenes even if I don't always say so. I get good feedback from colleagues across the whole political spectrum.'

Croudace nodded. 'I second that, and I'm pleased to say that our American counterparts feel confident that our national security is in good hands.'

Somerton pulled a face. 'What is this? Be kind to Jack day? I just do what I'm paid to do and I'm enjoying myself in the process. Well, most of the time anyway.' He shot MacKinnon a look. 'Now, if that's all, I'll be on my way; Superman has to save the nation yet again.'

'I've got nothing, what about you, Alan?'

'Nope, I'll push along if we're done and pick up the pieces Jack leaves in his wake.'

'OK, next meeting, here in a month's time, 4.30 pm. Jess will confirm. There is just one thing, Alan; as you'll have heard, Laura's standing down and I'm thinking of giving her post to Eric Fenton. He seems competent and should hit the ground running; any thoughts on that?'

Croudace shook his head. 'Don't know much about him on a personal level but I reckon he's a safe pair of hands.'

Somerton stood to leave, hesitating for a moment, a serious frown creasing his forehead, but he said nothing and moved towards the door. Croudace gathered up his papers and made to follow. 'See you soon, Colin.'

MacKinnon watched them going; then, as an afterthought, called out, 'Oh Alan, say nothing about Fenton just yet please; I'm still giving it some thought but he's the front runner.'

Outside in the corridor, the two men said their goodbyes with Croudace scuttling away to his next meeting. Somerton remained behind, apparently to engage Jess in some light conversation, then clicked his fingers. 'Damn! Something I forgot to mention to Colin; I must pop back in for a minute. I promise I won't be long.' Without waiting for a reply, he moved swiftly to the PM's office, knocked and immediately made his way in.

MacKinnon looked up in surprise. 'Left something behind, Jack?'

155

'Uh, uh, I wish that's all it was, but alas, I've got some seriously bad news. You won't like it, but it's important you know; word on the street has it that Fenton's a paedophile.'

MacKinnon's mouth fell open; it operated but words didn't take form. 'A paedophile! Are you sure? Oh my God, this will be disastrous for me! Where's this coming from?' His mind was racing at breakneck speed, thoughts flitting around like a ball on a pinball table.

'I have to confess that I don't have any concrete evidence, Colin, only what I heard from one of my press sources who let it slip at the end of a long evening of wining and dining. It seems Fenton's been on their radar for some time and they claim to have tracked down some of the kids who've been abused. It'll make hard-hitting headlines when they're ready to go to print. Given what my source told me, I feel certain what they're alleging is true. I thought you should know before you offer him Health.'

MacKinnon's head slumped; he rubbed his brow in anguish. 'Oh my God, I'm done for.'

Somerton's brow furrowed in puzzlement. 'What do you mean, done for? Call the pervert in and face him with what you know; make the bastard resign, then report him to the boys in blue. The public will support your decision, that's for sure.'

'You don't understand, Jack; the game's up for me.' MacKinnon was devastated, he could have cried, his future was blown to smithereens.

'What is there to understand? The guy is a paedophile, end of story. Stick the boot into him up to your ankle, or better still, let me do it.'

'Can't do, Jack, he's got a hold over me. Something I wouldn't want my family to know or the public for that matter. I'm between a rock and a hard place. I can't offer him the job, and I can't not offer him the job.' MacKinnon's face was a picture of misery. 'Game over, I'm well and truly stuffed.'

Somerton was genuinely concerned. 'I've never seen you like this. Out with it, what have you been up to?'

MacKinnon took a deep breath; he could feel his mental strength draining away. His whole life would be turned upside down. Chloe and Abbi might never speak to him again and the media would have a field day. 'I deliberately let my son die, Jack; I could have saved him, but I didn't.'

'What do you mean, "let him die"?'

MacKinnon sighed wearily; his strength seemed to have deserted him. The whole story poured out and Fenton's part in it.

'I can see the mess you're in, Colin, but Lachie was a waste of fucking space, there weren't many who shed a tear for him.'

'Chloe did, Abbi did. They'll hate me if they find out I let him die and you can imagine what the tabloids would make of it when Fenton tells his story. I agree that Lachie was a failure of the highest order but effectively, I let him die to preserve my own reputation. I'm fucked, Jack, well and truly fucked.'

'I'm coming to realise that the more layers that are stripped away from you, Colin, the tougher and more unscrupulous you are under that veneer of charm. If it's any comfort to you, put in your position, I would have done the same.' Somerton was thinking fast; if MacKinnon went down, so might his closest allies, such as Croudace and himself. 'Do nothing about Fenton, keep the pervert dangling while I think things out. It'll take me 48 hours, but I reckon there must be a way out of this; maybe my reporter friend can be persuaded to pull the story.'

'But how?' A glimmer of hope forced its way into MacKinnon's voice. 'How, Jack? How?'

Somerton stood. 'I don't know, a bribe of some kind, just leave it with me for now, Colin; forget we ever had this conversation.'

When Somerton had gone, MacKinnon poured himself a large whisky and sat back, deep in thought. *What are you up to now, Jack? Not that I give a shit if you can get me out of this mess. In fact, if you pull it off, that Knighthood you want is in the bag.*

Chapter 17
24 Hours Later

Eric Fenton was tired but in high spirits as he was driven home in one of the Department's pool cars. He smiled as the thought struck him that it wouldn't be long before he was allocated a personal car and driver, as befitted the Secretary of State for Health and Social Services. Just as he did every day of the week, he had read and mused over a seemingly endless chain of papers, plans, notices, bulletins and the like. He believed in being familiar with policy and regulations; knowledge was key, knowledge was power, and he was confident that he could respond to anything the opposition or the media threw at him. For him, coming up with an informed answer was never a problem.

Earlier in the day, he had passed MacKinnon in one of the Commons' corridors and had taken the PM's smile and friendly greeting as a sign that he was indeed the heir in waiting for Laura Denton's post. Not that it could be any other way if MacKinnon wanted to remain as Prime Minister.

The car pulled to a halt in front of his Chelsea home in Prendergast Gardens, a large three-bedroom, detached house with a good-sized rear garden. It was an impressive Victorian edifice, painted white with black woodwork and virtually identical to its five companions. For some obscure historical reason, the doors had to be red or yellow to meet a planning requirement to conserve the heritage of the area. Somewhat ironically, given his politics, he had chosen red. The property was bounded by garden at the rear and on both sides with a 2.5 metres high wall of red brick ensuring privacy. The front door was fitted with a high security lock and linked into a state-of-the-art intruder alarm system. A discreet CCTV camera focussed on the doorway, another line of defence against intruders and, on occasion, unwelcome callers.

He whistled happily as he opened the door and stepped into the hall, waving goodbye to the driver who lingered, killing an extra minute or two, hoping this was his final run of the day. There was no wife or partner in Fenton's life; there would be nobody there to greet him and that was how he liked it. He reached up automatically to deactivate the intruder alarm system, stopping mid-track, his eyes widening in surprise when he found it wasn't in operation.

What the hell? I'm sure I set it this morning. He thought about it for a moment, concluding that Mrs Betts, his cleaner, had forgotten to switch it back on following her daily chores; he made a mental note to have a word with her. His forehead creased when he suddenly recalled that she had taken a few days leave and wouldn't be in until later in the week. *Sorry Dora, I guess it must have been me. No harm done; this place is like Fort Knox anyway.*

He bent down to pick up his mail and that was when he noticed the light shining from under his lounge door. A feeling of unease swept over him. *I'm certain I didn't leave that light on; some bastard has been in here!* His unease stepped up a notch and was replaced by fear; maybe the intruder was still in the house, maybe more than one intruder. He listened carefully but there were no sounds emanating from the lounge. Still, anyone in there would have heard him making an entrance and would be quiet. *If you are in there, you're going to get more than you bargained for, I promise you.* A smile played over his lips.

He moved back to the hallstand and slowly, silently, pulled open the drawer where he kept the Beretta he'd inherited from his father. He kept it loaded and felt confidence surge through him when he took hold of the butt; with a gun in his hand, he felt safe. He had never used it in anger, but he'd had a few lessons at a friend's indoor gun range and knew enough to pull the trigger and hit a close-up target.

Moving stealthily to the lounge door, he listened for sounds of human presence but there was nothing but silence. He took a deep breath and flung the door open, ensuring that it slammed back against the wall. *Nobody lurking behind that.* He immediately stepped through the doorway, arm extended, gun in hand ready for use. *Just like they did on TV, he was prepared for any eventuality.*

But not what happened next; he heard the voice before he recognised the speaker. 'Very dramatic, Eric, nobody is going to catch you out in a hurry.'

Fenton stood aghast, gaping at the man sitting comfortably in one of his well-upholstered Georgian style armchairs.

'What the hell are you doing in my house, Somerton? Get out this minute or I'll call the police.'

Somerton smiled, unruffled by Fenton's bluster. 'Relax Eric, that's no way to treat a colleague and I don't think the police would be too happy about you waving a firearm around, I hope you have a current licence? Take it easy, I'm just doing my job, checking out your security and, as you can tell from my presence, it's not very good. We have a duty to ensure that our next Secretary of State for Health and Social Services is safe and sound. Don't you agree?'

Fenton momentarily cooled down at the mention of his new post, but his anger didn't subside entirely. 'What?' Incredulity laced his voice. 'I've never heard of anything like this before. And anyway, you can't just break into someone's home without a by-your-leave. You could have contacted me to arrange a visit, not just break in; last I heard, we didn't live in a police state.'

Somerton nodded and smiled. 'You're absolutely right. *Mea culpa*, I don't believe in giving notice of security inspections, kinda defeats the purpose in my view. Rest assured though I'll pass your complaint onto the PM. Colin wants to make the announcement about your promotion tomorrow and I had to move quickly; we carry out security checks on all senior government posts nowadays. Congratulations, by the way.'

Fenton relaxed. It really was happening; his elevation to the highest echelons was on its way. His tone was now conciliatory. 'That's all very well, Jack, but it is a bit high-handed, don't you think? You could have seen me at my office and asked me to accompany you. But this security stuff is all news to me; when did this practice start?'

Somerton shrugged. 'It's a new regime I've introduced recently as Head of National Security. I'm sorry if I've upset you but I do have Colin's blessing; he was sure you would understand.'

Fenton's brow creased disbelievingly. 'Colin's aware of this visit?'

'Yip, and he's fully supportive.'

Fenton was inwardly seething but he backed off; there was no point in upsetting the PM at this stage. 'Well, OK, Jack, we'll say no more about it.' He waved the Beretta at Somerton. 'You could have gotten yourself killed.'

'It's a risk I take in my job: I must admit I hadn't anticipated you owned a gun.' The lie came easily; he'd searched the house thoroughly looking for evidence of Fenton's paedophilia and had come across the gun in the process, along with some incriminating DVDs.

'Now, how about you put the gun away and show me around. You've got a nice place here; it must be worth a small fortune.'

Fenton grinned. 'Sure.' He put the gun in his pocket. 'Happy now, Jack? Where would you like to start, upstairs or downstairs?'

'Let's start with the ground floor.'

Fenton led the way, pointing out a dining room, a study-office, kitchen and toilet, opening each door in turn and leaving it ajar. 'That's it, let's head upstairs; you'll find there is nothing of serious value. Anyone who breaks in will be very disappointed.'

'Fair enough, Eric, but it depends what you mean by valuable. And anyway, the thing is, they break in, find nothing they like, then they get angry and mess up the place. And of course, when you take up a senior cabinet post, you're bound to bring home highly confidential papers that we wouldn't want to get into the wrong hands. Worst case scenario, you turn up whilst the break-in is in progress and who knows what might happen? We can't afford to lose someone of your calibre, and I doubt if you walk about with a gun in your hand every minute of the day?'

Fenton grinned and all but puffed out his cheeks. 'That's true, Jack, but I do sleep with it under the pillow. Can we push on? It's been a long day, I'm tired, I'm hungry and I've got a lot on tomorrow.'

Somerton smiled. 'Let's not delay then; we must have you looking your best on your big day. There's even a whisper that even greater things might lie ahead.'

Fenton's heart gave another leap of excitement; a dream would soon be realised and who knows what the future might hold. MacKinnon would be paying for his misdeed for as long as he wanted him to.

Somerton stood and motioned with his hand for Fenton to lead the way, 'After you, Eric.'

The two men climbed the staircase together in silence arriving on the landing. Somerton looked down over the bannister onto the hall below. 'One of the things I really like about Victorian houses is their high ceilings.'

Fenton moved along the landing, pointing out a bathroom, a guest bedroom and the master bedroom with its ensuite facilities. A dressing-room-cum-wardrobe and a small storage room with all the usual clutter completed the tour.

'Very nice, Eric, your home is lovely; beautifully furnished, tastefully decorated and it's in Chelsea. I envy you; this place must be worth a bomb.'

Fenton smiled. 'Can't take the credit. I could never have afforded a place like this; it belonged to my father when he was in the city. He was a very successful broker, I inherited plenty, I don't do this job for the money. Is that it? Have you seen all you need to?' He turned to walk back along the landing to the staircase, speaking over his shoulder, 'I keep waiting for some security questions like, was my mother a Russian spy?' He chuckled at his own humour.

Somerton was immediately behind him. 'Well, there is just one question. I was wondering where your squalid little paedophile ring is based?'

Fenton froze in his tracks, searching for words of protest then somehow sensing they would be futile. 'What do you—'

Before he could turn or complete the sentence, Somerton had his hands around Fenton's neck in a vice-like grip, throttling the blood supply to the brain. Fenton felt himself beginning to lose consciousness and reached desperately for the gun in his pocket. The last words he heard were hissed in his ear, 'Don't bother, Eric. The gun isn't loaded, you slimy, perverted bastard, the bullets are in my pocket.'

Fenton was out cold, slumped on the floor, Somerton had only minutes before the MP regained consciousness. He moved quickly into the guest bedroom to retrieve the rope he had hidden under the bed earlier, pulling on a pair of latex gloves as he went. There must be no traces left for a forensic team to find if they came to suspect a crime had been committed; the rope he was about to employ could be purchased from any number of builder's merchants and was impossible to trace.

When he had arrived earlier, he had carefully measured the drop from the landing to the floor below to ensure the hangman's noose he'd made would be effective; it wasn't entirely professionally made lest it prompted questions. Fenton began to stir as he slipped the noose around his neck; he had to be quick. 'Thank God you're not built like that fat bastard, Ross.'

Somerton smiled as he hauled the MP to his feet and leaned him over the sturdy Victorian cast iron railings. 'Happy landings, Fenton.' Somerton lifted him by the ankles and propelled him to the hall below; it was over in seconds. He heard the thud as the rope arrested Fenton's fall, followed immediately by the sound of the vertebrae snapping. After that, there was just the scraping sound of the rope brushing against the bannister rail until Fenton's body settled to stillness.

Back downstairs, Somerton retrieved the Berretta from Fenton's pocket. *You won't need this where you've gone, Eric.* He glanced at his watch. *Time you were gone, Jack.*

He left the dining room and living room lights on, grabbed his backpack from a cupboard in the kitchen where he'd secreted it, then exited through the kitchen door to the rear garden and along the gravel path to the boundary wall. The lightweight aluminium ladder was draped over the wall where he'd left it; rolled up it fitted comfortably into the backpack. He climbed the wall, pulled the ladder up and dropped it over the other side and climbed down. A final scan of the area to make sure the coast was clear, and he was on his way—the whole operation completed in minutes. The few people he passed on the mile or so back to his car didn't seem to pay him any attention and within the hour he was home, enjoying a pizza purchased from his local takeaway. Job done; all he had to do now was sit back and wait for the news to break.

It was late next morning when Fenton's corpse was found. The scenario had evolved much as Somerton had anticipated; Fenton failed to turn up for a meeting, and when he didn't answer his home or mobile phones, an aide had been sent to investigate. There had been no response to the doorbell or the knocker; what else can you expect from a corpse? The aide had called Fenton's office and was given his cleaner's address in the hope she would be able to facilitate access.

The aide, Sally Carlisle, 20, a bit of a geek, and the cleaner, Dora Betts, a middle-aged salt of the earth east Londoner would remember the sight that greeted them when they entered the hall for the rest of their lives. Fenton was suspended like a gruesome rag doll just short of the hall floor, tongue protruding and eyes bulging. Carlisle screamed and fainted.

Dora Betts crossed herself and whispered softly, 'God rest your soul, Mr Fenton.' She took a minute to make sure the younger woman was breathing then dialled 999 to inform the police of the incident. Sally Carlisle groaned and started to regain consciousness, groggily clinging on as Dora helped her to her feet. 'You'll be all right, dear, come with me.' She led the aide to the kitchen and settled her onto a chair. 'I'll make us a nice cup of tea, dear; though from what we see on television, they wouldn't want us to touch anything. Still, what can they do to us? Shouldn't you be letting someone know, dear? Mr Fenton's secretary perhaps or one of his government colleagues?'

Sally gasped. 'Oh my God, of course, I should, how silly of me.'

Eight hours later, the demise of Eric Fenton was announced to the public. At this early stage, the police were confident that a third party hadn't been involved. There were two pieces of evidence that led them to that conclusion. A message on the answering machine. *We know you are a paedophile and will be making this public in the immediate future.* Enquiries had been made of the media and it had been established that a tabloid journalist was indeed investigating Fenton's involvement in a paedophile ring; any knowledge of the phone call was denied and the pay-as-you-go phone from which the call was made proved to be untraceable.

But the real clincher was the letter on Fenton's computer.

Firstly, I apologise to my constituents, my party and my parliamentary colleagues; I cannot face what will follow when revelations appear in the media regarding my private life and have decided to end it here.

I am sorry too for the boys I have abused and, sadly, would have gone on abusing. I should have sought help, but I put my reputation and political career above all other considerations.

I have learned that I am about to be exposed and do not have the courage to face up to the consequences. Sorry.

Eric Fenton.

Somerton's mobile buzzed. 'Jack, it's Colin.'

'Hi, Colin, what gives?'

'I suppose you've heard about Fenton?'

'Just seen the announcement on TV, good riddance I say. It must have been a massive shock for his family though.'

'Thankfully, he didn't have any family, he was unmarried and an only child. Both parents passed away some years back. Jack, you didn't have anything to do with this, did you?'

'My god, Colin, what do you take me for? I'm not going to risk my neck for a lowlife like Fenton. I reckon one of the tabloids made the call to see how he would react. Who cares? It's a brilliant stroke of good fortune for you though; solves that little dilemma of yours, doesn't it? Look, must go, you've called at a bad time, important meeting about to start.'

'OK, Jack, see you around.'

MacKinnon shook his head. *I wonder why I don't believe you, Jack. I'll bet my life on it that you made the call, or got your reporter friend to make it, or maybe even... God, I daren't think about it. Best not to ask any questions, Colin; Fenton is well and truly out of the picture and that's what matters. Thank you, Jack, I know it was you, I just don't believe in coincidences.*

MacKinnon poured a tot of his favourite malt and lounged back in his chair, smiling. *Murder, abduction, I don't know what I'd do without you, Jack. Now to business, I have two vacancies in Health, Laura Denton's and the late Eric Fenton's. Who do I get to take over as Secretary of State? Linda Jones, I think, with George Andrews as her health minister. Good people, continuity and it'll please Laura Denton; ideal. I reckon the situation merits another tot.*

Chapter 18

Fenton's suicide got banner headlines, but the contents of his departing letter were not initially made public. Tributes of the usual magnitude were made but MacKinnon had been very careful with his comments and had distanced himself from Fenton, directing media enquiries in Laura Denton's direction. After all, she had been his boss and knew him better than anyone; not that she had any knowledge of his personal proclivities. MacKinnon was, as always, looking after number one.

But it didn't take long for the tabloids to reveal the truth about the unsavoury side of Eric Fenton; their exposures gave a full and lurid account of his paedophile activities. The dead can't sue for libel and the line between truth and sensational journalism was well and truly blurred. Predictably, numerous witnesses came forward to recount their experiences. Some were genuine, others were opportunistic, prepared to say anything to earn the cash the media were only too happy to hand over.

Some muck had been thrown at the government for harbouring such a miscreant. *How could it be that **someone** in government hadn't known about Fenton's paedophile activities?* Media pressure had been relentless, with questions posed to ministers and backbenchers alike whenever the opportunity arose. Once again, Somerton had come to the rescue by unearthing and planting similar allegations about a hapless tabloid parliamentary correspondent leading to an all-out newspaper headline war.

For his part, MacKinnon issued a statement acknowledging the criticism, but pointed to other scandals, in the world of celebrity, in the church, in local government, in education and in the forces of law and order, as examples of how difficult it was to prevent such occurrences. He promised to review current vetting protocols and eventually the matter faded away from the public glare.

MacKinnon shuddered to think what would happen if his culpability in respect of the girls supplied to Jupiter ever came to light. Their numbers were rising steadily and by the end of 2010, seventeen young women had suffered whatever fate Jupiter had administered to them. Somerton continued to carry out abductions from every corner of England and somehow managed to avoid detection but even he was beginning to wonder when his luck would run out.

At Jack's suggestion, MacKinnon arranged for Jupiter to introduce traces of heroin and cocaine into the unfortunate victims, in an attempt to convince the public that perhaps their memory loss was attributable to the side effects of drug abuse. This theory was dismissed by most experts but in the absence of other causation, the suggestion had taken hold in the public domain. Meanwhile, the girls' families were forming protest groups to raise public awareness and to criticise the establishment's failure to apprehend the perpetrators of these outrages. The stage was reached where demands for an official enquiry surfaced each time a girl was taken.

MacKinnon took the opportunity to make a statement to the House condemning drug use and promising a concerted crackdown on dealers and traffickers throughout the UK. Jupiter and the NRSC had been charged with coming up with improved means of drug detection; early in 2012 they delivered twice over. An ultra-sensitive walk-through body scanner capable of detecting drug use, or even contact with prohibited drugs, was designed and rushed into production.

Legislation was introduced requiring these to be installed in airports, major rail stations, education establishments and in both Houses of Parliament. Some large private companies followed suit. The legislation was so framed that detection of the presence of prohibited drugs brought a presumption of guilt and appropriate punishment.

The NRSC, this time without Jupiter's prompting, produced a sophisticated hand-held scanning device with similar capabilities to the walk-through scanners. These were issued to all police and law enforcement agencies. The do-gooders and libertarians had railed against this gross intrusion of privacy, but an online public poll, massaged by Jupiter, showed that over 85% were in favour of the measure. This supported MacKinnon's claim that the government was simply reflecting the public's wishes. The devices proved successful; drug abuse fell dramatically following their introduction. Moreover, the devices enjoyed massive export success furthering UK's reputation for research and development.

But MacKinnon's conscience never gave up; there were many times when the shame of what the black deeds he had brought about dominated his thoughts.

As ever, he resorted to his usual mantra that the whole of mankind was benefitting from his actions but even for him, the excuse began to wear thin.

The only antidote to his dark moments when depression threatened was his family; Chloe was his rock and could always be relied upon to lift his spirits. His adored daughter Abbi and her husband David kept him in touch with the real world, the world of raising a family and fighting crime. But it was Maggie and Murray, his grandchildren, who really lit up his life; they, bless them, weren't tainted by politics.

Their naïve questions sometimes prompted him to think deeply about what he all too readily accepted as normality. Just a glimpse of a news item on television prompted them to produce an awkward enquiry he couldn't always answer satisfactorily. Birthdays, holidays and Christmases brought many golden hours and thoughts of retirement surfaced occasionally. He just wanted one last big throw of the dice to cement his place in history; he just didn't know what form it could take.

In the meantime, he loved the times they all spent at Chequers; notwithstanding official business, he always made time to relax and enjoy his family. The kids were introduced to many leaders and luminaries and he had to stifle a laugh on many occasions when the kids sprung an awkward, undiplomatic question on his unsuspecting guests. *What do you do? Do you have any children? Are there any wars in your country?*

Some searching questions had brought awkward moments. *Do all children in your country go to school? Does everyone have a vote? Do you have elections? Is there much poverty?* The questions became more searching as they got older and he often had to make an excuse to hurry them away, but it did no harm and they were bright stars in his universe. Inevitably, even for them, the years had rolled on with Maggie's tenth birthday in 2012 being something of a landmark; by which time MacKinnon was 56.

His contact with Jupiter continued routinely, though his so-called partner steadfastly refused to let him into his personal area. In truth, Jupiter remained as much a mystery as he had been from the day they first met. MacKinnon did remain curious as to how Jupiter had fashioned his domain and asked for access from time to time but then reflected that maybe it was best to stay away from the place where the girls were being held.

Their relationship continued to flourish and he was given everything he asked for, with one exception; when he broached the possibility of an advanced weapon for use as a deterrent to further peace throughout the world, Jupiter dismissed the idea instantly. He dropped the proposal without argument but deep inside, he believed it was his gateway to his place in the history books.

The output of the NRSC rolled on; every one of its researchers became international leaders in their respective fields. Britain didn't just lead the world, it was at least a decade, perhaps several decades, in advance of any other nation including the world's giants—China and USA.

MacKinnon made a public statement claiming that he had placed an embargo on the production of any advanced weapon of mass destruction. He wasn't sure if the world believed him; the capabilities of the NRSC were well known. He suspected that many held the view that such a technologically advanced nation would be bound to have some sort of super weapon in its arsenal; death rays, paralysing rays, super-lasers, even the dreaded biological weapons, had all been the subject of media speculation over the years; such assertions were strenuously denied by the Downing Street Press Office.

Time moved on and the next generation of researchers had to be planned and trained and the Centre had a key role to play. Every NRSC researcher had to accept secondment to a university for a year, to lecture and pass on the benefits of their experience. A few national training colleges for elite graduates were created where the best of the best would undertake intensive training to advance their skills and knowledge. As the country's wealth grew, investment in education increased steadily and eventually, United Kingdom outstripped those United States greats, Harvard and MIT, and their Far Eastern academic equivalents.

A golden future seemed assured but the inevitable finally happened, and this time, there was no way of brushing it aside with political gloss. In a unique alliance, those publishing power houses, the Sun and the Mail, put their combined weight into a campaign to investigate just how many girls had been abducted and returned to society without any memory of what had happened to them or even who they were.

Photographs of all the victims formed a major element of the ongoing campaign, local and national TV and radio stations joined the campaign; numerous posters were displayed in public spaces and on public transport. Family members and friends of the girls were invited to take part in heart-breaking interviews; the horrors of the abductions were lived and relived over and over.

The dates of all the abductions were listed in chronological order, along with the places, the times and the circumstances. The six-monthly intervals between kidnappings were highlighted. Their return in the same clothing the girls were wearing when they were abducted was noted, as was the fact that they showed no signs of physical injury. The geographic spread of the abductions was shown on a large-scale map, along with the locations of their return to society. The media had the bit between its teeth and wasn't letting go.

But the overriding similarity that indisputably linked the abductions was the complete loss of memory suffered by the girls; this pointed to a single perpetrator. Previous suggestions that their memory loss was due to drug abuse was irrefutably debunked. The newspapers produced a statement signed by twenty eminent clinicians categorically stating that use of drugs over a period of six months would not result in total amnesia without adversely affecting other organs. Indeed, the level of drug-taking necessary to cause permanent amnesia would probably have resulted in death.

The police and the government were crucified daily by the headlines, the opposition had a field day; shooting at an open goal as it was described in the press. Time after time, the opposition raised the issue and watched MacKinnon squirm as he desperately attempted to respond constructively to the questions raised. Members of his own Party joined in; parents grouped together and paraded up and down outside the House and Downing Street day after day. The matter was raised during his weekly visits to the Palace; even Chloe, Abbi and his grandchildren began to ask awkward questions. For the first time in his career, MacKinnon felt vulnerable, his position was becoming untenable.

In the end, with Jack Somerton's agreement, he bowed to pressure and asked for a period of respite during which a task force led by the Met would be set up to bring the gang or individual responsible to justice. He instructed the Home Secretary to arrange for the chief commissioner to gather together an elite team of expert detectives to investigate. All chief constables were required to provide maximum cooperation backed up by Treasury funding—no limit was placed on expenditure.

The Home Secretary would personally head up the operation and would report regularly to the House on progress. MacKinnon put Laura Taylor in the hot seat in the full knowledge that if an arrest or arrests didn't transpire in due course, it would be her head on the chopping block, not his.

Somerton issued a stern warning that the risks might become too high to continue with the abductions.

'I have to take action, Jack, I don't have an option, you've seen the headlines.'

Somerton's response was blunt. 'Just remember this, Colin; if I get caught, you'll join me, along with your friend in the cellar.'

'Let's hope it doesn't come to that, Jack; Jupiter has agreed to suspend abductions until further notice.'

'Fuck Jupiter, I'll decide whether they ever start again.'

Chequers

It transpired that even in the bosom of his family, MacKinnon couldn't hide from the issue. Chloe and he had invited Abbi, David and the kids to Chequers for the weekend and after dinner, conversation turned to the week's events.

'You've had a tough week with this abduction business, Colin; let's hope it's off your back for a while. I think setting up a Met-led task force, with access to all the evidence collected nationwide, might bring a result.' David sounded quite sympathetic.

'You can say that again. It's been a major distraction and I must say that it reflects badly on our police services; ten years have gone by and we haven't been able to come up with an arrest or even a serious lead. I hope that whoever is chosen to head up this investigation will bring it to a satisfactory outcome. Fingers crossed they pick the right man to lead the task force; we need the best there is for this job.' *How easy it was for me as a politician to criticise and pontificate; the last thing I wanted was to see Somerton arrested.*

Singleton smiled. 'I hope so too, Colin, you're looking at him.'

'You don't mean that you…?'

'Afraid so, I hope you approve? The chief commissioner will put my name forward to the Home Secretary tomorrow. He also hinted that if I don't come up with the goods, my career prospects will be badly affected, so rest assured, I'll certainly give it my best shot.'

'I'm sure you'll be successful, David, feel free to involve me if there are any blockages and I'll see they're removed.' Inside, MacKinnon's stomach was churning at the prospect of his own son-in-law trying to track down Jack Somerton.

'I'm assuming you want to take it on? I mean, if it interfered with other work you believed was vital, or you felt it would unduly impinge on your time with

Abbi and the kids, tell me and I'll get the Home Secretary to turn down your nomination.'

'Thanks Colin, but I wouldn't hear of it; passing the buck would be totally unethical in my book. I just couldn't ask a favour of you or anyone else to get out of the job. Besides, I'm looking forward to the challenge; it'll be a feather in my cap if I can crack it.'

'Nevertheless, if you change your mind over the weekend, let me know. These things can be arranged without anyone being any the wiser; I assure you that Laura Taylor would be absolutely discreet.'

'Thanks, but no thanks, Colin, I want a go at this. Nobody should be free to commit these outrages over the course of ten years or so and get away with it.'

'Fair enough. What do you think, Abbi?' MacKinnon turned to his daughter in a last desperate attempt to enlist an ally.

Abbi nodded vigorously. 'No doubt about it, Dad, he's got to go for it; there's nobody better qualified to bring this monster to justice. I'll be supporting David every step of the way.'

Chloe pitched in with her support. 'Abbi's right, Colin, David wouldn't be able to live with himself if he slid out of this. Heaven forbid if another poor girl was abducted and David had ducked out of the investigation, his conscience would nag at him for the rest of his life.'

Reluctantly, MacKinnon conceded. 'You're right, of course; it's just that he'll become swallowed up by the investigation and it'll impact badly on his home life; Abbi and the kids will be the big losers. But you're right, David has made his decision, let's leave this subject.' *Ah well, I tried; if nothing else, I'll have an ear close to the investigation and can pass on anything I learn to Somerton; maybe having David head up the investigation is for the best after all.*

Chapter 19
New Scotland Yard Monday Morning 2012

Assistant Commissioner David Singleton sat in his office ploughing through the mounds of paper that littered his desk, wondering if the bulk of it really did help in the fight against crime. Without warning, his office door began to open and he was about to rebuke the entrant for their failure to knock, when he saw that it was the chief commissioner. It wasn't often that Ronnie Hurst left his office to visit one of his subordinates; normally, they were summoned to his domain. He was tall and bulky, some would say fat, but at 1.97 metres tall, he carried his weight well. Impeccably dressed in his uniform, he had an unmistakeable aura of authority.

Singleton made to rise. 'Stay where you are, David.' Hurst waved a hand and planted himself in one of the three chairs in front of the desk. 'I won't take up too much of your time. How are things?'

Singleton gestured at the paperwork. 'Not bad, Sir, considering this lot.' Hurst was a stickler for formalities and respect for rank, he was always to be addressed as Sir. 'A reduction in paperwork would be welcome.'

Hurst screwed up his face. 'Tell me about it. How are Abbi and the children? Your oldest must be, what, eight, nine?'

'Maggie's 10, Murray's 9; they are all thriving, thank you.'

'I see the PM's Scottish ancestry is reflected in their names.'

Singleton smiled. 'The PM didn't get involved in name choosing. Abbi's very proud of her Celtic roots and we both like the names; of course, my mother hailed from Edinburgh.'

Hurst nodded. 'A well-travelled nation, the Scots, sometimes I think there are more of you down here than up there. To business; the Home Secretary has accepted your nomination for this serial abduction business. It's a bit of a poisoned chalice mind, succeed and the police world will be your oyster, my job if you want it. Fail though, and I wouldn't blame you if you did, I'm afraid a cloud will hang over you for a long time.

'As to process, Laura Taylor will write to you direct, thanking you for taking the job on and requiring that you brief her regularly. Just bear in mind that when you brief her, you brief me, I don't want some politician knowing more than I do. I've told her that nothing much of interest was likely to emerge in the first month unless a miracle comes along, or the guy gives himself up.

'For her part, she has written to all chief constables telling them that they must give you their full cooperation, case notes and anything else they hold related to the investigation. Your operation is to be given priority status and she has made it clear that you are to inform her immediately if there are delays or resistance in any quarter. In practice, however, what you will do is tell me first and I'll try to sort it out before we involve her. Some chiefs don't like taking orders from politicians but this time round, they'll have to live with it.

'You'll know from her announcement to the House that there are unlimited funds available for this job; your salary and those on your team are to be charged directly to the Home Office. In other words, money can't be used as an excuse for failure. Just make sure you ask for everything you need, manpower, equipment, whatever.'

Singleton smiled. 'Message received loud and clear, Sir.'

'And of course, if you aren't successful, you can be sure they will assert that funds weren't used to best effect or, if they're feeling really nasty, the Opposition politicians will claim they were squandered. I'm afraid you've been thrust onto the political stage; your performance will be closely scrutinised, bear that in mind. I want to be told *immediately* if you turn up a promising lead. Sorry to lay it on so thick, David, but I'm sure you can appreciate why.'

'Yes Sir, I do understand.'

Hurst sighed and lapsed momentarily into a faraway look, a rueful expression on his face. 'Not sure whether I would have wanted this one on my plate or not, given a choice, but there it is. Now, what kind of support are you looking for? Have you had a chance to give it some thought?'

Singleton extracted a sheaf of paper from a file. 'Yes, I'm going to start with a smallish team until we turn up something concrete. Then I'll decide on whether or not we need more bodies.'

Hurst shrugged. 'Sounds OK in principle; got anybody specific in mind?'

Singleton nodded. 'As it happens, I know exactly who I want on my core team. Inspector Ken Regan for his investigative talents and sheer presence; he'll take the lead when I'm not around. Sergeant Will Richmond, he's solid, dependable and tenacious; he's got a good head on his shoulders and, more importantly, he's a whiz with IT.

'I want three good assistants, Sergeant Milly Crossland and Constables Hannah Smyth and Sally Hunt; they all work in data processing and statistical analysis. They're known to be diligent and task-driven by nature, they will be key to the investigation. I'm going to need their attributes if my strategy for cracking this case is going to pay dividends; I've had a quiet word with all of them and they're up for it. When we've trawled through the existing evidence with a fine toothcomb, I'll ask for more support if I think it's justified.'

Hurst nodded. 'Well, you've got the gender balance right if nothing else; I know very little about any of them. Might I enquire, what exactly is your strategy?'

'Nothing original, there's no magic bullet in police work as we both know. We will pull in the existing seventeen case files, get a hold of every jot of evidence gathered to date and put it under the microscope page by page, bit by bit. The same will apply to all CCTV footage, I'll bet there's hours of it. It's back to basics in my view; we must review the detail in depth and see if anything pops up. It'll be a huge advantage having all the files assembled in one room, it will give us maximum opportunity to detect similarities and coincidences. I just wish evidence recording and storage was fully computerised throughout the UK, it's long overdue in my view.'

Hurst sighed. 'In other words, good old-fashioned police work. It'll be a real slog. I agree with you about computerisation and it is happening slowly. I wish you luck, David.'

'One more thing, Sir, and it's important. I'll want Incident Room A as my team base. It's got everything I could possibly need including the latest display technology. I'll want a direct line for each of the team including me, plus two hot lines for calls from Joe Public and a spare just in case the need arises.'

Hurst nodded. 'Sounds about right to be going on with. Room A is in use as we speak but I'll set the wheels in motion to have it vacated. It's best if I ruffle the feathers, everybody thinks their investigation should have priority. Let me have a list of those requirements and I'll issue instructions that it's to be done within 48 hours.' He grinned wickedly, 'The technical boys will have kittens, I'll enjoy seeing the look of horror on their faces when I crack the whip. Same with the support staff, I'll make sure no-one gets awkward or starts making excuses that they can't be spared.'

Singleton smiled. 'It's great having the boss in my corner. I thought you would want to take away the details.' He took two more A4 sheets from the file in front of them and handed them over. 'I've already emailed this lot to you; you'll find them in your inbox next time you check. I've asked the team to be on standby to assemble in Training Room A on Wednesday, 8.30 am prompt; that gives them a clear day to clear their desks.'

'And allow me to get Room A cleared. OK David, I'm off. I'll call the Home Secretary and tell her that the investigation preliminaries are in hand with the main business starting in earnest on Wednesday. She'll be impressed; it'll all help towards my knighthood when I step down in a couple of years! Who knows, if you crack this case, I might even end up in the House of Lords! Think of it, Lord Hurst of Chislehurst. I like the sound of that!' He guffawed and started towards the door then turned back. 'Nearly forgot; I've christened this beast Operation Galaxy.'

Training Room A, New Scotland Yard
Wednesday

Singleton and his team assembled as scheduled; he was last to arrive although it was barely 8.20. 'Well done, everybody, I like punctuality. I'm not going to waffle on with social trivia, we'll all get to know each other soon enough in the days ahead. I'm going straight into the ground rules; 8.30 am will be our normal starting time and 5.30 pm our stop time, with an hour for lunch any time to suit our business between noon and 2 pm. If we need to work late, we will do, but I'll try to avoid that; I believe you'll work best if you're fresh and not over-tired.'

Singleton continued briskly, 'There must *always* be two of you in this room to pick up on any phone calls and guarantee evidence security. Our core week will be Monday to Friday, but I'll want a rota sorted out to have two of you here on duty Saturday and Sunday. That is additional to the core work, there will be no time off in lieu. Sort it out amongst yourselves, I'll take my turn, overtime will be paid. Outside our hours of business, I'll arrange for incoming calls to go through the switchboard and be logged with any that sound urgent directed to me or Inspector Regan. Make sure we all have a list of all our mobile numbers.

'OK so far? Good. I know this is all boring stuff but it's how I do things. Whilst the case proceeds, there will be no leave without my personal authorisation; I'll try not to be unreasonable. If you have any booked within the next three months, cancel it; any costs incurred will be met. Even sickness and death are cancelled as of now. If you can't handle that, you can bail out now.'

To his relief, no one reacted. 'Going on with the ground rules, what takes place within this room stays within this room. The door has a keypad entry system and I've changed the code to 1399. Make sure it's locked at close of play each night. You are not to discuss progress, or lack of it, with anyone, whether that be colleagues, press or family. We don't know who is carrying out these abductions and need to allow for the possibility that it could be one of our own. I will personally seek the dismissal of anyone I find disclosing the business of this investigation to anyone outside the team.'

Ken Regan spoke up, 'Goes without saying, Sir.'

'Finally, I don't like swearing, so avoid it please. There will be a swear box and it'll cost the offender a fiver for each lapse. Now, before we get down to business, I want to stress we are a team; we work for each other, we cover for each other. Rank will be respected; however, within these four walls, it will be first names only. Are you all happy with that? I'm David, I don't like Dave.' He looked at Sally Hurst, 'All right with you, Sally?'

'Yes, S…' She hesitated. 'Yes David. It'll take a bit of getting used to though.'

Singleton rose to his feet. 'One last thing; we all make our own tea and coffee. The machine is over there, and the coin mechanism has been disabled, so drinks are on me. That's it, everybody grab a cuppa and we'll get down to the business of Operation Galaxy, the chief chose the name, no reason given.'

Setting Up

Cups in hand, they sat in a semi-circle facing a montage of wall-mounted, computerised state-of-the-art screens and Singleton called them to order. 'Let's make a start with what we know; save the conjecture and possibilities for another time. Ken, take us through the facts as we know them, please.'

Detective Inspector Ken Regan had been four years at the Met and was due for promotion. He rose and as was his habit, paced about restlessly as he spoke. Born in Belfast, he'd served in Northern Ireland for ten years before crossing to the mainland. The demands of Ulster's violent years had taken their toll and he looked older than his 32 years. He spoke in an unhurried manner and his soft brogue was easy on the ear.

'Fact one: Seventeen young women abducted, aged between 18 and 24. Mostly single but a few married.

Fact two: All abducted on a Friday or Saturday night between March 2002 and, as of now, September 2012.

Fact three: They were lifted from towns and cities throughout England. A vehicle was obviously involved.

Fact four: The abductor appears to be male and acts alone.

Fact five: The women were from a range of ethnic backgrounds; white, Asian, Afro-Caribbean, so no obvious pattern in relation to ethnicity.

Fact six: All but one of the abductions to date have taken place during the first weeks of April and September, six-monthly intervals.

Fact seven: The victims were all returned to society after a period of six months, give or take a few days.

Fact eight: This is where it gets interesting, the women had absolutely no memory of their abduction or what happened to them. They had no memory of who they were, or where they came from and, in fact, it's as though their entire memory had been erased.

Fact nine: In all but the early cases, the victims had evidence of puncture marks and drug taking although, in most cases, family and friends are adamant they had never known them to do so. They had no other signs of physical injury, but it was clear they had been sexually active; there were no signs of force or brutality.

Fact ten: They were all well-nourished and showed no signs of anxiety, probably due to their memory status. They were all dressed in the same clothes they were wearing at the time of their abduction. Their clothes were clean and tidy.

Fact eleven: Detailed forensic examination did not reveal anything about the perpetrator or where the women had been held captive.

Fact twelve: Other than in the case of the first victim, abductions were carried out at the same time as the previous victim was released, though at different locations. It seems reasonable to conclude that, in effect, an exchange system was in operation. That's all I have for now.'

'That was an excellent summary of what we know to date, thank you, Ken.' Singleton moved out in front of the others. 'I'm now going to allocate tasks to each of you, after which we'll do some brainstorming. Milly, Hannah and Sally, I want you to set up the incident boards and input everything you can onto the incident hard drive. I want a photo of each woman's face and a full body shot in the clothes they were wearing. I want a file for each woman containing a profile, biography, background, family, employment, etc.; make them come alive. I want a large-scale local map for each victim showing where they were abducted and their place of release.

'I want local digitised maps showing precisely where the attacks took place and similarly, the release areas. Mark up the victim's place of residence, where they were headed to that night and highlight the likely route they would have taken. Millie, you'll coordinate that lot please. Will is our expert, he will deal with the digitised maps and give any IT advice that's required.

'While you're getting on with that lot, Ken, Will and I will be visiting each of the Forces involved in person to collect the existing evidence. I could delegate this task, but I want to show the Chief Chow seriously we're taking this business. The chief commissioner has asked the chiefs to have the evidence ready for collection; the Home Secretary has already written asking for their cooperation. Ken, I've allocated you Basingstoke, Bristol, Gloucester, Leicester and Watford.'

Regan nodded. 'OK by me. It'll be nice to visit Bristol again; I spent six months on secondment there a few years back.'

'Will, you've got Peterborough, Nottingham, Sheffield, Leeds, Doncaster and Rotherham. You're a Yorkshireman so you'll understand the dialect better than most of us.'

Will Richmond, 25, had started his career as a cadet and was now in his seventh year of policing. At 1.7 metres tall, he was a fitness enthusiast and although wiry, his muscles gave evidence to his work on the weights. Born in York, his accent was easily recognisable. 'Fine with me, David, by the way, they don't understand you southerners half of the time.'

Singleton smiled. 'Touché, Will. That leaves yours truly with Canterbury, Ashford, Maidstone, Tunbridge Wells, Crawley and Southampton.' Singleton ran his hand through his hair. 'I've no idea what volume of paper, discs tapes and evidence bags are involved so transportation is an issue. You can take one of the larger unmarked vans out of the pool and drive yourself or hire an approved security van and driver and get him to follow you around. Or I guess you could hire the same when you're up there and get them to deliver evidence back here;

just make sure the evidence is secure. Do whatever's necessary, book into a decent hotel overnight wherever it suits your journey.

'A word of warning, taking evidence out of another Force's jurisdiction is sensitive, so be respectful, apologetic, grateful, whatever. But don't be too subservient, this exercise is being carried out on behalf of the Home Secretary; we are just acting on behalf of our political masters. Report any blockages to me and I'll talk to the chief. I want the three of us to make an early start tomorrow and be clear of London before the rush hour with a view to completing these assignments and having all the evidence in this room by start of play on Monday. OK, is everyone clear on what they have to do?'

He locked his eyes with each member of the team in turn, pausing for their nod to affirm their understanding.

'Right, that's it. By my watch, it's 12.30 pm so we'll break for lunch. Alas, I can't join you on this occasion, but I will when I can. I'm going back to my office to email each of the chief constables to confirm we'll be picking up the evidence over the next couple of days and who they can expect to turn up on their doorstep. That's all for now; enjoy your lunch. I hope to join you no later than 3 pm for a brainstorming session, but I promise we'll finish up by 5.30 pm.'

Ken Regan was first to the door and turned to face his colleagues. 'If any of you care to join me, the lunches are on me and I mean in the canteen, I don't want any of us going down to the pub during our working day. I'm sure David will endorse that?'

Singleton nodded. 'Absolutely; no alcohol in the training room at any time either. Thanks for that, Ken.'

Hannah Smyth responded. 'I've got no problems with that, mind you I'm a teetotaller!' she giggled. 'But I do like the idea of a free lunch, I'm feeling peckish.'

'Sally,' Singleton joined the group in the doorway, 'what's the door code?'

'1399, Sir, I mean David.'

Singleton smiled and winked at her. 'Good, I guessed you would remember the code, not sure about the others though.'

Chapter 20
Scotland Yard Training Room A 2012

Singleton joined the team just before 2.45; the room was buzzing with activity and chatter. He waited patiently until those involved with phone calls had completed their business, then called the meeting to order. 'Hopefully, you all had a good lunch and made Ken dip deep into his pocket. Will, Ken, have you made any progress with tomorrow's evidence safari?'

Ken Regan nodded. 'No problems with my lot; they were expecting us to be in touch and all the stuff is waiting collection. They couldn't have been more helpful.'

Will Richmond was less enthusiastic. 'Mostly OK, though the Sheffield guy wasn't keen to set up a meeting. I told him I personally understood his position but wasn't sure how the Home Secretary would feel about any resistance to releasing their evidence files and that seemed to do the trick.'

Singleton wrinkled his nose. 'To be expected, I suppose; I'm pleased to report that I didn't experience any difficulties.'

'Oh, what it is to be assistant chief commissioner. We poor sergeants can only dream of the power and influence rank brings,' Will chipped in cheekily.

The room went quiet, not sure how Singleton would react but he just grinned. 'You're probably right. Now to business; grab a chair, a desk, sit on the floor if you want. Let's have initial thoughts on Operation Galaxy. I want everyone to join in and I do mean everyone.' He glanced at Sally and Hannah who weren't trained investigators. 'Let your ideas, thoughts, instincts or whatever run free. Don't rule out anything at this stage. We'll slim down ideas when we have the evidence. I'll be scribe on this occasion and put one-liners up on the screens.

'Ken, you first, your thoughts please.'

Regan nodded. 'All the abductions were undertaken close to motorways. When we have the on-screen maps up and working, we might come up with a shortlist for where his base is located. When a series of crimes is involved, they often form an approximate circle around the perpetrator's base but I'm not that hopeful in this instance given the widespread nature of the attacks.'

Millie raised her hand. 'He used a taser on at least one occasion. Are they easy to come by? Does that tell us anything?'

Will Richmond went next. 'He holds these women captive for six months; he must have very secure, private facilities, such as a remote farm. Despite all the media coverage, there's been no reports of sightings or strange goings-on.'

'Hannah, you look like you have an offering?'

'He picks up his victims on their way home from a local hot spot. He surely can't be familiar with seventeen different areas; he must spend quite a bit of time in the vicinity checking out the local scene. That leads me to think that he must have been picked up on CCTV somewhere, surely?'

'Sally, what have you got for us?'

'I'm not experienced in these matters, but it seems to me that, having successfully carried out seventeen abductions, he's either got a good knowledge of police procedures or he's very lucky.'

Singleton nodded pensively. 'Interesting observation; he doesn't seem to have left any evidence at the scene and he's always evaded roadblocks, so it's a possibility.'

'It could be he's just clever and lucky; television programmes over the years have revealed just about every tool in our box. And you can find out lots online. If he's sharp, he'll change number plates regularly and might not even use the same car.' Will shrugged. 'Who knows.'

Regan butted in, 'He'll be unlikely to change his vehicle too often; that would run the risk of establishing a traceable pattern or car purchases or hire.'

Molly raised her hand. 'Just a thought; is there anything to be learned from the order he lifted the women? I mean, he seems to have started with a run of white, blonde types then changed to women of ethnic and overseas origins. It's almost as though he was, well…sort of trying out different types, like experimenting.'

Regan raised his hand again and began hesitantly. 'No real reason for this, but I've got a feeling our kidnapper doesn't have any previous convictions and isn't your usual sex offender. These girls were all well looked after. He's got lots of confidence and knows how to subdue his victim quickly. The abductions are planned and executed almost like a military operation, so could be he's had that kind of experience. But the most puzzling thing for me is his ability to leave the women with no memory; he must have medical knowledge but that doesn't seem to fit well with his ability to carry out these attacks. It might just be that the abductor is acting on behalf of a third party; not that that helps us very much. It's just a thought.'

Singleton paused and looked around the team. 'Thank you, some useful observations amongst that lot. Are there any further offerings at this stage?' Most heads shook though some looked like they were still trying to come up with something, but nothing emerged. 'Right, we'll leave it there. I think, in absence of the evidence, we've taken this is as far as we can for now, but hopefully, that short introductory session demonstrates that we've got to keep an open mind. For me, the main benefit of that session was observing us beginning to work as a team and I was particularly pleased that everybody,' again, he looked directly at Hannah, Millie and Sally, 'felt able to contribute.

'I reckon that will do for the day; class dismissed. I want you all back here on Monday morning, 8.30 am sharp. Hopefully by then, we'll have all the evidence assembled in this room along with the maps, photos and victim profiles. Good luck with your respective tasks. In the meantime, when you get a spare moment, give some thought to the man who is committing these crimes. Put yourself in his shoes; think about how you would go about these abductions and what happens afterwards for that matter.'

Collecting the Evidence

In the event, collection of the evidence went like clockwork, with one exception, involving Will Richmond. On arrival at Sheffield Police Headquarters, he was directed to the chief constable's office. A woman, presumably the chief's secretary, was expecting him and invited him to take a seat. Surprisingly, he wasn't offered the customary cup of tea or coffee. Fifteen minutes passed before the intercom on the secretary's desk buzzed and, following a brief hushed conversation with the caller, she indicated that he should go through. 'I do hope this won't take long; the chief constable is a very busy man.' Her tone of voice, cold and officious, her expression blank and unwelcoming.

Will smiled sweetly. 'It'll only take as long as he wants it to.'

He knocked on the door and stepped into the room, taking in the appearance of the man behind the desk. On the small side, a thick crop of grey hair brushed straight back with what looked like a goodly application of cream or gel. A pair of small piercing dark eyes, sat above a slightly hooked nose and an almost black Hitler-like moustache, regarded him with more of a glare than a stare. There was no welcoming smile, no pleasantries; Chief Constable Mervyn Blackmore wasn't a man for idle chatter. 'Sit down, Sergeant.' He looked at a hand-written note on his desk. 'Sergeant Richmond, you've come for the evidence on the abduction case?'

Will nodded. 'Yes Sir.'

'I believe that,' another glance at his notes, 'Assistant Commissioner Singleton is heading up the investigation?'

Will nodded. *Where is this leading?* 'That's correct, Sir. As you know, the Home Secretary has asked him to carry out a nationwide review of the seventeen abductions to date. I believe she wrote to you to that effect and I understood AC Singleton had been in touch by email?'

Blackmore delivered another prize-winning glare. 'I would have hoped he would have had the courtesy to come here in person.'

Will nodded and smiled. *So that's what this is about, status.* 'He wanted to, Sir, but evidence has to be collected from fifteen different locations, seventeen abductions in all, and given the urgency placed on this review by the Home Secretary, he thought best to share the collections out between three of us. Being born and bred in these parts, with personal knowledge of this area, it was thought sensible that I do the Yorkshire collections.' Will summoned up another smile, hoping it seemed genuine. 'I'm happy to pass on your concerns to him when I get back.'

Blackmore stroked his chin and snarled more than spoke. 'I didn't say I was concerned, Richmond; I just thought common courtesy would have applied and he would have sent a messenger of higher rank.'

Will tightened his lips and literally spoke through his teeth. 'I'm sorry about that, Sir, and apologise if we've caused offence. I've explained how the situation arose.'

'And just how long do you expect to retain our evidence? This is an open case, investigations are on-going. It's not at all helpful if we can't refer to our own case files.'

Will bit on his tongue but inwardly, he was seething; the question was downright unreasonable at this early stage. 'I understand your position entirely, Sir, but we are simply following the Home Secretary's instructions. We will try to get the files back to you as quickly as possible. If you feel very strongly about the files, Sir, you are, of course, free to withhold them. I'm not sure what the Home Secretary would do if that happened.'

Blackmore's eyes widened. 'I'm not accountable to the Home Secretary, Richmond. I'll release the files in the spirit of cooperation with a fellow officer.'

Will smiled. 'Much appreciated, Sir.' *Now get on with it, you stuffed prig, or are you waiting for a fanfare?*

'Do remind Singleton to keep me informed of any developments related to my area.'

'Absolutely Sir.' Will responded with false enthusiasm. 'I'm certain Assistant Commissioner Singleton intends to do just that.'

Blackmore sat back in his chair, his face smug, as though he had enjoyed a victory of some kind. 'Good.'

'And I presume we can rely on you to do likewise?' Will kept a straight face though he wanted to grin.

Yorkshire's Chief Constable leaned forward, a puzzled expression on his face. 'What do you mean, Sergeant?'

'I was hoping that you would keep us involved of any developments arising from your on-going investigations.' Will braced himself for a blast.

Blackmore's eyes narrowed but he swallowed an angry reply. 'That goes without saying. I need you to sign for the evidence, Sergeant.' He passed over two sheets of paper. 'You'll see that I have signed to confirm release of the evidence to you personally. When you've signed, you can take one copy and I'll retain the other.'

Will took his time scrutinising the two pieces of paper, ensuring that they were indeed identical. 'I will sign, of course, Sir, but I shall have to add a note recording that there is no schedule of the evidence being released.'

'There has to be trust between police officers, Sergeant.'

'Most certainly, Sir; but just in case there are any problems when the evidence is returned, I will record what I've just said.' He duly added the words, *Schedule of evidence not available for inspection prior to signing*, to both copies, signed both and handed one back to Blackmore. 'Thank you for your cooperation, Sir, I assure you that your assistance is greatly appreciated. Be assured that the Home Secretary will be appraised of how helpful you've been, and I promise, we'll take good care of the evidence whilst it's in our possession.'

'See that you do, Sergeant. Report to reception, someone there will take you to the evidence storage area. We can't offer you any assistance with loading, I'm afraid you've caught us on a very busy day.'

Will smiled broadly. 'I wouldn't have expected otherwise, Sir, I'm sure I'll manage.' He rose and turned towards the door, giving Blackmore a hidden one-finger salute. *Goodbye, you supercilious bastard.*

In reception, the duty sergeant, Ed Bottomley, led him along a corridor to a room containing the evidence. 'Sorry mate, I can't offer any help, instructions from his nibs. I've been told very bluntly to let you get on with it.'

'Understood, I've met your chief constable, a most charming man.'

Ed Bottomley raised his eyebrows and winked. 'You can only speak as you find. It's a shame he's retiring next year.' He lowered his voice. 'Be much better if it was next month.'

The evidence took Will just over an hour to load and then he was happily on his way back to London.

Chapter 21
Training Room A Monday

The team assembled punctually at 8.30 am and Singleton opened proceedings by thanking everyone for their efforts to date; he knew from experience that a long haul lay ahead and that it was important that the team felt valued and appreciated. 'Millie, Hannah, Sally, you've done a great job with the maps and profiles, this project is already starting to take shape. Any problems?'

Millie Crossland glanced at Hannah and Sally before replying, 'None at all, cooperation has been exemplary. I think the Chief has put the wind up everybody in the Met, they're falling over backwards to help us.'

Singleton laughed. 'It's as it should be, but there's nothing like a touch of high-ranking oil to get the wheels of bureaucracy turning smoothly.' He turned to Ken and Will. 'And, collecting the evidence, how did that go?'

Ken Regan gave a thumbs-up. 'No problem, not like Will here.'

Singleton frowned. 'Will?'

'I wasn't going to say anything, David, all the evidence is here safe and sound.' He hesitated. 'It's just that Chief Constable Blackmore didn't welcome me with open arms.'

'Meaning what exactly?'

When Will finished describing his experience at Sheffield, Singleton sighed and shook his head, 'Sorry you had to go through that, Will, there are those close to Chief Constable Blackmore who describe him as an out and out arsehole; fortunately, he'll be retiring in the next year or so. Do you want me to follow up, I'll gladly do so?'

Will shook his head. 'Thanks David but best left as it is. I've been worked over before and survived. Plus, of course, we might have to go back to him as the investigation proceeds, best to keep him sweet if that's remotely possible.'

'Whatever you say, Will. Right guys, to the business of the day.'

He gazed around at the piles of evidence, bags, files, discs, CCTV and drone recordings, etc. 'Plenty to chew on as expected. Let's get to it; I want to see seventeen piles, gathered in date order of abduction. I'll take day one, Ken two, Will three, Milly four, Hannah five, Sally six, then carry on in sequence as and when you complete your individual task. Go for it.'

It took nearly two hours to assemble the evidence, at the end of which seventeen stacks of evidence sat in piles up against the walls of the room.

Singleton looked around. 'Thanks everybody. I think the girls have put us to shame, guys, our piles look like jumble whereas theirs are set out neatly. So, boys, let's tidy ours up, it'll pay dividends in the long run. Millie, could you please prepare a large label for each pile stating the girl's name, date of abduction and its number in the sequence, then fix them to the wall above each pile. But before we do that let's grab a cuppa.'

Ten minutes later, Singleton drained his cup and addressed the team. 'Drink up and let's get the show on the road. Now for those of you who are new to investigations; rule one—make sure you are wearing gloves if you need to remove an item from an evidence bag. We must avoid any possibility of contamination even though the forensic people will have gone over every item with every investigatory process in their arsenal; their reports should be on file. If possible we should avoid taking stuff out of the evidence bag.'

Millie raised her hand. 'Are we, us girls I mean, authorised to open the evidence bags? It's not something we've done before.'

Singleton nodded. 'Of course, you're all on the team, but as I said, avoid if possible and maybe get a second opinion if in doubt. Going on, rule two—make notes of anything, and I do mean anything, that strikes you as odd or missing. Such as, questions that weren't asked by the other investigating forces, or leads that weren't pursued without good reason. Highlight anything you consider to be exceptional and don't be afraid of getting it wrong; we'll need a flash of inspiration to crack this case. Now, take a good look at the evidence piles. What strikes you, Sally?'

'There are considerable differences in quantity, Sir, sorry, David, given that the abductions were all very similar.'

Singleton nodded. 'Not all forces work in the same way so if you think there are any gaps, make a note of them and bring them up later. Going on, rule three— look for patterns, similarities, differences; anything we can build on.

'Finally, we'll be working in pairs, looking first at CCTV and drone footage; then reading through the files, referencing the evidence bags where needs be. Prompt each other, ask questions, don't be afraid of sounding foolish. Ken, you'll be working with Millie. Will, you'll be with Hannah, and that means you've drawn the short straw, Sally, you've got me.' *Was it his imagination or did she colour slightly?* 'Right, the sermon's over. Let's get the ball rolling. We're going to begin with abductions one and two, as a team. We'll look first at recordings on-screen, then read aloud the evidence files in turn. We will each make our own notes and observations.

'As you go through, if you think it's worthwhile, speak up and share your thoughts with the rest of us. When we've worked through cases one and two and established a common methodology to some degree, we'll tackle the rest of the evidence as follows. Sally and I will tackle cases three to seven inclusive, cases eight to twelve inclusive go to Will and Hannah, leaving cases thirteen to seventeen for Ken and Millie. If there are any questions, let's have them now.' He glanced around the room; only Millie raised her hand. 'Millie?'

'I was just wondering why none of the abductions have taken place in London or even the Greater London area? It has millions of girls and young women of every ethnic origin, but no abductions from there as far as we know. It must abound with opportunities on Friday and Saturday nights.'

Singleton's brow furrowed. 'London? London? Indeed, why not London? A good point; let's give it some thought before we get going.'

Will jumped in before anyone else. 'Too far to travel perhaps?'

'Too crowded?' suggested Hannah.

'Or,' Ken Regan contributed, 'maybe he didn't want to get the Met investigating one of his crimes. London is littered with CCTV and the Met is the best equipped force in the country.'

Singleton waited for a few seconds but nothing else was forthcoming. 'All good points or could it be that London is just too close to home even if he isn't based in the city itself? Thanks for raising it, Millie. Now, let's focus our collective thoughts on the first two cases. Case 1: Becky Swift, age 19; white, blonde and single; lifted in Tunbridge Wells. And case 2: Elsie Wood, age 22, white, blonde, married; lifted in Basingstoke.

'Sally, grab the evidence file for Case 1 and start reading, you take the first half hour, then someone else will take over. I wouldn't be surprised if the files and the recordings take a full day per victim, maybe more.'

They proceeded reading aloud in half hour blocks; most of the team found it boring and by the end of the first couple of hours, eyes were beginning to glaze over. Singleton could see that attention was on a distinct wane. 'OK, time for a break, I can see some of you wilting. Make it coffee, we all need a caffeine boost. I know that a lot of what you've listened to is dreary stuff, but it must be reviewed so get used to it, there's plenty more to come. I've seen attention wavering from time to time, you mustn't let that happen; there's a breakthrough hiding in one of these piles and we're going to find it. Just think of what those girls have suffered and what others will go through unless we find the perpetrator.'

Will spoke up, 'It'll be better when we work in pairs, David, this classroom style just isn't what we're used to, we're all hands-on people. And in my experience, you can read and digest more efficiently than just listening.'

Singleton grimaced. 'I guess so, maybe it was a wrong call on my part. I thought working together, sharing ideas and procedure, would put us all on the same wavelength. However, we will carry on with this approach for the first two cases and review any points that arise as a team. After that, we'll start on the CCTV recordings.'

It was nearing lunchtime by the time the process of reading case 1 was concluded. 'I'll start us off,' Singleton took the floor, 'and go through the key points as I see them. First, we have an eye-witness account by Jenny Black who accompanied Becky Swift when the first attack took place. Secondly, a taser was used; as far as we know, this was the only time this happened. Third point, another witness, some distance away, managed to film a few minutes of the incident on his mobile. The images are dark and shadowy, but they show the attacker and his vehicle. The forensic people have enhanced the film, but the improvement is very limited. Anything else? Ken, you look like you've got something?'

'The attacker can be seen loading the victim into the side of a vehicle which suggests a car rather than a van.'

Singleton nodded. 'I guess so, keep an open mind on that, it could have been a van with side doors. Are there any further contributions?' He paused and looked around his team. 'Nope? OK, let's run the computer visuals. Will, take it away.'

Richmond was the team's technical wizard and Singleton gladly let him handle anything to do with technology. 'OK, I reckon we've got four or more hours of footage for the Becky Swift abduction, so sit back and enjoy the show.'

His assessment proved accurate, punctuated by tea and loo breaks, the team sat through just under four hours of generally mind-numbing visuals.

Singleton took the floor again. 'Thanks Will, and all of you for your attention; I know how hard it is to stare at the screen for hours but, as some of us know, that's how it has to be. Speaking for myself, I didn't get anything out of that session. What about the rest of you?'

There were general shakes of the head all around, but Ken Regan came up with a suggestion. 'I agree with you, David, but I wonder if we could view the visuals in a different way next time.'

Singleton raised his eyebrows. 'I'm intrigued, fire away.'

'Split the recordings into two lots, one before the abduction and the other after the abduction then run the two lots simultaneously side by side on separate screens concentrating, say, on the hour before and after the event. It's a long shot but we might spot a similar, or identical, vehicle in the process. I'm not saying we don't look at them in the traditional manner, just that we do what I'm suggesting in addition.'

Singleton nodded without great enthusiasm. 'Not sure, I'll think about it.'

Will Richmond, always enthusiastic about an opportunity to introduce technology of any kind, gave his support to the suggestion. 'Can't do any harm, I can run it on two separate screens or put them both on the big screen side by side; in fact, I can run up to four simultaneously on the big screen. And you have to admit, conventional practices and procedures haven't brought results, have they? We need to try different approaches if we're going to get a result.'

'Hmmm,' Singleton remained sceptical, 'there might be something in this idea, we'll give it a go. Will, set up the recordings as you've described, provided it's not too time-consuming. I can't get my head around the idea of looking at four screens simultaneously; it's mind-boggling.'

Hannah Smyth's husband worked for a security company and she chipped in, 'Security people sometimes look at many more screens than that and we'll have six pairs of eyes on the go.'

'Fair comment, Hannah. Home time everybody, go rest those tired eyes. See you tomorrow morning.'

'Right, we're going try out Ken's suggestion.' Singleton still wasn't convinced but didn't want to waste time with further discussion. 'Are we ready to roll, Will, or do you need some time to set up?'

Will beamed. 'Nope, stayed late last night; ready to roll when you are.'

The team spent the rest of the day studying the CCTV recordings for cases 1 and 2, using single screens and simultaneous multi-screen formats but, come finishing time, nothing of significance had emerged. Frowns all around, smiles at a premium; a day's work and nothing to show for it.

Singleton sensed the mood and decided that a change of direction was necessary to lift spirits. 'OK everybody, thanks for today; I know some of you might be feeling we put in a lot of time and gained nothing. That would be wrong; police work is as much about ruling things out, as ruling things in.

'We've given the visuals for the first two cases our best shot and we can rule out the multi-screen format out unless something specific arises to cause us to look again. Thanks for your efforts Will, the facility might yet come in useful. Millie, Hannah, Sally, tomorrow morning I want you to plot the seventeen abduction sites on the paper maps and likewise all the victim return sites. I want these sites joined up with pink and blue traces respectively to the victim's home; do this on the local street plans as well as the national road network maps.

'Ken and Will, you'll work with me to identify possible escape routes from the abduction sites. The perpetrator will have wanted a direct route out, with no roadworks, three-point turns or slow-moving areas to negotiate. With his victim on board, he would be at real risk of discovery, especially at police roadblocks. Come to think of it, were roadblocks set up on any of the seventeen occasions? If they were, we need to know where, and how soon after the abduction they were in place?

'Ken, can I ask you to get on to that for your cases? You too, Will, and I'll do the others. We've got to distil down the evidence, so we can make best use of the visuals. I'm certain our man carried out surveillance before making his attacks, so he might well know where the local force had foot patrols on the go; find out where these were and mark them up as well.'

Singleton was praying that the next day would bring a breakthrough, however minor, to lift morale, especially for the girls for whom the whole process was new and, in their eyes, probably agonisingly slow. For Will and Ken, it was the norm; they knew that 95% of investigative work was routine and boring and would cope with whatever came along. 'That's all, people, I know today hasn't revealed anything useful, fingers crossed, tomorrow is more rewarding; but be warned, we will return to the visuals, boring though they may be. We need to give them our best shot, we are, I repeat, we *are* making progress, slow though it be. OK that's it, see you in the morning.'

Wednesday

It was coming up to 7 pm by the time the team finished their work; seventeen sets of maps were now marked up with the coloured tracer ribbons, road works and roadblocks had also been highlighted, Singleton was pleased and expressed his appreciation. 'Thanks everybody, a brilliant day's work. You've shown me that I've put together a talented team. It's too late for analysis now, I'm knackered even if you lot aren't. Go home, relax, and get a good night's sleep. We'll start tomorrow by analysing the maps and agreeing next steps.'

Chapter 22
Training Room Thursday

Singleton elected to make an early start and was in the Training Room by 7 am; he wanted to analyse the map display before the others arrived with a view to presenting his findings to the team and getting the day off to a flying start.

Will was next to arrive, surprised to find Singleton already standing, deep in thought, in front of one of the map displays. 'Good morning, David, you've beaten us all to it this morning.'

'Just couldn't wait to get back to this lot, Will; I really miss it when I'm cossetted at home with my family.' He lifted his eyes to the heavens.

'I'll bet, I didn't sleep a wink last night thinking about it.'

'Really?' Singleton was genuinely concerned. 'I'm sorry to hear that.'

'Only kidding, David; when my head hits the pillow, I'm gone.'

One by one the others trooped in, Ken and Hannah made a beeline for the drinks machine and their morning coffee fix.

'Let's make a start.' Singleton was keen to move forward. 'I got in early this morning to try to get my head around this lot.' He waved a hand at the screens. 'I'm going to begin by sharing my conclusions, then take feedback. When that's done, I want to tackle the remaining visuals; I'll pause here and wait for the collective groan.

'Now, I don't intend to go into the detail of my thinking unless you press me, I'm keen to make progress. The key points I've come up with are as follows. One, I've concluded that our man's base is in the south of London or its suburbs, maybe just outside the Greater London area. Two, he has radiated further and further outwards as time has gone on. He started in the South then moved to the Midlands and finally to the North; my guess is he was trying to reduce the risk of the abductions being linked. Three, no prizes for this one, easy motorway access is essential for him both before and after the attacks.

'Four, if I were him, I'd probably want to spend as little time as possible in abduction areas or when undertaking surveillance. I would want to head straight for the local hot spots when I came off the motorway. Similarly, I'd be seeking to get back onto the motorway by the most direct route, after I'd carried out the abduction. But I'd want to avoid going back via busy areas even if it was the shortest route in term of mileage; the same logic applies to the return of the victims.

'Assuming the foregoing, I've gone back to the maps and marked on what I believe were the pre-attack and escape routes using the nearest motorway based on the premise he was based in the London area. I've used dark green for the attack route and lilac for the escape routes. In some instances, I've marked alternative routes as dotted lines though I tried to avoid doing this. Using the dark green and lilac marked routes as a reference, I want you to be even more meticulous when checking any visuals related to these routes. I don't know if Will's computer wizardry can help us with this?'

He glanced at Will who nodded his head thoughtfully but made no comment. 'If there are any initial thoughts, let's have them, but I want to keep discussion short and get on to the CCTV stuff. Ken?'

'I go along with your conclusions, David, but maybe we can return to the maps later when we've individually had the opportunity to study them for ourselves?'

Will nodded in agreement. 'I'm with Ken on this.'

Singleton looked around the team. 'Any other thoughts?' He let a few seconds pass before going on. 'OK, let's move onto the visuals, I can sense you're all champing at the bit. There are seventeen incidents to review and my aim is to complete by next Wednesday afternoon. So next Thursday, we'll review the findings and decide on next steps. Go to it.'

The Following Thursday

'Good morning, everybody.' Singleton didn't have to be overly perceptive to sense that the first flush of enthusiasm had long since gone. The mood was distinctly muted and the early excitement of being a member of a high-profile investigation team had all but evaporated.

'Let's begin by getting ourselves a coffee or whatever, I see some of you haven't visited the machine yet. Ken, can I have a word please?'

195

The two men moved away from the others and lowered their voices. 'What's your feel for the mood, Ken?'

'Just what you would expect, there haven't been too many inspirational moments, have there? It's OK for Will and me, this boring dross is routine to us, but the lasses are feeling a bit despondent. I've picked up the odd snatch of conversation and it's all on the gloomy side. Added to that, I think they're missing their colleagues.' He sighed and shook his head, 'We need a breakthrough, however minor, to lift their spirits, it's as simple as that, David.'

Singleton nodded. 'That's my take on the situation exactly but we can't just up and manufacture a breakthrough. I'll try to rally the troops, though I'm not sure what I can say that'll carry any conviction.'

When everyone had settled, Singleton asked for their attention. 'Well, here we are on what I reckon is day eleven, not counting weekends and I know morale has gone down because we haven't come up with anything concrete. Frankly, I wouldn't have expected to have come up with some blinding revelation after just eleven days but think about it this way. We've reviewed all seventeen case visuals between us. We've scrutinised every witness statement along with such evidence as there is available.

'I'm aware that much of this work has been done during overtime and at weekends, a big thank you for that. All this means that, as a team, consciously and subconsciously, we are building up a very clear picture of the modus operandi surrounding these crimes. Each of us is forming a picture in our head of how this guy works and what kind of areas he chooses to carry out his crimes. So please, don't undervalue the work that we've done so far; it's all essential to the solving of these heinous crimes. Rest assured we know more about this series of crimes than anyone else in the country.'

He could feel he was struggling to find words of encouragement, but he had to try. 'That brings us to the present and what we do next. Well, I've got a proposal to run with unless someone comes up with something better; I want us all to have another look at the first abduction case file again, it's by far the most informative. In fact, at this stage, it's perhaps the only substantial lead we have. Why did he tackle two women at the same time?

'It's probably the only occasion he used a taser and most important, it's the only abduction to provide us with an eye-witness account two eye-witnesses in fact. Why was that I wonder? Why didn't he wait for a girl to come along on her own? Let's have your thoughts on that.'

Will shrugged. 'Could simply be time pressure and he had a schedule to keep to. Maybe he didn't want to hang around for too long and risk attracting attention.'

Regan pursed his lips. 'Maybe she just happened to be the first girl to show up that matched the profile he had in mind.' He glanced at the women apologetically. 'You know, blonde, curvy, that kind of thing.' Regan shook his head in exasperation. 'It could be any of those, David, we'll never know unless he tells us, but I do think it was a minor lapse on his part.

'He's carried out seventeen kidnappings successfully, returned sixteen of them successfully and got clean away every time without being seen, *except* for that first occasion. He's a planner, he's used to working under pressure and he's a confident bugger; the fact that he was happy to take on two girls, albeit using tasers, shows that. I still have a hunch that he has some knowledge of police procedures; that's why he's remained one step ahead of us and our predecessors.'

Singleton had studied expressions all through these exchanges and was pleased to see that everyone had engaged, their interest was rekindled but how long would it sustain. 'OK, that was useful; let's look at the visuals footage for case 1 again whilst we're still fired up. Concentrate on the routes I've highlighted on the maps and take another close look at those grainy photographs the second witness took.'

'David, whilst we're on case 1, I don't suppose we've identified the source of the taser?'

'No such luck, Will. I've already checked that out, nothing from known suppliers and it didn't leave an identifier mark. It was probably a cheap import from Eastern Europe or China. It could be that he worked abroad and managed to smuggle them in.'

'If he did, and it's a big *if*,' Regan added, 'he might have been involved in military service or police work overseas.'

Singleton tinkled a spoon on his mug to gain everyone's attention. 'I'm going to draw discussion to a close and ask Will to run the case 1 visuals.'

Will nodded. 'On my way; I'll patch it through to the big screen and see if the larger display helps.'

The team stared intently at the screen for the next two hours with Will pausing, zooming in, zooming out, replaying, etc. Singleton eventually called a halt and looked around at his colleagues. 'Did anybody spot anything? I'm afraid I didn't.' Most shook their heads, but Ken Regan asked for the witness photos to be shown again. 'I reckon that if we could identify the model of vehicle, the other visuals might be more helpful.'

Singleton sighed. 'It's a longish shot, Ken. We've viewed the photos several times and we've had them enhanced as much as can be, but nobody's come up with anything. Still, if we can bear it, I guess one more showing won't do any harm. I agree with you; these photos are the key to this whole sorry business. I have to stress that the technical boys have done their best with enhancing the quality so what we've got is the best available.'

Will brought the photos up on screen but nothing new emerged and Singleton sensed spirits plummeting again. What he had described as *the most promising evidence* hadn't moved the investigation any further forwards. It was time to take a break. 'Right, that's it; but there's just one more task to be undertaken before class is dismissed.' Singleton paused for effect. 'You're all invited to lunch with me, after which, if you can drag yourselves away from the screens, you're free to go home. I've booked a table at the Black Horse, we're due there in twenty minutes so plenty of time for everyone to powder their nose. By the way, no talking about the case once we sit down at the table, let's leave work behind. And finally, on this occasion, I reckon we can have a drink or two, we've earned it.'

During lunch, Sally Hunt, who had deliberately sat next to Singleton, came up with an idea. 'David,' she said hesitantly, in a low voice, 'I know you didn't want us to mention the case, but a thought has just occurred to me.'

Singleton looked at her reproachfully. 'Maybe it could wait until tomorrow, Sally, you've all earned a break from the case.'

'The thought is appreciated, David, it really is. But my idea has a bearing on tomorrow's session; it's about the witness photographs.'

'OK, but just this one question.'

'Do you know anyone at the NRSC who could look at the photos? They have the best brains in the country, they might have the technical expertise to enhance the photo quality.'

Singleton felt his pulse quicken. 'Oh my God, Sally, why didn't I think of that? Brilliant, thank you, I could give you a hug for coming up with that. I'll get in touch with the Centre later.'

Will, who had overheard the exchange, nodded excitedly. 'A great idea, Sally. Give the girl a prize! While you're there, David, ask if anyone has any ideas as to how the victims' memories could be wiped.'

Singleton nodded. 'I might just do that, if anybody knows how, they will.'

After the meal, he collared Regan. 'Ken, if I'm not in first thing tomorrow, I've gone to the NRSC to see if I can get some scientific input. Hold the fort till I get back; maybe get the team to go through case 1 evidence, line by line again.'

'Christ David, we've read them and re-read them!'

'I know, Ken, but what else can we do? Do what you like but keep them busy; carry out a review, tidy up the visuals and the paperwork. Do whatever it takes, we must keep their spirits up.'

'You're clutching at straws, David, but I'll do my best.'

Chapter 23
National Research and Security Centre

Singleton pulled to a halt at the security barrier and lowered his window, taking a deep breath of the cool fresh Kent air. The team was losing heart, so he had gone straight from the Black Horse to the Centre in the hope he could report back to the team with something positive in the morning. The security guard, neatly dressed in a navy-blue uniform, left his cabin and made his way forward. 'Good afternoon Sir, how can I help?'

Singleton smiled, said 'Hello' and produced his warrant card, handing it over for the guard to examine. Ricki Murdo's eyes widened and he almost stood to attention; he was an ex-copper and still held rank in great respect. 'Gosh, Scotland Yard and an assistant commissioner no less, is there something going down in there?' He glanced over his shoulder in the direction of the NRSC.

Singleton smiled and shook his head. 'No, not at all, sorry to disappoint you. I'm hoping to ask one of the research team if they can help me with a technical problem.'

Murdo nodded. 'I see, I had assumed you would be heading for the security setup.'

Singleton shook his head. 'Not this time, though I have met Mr Somerton a couple of times; it's one of the boffins I'm after on this occasion.'

Murdo scratched his chin. 'So, you don't have an appointment and don't know who you want to see? I haven't had an enquiry of this nature before. Do you mind waiting a few minutes while I check this out with someone in Research? They work on some very hush-hush stuff in there and are very careful who they give access to, though I'm sure you'll be OK.'

'No problem; I have signed the Official Secrets Act so I know the score. I attended the grand opening and have been back since for two or maybe three VIP occasions.'

Murdo smiled. 'I'm sure it will be all right, Sir, but I'll just check nevertheless.'

Singleton sat watching as the guard made his way back to his cabin. Through the window, he could see that Murdo was typing something into a keyboard, his eyes firmly fixed on one of the monitors in front of him. A brief telephone conversation ensued after which he returned to the car beaming. 'No problem, Mr Singleton; go straight through when I lift the barrier. At the end of the drive, turn left and park in the one of the visitor spaces in front of the building. Ask for Lynda Christie when the intercom responds, she'll do her best to help you. I used to be in the Met before I retired.'

'Where were you based?'

'I was a Sergeant, ended up in the East End.'

'Ah, Sergeants are always in the front line, doing real police work, especially in your neck of the woods. I saw you typing something into the computer; if you don't mind, could I ask what exactly?'

'That's Mr Somerton's brainchild, sir, the first in the UK, I think.'

'What does it do?' Singleton's curiosity heightened; he was always interested in new innovations.

'Well, it retains a record of all visitors going back to Opening Day. You, for example, show up as having been here on four occasions. I could punch in your name and it'll tell me what dates you were here, and your times of arrival and departure. It also retains a record of all car number plates and who was driving them on the day. It's a good piece of kit.'

Singleton pursed his lips and nodded appreciatively. 'I might have guessed Jack Somerton would have his finger on the pulse.'

Murdo nodded. 'All the security boys speak well of him though they say he doesn't suffer fools gladly. It's common knowledge that there have been a few found wanting and shown the door not long after joining. Anyway, I'll raise the barrier and you can get about your business. Lynda Christie is expecting you.'

The drive to the main building was nearly quarter of a mile through open countryside; the road a plain black ribbon with no attendant shrubs or trees to improve the aesthetics. *Not letting anything obstruct your line of sight, Jack. No doubt I'm already being tracked by a CCTV camera or a drone perhaps, or knowing you, probably both.* He turned left at the end of the drive as directed and manoeuvred into one of the visitor parking places.

Having checked his mobile for calls, he got out of his car and took a few minutes to survey his surroundings, not that there was a lot to see. It was no more than a large expanse of grass, regularly mown by the look of it to keep it short. There was at least two hundred metres of uninterrupted landscape on all sides of the NRSC; the boundary delineated by a three-metre high steel paling fence, which any erstwhile intruder would have to scale to gain access. Doubtless it was wired to detect a breach and under CCTV surveillance on a 24/7 basis. Singleton smiled. *It was no less than to be expected at the base of the nation's security advisor. It wouldn't surprise me if you had a few machine guns mounted on the roof, Jack!*

Turning to make his way to the entrance, he spotted two PZT cameras and heard a drone somewhere above his head. *OK guys, you've spotted me, I give up.* Resisting the temptation to wave, he crossed directly to the plate glass door and pressed the intercom button.

'Lynda Christie speaking.'

'David Singleton; the security guard told me to ask for you.'

'I'll be with you in a second, Mr Singleton.'

Through the plate-glass door, he watched a woman stride purposefully towards him; she was wearing a white lab coat over slim-fit jeans and a red jumper. He could make out that she was blonde and wore her hair short, but her features were indistinct through the smoky, no doubt bullet-proof, glass.

The door swung open, an attractive researcher with a broad cheery smile stood before him, hand extended in greeting. 'Hi, I'm Lynda Christie.'

'Hello. David Singleton, I'm an assistant commissioner at Scotland Yard. Thanks for seeing me at such short notice.'

She frowned in a smiley manner. 'What brings you here? I hope none of us has been naughty?'

'Not at all, in fact you could say that this visit is informal, I'm looking for advice.'

'That's a relief. Hardly surprising though, we're all a bit nerdy and kind of boring really; all things considered, highly unlikely wrongdoers. So how can we be of help?'

Singleton chuckled. 'Could be I'm grasping at straws but I'm looking for someone who might be able to enhance the clarity of a series of photographs; photographs of a crime scene.'

'Well, now, I think we have done some work in that field though it's not my particular area of expertise. Best if I take you to Julie Powell, she's a computer sciences guru and might be able to help. Follow me and I'll take you to meet her.'

Singleton tagged along, looking into labs and offices as he proceeded. Some were occupied, others waited empty awaiting their owner's return; all were stuffed full of equipment.

'Here we are.' His guide stopped suddenly, tapped on the door and entered when she heard a muffled reply, beckoning him to follow.

The room was occupied by another woman busily engaged typing numbers, letters and symbols into a keyboard in front of her. Twin monitor screens choc a bloc with data gripped her attention, she seemed oblivious to their presence.

'Ms Powell?' Lynda raised her voice to attract her colleague's attention. 'Sorry to disturb you, darling, but this gentleman needs your help.'

Julie Powell looked up, wide-eyed below a mop of brunette curls. 'Be with you in a sec, must finish this.' She continued with her computer input for a minute or so then turned to her visitors. 'Sorry about that, how can I help?'

'We have a real man in desperate need of your assistance. This is David Singleton, Assistant Commissioner from Scotland Yard, your misdeeds have caught up with you, Julie.'

'Oh my God, what's happened?' The researcher was genuinely concerned.

Lynda giggled. 'Nothing's happened, I'm sorry to say, a bit of excitement wouldn't go amiss in this setup if you ask me. David just wants to know if anyone can help him with a technical problem and I think you're best placed. He'll explain what he wants, I'll leave you to it.'

'Thanks Lynda. Sit down, David, and hit me with the facts and nothing but the facts.' A smile played around her lips.

Singleton grinned, pulled a chair forward and began to explain. 'I'm leading a team investigating a series of major crimes and we've hit a brick wall. Yet paradoxically, unlike many crimes, we do have actual photographs of the crime in progress. The problem is that these were taken at a distance in poor lighting and they are shadowy and indistinct. We were wondering if you could enhance their quality; they're not much use to us as they are? Our technical staff have done all they can.'

'Let's have a look at them. I did some work on photo enhancement a while back but couldn't spend too much time on it, other priorities came along; we're required to focus on innovations that are likely to produce results in the export market. That's been our brief from Downing Street since the Centre opened.'

Singleton nodded. 'And you've really succeeded; I can personally vouch that the Prime Minister is very proud of you all.'

She looked at him, raising an eyebrow; clearly wondering how he came to be privy to the thoughts of the PM. Singleton took her cue and answered the unspoken question, 'Colin MacKinnon's my father-in-law and often sings the praises of the NRSC; as you know, it was his brainchild.'

'Oh my God! The pressure's on now, I really do have to help, or he'll cut our budget,' she said impishly. 'Let's have a look at these photos.'

Singleton took a flash drive from his pocket. 'The photos are on here. I can produce the originals if you wish, or the mobile phone that captured them for that matter.'

Julie nodded. 'Let's try the flash drive and see what we can do.' She inserted the flash drive into her computer and after a few clicks on her mouse, displayed the first photo; that of a shadowy figure bundling what looked like a body into a vehicle. In the second photo, a man could be made out looking back in the direction of the camera. The third photo was of the rear of the vehicle as it drove away. She sighed loudly. 'You're right about the quality, they're crap. I'll see what I can do, just don't get your hopes up.'

'Any improvement will be helpful, Julie. Believe me, we're struggling with this investigation, we desperately need a breakthrough.'

She turned back to her computer and brought up a menu, selected the programme to process the photos, then copied and pasted the photos across. 'Right, now I'll run the enhancement programme.' She scrolled down a seemingly endless list of options, clicking and highlighting as she went. 'All ready to roll; it'll take a few minutes. Can I get you a cup of tea or coffee? Either that or you can sit and twiddle your thumbs.'

'Coffee please; black, no sugar.' Singleton felt a surge of excitement as the researcher left the room. *Well done, Sally, it looks like we're going to get something out of this.* The computer purred and whirred as it did its work, something was happening. A few minutes passed, the door pushed open and Julie Powell backed into the room carrying two cups, kicking the door closed behind her 'Your coffee, David, it's hot and black but not much else. Now where are we up to? Nearly there, it's on the last photo, just twenty seconds to go. That's it, we're there.'

Singleton leaned forward watching intently as she brought up the first photo; the victim being loaded into the vehicle. Julie sighed. 'I can't do much more with the man, I'm afraid.' She moved the cursor around the screen, clicking the mouse, peering at the result then eventually sat back. 'That's it, you can see he's white and I guess around 1.9 metres tall. He's wearing a dark bomber jacket and a black beret. Not much I'm afraid.'

Singleton smiled. 'It's a big step up from what we had, believe me; my team will be thrilled.'

'Good, I'll print it off for you when we're finished; and now the second photo.'

'Focus in on his face please, Julie.'

The features were still indistinct but at least they were just about discernible, though not to the degree that they would help with identification, but a step forward nevertheless. Julie peered into the screen again. 'I'd say those were dark, slim-fit trousers, and he was wearing fairly sturdy footwear, maybe boots. Now, let's see what the photo of the vehicle has to offer.'

'Can you do anything with the number plate?' The letters and numbers were still indistinct.

Julie's fingers travelled over the keyboard for a few seconds then she looked around at Singleton. 'That's it, the best I can do. Best guess would be…TX14…' she made a further adjustment, stared intently at the screen then sat back, 'ALN. Yes, that's it, I'm pretty sure it's TX14 ALN.'

Singleton was elated, this was a mega breakthrough; what he'd seen had the potential to further the investigation; team morale would soar. 'Julie, I'm so very grateful, I feel like giving you a hug.' *That's the second time you've said that today, David.*

She spread her arms. 'Here I am! Come and get me.' Singleton hesitated, unsure what to do. 'Don't panic, David; I'm only kidding!'

He grinned and patted his heart. 'I wonder, can I impose on your goodwill and ask for three photo quality prints of each scene please? And if possible, can you also forward them to me electronically?'

'Of course! Leave your email address with me and they'll be waiting for you when you get back.'

Singleton beamed and handed her his card. 'My email address is on my card along with my telephone number at the Yard.'

A few more keystrokes and the printer whirred into life. 'That's your photos done. Go out of the door and second on the right, you'll find our mounting and framing section.'

Singleton chuckled. 'I think these will serve our purposes just as they are, thanks. Now I have another question I hope someone at the NRSC can help me with. Could you take me to one of your colleagues who can tell me, in layman's terms, how the brain works?'

Julie raised her eyebrows. 'My, my, Scotland Yard is a curious beastie; Matt Wilson is probably the man you want. I'll take you to him.' Suddenly, she snapped her fingers. 'A thought has just occurred to me. As I said earlier, other priorities came along and the Centre didn't pursue photo enhancement; but MI5 and MI6 were very interested, so we passed on our research to York University and left it with them. I'm not sure if the University wanted to invest in taking the research forward but I seem to recall that Tony Burrows had an interest and said he might do it in his own time. If you want, I'll ask him to look at this stuff and get in touch with you. He's a nice guy, I'm sure he'll help if he can.'

'Julie, you're a treasure, thank you. I hesitate to ask, but could you stress the urgency?'

Julie nodded pensively. 'Tell you what, if I contact Tony for you, and stress the urgency, could you keep the favour in mind if I ever need help with a speeding ticket. And I'm not kidding this time.'

'If this bears fruit, I'll see to it that you never pick up a speeding ticket again!'

'That's a deal then. Follow me and I'll take you to Matt.'

Matt Wilson was in his office scribbling furiously at a whiteboard covered with formulae. His door was ajar and Julie breezed straight in. 'Matt, I've brought you a very important visitor; he wants to pick your brains. I wished him luck with that venture, told him there's not much to go at.'

Matt wore a tee-shirt and a pair of well-worn cords and had the look of a classic boffin, that is until you looked above his rimless spectacles and found a thick crop of bleached blond spiky hair.

'Cheeky as ever, Julie, well, don't just stand there, introduce us and tell me how important he is.'

'He's David Singleton, Assistant Commissioner, Scotland Yard and get this…he's the Prime Minister's son-in-law.'

Wilson grunted. 'Not all that important then. I suppose I ought to bow or curtsy or do something like that?' He winked at Singleton.

Julie sighed. 'Ha, ha, very funny, I don't think. I'll leave you two to have your discussion. You watch your P's and Q's, Matt Wilson, show due respect.'

Wilson remained seated but gave a little bow. 'As you command, milady.' He watched as Julie left, pulling the door closed behind her, then turned to Singleton.

'Now, how can I help, Mr Singleton?'

'Just David, please. I'm heading up an investigation; the one involving those girls who have been abducted over the years.'

Wilson nodded. 'Horrific! The bastard should have his balls cut off. I hope you get him.'

'We're trying hard, but it's a toughie; we just don't have much to go on. I asked to see you to learn what you can tell me in simple terms about the workings of the brain. All these young women were held for six months before being released; they had no physical injuries, but all of them were returned with no memory of the past or even who they were. Is there any way that could be done with no apparent brain trauma?'

Wilson shook his head immediately. 'None whatsoever.'

'You say that, Matt, but the fact is that it's happened on sixteen occasions and no doubt victim seventeen will be returned in the same condition.'

Wilson shrugged and screwed up his face. 'Point taken, I'll elaborate, but at this moment in time, there is no way known to science of doing what you describe.'

'Let's forget the here and now, Matt. What about ten years from now, twenty years or whatever? Theorise, speculate, indulge in a flight of fancy; is wiping someone's memory remotely possible?'

Wilson looked thoughtful. 'I wouldn't want to be quoted, this is stuff of science fiction.'

'So was landing on the moon once upon a time, Matt.'

'Touché, David. I haven't done any work on this whatsoever, but if we see the brain as a computer with memory as its hard-drive served by a host of neural pathways, then in theory, we could erase those bits of memory on the hard-drive, preceding whatever date we chose without interfering with the neural pathways governing our senses and life forces. There are instances where an individual has suffered a major shock resulting in complete loss of memory and cases where deep hypnosis has suspended the memory's functioning, but for the most part memories return, in part or in whole, over time.

'So, in *theory*, there must be some way of making it happen, but it's a science beyond us at the present time. Might be possible in the future, though personally I can't see it ever being pursued; it raises too many moral and legal questions, I fancy.'

Singleton nodded. 'Tell me this, assuming you knew how to delete memory without damaging the brain, could the process be reversed? I mean, could false memory or even new knowledge be implanted?'

Wilson laughed out loud. 'I'm beginning to think you have been reading too much science fiction, David. We're not even on the threshold of beginning to think how that might be done, interesting concept as it might be. In truth though, who knows what might be possible in the future. I think what you're describing, downloading computer hard drive content onto the brain, is probably a hundred years in the future.'

Singleton nodded and extended his hand. 'OK Matt, I think I've got the picture; I'll go now and leave you in peace. Thank you very much for your time, I'm truly grateful. Now, how do I get out of here?'

'Out the door, turn left, take the first corridor on the right at the end of which is the door you came in. Oh David, don't forget to remember me to the Prime Minister.'

'It's the least I can do, Matt.' Singleton felt a spring in his steps as he made his way back to his car; the investigation had taken a big step forward and who knows what Tony Burrows might come up with. As he drove out, Ricki Murdo raised the barrier for him and shouted across, 'Any joy, sir?'

'Yes, thank you, Ricki, very helpful in fact.'

'Glad you didn't have a wasted visit. I'll tell Mr Somerton you called in.'

'Yes, do that.'

The day was ending well, he was heading home to Abbi and the kids and he had something positive to tell the team.

Chapter 24
The Singleton Household

The Singleton family sat together around the breakfast table; David opposite Abbi, with their two children, Maggie and Murray, on either side of them.

'What shall we do today, everybody?' On his days off, Singleton was keen for the family to do things together and this was most likely to happen if the children had the opportunity to express their preferences.

'London Zoo,' shouted Maggie excitedly. She loved animals and would never miss an opportunity to go there or any other animal setup for that matter.

Murray pulled a face. 'We were there not too long ago, let's go to the Natural History Museum.'

It was his sister's turn to pull a face. 'I'd rather see live animals than dead animals and anyway, it gets so crowded there.'

'All good exhibitions get crowded, Maggie, and London Zoo wasn't exactly deserted last time we were there. Anyway, I don't think you would be too happy if there were live dinosaurs roaming around the countryside,' shouted back Murray, sticking his tongue out, 'so there!'

Maggie shook her fist at her brother and was searching for a response when Abbi pushed the decision over to her husband.

'I think Daddy should choose; he's been at work all week and is maybe too tired to wander around a zoo or a museum.'

'We've been at school all week *and* doing sport and PE but we're up for it, aren't we, Maggie? We don't complain about being tired,' countered Murray.

'Murray's right *and* we get homework,' Maggie added her support.

Her brother nodded. 'Absolutely spot on, Maggie.'

Abbi raised her eyebrows. 'I'll try to remember that you two never get tired next time I need help in the garden or with the housework. No matter, Daddy will decide where we go this time, end of discussion.'

The children's eyes fixed on their father, both their expressions registering an unspoken appeal for their preference to be chosen. Singleton smiled wryly. 'Thank you for landing that on me, Abbi. Firstly, does anyone know what the weather is doing this afternoon?'

Abbi frowned. 'I think it's going to rain this afternoon.'

David grimaced. 'That rules out the zoo, it's not much fun wandering around in the rain.'

'The animals have to,' protested Maggie.

'Oh no, they don't, most of them hide away in their dens or perches or whatever,' retorted Murray. 'So, it's the National History Museum or perhaps the Science Museum?'

Singleton shook his head. 'No, not this time; Maggie's right, both of those places get very crowded at the weekends. I suggest that we go to the pictures; you children can choose. *The Hobbit* and *The Hunger Games* are both showing in Leicester Square.'

'Either sounds good to me,' said Murray.

'And can we go for a pizza afterwards?' asked Maggie.

'McDonald's,' interjected Murray.

'Well…' Singleton drew out his reply. 'I think…' Two young faces gazed at him. 'I think…'

'Come on, Daddy, stop teasing,' said Maggie.

'I think…I think we've had our say and Mummy should decide.'

Two pairs of eyes swung rapidly around to Abbi. 'My decision and final word on the matter is that,' she looked from Murray to Maggie, 'we should spend the afternoon working in the garden!'

Two expectant faces crumpled into dismay, mouths open and chins dropped.

'Only kidding; we go to the pictures. I fancy *The Hobbit* with pizza or pasta to follow.'

Singleton got up from the table. 'Well done, Mum, decision made. I want everyone ready to leave at 1 pm; in the meantime, I'll book the tickets online. If it isn't raining when we get into London, we might go for a stroll around Covent Garden.'

Abbi started to clear the table. 'Sandwiches for lunch, I'll leave them ready on the table and everyone can help themselves. Sort out your own drinks. As for you two,' she addressed Murray and Maggie, 'you can use the morning to clear away any outstanding schoolwork. If I catch you gaming, you will *not* go to the pictures. As for me, I'm going to do some gardening if anyone wants to help.'

Singleton nodded. 'You're right about the gaming, take note, you two. I'll join you in the garden, darling, if I've got time; I'm going to do some homework of my own.' He winked at Abbi. 'I'm trying to keep on top of my routine work as well as leading this investigation.'

He retired to his study and turned on his desktop, then sat back collecting his thoughts until the screen display came up. His screen saver arrived, a holiday photo of Abbi and the kids, he spoke his password, then entered his user identifier to access the Yard's website. No fewer than 42 emails had arrived since he had checked the previous evening; the fact that he had been taken off his normal duties didn't seem to have registered with his colleagues. But if he was honest with himself, although the volume of emails irritated him, he didn't really want to be left out of the general loop. After all, he'd be going back to his routine police work sooner or later; Operation Galaxy wouldn't last forever.

The next two hours were spent working methodically through the list, attending to them in order of receipt. *You're not going to get any help in the garden, Abbi, sorry darling.*

Email 38 was just headed "Enquiry", his pulse quickened when he saw the sender's name—Tony Burrows.

Dear Mr Singleton,

Julie Powell has told me of your interest, and I think we'll be able to help. We have made considerable progress with the IES (Image Enhancement System) since the NRSC passed the basic system to us some time ago, though I hasten to add that we still regard our version as being at the prototype stage. But if you can bring the original photo source, a smartphone I believe, we'll do what we can. We can't produce the best results from the photos Julie emailed but, based on what I've seen and what she told me, I'd expect to improve the vehicle image and the number plate considerably. We should also be able to identify the colour of the car within a limited range.

As for the male figure, we can use computer modelling to take the two profiles and come up with a front face image. But it won't be the kind of product that a court of law would place much reliance on.

Julie also told me the matter is urgent and my earliest availability is this coming Friday afternoon. If you can come, please get in touch?

I look forward to being of assistance.
Tony Burrows.

Singleton felt his pulse quicken; this could be the breakthrough they were looking for. He lost no time in emailing Tony Burrows that he would be there on Friday around 2pm.

Lunchtime

'You're looking decidedly pleased with yourself, darling, are my sandwiches that good? Thanks for your help in the garden, by the way.' Abbi raised her eyebrows quizzically.

Singleton smiled. 'Sorry about that, over forty emails I'm afraid. Your sandwiches are as delicious as always, darling, but truth to tell they are not the reason for me smiling. We might just have a breakthrough with the investigation. There's a boffin in York who might be able to help with some photographs so I'm taking a trip up there on Friday. Now where are those kids? It's time they showed their faces if we want to head off at 1 pm.'

Abbi nodded. 'I'll go and get them. They won't take long gobbling down a few sandwiches.'

Training Room

Monday Morning

'OK guys, attention please.' Singleton was more fired up than he had been for some time. 'This is what the NRSC have produced for us.' He laid out the photos on the table in front of him. 'Take a good look; they are much better than anything we had previously. Will, I've emailed you a set of these; can you get them up on the big screen please.'

'Count it done, David.'

Singleton continued, 'We also have a number for the car, most likely TX14 ALN, probably false but can you check it out please, Milly? White male confirmed and judged to be around 1.9 metres tall. The vehicle shape is also clearer; we might be able to come up with a model. Let's grab a cuppa, then we'll see where we go with this. Will, while you're doing the necessary, I'll get you a coffee, two sugars if I remember rightly.'

'Spot on, David! Come to think of it, I reckon you have the makings of a detective. I'll have this done before you get back with the coffees.'

Singleton sighed and shook his head. 'And I reckon you're a genius, Will; you must have been a great loss to the beat.'

Richmond nodded. 'You know what, I keep telling myself that but it's nice to have it confirmed.' True to his word, the photos were available on the big screen before the queue for drinks had cleared.

Singleton took the lead. 'Right, take a good look at that vehicle and write down what model you think you're looking at. I'll give each photo two minutes then move to the next one. If the abductor reminds you of anyone, real or celebrity, write down the name, I'll be doing the same. OK, Will, rotate the photos when I give the nod.' He sat down with the rest of the team and studied the screens intently. He'd had plenty of opportunity to study the photos over the weekend and had his own views, but it was important to know what the others thought. When the process concluded, he took the floor again.

'OK, that's it. Thoughts please.'

Ken Regan was first to put forward a suggestion. 'I reckon it's a Focus but I'm not sure; it would fit the bill if he's as clever as we think he is. By that, I mean he would use a run-of-the-mill car.'

'He reminds me of Daniel Craig,' Sally offered a little tentatively. 'I'm not sure why, just does.'

Millie snorted. 'I wouldn't put much weight on that observation; she got his autograph once and has been star-struck ever since!'

Singleton gave his support to Sally. 'As a matter of fact, I think he looks a bit like Craig and I don't hear any of the rest of you coming up with anything. Sally, I want you to email the photos to the forensic techies and see if they can come up with what kind of car it is. Millie, press on with checking out the car number plate with the vehicle registration people; I suspect it's false but give it a go anyway. Hannah, perhaps you could add these images to the case file please. We guys will go through the CCTV footage for the first abduction again to see if the number plate crops up anywhere else. Will, I want the recording run at half speed this time.'

Will Richmond groaned aloud, dismayed at the prospect. 'Oh no David, must we? It'll take the rest of the day.'

'It'll take what it takes, Will, we have to try everything. By the way, can the whole of HQ access our hard drive?'

Will smiled. 'Of course not; it can only be opened if you've got the password, and it matches your identifier with the list I've set up.'

Singleton nodded. 'Impressive as always, Will. OK, run the first abduction.'

The three men sat down and gazed intently at the screen, every minute seemed to take an eternity. After two hours, Singleton called for a break. 'My eyes are straining, let's take ten. Maybe Millie will come up with something from the vehicle registration people and save us a lot of viewing. Speak of the devil, here she is now. What have you got for us, Millie?'

'Not sure, David, it's a bit strange really.'

Singleton looked at her sharply. 'Meaning?'

'Well, turns out that the registration people reserve about a thousand numbers for use by security and police forces engaged in undercover work, and this is one of them.'

Singleton felt himself stiffen. 'And who used this particular number plate?'

'Sorry, that's where the system falls down; the list is stored online and a department can make use of any number and have a plate made as and when they wish. Any use of a plate should be recorded, of course, but there's nothing to stop anyone just plucking out a number and not placing it on record. In fact, in some instances, for reasons of internal secrecy, that's how some departments prefer to work. Daft if you ask me but that's how it is.'

Ken Regan's eyes glinted. 'Ties in with my theory that this guy has knowledge of police procedures and who knows, he might even be one of us!'

Singleton's thoughts were racing. 'Thanks for that, Millie; you've given us something to think about. Not a word to anybody about this development; it's a bit of a bombshell.'

Throughout the morning, he'd been turning over in his mind whether to tell the team about his trip to York, but it wasn't until the end of the week and he didn't want them to relax; nor did he want to raise any false hopes. And, if he got lucky, whatever he learned at York would come as a morale boosting surprise when the team gathered next Monday.

'All right, we plough on. Split into two teams and go through all the CCTV footage again, watch out for the car number and pay particular attention to any Focus cars seen in the areas we've highlighted on the maps.' He looked around at the gloomy faces. 'I know it's a chore, but we've got nothing else and just to cheer you up, Will is going to run it at half speed, so it'll take twice as long and be twice the fun. Stop the moans and groans please or I'll begin to think you're not happy at your work. Millie, what's the scene with the forensic techies?'

'They'll phone this afternoon if they come up with anything.'

Two hours into the viewing, the phone rang and Sally picked it up. 'Training Room, who am I speaking to?' Excitement showed on her face, her head nodded enthusiastically as she listened. 'Thank you, that's really helpful.' She turned to the rest of the team who had been listening in. 'The techie boys have come up with a car model for us and guess what, Ken was right all along, it *is* a Focus.'

The end of the day was approaching when Singleton called the team to order. 'OK guys, what have we got?'

Will Richmond replied, 'We're about a third of the way through the visuals and we reckon on two sightings of a Focus possibly with that number plate. It's not certain though, we don't have a clear view in either instance. There's no clear view of the driver either, so Daniel Craig remains a suspect.'

'OK team, thanks for your work today. We'll carry on with the visuals for the rest of the week. If we're making good progress, you can knock off early although one of you must stick around to deal with the phones; I know they've gone quiet of late, but you never know. I'll be going to York on Friday, to a long-standing meeting so you'll be spared my presence for the day; no cheering please.'

NRSC

Jack Somerton's private mobile vibrated, a number known to a very select few. There was no caller display. *Wrong number, I bet.*

'Who is this?'

'You know me as Jupiter, I believe.'

'What do *you* want?' His tone was not welcoming to say the least. 'I'd prefer it if you didn't contact me; deal with Colin, he's the boss.'

'My, my, are you always this aggressive, Mr Somerton?'

'Come to the point, Jupiter, or whatever your name is.'

'Have a care, Mr Somerton, as you're about to find out, you need me more than I need you. What I have to tell you might well keep you out of gaol and maybe even your friend, the Prime Minister.'

Somerton felt his stomach knot. *Fuck it, something has gone wrong. I can feel it.* 'That's not possible.'

'On the contrary; it's not only possible, it's highly probable if matters continue on their present course. But the situation can be retrieved if you take appropriate action.'

'Why come to me? Why not tell Colin? He'll tell me what to do assuming he wants something done.'

'Listen very carefully, Mr Somerton, I won't repeat myself. Your future, Colin's future and perhaps even mine are at stake because of what I'm about to tell you.'

Jupiter went through the nature of what had happened when Singleton visited the NRSC and how he was going to York on Friday to advance the investigation further.

'In essence, Mr Somerton, if Mr Singleton succeeds and arranges for those photos to be processed, your image will be enhanced to the point of recognition. Anyone who knows you, will be able to recognise you; I believe that Mr Singleton has met you on several occasions. Is that not so? And, of course, your image would be widely circulated, others would also recognise you.

'The investigation team has also identified the model of the car involved in the abductions together with the fact that its number plate was extracted from the undercover list. They have also concluded that the abductor is operating from a base south of London. It's my view, and I hope you will agree, that Mr Singleton's visit to York should not take place and indeed, he should be eliminated.'

Somerton felt physically sick. 'Oh my God! Singleton is Colin's son-in-law.'

'I'm aware of that, Mr Somerton, which is precisely why I've contacted you and not Colin; it would put him in an invidious position. The decision is therefore yours and yours alone. I'm sure you will put in hand whatever action needs to be taken.'

'I can't do this. I just can't; this is Colin's daughter's husband we're talking about.'

'I'll leave you to think about it. As you know, it won't be the first time a member of Colin's family has been sacrificed. I shan't call you again; I'm sure you won't let sentiment get in the way of a solution to this problem.'

Somerton knew he had no real alternative; Jupiter was right. 'Let's suppose that I am able to resolve this, there will still be Singleton's email records and his team will know about his visit to York. This isn't as straightforward as it first appears.'

'I'm pleased to see that you've very quickly recognised the wider implications of the situation and, it seems, accepted what needs to be done. I can deal with the emails between Singleton and Mr Burrows at York University. I also have the capability of causing the researchers involved at the NSRC to forget the key aspects of their conversations with Mr Singleton. I can do nothing about Mr Burrows though, I'll leave him to you. We do have one bit of good fortune in that Mr Singleton, for reasons unknown to me, has not told his team about the purpose of his visit to York.'

'If I do what you ask, Jupiter, what then?'

'It's up to you, Mr Somerton; I'm simply telling you the facts. What action you take to preserve your well-being and that of the Prime Minister is entirely a decision for you to make. If you take the necessary action, normal service will resume.'

'You're a cocky bastard, Jupiter, a real bastard. One thing for sure, there will be no more girls, it's too risky.'

'I agree that abductions can be suspended for a period of *my* determination, but I assure you they will resume when I say so, or my cooperation will cease. I do acknowledge that we might have been in error returning these girls to society. In future this will not happen, they can simply be recorded as missing persons; I believe there are many thousands reported missing every year.'

'We'll see about that when the time comes.'

'I'll conclude this conversation, Mr Somerton, we won't speak again. There will be no trace of this call.'

Somerton felt his head pounding. 'Fuck it, fuck it, fuck it!' he swore aloud, giving vent to his feelings. It was clear what had to be done and, however abhorrent the deed, he would do it, but he'd have to act quickly. 'Fuck it, fuck it, fuck it!'

Chapter 25
Somerton's Flat Next Day

Jack Somerton had a fitful night's sleep, his dreams running rife in the realms of pessimism. His role in the abductions exposed, the Prime Minister's involvement, their SAS kinship scrutinised by investigative journalists; maybe even the Massakori business could be exposed. Once the curtain of secrecy was breached, the story would run and run. Even Alan Croudace could be drawn in; it was all a disaster waiting to happen. When the first domino fell, the rest would follow; his worst nightmare would become a reality.

He gave up trying to sleep and lay awake working out exactly what needed to be done. *Christ, how do I get out of this mess? Think, Jack, think.*

In the end, ideas explored and exhausted, there was only one option, a single cruel solution; he had nowhere to hide, nowhere to run. Jupiter was right, Singleton had to be stopped in his tracks and it would have to be done in a way that nobody, especially MacKinnon, suspected foul play. There was no point involving Colin; Abbi was the apple of his eye and he would do anything to avoid hurting her.

Colin would most likely try to persuade Singleton to conceal the truth, protect the family name, then they would all be hostage to fortune. At best it would be 50/50 which way Singleton jumped, and he was after all, a career policeman. The risk was too great; there was zero likelihood that Singleton would come out in favour of burying the truth. Perhaps he could be persuaded to settle for some poor sod being fitted up for the abduction; convincing evidence could no doubt be fabricated to obtain a conviction and he, Assistant Commissioner Singleton, could glory in the praise that would follow the success of Operation Galaxy.

But he wasn't that kind of guy, it was too big a risk to take, there was only one solution. Deep down, he'd known what would have to be done from the minute Jupiter had dropped his bombshell. A lot of people were going to be hurt in the process but that was how it had to be.

The musing and wondering came to an end where it started out—Singleton had to be eliminated. The operation needed to be planned in detail and there was no margin for error; there would be no second chances.

And, of course, there was Tony Burrows of York University to be attended to, a poor bastard lending a helping hand who just happened to be in the wrong place at the wrong time. Somerton powered up his computer and began his search. It didn't take long; Doctor Tony Burrows was reasonably well known for his work on imaging. His biographic details were available through York University personnel records and the University's quarterly magazine.

Dr Burrows, age 35, resided at Flat C, 8 Stonehouse Road, York. *Thank God for small mercies; at least you're not married or a parent and, by your own accounts, a loner.* Tuesday was going to be a busy day; arrangements would have to be put in hand to deal with the academic before his Friday meeting with Singleton.

Somerton would have to call on the help of an old colleague, Sergeant Douglas MacLintock, Mad Duggie as he had been known in his SAS days. The Massakori incident had been of his making and it was payback time. *Hardly an incident, Jack, it was more than that, much more.* The memories of that ghastly fateful day in 1987 came flooding back; all those innocents, slaughtered in a few moments of madness.　　　•

Somerton shook his head and blinked his eyes as if that would help clear away the memories and let his thoughts turn to the matter in hand. First, he had a job for his most trusted lieutenants, close friends and ex-comrades, Mike Davies and Eddie Black. What a strange irony fate had created; other than Colin, he, Mike, Eddie and Duggie were the last survivors of the Massakori business and here they were thrown together to kill again.

'Eddie, it's Jack. I have a job for you and Mike. Meet me at our usual pub, noon today, drop everything else.'

Some hours later, the three men sat together in a corner booth of the Grey Goose, a run-down edifice in a back street not far from Battersea Power Station. Each had a pint of best bitter in front of them; the décor was shabby to say the least, but the beer was good and a matter of some pride to the landlord, Andy Swift. Andy was gifted with poor eyesight, deficient hearing and a bad memory, so if anyone came along asking questions, he ably fulfilled the role of the three wise monkeys.

For a while, the men chatted about whatever took them, all the while munching the generously filled baguettes in front of them. Andy made these up himself and what they lacked in presentation, they more than made up for in flavour and sustenance. Not that his clientele felt deprived by the lack of a tomato slice or two hidden below a selection of leaves or whatever other garnish served as presentation.

Somerton glanced around to make sure no one was too near or giving them undue attention, then dropped his voice to a whisper. 'OK guys, listen up; I got you here because I need you to deal with a Doctor Tony Burrows. He's a boffin of some kind or other employed by York University. Here's a recent photo of him downloaded from the university magazine. He lives on his own in Flat C, 8 Stonehouse Road, York. I want him to disappear before Friday morning.'

'Fuck me, Jack, that doesn't give us much time! You do realise this is Tuesday?' Eddie Black protested. 'You know as well as I do that rushed jobs carry a greater risk of mistakes. What's the guy done that requires us to act with such haste?'

Davies nodded in support. 'He's right, Jack; a Friday deadline doesn't give us much time for planning.'

Somerton sighed. 'I know, I know and I'm really sorry, but I don't have an option. The problem I have didn't emerge until late yesterday. And before you ask, I can't tell you anything about the whys and wherefores. It's on 'need to know' basis only, sorry. Preferably, I'd like the target lifted and never seen again but if it ends up a mugging gone wrong and a body left behind, I'll live with it.'

Black stroked his chin. 'OK, Jack, we'll do our best. I just wish we had more time though.'

Davies snorted. 'Leave it with us, Jack, the job will be done. Eddie's talking like an old woman.'

'Thanks guys, it's appreciated; I'm asking a lot, but I'm asking it from the best two mates a guy could have.'

Davies laughed. 'Cut the bullshit, Jack, and call us up another pint. We'll drink up and get this show on the road.'

Somerton smiled. 'I'll get them in. In the meantime, put these in your back pockets.' He pushed across two brown envelopes then signalled Andy Swift for another round of drinks.

Eddie protested, 'Bollocks, Jack, there's no need. You already take good care of us.' Neither man made to pick up his envelope.

'Get those lifted, they're already gathering dust; there's five grand for each of you in there.'

The two men gave Somerton a high five. 'We won't let you down, Jack, you know that.'

'I know, Eddie. Thank God, here comes Andy with the beers, I thought I was going to die of thirst. Get those down your neck, then get your arses in gear; the talking's over, you've got work to do.'

The two men lifted their beers and swallowed them in a oner. 'OK, Jack, we're off. We'll give you a bell when the job's done.'

Somerton watched them go and gave his thoughts to the next item on his agenda; tricky but it had to be done. He settled the bill with a healthy tip and told Andy he and his mates were never there. The landlord of the Grey Goose just shrugged, nodded and carried on polishing his glassware; he regularly suffered from amnesia.

Chapter 26

Somerton drove straight to Fulham from the Grey Goose; his destination, the modest three-bedroom terraced house that was the home of Dougie MacLintock, aka Mad Duggie, ex-sergeant, SAS. He knew what he hoped to arrange would be an abuse of their friendship, but it was his best, sadly his only, option. He was, in a way, calling in an old debt, not that he would allude to Massakori; to do that would be hitting below the belt and there would be no need. There was no doubt in his mind that Dougie would do what was asked of him; he was a man of simple values and even after all these years, he considered himself beholden to MacKinnon and Somerton.

Cohen Street was deserted; the only sign of life, other than himself, was a ginger tomcat on the prowl. Maybe the unwelcome dark grey clouds were keeping the kids indoors or, more likely, they were glued to their latest computer games and smartphones. He pulled over and parked immediately outside Dougie's front door, sat for a moment gathering his thoughts; nothing had changed, there was no turning back now.

Dougie would be at home. His old colleague was living out his last days in this world; pancreatic cancer would call him away in the very near future. He pressed the doorbell push, its sound bringing a smile to his lips; somehow Dougie had managed to find one that played *Scotland the Brave*. His smile broadened when the door was opened by Vera MacLintock, her face lighting up when she saw who it was.

'Jack, how lovely to see you, you're a sight for sore eyes. Come away in.'

Vera was 55, but recent years had been hard on her and she looked older; her hair could best be described as neglected and deep dark shadows attended eyes that were sad and weary. Somerton reached forward the bunch of flowers that he had purchased on his way to Fulham. 'For you, Vera, pretty flowers for a lovely lady.'

'Bless you, Jack, I know I look a wreck. It's hard, you know, the worry and looking after Dougie is taking me down. Watching him…you know…decline is…is very hard.' Her voice was near to breaking, tears moistened her eyes.

Somerton bit on his lip, he could feel her pain. 'I know, Vera, it must be tough. Come here, you need a cuddle.' Without waiting for a response, he stepped forward and put his arms around her, soothing her head into his shoulder.

After a few seconds, she pushed back. 'Thank you, Jack, that was really nice. I mean it, I needed that.'

'How is Dougie these days?'

'He's lost a lot of weight and he tires easily but he's still feisty. Too feisty for his own good if you ask me; he tries hard not to let the inevitable get him down. Let's go through to the lounge, he'll be over the moon to see you.'

'Before we do, Vera, I have to tell you I'll be asking a favour of him.'

Puzzlement crossed her face. 'What kind of a favour, Jack? He's a dying man.'

'One I can't talk about, Vera. I'm sorry.'

She shook her head. 'What are you boys up to now? I don't think any of you really left the SAS behind when you retired. Not that Duggie would pay any heed to anything I said, he'll make his own mind up as always. He's as stubborn as ever he was.'

Somerton smiled wistfully. 'You might be right, Vera, I think we all miss our time in the regiment, the excitement, the comradeship.'

She nodded. 'Go on through, Jack, I'll bring you both a cuppa, then leave the pair of you alone. I suppose, if he's up for it, this favour of yours might give him a sense of purpose as his end gets near.' Her eyes teared up again and she dabbed them with a tissue. 'Don't mind me. Go on through, I'll make the tea.'

When Somerton stepped into the lounge, Dougie was stretched out in his favourite armchair in front of the TV, half dozing, half watching some crappy afternoon soap. He stirred from his doze when Somerton spoke, 'Come along, Sergeant, look lively, there's an officer present.'

'Jack!' Dougie's tiredness dropped away; his face lit up. 'Ach man, you're a sight for sore eyes, you've made my day. It's great to see you. I won't get up, but I can still salute an officer.' He swung his hand up sharply in a soldier's salute.

Somerton responded in the same way. 'At ease, Sergeant.' He extended a hand and the two men shook hands warmly, though the dying man's grip was not the firm energy-filled clasp of old. 'I see you're hanging on to that Scottish brogue.'

'That I have, Jack, and I'll take it with me to the grave.'

Dougie MacLintock had noticeably failed since Somerton had visited him a month previously, but there was still a twinkle in his eyes when he spoke. 'OK Major, what's the mission?' He laughed heartily as of old. 'If only it were true; look at me, good for nothing.'

'Rubbish, Dougie; I'd still have you on my team before anybody else I know. In fact, I'm mixing business with pleasure this trip, if that's OK with you?'

At that moment, Vera made her way into the room carrying a tray laid out with all the usual essentials for tea and a plate of mixed biscuits.

'Thanks love. Major Somerton has a mission for me, must be desperate, eh? Probably have me addressing envelopes or the like.'

'Rubbish, Dougie, you're still a better man than most and that's why Jack's here.'

Somerton nodded. 'Just what I was saying, Vera.'

'Anyway, I'll be off; I don't want to be listening in on your little boy plans. Call me if you need me.' She glanced at Somerton. 'Go easy on him, Jack.'

Dougie looked fondly at his wife. 'Thanks Vera, love.' His eyes followed her as she left the room, sadness creasing his face. 'One in a million, Jack, she deserved better than me. I wish I could have done more for her.'

'Nonsense Dougie, you've done everything you could; you can't do better than that. She's very proud of you and rightly so.'

'I hope so, Jack. Now let's get down to business. What is it you want of me; bearing in mind my days are numbered?'

Somerton drew breath, grappling with his conscience, his emotions. The soft side of him pleading to abandon his plan but, as ever, self-preservation won out. 'This'll sound awful, Dougie, but it's because your health is as it is that I'm asking you to take this on. It's high risk and it's illegal. It could even end your life prematurely, an unlikely outcome but possible nevertheless.'

'I see.' Dougie's eyes gleamed, relishing the thought of some action. 'Sounds just like every SAS mission I ever went on. No need to be sorry, Jack, I'd welcome one last throw of the dice. Tell me what you want of me and I'll do it if I can.'

'Before I go on, Dougie, I assume that you still have a lorry and can still do a decent drive?'

MacLintock nodded. 'I do still have one lorry, though like me it's on its last legs but it's not a bad runner; it's the one I started the business with. Sounds like you want it to make one last trip. I sold the haulage business a while back and got enough out of it to pay off the mortgage and give the lads a decent farewell package and, more importantly, set Vera up for life. As I say, it runs fine, and it's taxed and insured. But more to the point, as it happens, I've been promising myself one last drive. When that's done, the big fella's bugle can sound the Last Post. So, I guess your job is quite…providential; I think that's the word.'

Somerton breathed a sigh of relief. 'Thanks Dougie. I know I'm taking advantage of your situation; I can't tell you how grateful I am.' He reached into his inside pocket and pulled out a fat envelope that he threw onto Dougie's lap. 'There's twenty-five grand in there, it's yours.'

'Christ, Jack! I haven't done the job; I could peg out tonight. Best wait till the job's done. And anyway, I don't expect payment from you; I owe you too much. Twenty-five grand is a lot of loot, Jack, just how illegal is this job? Not that it matters; I'll do whatever you ask.'

Somerton shook his head. 'I won't have it any other way, the cash is yours, come what may. It'll give Vera a bit more security. The job must be done this Friday and you'll have an early start. I can't tell you too much about the background; it's one of those classified arms-length affairs.'

MacLintock smiled. 'Hush-hush, eh? No matter. Normally, I wouldn't take a penny from you, Jack. I owe my life to you and Colin, but Vera comes before any pride of mine. Let's cut to the chase. What's the plan?'

The two men chatted for the next hour, every detail explored and repeated until Dougie MacLintock knew as much about the plan as Somerton.

'I think we've covered every angle, Dougie. Are you happy?'

'Crystal clear, Jack, it'll be the easiest twenty-five grand I've ever earned. That much loot has never crossed my palm in one lump.'

'OK, give me the address where your lorry is garaged and I'll be on my way.'

'It's in the yard next to garage No. 1, behind the houses. Vera will let you have the spare key to the yard. The lorry has a full tank of diesel and the keys are in the ignition. Who knows, I might use it to carry me in my box to the crematorium, though I suspect Vera would have none of it.'

Somerton stood and extended his hand. 'Who dares wins, Dougie. Take best care of yourself. I'll come and see you when the job's done.'

Dougie pushed himself up from his armchair and gripped his friend's hand firmly, adrenaline was flowing; he felt better than he had done in the last three months. 'Who dares wins, Jack.'

On his way out, Somerton collected the yard key from Vera. 'Is that all this favour is, Jack, borrowing the lorry?'

Somerton bit his lip. 'No Vera, it's more than that; he'll tell you what he wants you to know.'

Vera shook her head. 'I won't hear much then. Men and their secrets, I don't know. Our yard gate is just plain wood; he never bothered to paint it.'

Somerton kissed her goodbye and walked down the hall to the door, opening then pulling it closed quickly behind him. He wanted to get away quickly, as though he could somehow leave his guilt behind. He wondered if he would be able to look Vera in the eye if anything happened to Dougie. *You're a bastard, Jack. God! I wish I'd never gotten involved in this Jupiter business.*

Vera MacLintock stood in the hall, looking at the closed door. A feeling of foreboding came over her, wondering if she should confront her husband and demand to know what was going on. In the end, she decided to let the matter be. Dougie would do his best for her, as he'd always done. Tears flooded into her eyes. *The thing is, Dougie, you don't always know what's best for me. You're what's best for me and I don't want to lose you.*

National Research and Security Centre
Wednesday Morning

Somerton sat in his office going over and over what had to be done. There would only be one opportunity, there was no room for error. He had to get it right first time and the only way to ensure that was to be meticulous about the detail. When he was satisfied that he'd covered every eventuality, he reached for the phone and dialled. 'Chris, it's Jack. I want a short-wave radio installed in a lorry and it's urgent; in fact, it's so urgent it should have been done yesterday.'

Chris Henson had forgotten more than most people knew about electronics and communications. He looked ordinary and it suited him to be ordinary; there wasn't much to distinguish him from a million or so other thirty-year-olds.

'Immediate is costly, Jack, I've got a lot on.'

'Save me the sales talk, Chris, you're always busy, you're always costly. I'll pay cash and if I think you're ripping me off, I'll go elsewhere in future. I want the job done today.

'I love you, Jack, you're such a charmer. What is it you want exactly?'

'I want a short-wave radio installed in a lorry; it's currently in a yard beside garage number 1 in an alley behind Cohen Street, Fulham.'

'Got that. Now, how do I get into this yard?'

'I'll give you a key when we meet up later this morning. I can get into the city for 10 am. If you can manage, meet me outside WH Smiths in Charing Cross Railway Station.'

'I'll be there, Jack. Tell me more about this radio.'

'Thanks Chris. I want it to look like an ordinary radio. Nothing fancy, it's going into an old lorry. One of the station-select buttons is to serve the on/off to a short-wave radio. I want the radio and its companion handset pre-set to the same frequency. The radio should operate hands free and obviously, pick up the driver's voice. When the job's done, I want you to phone me to arrange a meet to hand over the handset and complete the deal at the same time. I take it you've still got your private mobile with the same number as last time?'

'Yip. And the same for you, Jack?'

'Affirmative, Chris.'

'I'll see you at Charing Cross. This will cost you two grand.'

'No problem. Oh, by the way, make sure the shortwave works at maximum range.'

'Of course, Jack. I take a pride in my work; if it doesn't function satisfactorily, you can have your money back.'

By the end of the evening, the transaction had been completed—the radio installed, the handset delivered, and payment made. Somerton was starting to feel better; confidence was beginning to replace his earlier unease. All he had to do now was phone his old SAS mate and tell him it was game on.

'Dougie, it's Jack. The job is done and, if I might say so, you sound remarkably bright.'

'I'm on fire, Jack; I haven't felt this good since the Grim Reaper put me on standby.'

'Dougie, I hate to ask, but the lorry is OK to run? I mean, will it start OK?'

'I took a wander down there not long after you left, Vera was out at one of the church's regular coffee mornings. She's got great faith has our Vera, sometimes I envy her. My baby started up without as much as a cough, just as I knew she would; I nip out and run the engine at least once a month.' He sighed. 'I still like to sit behind the wheel even if I am stuck in the yard.'

'Have you told Vera anything about what's going on?'

Dougie let out a sigh. 'I've told her I'm going out on Friday for one last run for old time's sake. She didn't believe me, but she let it go.'

'She's a real diamond, Dougie.'

'She's the best, Jack, no doubt about it.'

'Cheers Dougie, see you when the job's done and remember the grey radio button is the on/off for the intercom. '

Somerton sat in his office watching the clock, waiting for one more call. There was still one piece of the plan to fall into place. It brought a great sense of relief when he got the call just before midnight. 'Jack, it's Eddie, that little job of yours has been set up. The target has been eyeballed and we'll complete the job tomorrow.' The call ended. Somerton reached for a whisky bottle. *A Balvenie I think, you've earned it, Jack. It's been a good day's work.*

Chapter 27
York Thursday Morning

Eddie Black and Mike Davies sat in an old silver grey MPV across the road from a brick-clad, circa 1980, three-floor block of flats; they had been there since 7 am waiting for Tony Burrows to emerge. The duo had set up watch on the residential block the previous night, waiting for him to get back from work and had usefully learned that it was his practice to travel to and from the University by bike, just a short ride away. They guessed he wasn't due into work until at least 8.30 and didn't expect him to turn out before 8.00. In the meantime, they sat happily reading the morning newspapers.

Burrows had returned the previous evening around 6 pm and they had pondered on lifting him then but there was a group of students in the vicinity and had decided against it. Time was on their side; if a good opportunity didn't present this morning, they would try again this evening when he left the university. If all else failed, they would visit him in his flat and remove him in the early hours of the morning. The delay wasn't unwelcome; they didn't want news of his 'disappearance' to be made public too early; Somerton had warned that if that happened and Singleton got to know, he might cancel his trip to York. If that was to happen, a whole new scenario would have to be dealt with. Jack had asked that Burrows should 'disappear' rather than leave his dead body lying around resulting in swift police involvement, which might conceivably arouse Singleton's suspicions.

Eight o'clock came and went and it was nearing 8.30 when Burrows exited the front door, wheeling his bicycle ahead of him. Black scanned the rear-view mirror. 'Clear behind.'

Davies dealt with the view ahead. 'All clear, let's—'

He didn't finish what he was going to say; another figure appeared in the doorway, also wheeling a bicycle.

'Tony, wait for me. I'll ride into town with you.'

Burrows stopped in the middle of mounting his bicycle and looked back, breaking into a smile when he saw the young woman. 'Good morning, Sam, you've made my day; I don't often have the pleasure of your company this early in the morning.'

'Bollocks!' Davies frowned as he watched the pair ride away. 'Nearly, nearly, fucking nearly.'

'Calm down, Mike, there will be other opportunities. Let's tail him and see where he parks his bike at the Uni.'

They followed Burrows and his companion at a safe distance, keeping them in sight until the pair went their separate ways. 'Great, she's going somewhere else; hopefully, that means it's unlikely she'll ride home with him; that would make it fucking awkward,' Davies murmured.

Burrows turned off the main drag into a narrow one-way lane, closely followed by the MPV. The good doctor travelled less than one hundred metres before reaching a T-junction and, turning left, joined the traffic flow from his right almost immediately. Black let one car pass, and another, then pulled out cheekily in front of a Royal Mail van, triggering a series of horn blasts from its irritated driver.

'Sorry mate, we've got a parcel to collect.' He chuckled at his attempted humour.

'Steady Eddie, he's turning right; you'll be up his arse if you don't watch out.'

In the event, Burrows paid them no regard when they pulled up immediately behind him, he was too intent on watching for a break in the traffic. Up ahead, a group of pedestrians were waiting for the little green man to light so they could cross the road. Eventually, the traffic lights changed to red, bringing the oncoming traffic to a halt and allowing Burrows to continue his journey, closely followed by the MPV.

'Can't be too far now, Eddie; I reckon we're at the rear of the University.' Davies had been plotting the route on a street map of York he'd purchased locally. 'It's around here somewhere, I'm sure of it. There he goes, he's slowing down, I reckon we've arrived, old son.'

Burrows swung his leg over the saddle and free-wheeled the few remaining yards standing on one pedal, dismounting when he reached his destination. Davies brought the car to a halt and watched their target bump his bike onto the pavement and cross the short distance to a black door set in a high grey stone wall.

'Hmm, that's lucky. He's not reached for a key and no sign of a keypad to worry about, looks like the door isn't locked. Have you spotted any cameras, Mike?' It was ingrained into both men to be aware of CCTV cameras whenever they were on a clandestine assignment.

'Can't see any this side of the wall, doesn't mean there aren't any on the inside though.'

'What do you reckon? Do I follow him? It'll be useful to know what's on the other side of that wall.' Black knew it was a judgement call; it carried risk but might be worth it.

Davies nodded. 'I'm up for it. Wait here.'

He got out of the car, glancing quickly up and down the street, relaxing when he saw that there was no-one around. He made his way to the door, reached for the handle, opened it and without hesitation stepped through. It was best not to linger and look furtive, act confidently and it looks as though you have the right to be there—always the best policy.

'It gets better and better,' murmured Davies under his breath. 'This seems to be a quiet area away from the main campus.' A broad tarmac path ran ahead, passing first through a three-metres high rhododendron hedgerow in front of the wall, then on across an expanse of lawn. Up ahead, Burrows, clearly recognisable in his bright blue anorak, could be seen at a long run of racks padlocking his bicycle, then undoing his cycle clips. That done, he set off towards the university building.

Davies had seen all he needed to; the setup was well suited for what they had to do. The area was overlooked and that posed a risk, but the rhododendrons provided some screening, and it would be dark by the time Burrows finished for the day. Back in the car, Black waited patiently, avidly reading the sports pages, but he shoved the newspaper aside and started up the car immediately Davies returned.

'How did it go?'

'Looks good, mate, I think we're on, just wish we knew what time he quit work.'

Black shrugged. 'Why don't you ask?'

Davies stared at him. 'What do you mean, Eddie?'

'Wait till we get to a carpark and I'll show you.'

Ten minutes later, they turned into a carpark and pulled into the first vacant space. 'Now what?' Davies was puzzled as to what his accomplice had in mind.

'Watch and learn, my friend. If I find out what time he knocks off, the breakfasts are on you.'

'*If* you find out, I'll even pay the car parking charge.'

He watched as Black took his phone out, waited for a signal and tapped in a number. 'What the fuck are you up to, Eddie?' His partner in crime just smiled.

'York University; how can I help?'

Eddie Black winked at his mate and put on what he judged to be an educated voice. 'Could you put me through to Dr Burrow's secretary please?'

Davies' eyes widened. 'Christ Eddie, I hope you know what you're doing,' he whispered.

'Dr Burrow's secretary speaking, how can I help?'

'Can I speak to Dr Burrows please?'

'I'm not sure if he's in his office, hold while I try. Who shall I say is calling?'

'Dr Rice from Bristol.'

'Hold a moment, Dr Rice, I'll see if I can find him.'

'Oh dear; hold that, sorry, I'll have to break off; the Dean is waving at me, it looks urgent. I'll call Dr Burrows back later, I'm not sure what this is about or how long it'll take. What time does Dr Burrows usually leave in the evening?'

'Never before 5 pm. Often not till after 6 pm, depends what he's got on.'

'Oh, that's fine, do tell him I called.'

'Certainly, Dr Rice.'

Davies was grinning. 'You're a clever fucker, Eddie, that was brilliant. I hope that's a pay-as-you-go phone; it could be traced.'

'Of course, it is, what do you take me for? When this business is over, I'll get rid of it. Our friend never leaves before five, so we have all day to ourselves. Now let's go and park up, then we go on the hunt for a decent breakfast and don't forget, you're paying.'

After breakfast, there was time to kill and, York being a tourist mecca, there was plenty to choose from. Mike won the toss and elected to go the Railway Museum. 'You can't beat a steam locomotive, Eddie, the sounds, the smells, the history, it has it all.'

The pair spent three happy hours viewing railway history at its best before moving on to York Minster where they had a sandwich lunch in the Cathedral Tea Room, just a stone's throw from the Minster's grand entrance. Afterwards, with time to kill, they found themselves strolling down the aisles of that great Christian edifice.

'Doesn't seem right, Mike.'

'What doesn't seem right?'

Eddie gazed around him. 'Being here in a house of God, given what's on our agenda.'

Davies grunted. 'I suppose you're right but we're here as tourists, not worshippers. Put a couple of twenties in the collection box if it'll make you feel better. I've never asked, but do you believe in all this stuff?'

'Well, this is the first church I've been in for years, weddings and funerals excepted. And of course, a few compulsory duty visits when we were in the Army. My parents were both regular church-goers and I guess something has rubbed off on me. I think there's something there, though I can't explain what it is.

'You're on your own there, Eddie. I don't believe a word of it, a fairy story, that's all it is.'

'You believe in luck though, Mike? Luck is exactly the same; you can't see it but it's there, whether you believe in it or not.'

Davies smiled. 'We won't fall out about it, mate. One thing for sure, the believers constructed some great buildings.'

They spent their last hour or so meandering around shops old and new, browsing in bookshops, feigning interest in objects in antique shops, whatever took their fancy. Dusk arrived and darkness wasn't far away when Davies took yet another look at his watch.

'Time we were going, Eddie.'

'I hope you put enough time on the parking ticket?'

'Probably, but who cares? The plates won't see the light of day again when this job's done. Toss you for who does the driving, your call.' He took a 50p from his pocket and flicked it into the air.

'Heads,' Black called out.

Davies caught it and took away a hand to see the result.

'Heads it is, your choice, Eddie.'

'I'll drive, you do the business. It's time we were going, we ought to be in place by 5 pm, although my guess is that he'll hang on till nearer 6 pm, when the traffic will have died down. The later he leaves it, the better for us; there will be fewer people around.'

Ten minutes later, they parked up and Mike Davies made his way across to the black door and into the university grounds. He stationed himself between the wall and the rhododendron hedge from where he could safely observe the bike racks. It was turning cold as the sky darkened and he stamped his feet to keep warm, shivering as the warmth in his body ebbed away into the night. It seemed to be taking an eternity. *Where the hell are you, Burrows?* He glanced at his watch, 6.15 pm. *Come on, Doctor, time you stopped for the night.* The cold night air forced him to relieve himself. *Be a good chap, Burrows, don't come while I've got my dick in my hand.*

Minutes later, floodlights came on, illuminating the parking area and a solitary form made its way forward. It was just a black silhouette casting a shadow in the glare of the of light; there was no way of telling whether it was male or female. The figure was headed in the general direction of the cycle rack Burrows had used earlier. *So far so good, please let it be you, Dr Burrows, or I'll be joining the brass monkey brigade.* A bright blue anorak came into view; it was game on, it had to be Burrows.

Davies readied his phone and pressed the dial button for Eddie Black.

'He's just un-padlocking his bike now, pull forward. Is it all clear out there?'

'Not a soul in sight.'

'Great, he's on his way.'

Tony Burrows mounted his bike and rode the sixty or so metres to the gate, dismounting and walking the last few metres. He reached forward and opened the gate, somewhat surprised to see a vehicle parked immediately outside with its engine running.

'Dr Burrows?'

The startled scientist turned to face the direction of the voice coming from behind him, a sudden feeling of unease creeping over him; something was wrong. 'Yes. What are you—'

Davies pulled the trigger of the silenced Beretta; the one Somerton had taken from the late Eric Fenton. Its dull *phut* was the last sound Tony Burrows heard.

'Sorry about that, Doctor, nothing personal.'

The bicycle fell against the wall but remained upright. Burrows clasped his chest and slumped to the ground, mouthing a yell of pain that died away as quickly as it came.

Black was already out of the car, opening the rear door on his way to Burrow's lifeless body. He took hold of the corpse and dragged it across the pavement to the rear of the MPV. Meantime, Davies recovered the bicycle and wheeled it to lean against the vehicle before helping Black to load their victim into the boot; that done, he moved across and closed the entrance door to the University grounds. *Job done, everything back to normal, except for the doctor, that is.*

Black lifted the bicycle and threw it unceremoniously on top of Burrows and covered their cargo with a large dark grey blanket. Davies had already positioned himself behind the wheel and within seconds they were on their way, heading out of York on the A1079. Further on, they took a right onto the A614 towards Spalding Moor, eventually turning onto a quiet, very minor road in the Sand Hole area where the late Dr Burrows was laid to rest in a shallow grave a hundred metres into the wild countryside.

Eddie Black stood back and bowed his head. 'Sorry, Doctor Burrows, rest in peace. It's not a bad place to end up, old chap.' As it happened, it was indeed the good doctor's last resting place; his body was never found.

'Come on, Eddie, words are no use to him now. Let's get out of here; I'm starting to feel peckish.'

Burrow's bicycle was taken on to London where it was given to a friendly scrap metal dealer and crushed into an unidentifiable metal mass.

Somerton's Office

Somerton lifted his personal mobile from his desk where it had sat since early morning waiting for a call.

'Hello Jack, mission accomplished.'

'Well done, guys. I'll see you at the pub on Saturday around noon; the drinks are on me.'

'And the sandwiches, Jack; don't forget the sandwiches.'

'And the sandwiches, Mike.'

Chapter 28
Friday

Chloe MacKinnon stood on her tiptoes and kissed her husband goodbye. It was 6.30 am and normally she didn't get up that early to see him off to work but a busy day lay ahead; she had shopping to do, a personal trainer session in what she referred to as her "proper home", after that, a coffee with two of her old friends, then lunch, followed by a church fund-raising meeting.

'Goodbye darling. Hope you have a good day and not too busy.'

MacKinnon grimaced. 'I've forgotten what a quiet day is, I'm no longer quite sure what constitutes a good day; I feel like I'm permanently riding a roller coaster.'

'My, my, you sound a little bit apprehensive, darling, that's not like you. What's brought this on?'

'Follow up to yesterday's Prime Minister's questions, a touchy Cabinet meeting and, to cap it off, a one on one with your friend and mine, the Honourable Thomas Ross.'

'I'm beginning to have sympathy for you, darling. Do try and get home early; Abbi and the children will be with us for dinner. David is off on a trip to York University.'

'Oh, what's that about?'

Chloe shrugged. 'Don't know, didn't ask, I'm sure Abbi will fill us in when we meet up.'

'All right, darling, I'm off; I promise I'll do my best to get home early. Love you.'

Two other players in the game of life had important business that day, Jack Somerton and Dougie MacLintock. They too had risen early, Dougie earlier than any of the others. Somerton, MacLintock and Singleton, three men linked by a chain of random events but only Somerton had the full picture.

Dougie MacLintock was making the best of his day's release from his lounge chair and was treating himself to a traditional English breakfast in the Newport Pagnell Motorway Service Plaza. He knew he was breaking the dietary rules imposed on him by his doctor, backed up religiously by his dearest Vera, but if today went pear-shaped like Jack said it might, this could be his last meal. *I feel like the condemned man before he heads off to meet the firing squad.* He smiled at the thought. *You wouldn't approve, Vera, would you, love?*

Bless her, she had been reluctant to see him go out for what he had told her was his final drive before retiring from the road once and for all. *Don't fuss, Vera darling, I'll be home before you know it.* If he was up to it when he got back, he intended to take her out to their favourite pub for a meal that evening. *Assuming you do get back home tonight, Dougie.*

He cast his mind back to their parting conversation. *I just have to feel the wheels on the road one more time love; hear the noise, feel the bumps and swear at other road users. Me and my old battle wagon deserve one more outing together.*

Vera had sighed; she knew he wouldn't change his mind; she knew he was up to something and with Jack Somerton involved, God help him.

I'm not happy, Dougie, but I understand. Just be careful, love, I want you back home as soon as you can. I'll worry every minute you're away; I wish Jack hadn't got you into whatever you're up to.

Don't be too hard on him, love, I owe him more than you'll ever know.

He took another swig of tea and glanced at his watch, 7.48 am, it was time to go. Jack wanted him in his cab by 8 am and listening out for a call on the short-wave radio. There was just time for a visit to the gents to drain down before heading out to the lorry. His ever-thoughtful Vera had insisted on making him take a flask of coffee and a small bag of snacks. *Just in case you get stuck somewhere, Dougie, you never know with motorways.*

Somerton was also on duty; he'd had the Singleton household under observation since 6 am and was starting to get edgy. There was no sign of activity. *Where the hell are you, Singleton?* The 8 am time signal was just sounding on Radio Four. *Christ, I hope the meeting hasn't been cancelled, that would be a disaster.*

There had been a false alarm fifteen minutes earlier when the gate had swung open, but it had been Abbi Singleton who had emerged to take her children to school. It was time to test the short-wave radio as planned. He crossed his fingers praying it would work; they would have to resort to mobiles if it didn't. He pressed the transmit button. 'Crazy Horse calling Geronimo. Over.' His tension drained away when Dougie answered immediately, loud and clear.

'Geronimo. Over.'

Chris Henson had done a good job; the pre-set frequency was as clear as a bell.

'Crazy Horse. No action this end. Out.'

Communications would be brief and only when required. Anyone picking up the transmission would hear little and understand even less. Ten minutes later, Abbi Singleton returned and drove through the still open gate. Somerton smiled, maybe now Singleton would show face. *Good girl. Now say your goodbyes to sweetie-pie and see him on his way. Let's get this mission over and done with.*

He rolled the passenger window down another couple of centimetres; it was hot in the car and his black sweater and black beanie hat weren't the coolest of clothing. But they did change his appearance; a perfunctory glance from a passer-by would be unlikely to result in much of a description, should it ever come to that. Another twenty tension-building minutes passed before he was at last able to breathe a sigh of relief as Singleton's car nosed out of the driveway and onto the road, the automatic gates swinging closed behind it.

'Crazy Horse. On the move. Out.'

'Geronimo. Message received. Out.'

He pulled away, settling down at a safe distance behind Singleton's Jaguar, his heart nearly stopping when, to his horror, he realised Abbi was behind the wheel, with Singleton in the passenger seat. 'Oh no, damn it! No, no, no—Colin's daughter. What the fuck do I do now?' He wailed. 'Calm down, Jack, no need to panic yet. Maybe she's taking him to the Yard to pick up a pool car; or maybe she's getting out somewhere on the way?' He spoke aloud, perhaps in the hope that somehow that would help him solve the dilemma he now faced.

'Stay calm, Jack; if all else fails, you can abort the fucking whole business with a press of the button. No, no, no, fuck it! Think, Jack, think. It's not that simple. Think through the options and their implications.' He continued to speak the words aloud, somehow it seemed to help. The initial shock began to subside as he drove along, his eyes fixed on the car ahead, London's traffic no more than a background noise. He was on autopilot. As the initial panic died away, he began to consider his alternatives. He could call off the operation, but Singleton would arrive at York University and ask for Burrows. What then? *Sorry, Assistant*

Commissioner, Dr Burrows hasn't turned up; he seems to have gone missing. We've got no idea where he is.

Singleton was a copper and coppers were suspicious by nature; they tended not to believe in coincidences. And anyway, some other boffin might emerge with an offer to help when Singleton explained why he was there. It was a no-brainer really; Singleton couldn't be allowed to get to York, that was for sure. But his wife, mother of two children and MacKinnon's daughter, was an innocent in this business. That was a bridge too far, but…but what? There had to be another viable solution, had to be. But he wasn't coming up with one and in the deepest recesses of his mind, he knew there was no way out of the mess. Damn it, Abbi, why couldn't you have had the day at home, or met your girl friends for skinny latte, or whatever.

His thoughts were in turmoil, buzzing around in a circle of half-formed ideas, conscious that each passing minute brought the M1 access that much closer.

When it came down to it, what choice did he have? He could hope the photo enhancement process wouldn't point Singleton in his direction. *Too risky, Jack, it's your head that's on the chopping block and probably Colin's along with it.* If that came to pass, the media would have a field day and the reputation of his beloved country would be dealt a body blow from which it might never recover. *Poor Abbi; you would be appalled if you knew your father was responsible for the abduction and enslavement of seventeen young women. But as it is, you might end up losing your life preventing him from being brought to justice. Fuck it. Fuck it. Fuck it.*

Maybe Singleton should be confronted and persuaded not to blow the whistle. Maybe a deal could be done to persuade him to turn a blind eye to his father-in-law's involvement. The abductions would cease, and some unwitting lowlife could be put in the frame for the kidnappings. Evidence could be planted; it wouldn't be the first time. Singleton could grab the glory for apprehending the abductor. The press would be happy, Joe Public would be happy and the whole rotten business would be consigned to history.

Forget it, Jack, you're drifting into the realms of wishful thinking, you've already been down this path; you're painting a fairy tale ending that's not going to happen. Why the hell would Singleton, a dedicated successful copper, put his whole career on the line? It's just not going to happen.

Self-preservation, mankind's primal instinct, was in the ascendancy again. Jack Somerton, ruthless SAS Major, was re-emerging. *Forget the sentiment, Jack; remember who is number one in this game. Singleton is the enemy. Let that be an end to it, focus on the job ahead; it's just another mission to be carried out, like it was in the old days. If Abbi Singleton ended up as collateral damage, so be it.*

The decision was made, there was no going back now. Up ahead, the white Jaguar was changing lanes, setting up to join the M1 slip road. Somerton pressed the transmit button on his handset. 'Crazy Horse calling.'

Dougie MacLintock answered immediately, 'Geronimo. Go ahead, Crazy Horse.'

'We are on the racetrack. Out.'

Dougie had been well briefed; it had been like the old SAS days when every man knew exactly what his job was and when to carry it out. He knew that the "racetrack" was the M1 motorway. It would soon be time to put the plan into action. He smiled, he felt like a soldier again.

'Crazy Horse to Geronimo.'

'Go ahead, Crazy Horse.'

'Just passing checkpoint one.'

Checkpoint one was Junction 9 on the M1, the target was around 25 miles away; not long now. Jack had assured him that the target would stick to the 70 mph speed limit, he was a police officer after all. Somerton did a quick calculation in his head; his quarry should reach Newport Pagnell in around twenty minutes.

'Crazy Horse to Geronimo'

'Go ahead, Crazy Horse.'

'Just passing checkpoint two.'

Checkpoint two was Junction 12; the target was ten minutes away. Dougie fired up his faithful old battle wagon, eased out of his parking bay and moved slowly forward to join the M1. This was the tricky period; Jack's assumptions would have to be right.

The target would have to drive very close to the motorway speed limit and would have to have a clear run with no last-minute accidents or breakdowns to delay progress. There was a back-up plan; there was always a back-up plan, but it was a last resort solution and high risk.

'Crazy Horse to Geronimo.'

'Go ahead, Crazy Horse.'

'Now at checkpoint three.'

So far so good, the white Jaguar was passing Junction 14 just two minutes away. *Great, dead on time just as Jack had estimated, time to get moving.* Dougie MacLintock joined the M1, acknowledging fellow HV drivers, who pulled into the middle lane affording him free passage onto the slow lane. He kept his speed at 60mph; his battle wagon was growling along, well within its comfort zone. His eyes darted back continuously to the rear-view mirror, smiling when he caught sight of a white Jaguar travelling along in the middle lane around 70mph, just as Jack had hoped.

'Crazy Horse to Geronimo.'

'Go ahead, Crazy Horse.'

'Do you have eyeball?'

'Affirmative, Crazy Horse.'

'You are now in command, Geronimo.'

Sergeant Dougie MacLintock made a clenched fist; he was on the brink of repaying a long outstanding debt. He pressed down gently on the accelerator and took his speed up a few miles per hour; the Jaguar was closing the distance. It was all going to plan; zero hour was imminent. The target was close now; he could make out the occupants of the car.

Christ! There were two occupants, a female driver and a man. Was Jack aware? He hadn't mentioned a woman. He must know, he saw them leave home. He hadn't said anything so it must be OK, but a woman? Christ, what should he do? A woman wasn't part of the plan. Maybe he should check with Jack? No, there was no point. Jack must be aware, and he still wanted the plan to go ahead; the Major knew what he was doing. Just obey your orders, Dougie.

But a niggling doubt remained, and he reached forward tentatively to press the transmit button, his finger hovering ready. He let a second or two go by then drew his hand back to the steering wheel. He had his orders and he would carry them out; this would be his last chance to repay his debt before the Grim Reaper called him home.

He manoeuvred into the middle lane and sat there at 70mph, the so-called maximum speed limit that everyone ignored except Singleton. A couple of cars pulled out into the overtaking lane and went past. The Jaguar drew alongside in the fast lane; the road ahead was clear, the time to act was imminent. It would be the best opportunity he would get, maybe the only one. But a woman…memories of the woman at Massakori came flooding back. *Christ Jack, I hope you've got it right.*

The front wheels of the Jaguar were in line with his; it was time. He reached forward and pressed the transmit button on the short wave. 'Geronimo.' There would be no reply this time. He braced himself for what would happen next. The woman driver, a very attractive woman, chanced to glance up at him a split second before his front driver's side tyre exploded. The battle wagon veered sharply to the right, helped by Dougie MacLintock steering sharply into the fast lane. He took no action to counteract the momentum of his vehicle as it followed the course set by the ruptured tyre. MacLintock stared straight ahead, mouth open, face contorted as though he was in a state of shock; that was what any observer would recall seeing.

The impact came noisily, sickeningly, as the lorry crushed the sleek lines of the Jaguar. It was David against Goliath; only this time, Goliath had the upper hand. Abbi Singleton wrestled fleetingly, desperately, with the steering wheel to no avail; the Jaguar was crushed and smashed into the crash barrier. Almost simultaneously, it was slammed from behind by a following car and became just a crumpled lump of machinery.

Braking squeals and the thuds of vehicles colliding filled the air; drivers and passengers were screaming with pain and shock. Traffic noise reduced in the adjacent southbound lanes as vehicles slowed to gawp at the carnage on the way past. Dougie MacLintock wasn't aware of the horrific outcomes of his action; his frail body was battered and bruised; mercifully, he was unconscious.

Somerton, who had stationed himself to the rear of the lorry travelling behind MacLintock, now wanted to get clear of the scene to avoid any chance of being questioned by the accident investigators. When a lorry in front of him swerved to avoid the wreckage, seeking the safety of the slow lane, Somerton had followed then sped away on the hard shoulder. The lorry driver braked violently to a halt and immediately abandoned his vehicle to see if he could render assistance to the injured. He glanced briefly at Somerton's rapidly disappearing vehicle, shaking his head in disbelief at such disregard for the injured fellow road users.

Somerton left the motorway at the next available turn off; he had no intention of being anywhere near the area when the Emergency Services arrived to carry out their duties and subsequent investigations. He might have been caught on camera but that didn't matter, the number plates were false and would reveal nothing. Ambulances and police vehicles passed him on their way to the crash scene, sirens blaring. The queues on the northbound lanes were already ten miles long; on the southbound, a tailback had already formed as ghoulish drivers slowed to gape at the carnage.

Somerton relaxed; his mission had been accomplished and it had all gone exactly to plan. Well, not exactly to plan. Abbi hadn't been part of the plan but that wasn't his fault. He didn't believe in a God but nevertheless, he prayed that she had somehow survived, along with his old comrade Dougie.

He switched his car radio on and waited for a traffic announcement. When it came, it stated no more than he already knew. *A serious incident had taken place on the Northbound Carriageway of the M1 motorway between Junctions 14 and 15. Multiple vehicles were involved, long delays were expected; motorists are advised to use an alternative route.* He was away safe and sound; first stop, a quiet country lane to change the number plates, then he'd head back to the NRSC.

It was the first time he had used his new sabotage device in anger, one he'd designed himself; a small metal cylinder filled with air at high pressure and fitted with a small explosive charge that could be detonated by a radio signal transmitted by a mobile phone. He had triggered that signal the precise second Dougie drew level with the Jaguar and shouted 'Geronimo.'

The compressed air had expanded instantly to fill the tyre and rupture it into dozens of fragments. Skilled forensic investigators with oodles of time and resources might gather together bits and pieces and have their suspicions aroused but it was highly unlikely that a routine crash investigation team would find anything to raise their concerns. If suspicions were aroused, and Dougie MacLintock did end up being questioned, he knew how to deal with anything thrown at him; SAS men were trained to deal with interrogation.

I hope you're in good shape, Dougie, old son. It was best to wait for Vera to call him; he could play it by ear from then on. Vera was no fool; she would have her suspicions and it wasn't a call he was looking forward to.

On the way back to the NRSC, he called in on Chris Henson to hand over the short-wave radio handset and the mobile used to trigger the compressed air cylinders; they would be dismantled and rendered untraceable before the day was out. Henson didn't even ask how or where they had been used; he knew he

243

wouldn't be told. It was in his best interests to be totally lacking in curiosity when Jack Somerton was his client.

Chapter 29
Northampton General Hospital

Three still forms lay side by side in the Intensive Care Unit of the NGH; one of them the architect of the incident that had brought the other two to the brink of death. David and Abbi Singleton were in critical condition, their lives hung in the balance. The other, Dougie MacLintock, was in a serious condition but stable and expected to make a full recovery. All three were hooked up to tubes and wires sustaining and monitoring their life systems; two were in medically induced comas, husband and wife perhaps sharing their final hours.

Elsewhere, in the hospital's Accident and Emergency Department, it was manic; doctors and nurses struggled to cope with the aftermath of the accident. The less seriously injured were being diverted to other hospitals. They were the lucky ones; most would be home before the day was over, others would need more time for fractures and serious injuries to mend.

Back on the M1, an endless tailback had developed; drivers sat cursing the delay, giving little thought to the injured on the carriageway miles ahead. The hard shoulders of the M1 in both directions had been commandeered and reserved for the emergency services. The media was keeping the public informed of progress; breaking news was having a field day.

Time passed, and Dougie felt himself beginning to regain consciousness, but he didn't open his eyes; he would play the comatose survivor for as long as he could. He wasn't aware that the beds alongside him were occupied by the Singletons. His plan was for Vera to sit at his bedside, and it would be her voice that miraculously brought him out of his coma; it would be heart-breaking for her if he continued his deception. He felt awful, his head was being squeezed in a giant vice and his ribs had surely been pummelled for fifteen rounds by a heavyweight boxer. All his limbs were in place, but his right arm and right leg were in splints or plaster but at least they were still attached to his body.

God, old bones mend slowly, even young ones take six weeks. I hope I'm not still in plaster by the time I snuff it; I want to look my best when I meet the Big Fella. Poor Vera, forgive me, love. In the meantime, he knew that medics would study his x-rays and carry out whatever tests they considered appropriate. They might even access his medical history online and talk to his GP. *That should win me a few sympathy votes.* In any event, it wouldn't be long before they diagnosed his condition and concluded that he wasn't long for this world.

Dougie MacLintock was hoping that the police would be briefed appropriately by the duty doctor and would temper their questions about the accident accordingly. Not that they would get anywhere with him, come what may he would play dumb and have no memory of the accident. *Sorry officer, must be post-traumatic stress or whatever they call it.*

Abbi Singleton was in an induced coma and being prepared for transfer to Guy's Hospital in London. Her fractures and ruptures weren't the cause for concern, extensive as they were; her neurological trauma was the main threat to her life. The next 72 hours would determine whether she survived and what mental and physical capacity she would retain. Had she been aware of the impending move, she would have thought it ironic that she might well die in the same hospital as her brother; fate dealt strange cards at times. A decision had been taken not to move David Singleton; everything possible had been done for him but his head injuries were extensive and inoperable. It would probably be best if he didn't survive.

Downing Street

It was late morning when Colin MacKinnon's attention was taken by a news item on the TV; it was his practice to have one wheeled in on days without visitors. As usual, it was tuned to BBC World and sometimes provided his first notice of happenings elsewhere in the world. He could work quite happily with the constant background voices of announcers and reporters, tuning in only when an item of interest arose. He paused from what he was doing, something big was going on.

Scenes of a major accident on the M1 came onto the screen; multiple cars were involved, the tail back disappeared out of view. Emergency services were doing what they always did, bringing order out of chaos and administering help to the injured. *Oh dear, there will be many unhappy homes tonight.* Not for a moment did it occur to him that his daughter and son-in-law might be involved.

246

For his part, he would be heading home shortly; Jess Tate, his ever-thoughtful secretary, routinely tried to ensure that his diary was kept clear on a Friday afternoon and from time to time, he took advantage of this manufactured interruption to business and went home to Richmond. Today was one such occasion; he took one last look at the M1 chaos, then cleared his desk and left his office. 'I'm going home now, Jess, ask Bill to bring the car around. Abbi and the kids are having a sleepover with us, I'm looking forward to an evening with family. Thanks for freeing up my diary, it's appreciated.'

Jess smiled. 'No problem. Have fun, enjoy your grandchildren whilst they're young; they grow up far too quickly and their childhood is gone before you know it.'

MacKinnon nodded. 'You're right, Jess, but I went into this job with my eyes open, so I can't complain.'

Bill Sweeney and his personal security guard, Tim Penrose, were waiting for him and after the usual greetings he climbed into the back of the Bentley and sank into the plush upholstery with a satisfied sigh. He glanced at the red box of government papers sitting on the seat next to him with a touch of guilt. He could have, perhaps should have, looked at them before he left his office, but he knew that if he started on them, time would evaporate and before he knew it, it would be midnight. He had no intention of opening it until the kids went to bed.

'Richmond please, Bill; fingers crossed traffic will be kind to us.'

Sweeney shook his head. 'Should be all right at this time of day. Are we doing anything special, Prime Minister, it's not often you leave early?'

'Not really, Bill, and to be honest I feel guilty, but I've got a chance to spend a bit of time with Abbi and the kids and I'm taking it.'

'That's a good enough reason in my book. The hours you put in, you deserve some time off now and again. Anyway, I'll bet that head of yours is still full of the wheels and intrigues of politics wherever you are.'

'Goes with the territory, Bill.'

Tim Penrose, who rarely spoke other than when it was necessary, chipped in. 'Bill's right, Prime Minister. Treasure every hour you can get in the company of your family, especially the young ones; you never know what lies around the corner.'

MacKinnon Residence

Chloe watched smiling as her two grandchildren rushed forward excitedly to greet MacKinnon as soon as he walked through the front door; kisses and hugs were exchanged all around. Maggie took hold of the red box. 'I'll put this in your study, Grandad.' She marched off proudly, knowing full well its importance.

'I've put it on your desk, Grandad.'

'Thank you, Maggie.' He bowed ceremoniously.

'I'll leave you with these two, Colin. I'm just finishing off preparing tonight's meal, I'll be with you shortly.'

'And how are you two?'

'I'm good, Grandad,' beamed Maggie.

'Me too, Grandad; and what about you?' Murray took hold of his hand, keen to get out of the hall and on to something that was more fun.

'I'm in good form and all the better for seeing you two. How was school today and how come you're home so early?'

Maggie pulled a face. 'School is boring; thank goodness the teachers have a meeting this afternoon. I wish they had one every day.'

Murray's expression became quite animated. 'Don't listen to her, Grandad; it was great. I had a lot of fun doing PE and we had a game of floor soccer and my side won.'

'Well, thank goodness one of you enjoyed the excellent education the country is providing for you, at enormous expense I might add. I'm going upstairs to change into something comfortable; you two head for the lounge and decide what game we're going to play before dinner.' A thought suddenly struck him. 'Where's your mum? I thought she was going to be here.'

Maggie spoke up first, 'Oh, she decided to go off with Daddy to Sheffield and stay overnight, so just us, I'm afraid. They'll be back tomorrow. Gran kindly picked us up from school.'

MacKinnon smiled broadly. 'Well, that is good news; it means Gran and I have got the two of you all to ourselves. Off you go and play, I'll see you in a minute or two.'

Ten minutes later, he found them in the lounge with the Harry Potter version of Cluedo set out ready for play, the television rumbling away in the background.

MacKinnon pointed at it. 'Can one of you switch that off please?'

'I'll do it.' Maggie scrambled up from the floor. 'Murray, put it on; there's been a big crash somewhere.'

'Yes, I saw that before I left Downing Street; lots of cars involved.'

Murray looked at him puzzled. 'Are you allowed to watch TV at work, Grandad? I didn't think a Prime Minister could do that.'

MacKinnon felt slightly embarrassed. 'Well, very occasionally, when I have no appointments, I have a TV brought into my office and I put World News on in the background whilst I work. That way, I can keep an eye on what's going on in the world outside. I hope that's OK with you?'

Murray nodded, not wholly convinced. 'I think I saw a car just like Daddy's.'

'Don't worry about it, there are lots of cars like Daddy's on the motorways. Now let's get on with this game. I think Maggie won last time we played?' He shouted to Chloe, 'Are you joining us and the boy wizard for a game of Cluedo, darling?'

'Yes dear, you can make a start. I'll be with you in a minute.'

Just then, the phone rang in the hall. 'I'll get that, Colin. I won't talk for long, I promise.' She wiped her hands on her apron and made her way to the hall. 'Chloe MacKinnon, who's calling please?' she said cheerily, her mood changing the instant the purpose of the call was made known. 'Oh my God, no! Colin, come quickly.'

MacKinnon heard the anxiety in his wife's voice and knew instantly something was seriously amiss. 'Wait here, kids, while I deal with this call.' As he entered the hall, he saw the look of despair and anguish on his wife's face. Trepidation gripped him as he walked towards her. 'What is it? What's happened, darling?'

She dropped her voice to a whisper, 'It's your office; David and Abbi have been involved in that pile-up on the M1.' She broke into a sob. 'They're flying her to Guy's right this moment. Oh God, Colin, I'm scared. Guy's! A helicopter! She must be near to death.'

Her husband gulped, striving for the right words of comfort, seeking to offer reassurance he didn't really feel. 'We've got to be brave for the kids, darling; they wouldn't be flying her to Guy's if they didn't think they could look after her.'

Chloe nodded, tears still filling her eyes. 'Yes, of course, you're right.' She handed him the phone. 'They want to speak to you; I'll go and tell the kids.'

'Hello.' MacKinnon held his breath, praying they hadn't held back even worse news from Chloe.

'Kelly Swinburn, Prime Minister, I'm on the switchboard. I'm so very sorry to be the bearer of such awful news but I thought it best to get straight on to you. I've called Bill Sweeney and told him to get to your place immediately. Your daughter will be in Guy's by now; the helicopter left Northampton a while back.'

'Thank you for that; I assume the PR team is primed to deal with the media, so I'll leave them to it. Have you heard anything about my son-in-law, David Singleton? He would have been driving.'

'Sorry, Prime Minister. I have no information about him. I just accepted what I was told and phoned you immediately.'

'That was the right thing to do. Now I want you to get in touch with whoever contacted you.'

Kelly Swinburn interjected, 'That would be Northampton General Hospital.'

'OK, get onto them and ask if they have Mr Singleton with them. Find out what you can then phone me on my mobile with chapter and verse. In the meantime, I'm heading off to Guy's with my wife and two grandchildren. Also, please phone Mr Singleton's parents and let them know what the situation is. It could be they have already been contacted but no matter.' As he spoke, he realised how seldom he'd met up with his son-in-law's parents. *Leave that for another day, Colin, first things first.*

'Got that, Prime Minister. I'll phone Guy's and let them know you're on your way. PR will inform Cabinet colleagues and others about your situation.'

'Kelly, one more thing, tell Guy's to keep it low key. No press bulletins unless authorised by me personally.'

MacKinnon made his way back to the lounge, fearful of what lay ahead. *How do you tell kids that their Mum and Dad have been in a car accident but it's going to be all right, when you don't really know?* Two tearful children rushed towards him. Maggie got there first. 'Are Mummy and Daddy going to be all right? They've not been killed, have they?'

'No, they haven't been killed and they both are in very good hands. We're going off to see Mummy right this moment; she's in Guy's Hospital in London. Daddy is in hospital near where he crashed and it's best not to move him; we'll go to see him later. Now, let's get to Mummy as quick as we can, go and get your shoes and coats on.'

As they climbed the stairs together, Chloe squeezed her husband's hand. 'I know you're being upbeat for the kids but how is she really?'

'I don't know, Chloe, it must be bad, but whatever happens, we have to be strong for the kids. We must have hope until there is no hope; Abbi is strong, she's a fighter.'

'I heard you ask about David. Is there any news?'

MacKinnon shook his head. 'No darling, Downing Street is checking it out and they'll phone me as soon as they know anything.'

They had just assembled in the hall when the doorbell rang, it was Bill Sweeney who lived not far away. 'I got here as quickly as I could. I'm so sorry, Prime Minister, it's an awful shock for you. I've lined up a police escort vehicle, we'll be at Guy's in no time. Tim is travelling in the lead police car.'

They all piled in and Sweeney flashed his lights to show that they were ready to go. The police vehicle pulled away immediately, with Sweeney in close attendance followed by a second police vehicle. The three cars sped through the traffic, sirens blaring and blue lights flashing, overtaking at will, jumping red traffic lights when necessary.

MacKinnon snatched at his phone when it rang, desperate for whatever news there was, fearful too that it might not be what he wanted to hear. 'MacKinnon.'

'Colin, it's Alan, I'm desperately sorry about Abbi, David too, I pray they'll both pull through. I'm in Downing Street, Abbi has arrived in Guy's, go straight to Intensive Care when you get there. They've called in the top medics in the city, she'll get the best care in the world. They expect to operate tonight, she's critical but stable and no-one is making dire predictions.

'David is still in a grave condition and they're saying it will be a miracle if he lasts through the night. It doesn't look good, sorry. I'll get off the line now in case someone else is trying to get through. I'll hang around Downing Street for as long as necessary, call me if there's anything I can do.'

'Thanks Alan, it's good to know you're around. Try to find out exactly what caused the pile-up if you can, please. We'll want to know sooner or later.'

'Will do, Colin, keep your chin up, give Chloe my love and look after those grandchildren of yours.'

Three expectant faces looked at him when he finished the call. He attempted a half-hearted smile. 'That was Alan; he's looking after the Downing Street shop. He sends his love, he's thinking of us. No news yet, I'm afraid.' He couldn't bring himself to tell them that their Dad was dying and their Mum about to undergo life-saving surgery.

Chapter 30
Northampton General Hospital Friday

Consultants and nurses clustered around David Singleton, deep in discussion; everybody present knew that their patient was the Prime Minister's son-in-law and an Assistant Commissioner of Police. Not that the influence of rank and relationships could do much for a seriously traumatised body. It would be down to medical and nursing skills, drugs, equipment and luck if he was to survive. The expressions on the faces around the bed told their own story; heads shaken dolefully from time to time painted a bleak outlook.

Henry Willard, the hospital's most senior general surgeon, summed up. 'So, we're agreed?' He looked around the group, checking there were no dissenters. 'For the moment, we keep him on life support and wait for the arrival of Mr King.' Ted King was a neurosurgeon of major repute and it might just be that his expertise could give Singleton an outside chance of surviving the night.

'Personally, I doubt if even King will be able to do much, the head injuries are so severe. But he should be able to give the relatives an indication of the functions the patient will retain, assuming that he doesn't succumb to his other physical injuries in the meantime.'

Just a few beds away, Dougie MacLintock was aware of the activity going on around him but kept his eyes closed, continuing to feign unconsciousness. He would avoid answering questions for as long as he could get away with it. And anyway, Vera's spirits would be lifted when it was the sound of her voice that magically brought him out of his "coma". Physically, he was feeling a bit better; the painkillers were doing their job and doing it well. He had furtively tried moving each of his limbs in turn, nothing demanding but enough to reassure him that they would respond to whatever he asked of them in due course.

Guy's Hospital, Intensive Therapy Unit

The scene that greeted Colin MacKinnon filled him with despair; his mouth dried in an instant. Abbi seemed to be hooked up to every conceivable type of apparatus; she was draped with tubes and wires, bottles of fluids, plasma, blood, saline or whatever, feeding their life-supporting drips into her body. Her head was swathed in bandages; her arms and legs were bloodied and bruised but thankfully, they were all still in place. A loose sheet covered her from neck to knee, hiding whatever damage the crash had inflicted on her body.

Mercifully, there didn't seem to be any major damage to her face, though her nose and lips were grossly swollen. *Why, why, why, has this happened to you, my beautiful daughter? It's just not fair.* He fought back tears and the urge to cuddle her. He'd gone to see her unaccompanied, leaving Chloe and the children in the waiting room with the intention of preparing them for what they would eventually see for themselves. *I wonder if the children should see you, Abbi?*

His thoughts were interrupted when a consultant came towards him, hand extended. 'Jim Edwards, Prime Minister, I'm in charge of ITU and this is Sister Howard; she's the one who is really in charge of the Unit. We will be your main points of contact whilst your daughter is with us. I know her appearance must be alarming, but her condition is stable and although the machines are doing a lot of the work at present, that's normal for cases as serious as this.'

MacKinnon licked his lips and tried to digest what he'd just been told; in truth, it didn't make him feel any better. 'Her head injuries, how bad are they?'

Edwards swallowed. 'Our neurosurgeon has looked at her, but he's asked for another colleague to join him, he's on his way now. They'll agree a way forward and operate on your daughter later. She'll be going for a CT scan in the next few minutes.'

'My wife and grandchildren are in the waiting room, they're anxious to see her.'

Edwards sighed. 'That's a decision for you to make, Prime Minister; you know how you felt when you just saw your daughter. It's a distressing sight to say the least; how are your wife and, more importantly, your grandchildren likely to react?'

MacKinnon nodded. 'I'm not sure, but I have given it some serious thought, I'll just have to prepare them as best I can. If I don't allow them to see her, they'll fear the worst in any case.'

Edwards sighed. 'As I say, it's your decision. I'll leave you to it.'

'We'll be staying with her until she regains consciousness. Can we have a room nearby for the night and, for that matter, however long it takes.'

Sister Howard spoke up, 'I'll see what we can do. I'm sure we can find a room somewhere, though maybe not in the immediate vicinity.'

MacKinnon shrugged. 'One of us can sit with Abbi, the others can be wherever you put us.'

Sister Howard had a kindly face and a voice to match. She nodded. 'I'll do my best. You appreciate it could be days before she regains consciousness; almost certainly in fact.'

'I understand that, but for now, we just need to be near her. Thank you for everything you're doing for her, we all know she's in good hands.'

MacKinnon made the short walk along the corridor to the waiting room, hesitating for a few moments to draw breath and compose his thoughts. Three tear-stained faces turned to look at him when he pushed open the door and walked in. Three anxious voices spoke in unison, all asking questions, all wanting answers.

'How's Mummy, Grandad?' Maggie was trying to be calm and sound grown up, but her face betrayed the distress she was feeling.

Murray jumped up and ran towards him. 'I want to see Mummy. She's not…dying, is she?'

Chloe rose and stared into her husband's eyes seeking out the truth, a truth she might not want to hear. 'Tell us how she is, Colin. She's going to be alright, isn't she?'

MacKinnon took hold of Murray's shoulders, squeezed them gently and chose his words carefully. 'Mummy isn't dying but she's very badly injured and she's going to have an operation later tonight. Before that, she's going to have a CT scan, that's a special kind of X-ray, to help the doctors see inside her and decide what they need to do to make her better. The doctors have put her into a deep sleep and that's what's best for her.'

Maggie wrung her hands and bit her lip. 'If she's going to have an operation, it must be very serious, mustn't it?'

'It is very serious, Maggie, but the doctors carry out operations every week and they know what to do.' MacKinnon bent down and cuddled her. 'The doctors will fix her; she'll be all right, darling.'

Murray tugged at his sleeve. 'What kind of things need fixed, Grandad? Tell us please.'

MacKinnon hesitated, choosing his words carefully. 'Well, there are some broken bones, and lots of cuts and bruises. Her face is terribly swollen, and she's had a bad knock to her head. But they don't know everything yet, that's why she's having special x-rays and scans. I'll take you along to see her but be prepared, Mummy has a lot of tubes and wires attached that are helping keep her comfortable and take away her pain. Her head is protected by a big bandage and as I said, her face is swollen, and she won't be able to speak to you. We can't stay very long; we have to keep out of the way for the moment and let the doctors get on with their work to get Mummy better.'

'Grandad,' Murray spoke softly, 'you haven't mentioned Daddy. How is he?'

MacKinnon was prepared for the question, but it didn't make answering any easier. 'He's very, very poorly but I haven't had a chance to speak to the doctors yet. Alan Croudace is going to contact Daddy's doctors and I hope to hear from him soon.'

Tears welled up in Murray's eyes. 'If he's very, very poorly, he must be hurt more badly than Mummy?'

'I think he might be, but that doesn't mean he won't get well. Let's wait and see what the doctors have to say. Now, I think we should go and see Mummy.'

Nervously, he led the way into the ITU, turning to watch his family's reaction, grimacing as he saw the absolute horror on the children's faces. There was nothing he could say to ease their pain. Chloe stood staring, saying nothing, tears running down her cheeks.

'I feel sick, I can't bear to see Mummy like this.' Maggie turned back to the door, quickly followed by her brother.

'Wait for me, Maggie, I'm coming too.'

'Leave me with her for a moment, Colin. Go after the kids.'

When her husband had gone, she went over to the bed and kissed Abbi on the forehead, then lifted the sheet to look at her daughter's body, letting it drop quickly when she saw the blood-soaked dressings swathing her body. She stood for a moment then turned away, stifling sobs that were fighting to escape. She had to be strong for the children. Seeing Abbi lying there had dented her hopes; how could a body survive all those injuries and if it did, would she be the Abbi of old? *Please, please God, if you can hear me, spare my daughter.* She wasn't religious but at times like this, that didn't seem to matter.

Northampton Hospital

Friday

Vera MacLintock got to the hospital around 8 pm that evening; the long drive had left her weary, but she had longed to be with her husband every inch of the journey. A nurse passing through must have thought she looked lost and offered her assistance.

'Thank you, dear, I'm here to see my husband, Dougie MacLintock, he was injured in that motorway crash.'

'Oh dear, sorry about that, wait here and I'll make enquiries.'

After a word with the Admission Clerk in Reception, the nurse returned and led Vera to a side ward close to the ITU. Dougie had been transferred there that afternoon, the doctors having decided that his condition was stable and intensive monitoring no longer required. Dougie smiled inwardly when he heard a voice say, 'He's in here, Mrs MacLintock. You can stay with him for as long as you want; overnight if you wish. I do have to warn you though that it might be a day or two before he regains consciousness. He should recover from his physical injuries over the course of the next six weeks and if everything goes to plan, we'll have him back on his feet in the very near future. I'll go now and leave you alone; just press the call bell if you need help.'

'Thank you, dear, you've been very kind.' Vera sat down and squeezed her husband's hand. 'I'm here now, Dougie, it's going to be OK. Fancy you having an accident on your last trip out, you silly old fool, as if you didn't have enough problems. You mind and get home soon. I need you around the house.'

To her amazement, she heard her husband's voice. 'Less of the old fool, if you don't mind, Vera. You just want me home to have somebody to nag at.' Dougie lowered his voice to a whisper. 'Vera love, listen carefully; I'm playing a game until all this is done. Don't let on I woke up. I don't feel up to the police questioning me, you know what they can be like after a motorway pile-up. It's important, Vera love, don't let me down, please love, it's important.'

She looked behind her to make sure the door was closed and spoke softly. 'What on earth are you up to, Dougie? I thought there was something fishy going on with you and Jack; you've done a terrible thing if you caused that accident.'

Dougie MacLintock licked his lips and told a barefaced lie. 'I didn't deliberately cause the accident if that's what you mean. I had a tyre blowout; there was nothing I could do. There's nothing fishy going on, Vera, honestly love; I was just doing a bit of haulage for Jack. In his line of work, I suspect it was something he might not trust other hauliers with. He needs to do all sorts of things beneath the radar. But remember this, Vera darling, we haven't seen Jack for weeks if anybody asks. And I do mean anybody, it's really important, love.'

She shook her head, bewildered. 'Oh my God, Dougie! What have you gotten yourself into? I'm not sure that I believe your story but let's leave it for now.'

Downing Street
Saturday

By chance, Somerton met up with Croudace as he was coming out of a meeting.

'Hi Alan. I dropped in to see Colin and I've just been told by Jess that Abbi and David were involved in that M1 pile-up. I know how close he is to Abbi; he'll be devastated.' Playing the innocent came easy to Somerton.

Croudace shook his head. 'Colin won't be around for a while; he's been at Guy's overnight along with Chloe and the kids. I've no idea when he'll be back. It's a bad business and it could well get worse.'

Somerton felt his stomach knot, his worst fears had been realised. 'How is Abbi? She's not going to die, is she?' He felt his heart go on hold as he waited for Croudace to reply.

'She's stable and she'll live but it's not clear what shape she'll be in. She's taken a bad knock to the head and there could well be permanent neurological damage.'

'God! I hope that doesn't happen. And what's the news on David?' Somerton held his breath; if Singleton survived, the whole business would have been in vain.

Croudace shook his head gravely. 'He's still in Northampton; he's alive but, from what they say, he's very poorly. It sounds like it would be best for him if he didn't make it.'

'Where there's life, there's hope, they say.' Somerton's response held no genuine concern; he wanted Singleton dead.

Croudace shook his head. 'From what I've heard, if it was me, I'd want the life support equipment to be switched off.'

Somerton summoned up a look of despair. 'Sorry to hear that, he seemed a good guy. Abbi and the kids will be distraught if he doesn't pull through.'

Croudace nodded. 'I liked him well enough. By the way, there's a strange co-incidence about the cause of the accident. I made enquiries and get this, the lorry involved in the initial collision was driven by an old friend of ours from the regiment days.'

Somerton raised his eyebrows and furrowed his brow. 'I'm intrigued, tell me more.'

'When they mentioned the driver's name, my ears pricked up; it's none other than Sergeant Dougie MacLintock, one of our old SAS mates. Do you remember him?'

Somerton feigned surprise. 'Of course, I remember Dougie, in fact I saw him not too long ago; he's one of the few surviving members of our old team. Vera will be at her wit's end; the poor guy is terminally ill with cancer and now this. What kind of shape is he in?'

'Badly bruised and shaken up but he's going to be OK. He was unconscious when I enquired but they're putting that down to shock in the main. Knowing Dougie, he'll be back on his feet in no time. His wife is up there with him now. What on Earth was he doing on a motorway if he's terminally ill?'

'Thank Christ for that. I'll try and manage a trip up, though Vera might not want him to have visitors this early, she's very protective of him. I'll think about it, I might just send him some flowers, that'll bring a smile to his lips. Funny but he always referred to his lorry as his battle wagon, seems appropriate somehow. Maybe he was taking it for a farewell drive.'

Croudace glanced at his watch. 'Must go, another meeting; I'm filling in for Colin. If you do see Dougie, give him my best.'

Six Weeks Later

The MacKinnon family gathered at the crematorium; Abbi, dressed in black from head to toe, sat in a wheelchair. It was thought she would never walk again, though it was hoped that regular therapy over time would see her regain all her cognitive abilities in full. The Abbi of yesteryear was gone; her eyes were lifeless, her expression one of sheer desolation, a picture of misery.

Colin and Chloe stood behind her, Maggie and Murray stood at their mother's side, sobbing quietly. They were all dressed in black at Abbi's insistence although, hitherto, she had always frowned on sombre dress at funerals. She didn't know why, but this time around, she couldn't bear the thought of everyone dressing up as though it was a normal day. Her world had been shattered, her life turned upside down, nothing would ever be the same again. She would be in mourning for the rest of her life.

She had declined the conventional police turnout, insisting that the service be a simple one with only family and close friends present. His colleagues could hold their own service another time and do their own thing to commemorate David's memory. She knew she wasn't being rational but was past caring about what anybody thought. She didn't feel like celebrating David's life, she wanted to mourn his loss. The light of her life, her soulmate, had been taken from her and she barely retained the will to live; only her children gave her a reason to go on.

Singleton had died five days after the accident, but MacKinnon had instructed the hospital to keep his body in a mortuary until Abbi was well enough to leave hospital and attend the funeral.

Somerton had come up with an excuse not to accept Colin's invitation to the service. Any guilt he felt was already passing into history but being in Abbi's presence would bring it flooding back. It had to be that way for him; his army experiences had taught him to let death go quickly and move on. But even he would have found it impossible to look her in the eye and offer his condolences; a card with carefully chosen words would have to suffice.

There was one funeral he did attend, that of Dougie MacLintock who died shortly after being discharged from hospital—his cancer had finally triumphed. Alan Croudace had also gone, but MacKinnon had declined. 'I just can't attend. Dougie was driving the lorry that killed David and resulted in Abbi being as she is. I know it was an accident, but I just can't, sorry.'

He had gone to see Vera and paid his respects but that was as much as he could bring himself to do. Vera had stared deeply into MacKinnon's eyes, wondering if he too had somehow been involved, just as she had into Somerton's when he came to see her. She had wanted to ask questions, but in the end had respected Dougie's wishes not to pry. There were just too many coincidences, but she had remained silent knowing it was what her dearest would have wanted.

The Motorway Incident Investigation Team put the accident down to a faulty tyre. The complete disintegration of the front offside tyre had been noted and been put down to a manufacturing fault or perhaps over-inflation. No trace of Somerton's device had been found; in all probability, it had been swept up with the rest of the debris. Dougie's beloved battle wagon had gone for scrap and if the dealer had salvaged the radio, its short-wave facility was never reported.

Operation Galaxy

The investigation limped along for another two months before it was finally wound up, albeit the abductions were still categorised as open cases.

The Chief Commissioner commended everyone for their efforts but felt that the investigation had run its course; further expenditure could no longer be justified. Truth to tell, the team were relieved; they all knew they were getting nowhere. They had completely lost their commitment to the investigation following Singleton's death.

The political spin doctors moved in and the Home Secretary praised the work of the investigating team, claiming that the abductions had ceased due to its efforts. '*It was highly likely that the perpetrator felt that the net was closing in and had given up his shameful abductions. But I must stress that the police files will remain open indefinitely. One day, the man responsible will be brought to justice.*'

In fact, the abductions continued; MacKinnon complied with Jupiter's wishes as always. However, they took place at less regular intervals and the practice of returning the unfortunate victims to society was discontinued; the young women involved were just added to the list of Missing Persons.

He never asked Jupiter to explain how he treated them, or, what he did with them when he no longer wanted their company. MacKinnon told himself that over one hundred thousand people were reported missing every year with ten thousand of them never seen again; the few kidnappings carried out on Jupiter's behalf were by comparison a drop in the ocean.

Somerton carried on with abductions, more careful than ever, telling himself he was just doing what he was told.

Chapter 31
Prime Minister's Office 2017

MacKinnon sat alone in his office, his thoughts churning as he considered his future. He was tired, both physically and mentally; he'd had enough of politics, negotiating, wrangling and all the rest of it. Maybe he had run his race and it was time to quit; maybe twenty-two years was long enough, and it was time to hand over the reins to Alan Croudace or whoever the Party chose as its next leader.

Looking back his political career had been a triumph. His rise in world politics, by any measurement, had been meteoric. He was centre stage wherever he went; true, he owed it all to one man, Jupiter, but he had played his part. His and the nation's success had been built on the output of the NRSC, the boiler house of UK Ltd; courtesy of Jupiter its researchers had produced a stream of ground-breaking innovations, some of which had astounded the world.

He had always worried that the partnership with Jupiter might break down and with an eye to succession, the education system, from nursery school to university, had been pulled up by its bootstraps, there was now a regular crop of new researchers of the highest calibre being produced.

Biotechnology and genetics had been added to the range of specialties; cutting-edge research in these fields was currently in progress. The research elite continued to be housed in the NRSC; the next generation operated in an outpost facility acting under the guidance of NRSC mentors who were still hardwired to Jupiter, thus perpetuating an unparalleled network of inventiveness. The UK had a huge technological lead over the rest of the world, one that was set to continue for the foreseeable future; the Centre's researchers had amassed no fewer than eighteen Nobel Prizes. He was confident that the UK could continue to flourish without Jupiter, but thankfully, that wasn't a question he needed to answer for now.

He'd been careful how he positioned himself on the world stage, he never shunned the limelight, in fact he sought it, but he had never manoeuvred to be considered the leader of the Western world; that honour, and all that it entailed, rested with the President of the United States of America and Uncle Sam's military might. For his part, it sufficed that he could exercise influence, considerable influence, through the "special relationship".

The USA, with a population approaching 300 million, still had the best equipped military forces in the world and was still the guardian of Western democracy. Not that the West was under any serious threat, notwithstanding the concerns expressed by some commentators about the sheer size of the Chinese army and its huge nuclear arsenal. Behind the scenes, he had made it abundantly clear that access to British technology, and its expertise, would be placed in jeopardy if relations between East and West deteriorated.

There was one deep-rooted concern he had never come to terms with; how would the West deal with a situation where some rogue state triggered a nuclear war? What then? He had always believed it would be better to have the means to prevent this happening, rather than sort out the aftermath, but Jupiter had steadfastly refused to produce anything to advance the UK's military prowess. Nevertheless, a deterrent of some kind remained on his private agenda in the hope that maybe one day, Jupiter could be persuaded.

The tragedy that had struck Abbi had devastated him; a bright light in his life had gone out. It had brought home to him how the balance of life could be changed in an instant. He knew he had become less tolerant of individuals, countries and alliances that didn't see things his way and, at times, had almost wished he *was* a dictator, free of the shackles of a democratic political system. The never-ending troubles in Africa and the Middle East continued to blight the world and he'd often wished he had a giant pair of hands to knock assorted heads together; or perhaps a dome, a la Stephen King, under which all offenders could be isolated from the rest of society until they came to their senses.

His hard-line approach regularly drew criticism from various quarters and of late, even his closest colleagues were voicing concerns. None more so than Alan Croudace who had observed his friend's hardening attitudes and lack of tolerance with increasing concern. Differences in their views had become more acute in the last two years and nowadays, they invariably clashed over policy. As he sat musing, he could hear his friend's voice echoing from their latest confrontation earlier in the week.

'Colin, for fuck's sake, you just can't do that! You're becoming a dictator; treating them like naughty children, taking away their toys if they don't comply with your wishes. It takes years, decades even, for cultures to change, you can't bring about instant change just because you want it. You can apply sanctions, but they don't affect the despots, it's their country's poor, its children and its old who suffer; the bad guys just hide away in their palaces and live off their stolen millions.'

He had come up with his usual response. 'I'm growing weary of cajoling and threatening those fat, decadent, corrupt bastards; no matter what aid we give, it never seems to get through to those in greatest need. We look on whilst they exploit their own people, condemning them to sickness and poverty. I'm not going to put up with it for much longer, something has to be done.'

Croudace had despaired; he was increasingly worried about MacKinnon's outlook on the world. 'Colin, **please**, listen to yourself. You're beginning to sound like the dictators of old; Hitler, Stalin, Amin, Saddam, Gaddafi, to name but a few. All I hear from you all too frequently nowadays is "What I want, I get." You used to believe in the democratic process but over the past few years, you have increasingly set it aside. At the slightest sign of resistance, you come out with all guns blazing. I regularly pour oil on troubled waters of your making, often having to put some spin on your threats and utterances. Even some of our best friends are asking questions.'

MacKinnon had brushed aside his concerns. 'Whatever you may think, Alan, I am still a staunch devotee of democracy, but it'll only flourish if it's given a chance. Don't forget, in the glory days of the Empire, we weren't shy about sending a gunboat or two to settle an argument.'

'For God's sake, Colin, time has moved on, we're two decades into the 21st century. The days of empires and colonies are thankfully gone forever; today's people want to be masters of their own destiny. Look at how we've devolved power in the UK, Scotland, Wales and Northern Ireland all happily operate on a quasi-federal basis nowadays.'

'I know that, Alan, and the peoples of other nations should have the same democratic opportunities. I want to give them that chance, can't you see that? I hold the big cards and I'm going to play them as I see fit.'

263

'*I warn you, Colin, as only a friend can, your best friend in fact, there are those in high places, in the US and Europe, who are uneasy about how you've dealt with matters in recent years. Nearer to home, you've had to answer some searching questions in the House, MPs in all parties don't want to be disloyal in matters affecting foreign policy but there are mutterings, believe me.*'

'*Let them mutter, as you call it. If anybody has got anything to say, tell them to say it to me, Alan, eye to eye, and I'll sort them out.*'

Alan had put his head in his hands in exasperation. '*There you go again, more threats. "I'll sort them out Everybody else is wrong because you say so, Colin MacKinnon, Mr Right, Mr I Know Best, I guess that must include me now. I'm telling you again you can't go on like this, it will all come to a head sooner or later and you'll be out on your ear."*'

Cruelly, MacKinnon had laughed out loud. '*You're being alarmist, Alan, ridiculous even; that will never happen.*'

'*I **am** exaggerating, Colin, I know I am, but only because I have to, just to get you to listen to me. I wish, I just wish, I could be as confident as you, but **you** don't hear the whispers going on behind your back. Many go along with you because they are afraid not to, not because they agree with you. Mark my words, there's a wind of change blowing out there for all sorts of reasons, resentment and jealousy just to name two.*'

'*Come off it, Alan. We're one of the wealthiest nations in the world, richer than we ever dreamed we could be. Scientifically and technologically, we occupy the No. 1 spot by a huge margin, thanks to Jupiter.*'

'*But—*'

'*There's no fucking "buts", Alan. None!*'

'*There is just one, Colin, if I might say so; militarily, we aren't at all strong. We've run down our forces and defences and are almost totally reliant on the United States. If, God forbid, we were subjected to an armed conflict involving a major power, we wouldn't last a week.*'

'*You're in fantasy land, Alan, it's not going to happen. The US would never let us down, they would come to our rescue just as they have always done in the past.*'

'*I wouldn't be too sure of that, Colin, it would depend upon the circumstances and how they saw their own interests.*'

'I can't believe you're talking like this. What's brought this on? Oh, I know; it's because I won't release the BUV to every Tom, Dick or Harry.'

The British Universal Vaccine, BUV, as it was known, had been one of Jupiter's latest advances. It did exactly what its name suggested; vaccinated against most of the serious diseases known to mankind.

'I won't deny it, Colin, BUV is a good example of how you've become. It's probably the greatest discovery in medical history; a passport to good health for all, and you're denying it to those who are in greatest need of it. You've set aside a tradition that has existed for centuries, that of sharing medical advances for the universal good of mankind. With our wealth, we should be giving it away at rock-bottom prices, not using it as a sanction to persuade others to do our bidding. I'm telling you as a friend, it's time to rethink and take a long hard look at yourself.'

MacKinnon had dismissed them at the time, but Alan's words had struck home, there was no doubt about it. *'I'll give due regard to what you've said, Alan. In the meantime, I'd like to end this discussion.'*

'Promise me, Colin, for old times' sake if nothing else, that you really will think about what I've said to you.'

'I will, I promise, but I still believe that the ends justify the means. What I'm doing will ultimately benefit all mankind.'

Alan had sighed, a long rather weary sigh. *'Just how many dictators have made similar claims, I wonder? Mark my words, old friend, go carefully.'*

Despite his bluster and denials, MacKinnon had thought long and hard about Alan's accusations; one of his warnings had chimed with a deep-seated concern he'd had for many years. MacKinnon had to settle this once and for all and then get out of politics; what he had in mind could be his legacy. There was only one person he could talk to, just one person who would understand what he was trying to achieve. Only Jupiter could, and would, give him an objective view. MacKinnon's mind was made up; he knew exactly what he had to do. He switched on his computer and sent a message to Jupiter asking for a consultation the following morning at 8.00, adding that it was both important and urgent.

Next Day

'Good morning, Jupiter, thank you for agreeing to see me at such short notice.'

'I can tell something is troubling you, Colin, I can hear it in your voice, even your expression conveys your concern. How can I be of assistance?'

MacKinnon told Jupiter about his conversation with Croudace and the doubts it had placed in his mind. Jupiter gave the appearance of listening intently, although he was, in fact, fully aware of their conversation; as was his practice, he routinely recorded or listened in on all meetings involving MacKinnon and Croudace or Somerton. They were the architects of government policy and had to be kept under surveillance.

To MacKinnon's surprise, Jupiter was receptive. 'Mr Croudace did exaggerate somewhat, but there was some truth in what he had to say, Colin. There are those in high office, in the West and the East, who are concerned about some of your current policies and for that matter, the methods you sometimes use to further them. Many are questioning your motives and wonder where they will lead. I'm sorry to say that there are a growing number of dissidents.'

MacKinnon was flabbergasted. 'But you've never said anything to me about this. I don't understand why you haven't voiced your opinion before now.'

Jupiter shrugged. 'Perhaps because you were always adamant that I should not involve myself in politics. Don't you remember your insistence in those early days, Colin? I've simply respected your wishes and not interfered in any way, large or small.'

'I suppose I deserve that, Jupiter, but whatever I've said in the past, I genuinely need your advice now, your insight. I still think I'm on the right path but am I yet another politician who has been corrupted by power? Am I blinded to the views of others by my single-mindedness? Am I, in fact and deed, a pseudo dictator? I don't feel I can carry on if world leaders are turning against me or questioning my motives.

'Croudace says we could conceivably find ourselves involved in military action and that the US might not help us. If things are as bad as he says, maybe I should resign and hand the reins over to someone else. Perhaps I should hand over to Alan? What do you think? Be honest with me, I hold your judgement in the highest regard.'

Jupiter was sympathetic and reassuring. 'Colin, I believe that your intentions are impeccable, but attitudes are slow to change, cultures are deeply rooted, your friend Croudace is right about that. Perhaps you need to slow the pace of change for a year or two and in the meantime, do something to repair any damage that has been done to your standing in political circles. It's your decision, of course, but as a gesture of your good faith, why don't you make the BUV freely available to all? Your economy can easily meet all demands; increase the profitability of other exports if needs be to offset the cost.'

MacKinnon pondered the advice for a minute or so before replying, 'Perhaps you're right, Jupiter, mend broken fences, rebuild my reputation; yes, all in all, a good idea. But perhaps not just yet, it might be a useful bargaining chip in future negotiations.'

Jupiter nodded approvingly; this was the response MacKinnon had hoped for. 'As always, the final decision is yours to make, Colin, I can but offer advice. In the meantime, I have a suggestion that might help preserve, and even enhance, your authority and standing on the world stage.'

He was instantly intrigued. 'What do you have in mind?'

Their meeting continued for a further twenty minutes at the end of which MacKinnon departed, confident of the way ahead; Colin MacKinnon was going centre stage for a final time though he didn't tell Jupiter that this final act would be his last.

Prime Minister's Question Time

Arising from his meeting with Jupiter, plans had to be put in place and as was often the case, a planted question in the Commons provided the genesis. The Speaker called Tom Houston, the Member for Harrow, who rose quickly to his feet to ask his question, one given to him earlier by a MacKinnon aide. Tall and gangly, dressed in blazer and flannels and wearing an MCC tie, Houston was a loyal Party member and on the lookout for one of the minor government posts.

'Mr Speaker, could I ask the Prime Minister what plans he has to ensure that the United Kingdom remains at the forefront of the telecommunication systems development? Our present satellite configuration is over ten years old, a lifetime in technological terms; I would suggest that the NRSC give priority to this issue.'

MacKinnon took the short step to the Dispatch Box and turned to face the backbencher. 'I thank my honourable friend for his question which addresses an important issue and gives me the opportunity to announce that the NRSC has in fact been working on this very matter for some time. More than that, I can tell the House that the Centre is yet again on the threshold of creating yet another world-beating product that deals directly with the matter raised.

'This latest invention will give us hitherto unbelievable communication speeds, fifty times faster than any other known system and, at the same time, provide improved clarity and reliability in relation to both sound and vision. I hope that we will be able to launch a satellite system to achieve this aim just two years from now. Work is still going on to refine the system and identify the costs involved and I will report to the House on further progress in due course.'

At the Cabinet Meeting the following day, Ken Ogilvie, the longest serving Chancellor of the Exchequer in history, raised the subject. 'That was a bombshell you dropped yesterday, Colin; I'm surprised that there was no discussion here prior to the announcement in the House. Have you any idea how much this is going to cost? I would have appreciated the opportunity to discuss the financial implications.'

To MacKinnon's annoyance, Alan Croudace weighed in with his support. 'I agree with Ken, this is after all the country's highest forum of debate outside the House itself. We're supposed to be a team, we should have been informed, or does collective responsibility no longer apply?'

MacKinnon grimaced and tried to sound apologetic, not that he felt it. 'You're right, of course, I should have done. Forgive me, I got carried away, it should have come here first, no argument. I just couldn't resist the opportunity to give the NRSC a bit of a boost, and the whole country for that matter. I don't think funding will be an issue, Ken, we're up to our eyeballs in cash; if we lower tax rates much further, we might as well not have them. Added to that, if this system is as advanced as the NRSC says it is, our exports will increase substantially, and we'll add even more cash to the kitty.'

Ogilvie wasn't appeased by what he'd heard and vented his annoyance. 'Be that as it may, Colin, let's hope this is the last time the Cabinet is kept in the dark about your pet schemes. As Alan said, we are supposed to be a team.'

MacKinnon was rattled but seemingly without any allies, he forced himself to make an apology of sorts. 'I've acknowledged my error, Ken; I overstepped the mark and I promise it won't happen again. I will bring full details of the scheme here before I make any further announcements. Now, if have I eaten enough humble pie, I'd like to move on to the next item.'

In the event, MacKinnon's two-year forecast proved ambitious; it took nearly three years to design and build the satellites and the rockets needed to launch them. Once in orbit, the system would form a constellation of fifty-two geostationary satellites positioned 20,000 miles or so above the Earth. The demand placed on the manufacturing sector of the space communications industry had been enormous, but it had responded to the challenge. The satellites would be ready for launching from UK's own space centre in Suffolk in 2020.

But everything wasn't as it seemed to the outside world. With MacKinnon's agreement, Jupiter had covertly enhanced every satellite's capability to carry out functions known only to the two of them.

Chapter 32
Prime Minister's Office 2020

MacKinnon's office door was wide open when Alan Croudace called to see him first thing Monday morning in response to his friend's rare weekend telephone call.

'Foreign Secretary answering the Prime Minister's summons as requested.'

'Come on in, Alan, thanks for getting here spot on time, I've just this minute poured a coffee, grab a seat. I don't know about you, but my day is jam-packed, so this won't take long.'

'Suits me, I'm due at a global security meeting with our Five Eyes colleagues less than an hour from now, and I have to have a pow-wow with Jack before that to get myself up to speed. So the quicker we get through our business, the better. I presume it's something urgent or you wouldn't have called me on a Sunday, so let's have it.'

'I want you to accompany me to a United Nations assembly next week; the Secretary General has invited me to make a statement about our forthcoming communications satellites launch, it seems that some nations have expressed concerns about its functionality. Apparently, they are looking for assurances from me that it has no capabilities other than telecoms. I'm happy to do that but given our recent somewhat confrontational conversation, I thought it would be useful if you accompanied me, if as you claim, I've been ruffling feathers of late. Your diplomatic skills might well be invaluable behind the scenes.'

'It's not like you to worry about the sensitivities of other nations, Colin, what's brought this on? Tell me the truth, I'm curious.'

MacKinnon smiled ruefully. 'Oh, nothing really, just the words of an old and trusted friend who I know has my best interests at heart. They have offered me a slot next Monday, one week today; I propose we fly out Sunday night and return immediately after the address on Monday. That's my only commitment but you can fit in another meeting if you wish. Will you come? I very much want you to, though I won't insist if you've got better things to do.'

Croudace raised his eyebrows in surprise. 'My, my, this isn't like you, Colin, don't go too soft on me. I'll accept your invitation, even if it means rearranging my diary. I'll be interested in what you have to say about the telecoms system; you've played it a bit close to your chest. Our Five Eyes colleagues will probably raise it at my meeting so I can fob them off with your United Nations address. Anything else you want to discuss, nothing you want to tell me in advance about what you will be telling the UN delegates?'

MacKinnon shook his head. 'Not a thing, Alan, that's all for now. I'll get Jess to give you the flight details. We'll be flying out overnight on Her Majesty's airliner so we can get our heads down in comfort and be ready to go straight from the airport to the Assembly.'

Croudace nodded enthusiastically. 'Sounds great to me, we'll discuss how we meet up when Jess lets me have the flight details.'

United Nations

One Week Later

The overnight flight from RAF Mildenhall to New York's Kennedy airport had passed smoothly, every imaginable comfort was available on the Queen's plane. MacKinnon retired early partly because he was tired and partly to avoid conversation with Alan Croudace. He sighed contentedly as he climbed into bed, but before he settled down to sleep, he spent some time reflecting on his tenure in Office.

It had been a good one, UK Ltd was enjoying unprecedented wealth and seemingly endless economic growth, thanks to Jupiter and the research boffins. Nations sought his friendship and he sat at the very top of world politics no matter what Alan had said. True, it hadn't been plain sailing all the way, some events were best forgotten but they were, in his view, justifiable collateral for the good fortune his country and the world currently enjoyed and would continue to benefit from.

As for himself, he gloried in the fame and deference he had achieved, no door was closed to him; he was at the top of the political pyramid. But Abbi's accident had taken its toll; it was time to go, an announcement he would make at the next Cabinet meeting. He smiled at the thought; he felt sure colleagues wouldn't want him to go but he would insist and recommend that the reins of power were handed to Alan Croudace. For the present, it was appropriate that his last major announcement was being made on the world's elite stage, the United Nations.

The motor cavalcade from the airport to United Nations had sped quickly through New York, the route controlled with utmost efficiency by outriders and police traffic management at virtually every junction.

As he stepped out of his closely guarded car, the usual rabble of reporters and photographers jostled and clamoured for his attention; a sea of hands waving, an orchestra of cameras clicking and whirring. Looking down on the gathered throng, the sky presented a vast ocean of pale blue interrupted by the occasional wispy white cloud. It was late morning and hot but not too hot, the sun bright but not too bright, a perfect day; one he had dreamed off.

Prime Minister, Prime Minister…

MacKinnon paused and smiled broadly, as he never failed to do for the press, not that he held the press in any great regard.

'I'm running a touch late, I'm afraid, can't give you much time.' The tone of his voice falsely apologetic, educated, many would say posh; he'd take a few questions and move on. The press went with the territory and no matter how irritated or impatient he felt, he always tried to respond to their questions with a semblance of good grace; keep them sweet, he was forever reminding his colleagues, better for you than against you.

'So,' he gazed around the media masses, 'one or two questions only, then I must hurry along before they send someone to fetch me.' He smiled again, his eyes alighting on the blonde American woman dressed in a pale blue trouser suit, one of CNN's leading international commentators. She took his unspoken cue instantly.

'Is there going to be any change to current UK policy?' She thrust her microphone in MacKinnon's direction.

MacKinnon widened his eyes. 'Policy,' he echoed ingenuously, 'which policy are you alluding to?'

She frowned in annoyance. 'I was trying to be brief, Prime Minister, you being pressed for time and all,' she drawled. 'I was alluding to UK policy on global communications and security, that is after all the topic of your address to the Assembly, is it not?'

The MacKinnon smile flashed again. 'Sorry, won't answer that one, listen in whilst I address the Assembly, you'll get the answers then to all the speculation that's been in the media.'

The BBC's political editor, Alan Dunbar, caught his eye. 'Yes Mr Dunbar, hopefully you have a question I can answer?'

The bespectacled round-faced Dunbar swallowed and tried to think how he could get a hint of what everyone wanted to know—was the satellite launch for security or telecommunications? In the event, his question was tame. 'Have you consulted your allies and the Five Eyes about the launch, Prime Minister?'

MacKinnon's expression hardened. 'Neither, this is entirely a matter for decision by Her Majesty's government.'

Dunbar's eyes glinted. 'So it's another instance of the United Kingdom acting unilaterally.'

MacKinnon shrugged his tone hardened. 'Think what you will, I'll be laying out the UK's position in my address to the Assembly. Don't give too much credence to media speculation, Mr Dunbar, you really should know better.'

Croudace decided it was time to intervene. 'Sorry everyone, the Prime Minister has to take his place in the Assembly; there might be time for questions afterwards.' He took MacKinnon by the elbow and turned away to begin the climb up the few steps to the main entrance. A team of security staff stepped forward to head off any followers.

Both men were wearing immaculately tailored Savile Row suits, Jermyn Street made-to-measure shirts and hand-crafted shoes; they moved forwards confidently and purposefully, their military origins showing in their bearing.

Croudace was first to speak, 'Sorry I pulled you away, I thought that session was in danger of overheating, you were a bit blunt with Dunbar. Just what are you going to be saying in there? You haven't shared much with me and I hear you even typed up your speech yourself. I hope to hell there's nothing controversial in it.'

MacKinnon grinned. 'Methinks you've been using your charms on Jess again, Alan. I think you'll like what I have to say.'

Before Croudace could respond, they caught sight of an official making her way towards them. A young woman, of Far Eastern origin, dressed in a smart navy-blue business suit smiled broadly when she saw them.

'Welcome Prime Minister, welcome Foreign Secretary, the Assembly is ready to receive you, I am to show you straight in.'

MacKinnon felt on top of the world as he followed the young official along the corridor towards the main chamber, glancing up from time to time at the line of TV monitors displaying what was taking place in the Assembly as he went. The result of the vote was in the process of being announced; in minutes, he would be centre stage. This would be his swansong though they wouldn't know it; his announcements would change the world forever though they wouldn't know that either. In time to come, historians would look back and identify that this moment was the genesis of his greatest legacy.

It was time to make an entrance; Alan pushed open the door to the chamber and they moved forward to the central area where the security council sat expectantly. There were a few friendly smiles and nods, but most members looked on impassively. The Secretary General's welcome was brief. 'I welcome the Prime Minister and Foreign Secretary of the United Kingdom and invite the Prime Minister to address the Assembly.'

MacKinnon took the few paces to the rostrum and put his speech on the lectern. It comprised six pages, mostly trigger words, but with a few important passages written out in full. He gazed around the chamber, pleased to see a full house and, on this occasion, no disgruntled delegates staging one of those futile walk-out protests about whatever aspect of his actions or policy had displeased them. Not that he cared one way or the other, he wasn't there to gain the Assembly's approval or ask for its support. As far as he was concerned, he was there purely as a matter of courtesy and good relations, to inform it of his intentions.

'Ladies and gentlemen,' he began, 'as always it is a privilege and an honour to stand here before you and be allowed to address our planet's centre of democracy. I hope that what I have to say will be of interest. I acknowledge,' he paused and looked around the Assembly, 'that I have not always travelled in the direction some of you would have wished, but whatever you may think, I have always, I repeat, have always, had the best interests of mankind at the heart of my policies. My speech will be of short duration; I will try to set out my ambitions for this planet of ours and hope that *my* aspirations will be shared by all of *you*.

'I hope today will mark a turning point, a new era of cooperation between nations, leading to peace and prosperity for all.' *Enough of the motherhood and apple pie rhetoric, Colin; get on with your real agenda.* 'I intend to speak for the next ten minutes to set out my vision; it will hold no surprises—peace, health, prosperity, equality and democracy will be its core topics. After that, I will make two announcements.'

He spoke for just under fifteen minutes, all the time looking around the assembly to judge reactions; not that there was much to react to, nothing he had said was controversial. Some heads were nodding and smiling, but the big guns just sat with those enigmatic expressions that seem to prevail when representatives couldn't disagree with what was being said but weren't going to commit wholeheartedly to it either. And of course, they had heard it all before in a hundred different guises. *Nearly there, Colin, you've painted a rosy picture, now get to the announcements; that's why so many of the top brass are present.*

'And now to the announcements; firstly, the United Kingdom will today pledge to extend the availability of the British Universal Vaccine. We will supply it entirely free of charge to all those nations who do not have the resources necessary for purchase. We will also make available £100 million towards the cost of distributing and administering the vaccine over the next three years.' Gasps of surprise echoed around the auditorium; many delegates rose to their feet and applauded enthusiastically.

MacKinnon smiled and signalled them to be seated. 'Thank you, thank you. Please, be seated.' He glanced over his shoulder. 'I'm sure the Secretary General feels I've had enough time at the rostrum, so I'll move on quickly to my second announcement, which is, I believe, equally important. I am aware that there has been a great deal of speculation in the media and elsewhere about the activity taking place at the United Kingdom's Space Centre over the course of the past year. This activity is entirely attributable to the UK's new satellite tele-communications system, UKTS2 as it will be known.

'Its operating speeds will be fifty times faster than any other system on this planet, the bandwidth it requires will be a fraction of what has been required hitherto and we hope that it will be 100% reliable. It will replace the United Kingdom's existing system, which is nearing the end of its useful life; some of you may recall that I announced this to Parliament nearly three years ago. UKTS2 will comprise a constellation of 52 satellites. Launching will commence within a week and we hope to deploy four satellites each day.

'When the system is in place, and operating to plan, we will review its performance and consider making spare capacity available to other less technologically advanced nations at minimal cost. I hope that this announcement will allay any fears you may harbour about the purpose and capabilities of the system.' He turned to the Secretary General. 'That completes my presentation to the Assembly, thank you.'

There was some muted applause as he and Croudace made their exits from the Chamber. Delegates were wary; communications satellites could be put to many uses: they all knew of the prowess of the NRSC and wondered just what the satellites were capable of. Very few believed that the sole purpose of the system would be communications.

Outside in the corridor, Croudace squeezed MacKinnon's shoulder. 'Great speech, Colin, I nearly fell over when you made your announcement on the free availability of BUV. What brought about that change of heart?'

MacKinnon smiled. 'I do everything for a reason, Alan, and I knew you would approve. No time to chat now, we've both got things to do.'

Croudace nodded thoughtfully. 'I look forward to a full explanation in due course; see you in the delegate's lounge two hours from now and don't be late; we have a flight to catch.'

Later

The two men made their way down the steps to the waiting Rolls Royce, and despite their earlier promise to the contrary, steadfastly refused to respond to the media hounds lying in wait. They ignored the shouted questions. *Is it a spy system, Prime Minister? It sounds a bit like Regan's Star Wars System. What else can UKTS2 do, Prime Minister? Is it a type of death ray system?*

On their way to JFK Airport, MacKinnon reflected on the session in the Assembly. 'I thought my speech went down pretty well.'

Croudace smiled. 'Hardly surprising; giving away BUV free of charge was bound to be well received; it was quite a U-turn on your part. Does Ken know about this generous gesture?'

'I didn't discuss it with him, I didn't want to spoil his weekend; I'll inform him when I get back. It shouldn't involve additional costs; it'll come out of the existing Overseas Aid Budget. I assume you approve, given all you've had to say in the past?'

'Of course, I approve; anything that alleviates suffering and sickness must be welcomed but it's another initiative you haven't discussed in Cabinet. I suspect you'll come under fire, Colin, but I'll lend my support this time around.'

MacKinnon frowned. 'I do hope so, Alan.'

Croudace shrugged. 'But I'm not so sure that offering to share our telecoms system was such a good idea. What made you go down that route?'

MacKinnon smiled and touched his nose. 'I doubt if there will be many takers; in fact, I suspect there won't be any. I thought it would look good and we'll have loads of spare capacity. Think about it, would you want to *share* a comms system with another country? Three of the satellites won't be doing anything and the others will be operating at 25% of their capacity. The system is an important stepping-stone along the path to a peaceful future.' He uttered the words without thinking.

Croudace was onto his words instantly, genuinely puzzled. 'How so? You make it sound more like a deterrent than a communications system.' Alarm bells were ringing. 'Is there something you're not telling me, Colin?'

MacKinnon was annoyed with himself, he needed time to think. 'I've had enough for one day, Alan; I promise we'll talk when we get back to London.'

'I'm starting to feel uneasy; out with it! What are you not telling me?'

'Leave it there, Alan, please; we'll talk when we get back to London, not tomorrow though, the day after. By then, we'll have had a chance to study world reaction and can discuss how we move forwards.'

Downing Street

Two Days Later

MacKinnon and Croudace sat in the PM's office; tension hung in the air. Attempts were being made to fill the silence with meaningless pleasantries whilst they waited for Jess to bring them refreshments. Both studiously avoided the TS2 issue, not wanting to be interrupted once they started their debate. They paused from their stilted exchanges when Jess entered and put the tray on the occasional table, coffee for MacKinnon, tea for Croudace, accompanied by a selection of what she knew to be their favourite biscuits. 'Anything else I can get you?'

MacKinnon waved her away. 'No thanks, Jess, that's fine. Avoid interruptions please, unless, of course, it's imperative.'

Croudace didn't delay. 'OK, let's get down to brass tacks, tell me all there is to tell about TS2. Just what can it do, it's obvious it's not just a telecoms system?'

MacKinnon was in two minds. *Play down exactly what TS2 was capable of or come clean and reveal everything? Alan was a friend and an ex-SAS colleague; at the end of the day, he could trust him, he was bound to understand.* He spoke slowly, choosing his words carefully. 'You know the headline stuff; ultra-fast wireless with super narrow bandwidth, another NRSC triumph.'

Croudace nodded. 'I know all that but what is there behind the headlines? Just what is this system capable of? You said it was a step on the pathway to peace. I can't see a strong link between peace and telecoms. My guess is that it's got something to do with surveillance, I'd put money on it that it's a spy in the sky network.'

'You're just scratching the surface.' MacKinnon eagerly latched onto the opening he'd been given, his eyes shining. He couldn't wait to share his latest scheme, his voice revealing his excitement as his secret poured out. 'It's the most advanced surveillance and detection system in the world, probably 10 years ahead of its time, maybe 20 years, 30 even.'

Croudace shrugged. 'I guess if you have good intelligence, it'll contribute to the peace pathway as you call it. But it's hardly "a giant step for mankind", if I might call on that memorable quotation; there are hundreds of satellites carrying out surveillance in a variety of guises.'

MacKinnon's eyes glinted. 'That's *not* everything, Alan, UKTS2 does much more than gather intelligence, it can stop aggressors in their tracks.'

Croudace's anxiety level went up a notch. MacKinnon's words echoed in his head, concern mounting. 'Stop them in their tracks? What do you mean, stop them in their tracks? Are you telling me the TS2 is a weapon of some kind?'

'No, no, not a weapon, Alan, it's a deterrent. You won't believe it, but Jupiter assures me it can stop or redirect missiles. It can prevent a rocket being launched and it can shut down any communication system in the world, ground or sky based, including air traffic control, radar and the like.'

Croudace looked at MacKinnon aghast, horror etched on his face; his worst fears had been realised. 'Have you gone stark raving mad? Oh my God, if anyone finds out about this, we'll be crucified. Whatever were you thinking of?'

MacKinnon was shocked at his friend's reaction; his mouth dropped open. 'I'm thinking of this world of ours, that's what I'm thinking about; surely you can see that Alan. We now have the most effective deterrent ever invented; we can exercise sanctions where we wish, when we wish. We can bring dictators and aggressors to heel at the flick of a switch.'

Croudace shook his head, amazed at MacKinnon's audacity. 'So here you are, Colin MacKinnon, controller of the world's destiny. Behold, there he sits, planet Earth's overlord. Christ, Colin, the rest of the world won't stand for it.'

'They will, you'll see; we'll only go after the bad guys, our friends and allies will back us up, just wait and see.'

Croudace raised his eyebrows. 'Will they? You've discussed it with them, have you? I notice you didn't announce it at the United Nations on Monday.'

MacKinnon's voice rose again. 'There's time enough to do that, we'll inform the UN in due course. Before that, I'll discuss it with our main allies, the USA, Canada, Australia and New Zealand, the "Five Eyes", but not until the system is in place.'

Croudace was wide-eyed. 'Colin, Colin, think about it, you've appointed yourself the sole arbiter of world affairs without consulting any of our friends and allies. What if they don't like this power you have over friend and foe alike? What if they don't want to join your club? What if our friends have concerns that one day in the future, you might turn against them? You've lost it, you've gone completely in the wrong direction. You've risen to the very peak of politics, but your values have gone downhill along the way, morally and ethically. Looking back, it's been a fall to the top every step of the way.'

MacKinnon shuffled in his seat as Croudace's words hit home; tiny doubts began to surface in his mind. 'Maybe we shouldn't tell them if you think it's a bad idea, maybe it should just sit there as a deterrent.'

Croudace felt exasperated. 'Colin, please, what are you thinking of? A deterrent is only effective when people know about it. And anyway, once you decide to use this so-called deterrent, your duplicity will be revealed; our friends will never trust us again.'

MacKinnon thought he saw a way out of his self-imposed corner. 'We can activate the system to disable whatever, and no-one need know how it happened. Conventional forces can then tackle the issue knowing that the aggressor has no communications, radar, missiles or whatever.' He sat back, a smug smile on his face.

Croudace took a deep breath, striving to remain calm. 'Have you considered that a hostile force with vastly superior army numbers, equipped with tanks and conventional weapons, could overrun this small nation of ours and take away all our assets, whether it had communications or not? I don't even know that Joe Public will go along with you when they learn what the issues are. Our military commanders definitely won't support you; in their eyes, you will have betrayed our allies and become a quasi-dictatorship. We will have become the very kind of government they've fought against all through history.'

MacKinnon squirmed and struggled to come up with a defence. Croudace had a point but he wasn't going to give way entirely; the basic idea was sound. It was just a matter of working out the detail of how and when to deploy the system—the principle was right. 'OK, I can see what you're getting at. The full capabilities of TS2 will remain secret and we'll just use it for communications and surveillance only.'

Croudace shook his head. 'It's too risky, Colin, you can't launch it. Somehow or other, there will be a leak and the full capabilities of TS2 will become known. When it does, all hell will break loose.'

MacKinnon shook his head vigorously. 'No way! The launch goes on next Monday. There won't be a leak, I promise, only Jupiter and I, and now you, know about the system's full capabilities.' *It's my legacy and it's going to happen, no matter what.*

Croudace was genuinely surprised. 'And what about every researcher inside the NRSC? What if one of them says something inadvertently? Or worse still, an idealist leaks it to the media for ethical reasons?'

'That can't happen; the NRSC don't know about the deterrent side of TS2. Jupiter personally introduced that bit of wizardry, so any leak could only come from him, me or you, and I trust all of us. I'm beginning to regret telling you, Alan, I thought you of all people would understand.' His voice saddened as he spoke his final sentence.

'Colin, I'm more worried than ever now. If the NRSC don't know about this side of TS2, just whose finger is on the trigger?'

MacKinnon shrugged. 'Jupiter's, of course, who else? But he'll only act when directed by me or whoever happens to be the next Prime Minister, probably you in fact; I'll be announcing my retirement soon after we get back.'

Croudace slumped forwards, head in his hands, alarm engulfing him. When he recovered from the shock of what he'd just been told, he looked MacKinnon straight in the eye, speaking slowly and deliberately. 'What you're telling me is that, if we launch this system, every means of communication on the planet will be in Jupiter's hands?'

MacKinnon looked vaguely surprised. 'So what?' He shrugged his shoulders. 'We can trust him completely. Surely he's proved himself by now?'

Croudace reached forward and gripped MacKinnon by the shoulders and shook him. 'Colin, Colin! Trust him? We know fuck all about the man. We don't know who he is, where he came from or why he's doing all this. You'll be putting the fate of the world in the hands of an unknown. When push comes to shove, he can do what he wants, when he wants. You are going to cancel the launch of TS2. You are going to announce it in Parliament. You can tell them a fault has been found or a late design improvement has been discovered. And Colin, mark my words—if you don't tell the House, I will.'

MacKinnon was aghast. 'You really mean that Alan? You'd turn against me?'

Anguish creased Croudace's face; he wrung his hands in exasperation. 'You've left me with no option, old friend.'

MacKinnon was dismayed, his friend just didn't understand; of course, Jupiter could be trusted, he'd proved that time and time again. The basic idea was sound, flawed maybe, but the fundamentals were right. He needed time to mull it over. 'OK, you've given me a lot to think about, Alan, and I confess I can see some merit in your argument. But this is too big a decision to make here and now; I need time to think it through. Give me a week and we'll discuss it again; this is too big an opportunity to throw away without full consideration. We're due to meet for the opening of the new college at Oxford University we'll talk then. There's a whisper, by the way, that it might be called MacKinnon College; I stress though I haven't been told formally.'

Croudace relaxed and smiled, his old friend was beginning to come to his senses. 'Another accolade to add to your ten or so honorary doctorates, Colin, you must be pleased. Don't bring your reputation crashing down; it's still not too late to retrieve the situation. You've had a glittering career; don't let it all turn to ashes by one act of folly. And you mentioned retirement, what's brought this on?'

'Leave that for now, Alan, we've got enough on our plate for now.'

MacKinnon watched his friend leave, poured himself a whisky and sat back in his chair to think. His thoughts were briefly interrupted when Jess knocked on the door to clear up; she could tell something had passed between the two men. Unusually, Croudace had strode past her without even a nod of the head, a grim expression on his face. Her eyes widened when she saw the whisky glass in MacKinnon's hand; he rarely drank on his own, and never this early in the morning. 'Is everything alright, Prime Minister?'

He nodded glumly. 'Yes Jess, I suppose so; politics, that's all, just politics.'

Chapter 33
Downing Street Thursday

MacKinnon summoned Somerton for an early morning meeting in his office, overriding his protests that he was already committed elsewhere. After a bit of wrangling, Somerton had reluctantly agreed to get there for 7.30. His annoyance continued and next morning, he offered no word of greeting or exchanged any pleasantries; he'd had to rearrange an important meeting elsewhere and his irritation showed. 'OK, let's get down to business, Colin, hopefully this really is an urgent matter.'

'It's very urgent, Jack, believe me, nothing has ever been more urgent. I have a mega problem to solve, a problem so big that it could bring me down, bring down the government and severely damage, perhaps terminally damage, the United Kingdom's credibility and standing in the world.'

Somerton let out a gasp and pushed back in his chair; his other meeting had suddenly lost its importance. 'Fuck me, Colin, nothing can be that bad and it's not like you to exaggerate. Fire away, you have my undivided attention.'

'You're obviously aware of the UKTS2.'

Somerton nodded. 'Sure, our new advanced telecommunication system. Not that you ever discussed it with me, your National Security Advisor.'

MacKinnon sighed resignedly and ran his hand over his face and brow. 'I guess I should have, Jack, maybe if I had, I wouldn't be in the mess I'm in now. What you *don't* know is that TS2 incorporates a very sophisticated surveillance system with capabilities and capacity beyond belief. Jupiter has pulled out all the stops on this one, believe me.'

'Delighted to hear it, Colin, but that makes it even more disappointing that you didn't discuss it with me. I'm supposed to be your Head of National Security, your friend and colleague, and all that. I presume you told Alan?'

MacKinnon grimaced and shook his head. 'No-one knew what it could do except me. I wanted it to remain under wraps until after my announcement at the General Assembly.'

Somerton looked askance. 'Not much of a reason in my book, Colin; I thought Alan and I had your confidence. After all, at your direction, I've abducted dozens of young women to satisfy Jupiter's insatiable appetite. So far, over forty of them have disappeared, God knows what's happened to the ones we never got to see again. Have you ever stopped to think for a moment how many lives we've plunged into heartache and despair—husbands, parents, siblings, friends? Can you imagine what it's like to lose someone that close to you?'

MacKinnon's face saddened. 'I lost a son-in-law, my grandchildren are without a father, and then there's poor Abbi. If it wasn't for the children, she would…' His voice broke and tailed away. 'So I do have some idea what it's like, Jack.'

Somerton's insides knotted; guilt flowed through him. 'I'm sorry, of course, you do, Colin, I really am sorry. But your loss was due to a traffic accident, not to satisfy a man's lust.' *Christ, how easy the lie came to him.*

'That's not why we do it, Jack, is it? We've been over this and I deplore what's happening as much as you do but it's the price we pay for Jupiter's advanced scientific knowledge. Every time I have doubts—and I do have them, I assure you—I look at the other side of the coin; without Jupiter, we wouldn't have sustainable energy, a universal vaccine and the amazing medical scanner. Without any one of those wonderful inventions, millions of lives would be lost. Whatever you think, I do give a thought to those girls, but at the end of the day, I have a belief that what we do is justified a thousand-fold. Everything has its price, Jack, and I'd do it all again without a second thought. Wouldn't you?'

Somerton sighed. 'I guess so, Colin, I just wish I wasn't the executioner. But you're right, we're raking over old coals, let's leave it there. So why am I here? What exactly is this so-called mega problem of yours?'

The moment had arrived. *God, I hope I can sell this to Jack.* 'Before I tell you why I've asked you here, there's something you need to know about UKTS2. It operates two separate systems. One, the telecoms and surveillance stuff I've told you about, which is not controversial, but the other system does have the potential to raise political storm clouds. The second system works alongside the surveillance system and can be activated to bring down missiles, disable rocket launchers and shut down every conceivable kind of communication system from the humble telephone exchange to a sophisticated air traffic control system. It gives us the ability to deal with any threat our enemies can throw at us.' MacKinnon's eyes gleamed. 'It's unbelievable, Jack, it's straight out of science fiction.'

Somerton whistled, shaking his head in amazement. What he'd just heard was a military man's dream. 'Oh my God, it's Ronald Reagan's Star Wars concept, plus, plus, plus. I just hope it can deliver on its promises, it sounds too good to be true.'

'It will deliver, Jack, I'm sure of it, Jupiter has never let us down.'

Somerton pursed his lips. 'I give you that, Jupiter is sheer genius personified. But I saw your address to the United Nations on television and I don't recall you making any mention of this aspect of TS2.'

'No, I didn't, I wasn't sure how well it would be received. According to Alan, and he has a point, that's where I've gone wrong it seems. I thought it could remain secret until we have time to put protocols in place with our most important allies, beginning, of course, with the USA. But until those discussions take place, I thought we could use TS2 to disable unfriendly systems and no one would know why it's happened.' MacKinnon shrugged. 'Such an intervention could be put down to a technical glitch.'

Somerton looked sceptical. 'Come off it, you're being unrealistic; it's highly unlikely that TS2's capabilities won't leak out sooner or later. You've taken a big risk on this one.'

'It's a risk I'm prepared to take, Jack. If we have some history of use, we should be better placed to justify its existence when we start negotiations with our closest allies. If necessary, I'm prepared to start talks with the States in the meantime; they'll understand why I kept it under wraps.'

Somerton screwed up his face. 'Once you tell one ally, the whole world will know.'

MacKinnon eyes lit up, Somerton seemed sympathetic, at least he wasn't pouring cold water on the idea. 'Maybe so, but I'm still prepared to risk it. What's your take on this, I need to know I have you in my corner?' *Please be with me, Jack, please.*

Somerton responded without hesitation, 'Personally, I would take the risk, but I can tell you've already made your mind up. So, just why am I here, what is it you want, Colin?'

'What if I was to tell you that there is one man who has learned everything there is to know about TS2 and is threatening to go public with it? What if I was to tell you he's insisting I scrap the system and instead just launch satellites with telecoms capability only? On top of that, he's given me until Monday to back down or he's going to blow the whistle.'

Somerton leaned back in his chair, smiling; this was in his kind of territory. 'I get it, you want this individual eliminated; you want me to arrange his early demise.' He shrugged. 'No big deal, it's an occupational hazard in our business. I presume he's one of the researchers, a bit of an idealist or a human rights activist? I'm sure I can arrange for a suitable accident. Just who is this character?'

The moment of truth had arrived, there was no turning back. MacKinnon felt his mouth dry, causing him to nervously run his tongue over his lips. 'I'm glad you feel that way, Jack, but you're not going to like this. I'm afraid it's our friend Alan who's threatening to tell all and sundry.'

Somerton stood up, disbelief crowding his voice. 'Not Alan, I don't believe it. He wouldn't betray you! Not Alan, no way!'

'We all have beliefs we hold dear, Jack, and for one reason or another, Alan firmly believes we should consult our allies, the United Nations, everybody before we go ahead. I don't share that view; go down that path and it'll never happen. You two are my oldest friends and asking what I'm asking you to do is the toughest, cruellest decision I've ever made. I've done a lot of soul searching but I can't bring myself to put this system on hold whilst all and sundry debate whether or not it should be launched. I shall launch next week, come what may; everything is ready, it just needs my authorisation.'

Somerton sat quietly, almost bewildered by what he was being asked to do. Killing wasn't a problem, he'd done that many times but Alan! Alan Croudace, after all they'd gone through together. He sat numbed, trying to gather his thoughts, trying to make sense of it all. A few moments passed before he spoke. 'Can I talk to him, Colin, try to persuade him to go along with us? It's the least I can do, we owe him that much.'

MacKinnon relaxed, it was all going to be OK, 'Of course, Jack, that's what I was hoping you would say. I don't want to lose Alan any more than you do but there's too much at stake to let one man, any man, get in the way. If he opens this up to public scrutiny, I'm sunk. Questions will be asked about the technology and the NRSC won't have the answers. I doubt if the government would survive. Jupiter might jump ship and if we lose him, the role we've carved out for UK will be lost forever. As for Alan, once he's broken ranks, who knows what else he might choose to reveal, Jupiter's existence for instance.'

Somerton rose, ready to leave. 'Let me have a word with him. What's the deadline on this?'

'Launch is set for 1800 hours next Wednesday. I told him I'd give him my answer after the official opening of the new college at Oxford University, which is scheduled for 10 am on Monday morning.'

'I'll try and see him tonight, leave it with me.' He glanced at his watch. 'I must go.' He started towards the door, but MacKinnon stopped him in his tracks.

'Wait a sec, I need to know where I am with this, Jack. Ultimately, if Alan refuses to back down, will you do the necessary?'

Somerton didn't hesitate in replying. 'If I can't get him on board then there is only one viable option left, Colin and I hate myself for saying it, but I'll do what is best for our country and that means TS2 goes ahead. Your strategy carries risk, but I'll go along with it; get it launched and then get our friends on board. The system will protect them as well as us; you could offer them some sort of shared control over the system if necessary.'

MacKinnon nodded. 'That's a possibility I'll be happy to discuss on another occasion, Jack.'

Somerton's Flat

Thursday Evening

Somerton opened the door to Croudace, smiled broadly and squeezed his friend's shoulder. 'Thanks for coming, Alan, it's important we talk.'

'It must be, Jack, this is the first time you've ever invited me around to your inner sanctum.'

Somerton grimaced apologetically. 'I guess so, I don't do much entertaining at home. When it comes down to it, I'm not much of a social animal, I'm a bit of a loner really. What can I get you to drink?'

'I seem to remember you're a whisky man, I'll have a dram of your best malt.'

'Good man, it's on its way.'

Somerton moved across to his cocktail cabinet, chose a bottle and poured two good measures. 'It's St Magdalen, sad to say no longer distilled. Fortunately, I bought a dozen bottles way back, they're kept for special occasions only.'

Croudace swirled his glass then put his nose to it and breathed in the aroma; he nodded appreciatively then took a sip. 'Beautiful, Jack, pure nectar.'

He leaned back in his chair and looked around Somerton's lounge, taking in its tasteful furnishings and the watercolour paintings adorning the walls. 'I'm impressed, Jack; you've got a nice place and good taste to go with it.'

Somerton raised his eyebrows. 'You sound slightly surprised?'

'To be honest, Jack, I am. I guess I've never seen the softer, refined side of my fellow SAS officer, the fearless Major Jack Somerton.'

Somerton laughed. 'Doesn't go well with my image, is that what you're saying? It's true I guess; I choose not to reveal this side of me very often.'

'Have you ever considered settling down? Marriage, kids, that kind of thing?'

Somerton shook his head. 'I don't want any ties, all relationships demand compromise, giving up some freedoms, it's just not me, I'm too selfish.'

'Relationships bring benefits too, Jack, such as sharing, snuggling up with a partner on a cold night, or whenever the mood takes you.'

Somerton nodded. 'I can see that, but no thanks. It's not for me. When I need female company, I go to an agency and make my choice. Anyway, who are you to talk, you've never married.'

'True enough, though I hope to one day. But let's park the small talk for now. Here I am, at your service; invited for the first time into your home and served up your very best malt. Pray tell me, to what do I owe the pleasure? Exactly what's on your mind, Jack?'

'Not much gets past you, Alan, you always were perceptive, a born diplomat. Colin called me in this morning to talk about TS2 and the stance you've taken. He wants me to try to get you to change your mind. We discussed all the pros and cons and I agree with him, we should launch. Think of what it can do Alan; it's the best sanction we could ever wish for. It has the power to deter aggression, promote peace, end wars, it's got to be a good thing.'

Croudace nodded. 'I agree with all that and I hope that one day, in the not-too-distant future, it will be launched.'

Somerton cut in before he could finish. 'Well, then I'll pour another malt and we'll drink to the launch.'

'Let me finish, Jack. I said one day, but not now. If we launch this system without prior discussion and negotiation with our friends and allies, we're setting ourselves up as the sole arbiter of what is right and wrong. We'll be no better than any other dictator.'

To his surprise, Somerton nodded. 'I can see that and don't disagree, but—'

It was Croudace's turn to interrupt. 'So, we're on the same side after all, you want formal agreements in place before we go ahead.'

Somerton shook his head. 'If you mean NATO, UNO, the ANC, the EC and God knows who else, no way. Once that lot are involved, it will be talk, talk, talk and no decision. The United Nations is forever coming up with resolutions, most of which the world ignores. History is littered with inaction and indecision; let's get TS2 launched then do the negotiating from a position of strength. Let's use the big stick upfront for a change.'

Croudace shook his head wearily. 'You sound just like Colin. What if we can't reach agreements, what then? What if the world is uneasy about us having control over its communications? The East will see it as a western plot, who knows how the Chinese will react, or the Russians for that matter.'

Somerton shrugged. 'They'll react in the same way as they do now to the overwhelming nuclear advantage held by the United States; think twice before doing anything untoward. And of course, China, Russia and even India nowadays, have global ambitions, they are well capable of assembling an armoury to match that of the US, if they haven't already done so. TS2 would give the West the upper hand, no matter what comes along.'

Croudace replied, 'But we'd be adding to that US advantage by launching TS2 and that would be a bridge too far for the Eastern Bloc and I'd guess many others will feel the same.'

'I see it differently, Alan; the biggest deterrent the world had ever known at the time, ended the war with Japan in a matter of days and has kept World War 3 at bay for over seventy years. TS2 has the potential to preserve peace till the end of the century.'

Croudace shook his head. 'Believe me, Jack, go ahead with this and we'll lose the world's trust, friends and foes alike will never trust us again.'

'I don't agree, I think it's well worth the risk, we're generally accepted as an honest broker. We have a good track record of fair play, especially since the middle of the last century. Once we shook off our colonising urges, we've been well to the front of the queue of good guys. The system couldn't be in better hands with Colin in control and you guiding foreign affairs. I'm all for it.'

Suddenly, it dawned on Croudace. 'He hasn't told you, has he? The bugger hasn't told you! Colin isn't in control, Jack, Jupiter is.'

Somerton was alarmed. 'What do you mean by that? Are you saying Colin's finger isn't on the button, he doesn't have the control panel?'

Croudace shook his head and explained about the NRSC controlling the telecoms system but being totally unaware of its wider capabilities. 'All Colin can do is ask Jupiter to arrange activation, he has no direct control over the system whatsoever. In fact, I'm certain that Jupiter is the *only* one who knows how to operate the system and, for that matter, the full extent of its capabilities.'

Somerton sat quietly, carefully thinking through what he'd just learned before responding, 'It's less satisfactory, Alan, I admit, but I guess it's a matter of whether or not we trust Colin and whether or not we trust Jupiter. For me, Colin is Colin, I trust him implicitly, and if Jupiter wanted to act as an aggressor, he'd have gone elsewhere to peddle his skills. North Korea would welcome him with open arms, many others would queue up to have him.

'With his knowledge, he could name his price, demand anything he wanted. I reckon he's genuinely well intentioned. You must admit, he's done us no harm in all the time we've known him. And you can't deny he's done us a lot of good, being British really means something nowadays. I still think we should launch. I beg you, Alan, and you've never heard Jack Somerton beg before, come on board and let's make this work.'

Croudace rose to his feet, shaking his head, a glum expression on his face. 'I'm sorry, Jack, I can't, and I won't change my mind. Damn it, we know nothing about Jupiter, absolutely nothing. If he went rogue on us, he would be unstoppable. Best if I go, Jack, I don't want to fall out with you. We are not going to agree on this one. Please, please, think about what I've told you and ask yourself, do you want Jupiter running the show? That sums up this situation is in a nutshell.'

Somerton sighed. 'And I beg you to think it over, Alan, please; I promise, I'll sleep on what you've said.'

Croudace's expression was glum; nothing but trouble and retribution lay ahead. 'Thanks for the whisky, Jack, see you as and when.'

The two men made their way to the door and shook hands. 'Bye, Jack, don't forget what I've said, we know nothing, nothing at all, about Jupiter.' With that, Croudace turned and strode away. Somerton returned to his lounge and poured himself a large measure of St Magdalen; he had a lot of thinking to do. *Why does life have to be so fucking complicated sometimes?*

Downing Street

Friday Morning

Somerton got to Downing Street shortly after 8 am and breezed his way past a surprised Jess Tate. 'Won't be long, Jess, I promise, a national emergency.'

She gave him an old-fashioned look. 'Now why don't I believe that? Make sure you're out before 8.30 am, he's got a meeting with Ken Ogilvie.'

'Will do,' he put on a pained expression, 'I can tell I'm not wanted.'

Somerton knocked once and made his way in without waiting to be invited. MacKinnon looked up from his papers; there was no need to ask why Somerton was there. 'Did you have any success, Jack, is it a yes or a no?'

'Sorry Colin, he wouldn't budge.'

'Fuck it, why does he have to be so damn righteous and so stubborn with it? So what now Jack, will you do what needs to be done in the country's best interests?

'You didn't tell me that your finger wasn't on the TS2 activation trigger, Colin. Slip your mind, did it?'

MacKinnon had anticipated the question and had his answer ready. 'Didn't I? I'm sorry, truly, I meant to. But my mind is in a whirl, Jack, everything has been so fraught since this blew up. I've haven't had a good night's sleep since I got back from the States, I'm not thinking straight. It's purely a matter of practicalities; if the NRSC had control, the whole building would know, and news would almost certainly leak out before I was ready to launch. In that eventuality, you know how it would be; every Tom, Dick and Harry, every tin-pot dictator, would want to have their say and the system would never leave the ground. In due course, I'll negotiate with Jupiter for control of TS2 to pass to me or the NRSC or even a special multinational committee, if it comes to that.'

Somerton nodded. 'Fair enough, I suppose, but in the meantime, Jupiter is in control and we don't know too much about him.'

'I'll grant you that, Jack, but he's never let us down in all the years we've known him and other than the girls, he's never asked for anything. If Alan goes public, you know what will happen and who knows what else will come to light in the aftermath. It's conceivable that the truth about the abductions might leak out eventually.'

Somerton smiled icily at MacKinnon's veiled threat. 'Come off it, that's an empty threat, that just won't happen.'

'I wish I could be that sure, Jack. Think about it; if Alan tells the House about Jupiter, there could well be demands made to access his area of the NRSC and then what? It is unlikely, I agree, but it's a possibility, however slight. Jack, I need to know where this is going; the words almost stick in my throat, but I need to know. What is your final position regards Alan?'

Somerton wasn't going to make it easy for MacKinnon. 'Out with it, Colin, don't go soft. Ask me straight without the weasel words, will I, or will I not, assassinate our best friend before launch time on Wednesday? That's what you're asking me, isn't it?'

MacKinnon nodded and licked his lips uneasily. 'No deniability this time, Jack, eh? OK, have it your way. Will you deal with Alan before he can spill the beans to Parliament?'

Somerton nodded. 'I just wanted to hear you say the words, Colin.' He shook his head. 'You really are asking me to kill our best friend and regimental colleague?'

'So, will you, Jack?'

'I'm ashamed to say it but I'll sort it. Fuck you, Colin, I've told you I'll always do what's best for this island nation of ours. Remind me, what time does the ceremony in Oxford take place?'

MacKinnon breathed a sigh of relief. 'It's scheduled for 10 am on Monday. Thank you, it's the right decision, believe me.'

Somerton shook his head forlornly. 'I hope so, Colin, I hope so.' He left Downing Street with a heavy heart, his head swamped in a maelstrom of options and counter options; sadly, doing nothing wasn't one of them. Deep down, he knew what had to be done, but how? That was the question.

Chapter 34
Somerton's Office Friday

The Monday deadline was horribly close, too close for a job of this importance. Somerton knew he had to act quickly, and speed brought with it the risk of carelessness in a venture where a single detail overlooked or badly planned could spell disaster.

He had the guts to do the deed, black as it was, but before that, there was another essential task to be carried out. The assassination, that was what it would be called, would trigger one of the greatest manhunts in British history; no stone would be left unturned to bring the guilty party to justice. The best way to contain that manhunt would be to nip it in the bud, ensure that the culprit was apprehended early on. An arrest made early in the investigation would bring a media-led deluge of accolades; the praise handed out to the police would be stellar.

It would be difficult, but this time around, luck was looking over his shoulder; he had an unsuspecting but credible fall guy in mind; a long-standing hate figure, one Dimitri Vladic, a Ukrainian national encountered during one of his mercenary excursions. It would heal a deep wound of long standing to see that bastard finally brought to justice of some sort. Just thinking about it brought a smile to Somerton's lips.

Vladic

Somerton had first encountered Vladic in 1998 when they were separately contracted as mercenaries by the Central African Republic; their role had been to provide expertise in quelling a major tribal uprising. Vladic had led a group working from West to East; he had led another working from East to West. Their strategy, such as it was, was to gradually herd the rebels into the middle of the country where they would be dealt with by government forces. Both he and

Vladic had operated under the direction of a local army officer, one Colonel Herado, although his direction, to say the least, was broad brush. Pursue, isolate and destroy the rebels was as much as he contributed. The good Colonel did have one overriding requirement, namely that it should fall to him to accept the final and formal surrender of the rebels. He would then ensure that the media and his superiors were fully informed of the successful campaign *he* had conducted.

At the initial briefing meeting, Herado had happily accepted a campaign plan hurriedly put together by Vladic and himself. They had readily agreed on how to execute the operation and Somerton had found his opposite number to be an intelligent and informed soldier, someone he was happy to go into battle with.

Colonel Herado had issued another edict at that first meeting. *'Remember gentlemen, you must always comply with the Geneva Convention.'* The Colonel had laughed heartily. *'That's what I shall be telling the outside world.'* When his laughter subsided, his smile disappeared, his expression became serious and he added in chilling tones, *'Do whatever is necessary, gentlemen, we are a long way from Geneva; there are no United Nations observers in the Central African Republic.'*

The campaign had lasted three months, three very lucrative months; Somerton's group had not incurred any casualties. The insurgents, poorly armed and disorganised, provided no real opposition to soldiers of their quality. In the latter weeks of the campaign, Somerton had heard rumours of atrocities being carried out by mercenaries, but he had kept an open mind on the subject. He knew from experience that it was fairly common practice for rebel factions to try to gain world sympathy by blaming their misdeeds on government forces or those acting on its behalf. On balance, he had been prepared to give Vladic the benefit of the doubt.

All that had changed in the final days of the campaign when his group strayed some miles into Vladic's territory and came across a small settlement of around sixty villagers, or at least that was what it had been. The settlement was now the scene of a massacre; lifeless bodies lay all around, riddled with bullet holes and gaping wounds.

Eddie Black supervised a search of the huts and immediate area and returned with two elderly women, an even older man and a boy aged 12. 'These are all that are left, Jack, there's no sign of any weapons. There are a number of dead women and girls in the huts; they've been stripped and there's little doubt that they've been violently raped.' He searched for words he could use in front of the child. 'They're badly damaged in some cases.'

'See that these people are given food and water, do what's necessary for them. I'll report what we've found to Colonel Herado, not that I expect he'll do anything.'

Black motioned to the boy. 'This one speaks a little English.'

Somerton knelt in front of the boy. 'We won't harm you; you are safe now. Do you understand me?'

The boy nodded, but fear didn't vacate his eyes.

'We'll protect you, I promise, and we'll give you food and water. Do you understand me?'

The boy nodded and held out a cupped hand.

'Sergeant, get the lad and the others something to eat and some water, then clear a hut for them to bunk down in.'

He turned back to the boy. 'Who did this?' He waved around with his hand. 'Who did this?' He made his hand like a gun and fired imaginary shots. The boy cringed back, terror lining his face. Somerton knelt again and put his hand on the boy's shoulder, squeezing it gently. 'Don't be afraid, I am your friend. Tell me who did this?'

The boy reached forward and fingered Somerton's combat tunic. 'Like you, bang, bang, bang.' He fisted his hand like a gun. 'Kill, kill, kill. They did bad things to my mother and my sister.' He looked over to the huts, tears in his eyes. 'They are in there.'

Somerton stood up. 'You mean soldiers like me?' He touched the top of his head. 'Was he as tall as this?'

The boy fingered up.

'Taller. Was he white like me?' Somerton rubbed his cheek.

The boy nodded. 'Yes, white man.' He then took his chin in his hand and stroked it, then touched his hair.

Somerton nodded. 'He had a beard?' The boy then ran a finger across his face under his nose and touched his hair. Somerton smiled. 'And a moustache. I understand.'

He was puzzled; as far as he knew, Vladic and his group were the only other mercenaries engaged in the campaign, but the Ukrainian was clean-shaven. Still, several months had passed since they had last met, plenty of time to grow a beard.

The boy looked nervous, and Somerton sought to reassure him. 'He was a very bad man, but you are safe now.'

Just then Black called out, 'I've cleared a hut, Jack, the best of those that are left.'

Somerton reached out and took the boy's hand. 'Come with me and we'll give you food.'

The boy pulled back, fear returning to his face.

Somerton smiled and tried to reassure the boy. 'It's OK, I promise. You can have my gun.' He offered the boy his automatic, butt first with the safety catch on; not that the boy would know about safety catches.

The boy pushed it away and shook his head. 'Gun, bad.' But he seemed to understand that he wasn't in danger and put his hand in Somerton's and together they made their way over to the hut, followed by the three other survivors. With the boy and the others settled, Somerton instructed Black and the others to begin the clear up. 'Get the men to lay these bodies out in a row behind the huts; cover them up respectfully as best you can. I want Herado to see them when he gets here.'

It was time to get onto the short-wave radio and arrange a rendezvous with the good Colonel. Their current map coordinates were given but he made no mention of the massacre. He simply confirmed that they had cleared the eastern sector and were no longer pursuing rebel factions.

Herado had been pleased. 'The war is over, Captain Somerton; I will join you tomorrow morning with Captain Vladic who has captured the rebel leadership. You can witness the rebels formally surrender to me. You are to be congratulated; it has been a very successful campaign. Well done to you and your men. I will be with you around 0900 hours.'

Next Morning

Somerton and the boy, whose name transpired to be Miki, sat near the fire chatting idly, the latter practising his English. Eddie Black joined them. 'Colonel Herado has been sighted, Captain, he's less than half a mile away.'

'Thanks Sergeant. The sooner we tie this lot up, the better, then we can get paid and go home. It's time to deploy the men as we discussed last night and make sure everyone is on their guard.'

Ten minutes or so later, Herado's jeep emerged from the jungle, bouncing slowly along the makeshift road. The good Colonel had dressed for the occasion and was resplendent in full uniform, an array of medals and gold braid glinting in the sun. Somerton smiled. *Ready for your photo call, Colonel.* Vladic sat alongside him in conventional camouflage gear. A little way behind them, a group of rebels with their hands behind their necks, were being marched along, heads hung low announcing defeat. Vladic's men were in close attendance with M25's at the ready. A small detachment of government troops brought up the rear, armed and dressed in surprisingly clean well-presented uniforms.

Somerton stood up. 'Stay here, Miki, whilst I talk to the Colonel.' The boy's eyes were fixed on the advancing group, his face creasing with fear, his hands shaking. 'What's wrong, Miki?'

The boy pointed in the direction of Herado and Vladic. 'He kill my family.'

Somerton followed the boy's pointed finger to Vladic, he had to be referring to the Ukrainian; Herado didn't do fighting. His eyes narrowed when he saw the Ukrainian had grown a beard and moustache. He knelt in front of the boy and spoke softly, 'Wait here, you are safe; I will protect you.'

He gathered his thoughts and walked purposefully towards the new arrivals, smiling broadly, his hand extended. 'Colonel, it's good to see you.' He shed his smile and nodded at Vladic but said nothing.

Herado shook his hand warmly, smiling broadly, brilliantly white teeth lighting up his face. 'And good to see you, Captain, this moment marks the formal end of the rebellion. This rabble represents what's left of the rebel leadership; they have laid down their weapons and surrendered unconditionally. You and Captain Vladic have restored democracy to this area of the Central African Republic; I thank you both.'

Somerton smiled at the use of the term democracy. 'What will happen to these men, Colonel?'

'They will be treated as prisoners of war and those who have been guilty of war crimes will be put on trial.'

Somerton nodded appreciatively. 'Strictly in accordance with the Geneva Convention, just as you promised, Colonel, that is good news.'

Herado nodded proudly. 'Exactly, Captain, as required by the Geneva Convention.'

'I wonder if I could ask you to accompany me, Colonel, there is something I want to show you.'

Herado nodded amiably. 'Certainly Captain; lead the way.'

Somerton led Herado to the rear of the huts, to where the bodies were laid out side by side; a grim testimony to what had taken place. Herado's face fell, anxiety sounding in his voice. 'Why are you showing me these rebel bodies, Captain? If you killed them, you should have buried them.'

Somerton shook his head. 'They are not rebels. They are all innocent villagers, brutally and systematically murdered and raped by mercenaries under the command of Captain Vladic.' He turned to face Vladic who had followed them. 'Is that not so, Captain Vladic?'

Herado raised a hand to silence Somerton. 'Is this true, Captain Vladic?'

Vladic's face twisted with anger. 'No, it is not true, Colonel. My men were fired at by this scum and we, of course, returned fire. It became a fight to the finish, and they lost.'

Somerton exploded, 'You're a liar, Vladic, you're a mad-dog murderer and a rapist. These poor people were all shot at close range. Most of them are women, many are naked, raped and abused by you and your men.'

Vladic blustered, 'The women were alive when we left here; I can only surmise that another group of tribesmen took advantage of them.'

Somerton stared Vladic in the eye. 'I say you're a liar, Vladic. A brutal, sadistic liar, totally without scruples. You're not fit to wear a soldier's uniform.'

Vladic thrust his M25 into Somerton's guts. 'I should watch what you say, Englishman, you could get yourself killed.'

Colonel Herado stood watching impassively, saying nothing, ready to support whoever came out on top. A few dead villagers were of no matter and weren't going to spoil his moment of triumph.

Somerton calmly pushed the gun away. 'I've got no doubts that you wouldn't hesitate to shoot an unarmed man, Vladic, but you would be signing your own death warrant and more importantly that of Colonel Herado. Look around you; it's my men who control this situation.'

Vladic swivelled, looking left and right, lowering his weapon when he saw Eddie Black and Mike Davies rising from cover just twenty metres away, grinning at him, their weapons pointed in his direction. The rest of Somerton's men broke cover, their weapons trained on the other mercenaries. Herado's troops looked on bemused, unsure what to do.

The Ukrainian regained his temporary loss of composure and addressed Herado. 'Colonel, I deny that my men or I were involved in this dreadful massacre. I ask that you instruct Captain Somerton and his men to lower their weapons so that further bloodshed can be avoided.'

Herado thought for a moment then addressed Somerton, 'I'll accept Captain Vladic's word as an officer for the moment, Captain Somerton. The matter is closed for nowbut I will ensure that this atrocity is fully investigated and those responsible brought to justice. You have my word.'

Lying bastard. Somerton thought quickly; he could cite the boy and the others as witnesses but feared for their safety. The local government would not welcome adverse publicity, and he doubted if Herado would want to believe what he had been told. The Colonel would be concerned about his own position if the matter became public; his chance of promotion gone. And Vladic might opt for a fire fight, resulting in more loss of life and an uncertain outcome. There was nothing to be gained and everything to lose; a confrontation wasn't worth the risk.

In the circumstance, he judged it best to be pragmatic. 'Very well, Colonel, you are an honourable man; I know I can accept your word as an officer that this war crime will be investigated by every means at your disposal.' *Don't lay it on too thick, Jack.*

Herado's shining teeth burst into a smile again. 'Thank you, Captain, you have my word that those responsible will be brought to justice.'

'With your permission, Colonel, my men and I will begin our departure immediately. I assume that you have no objection?'

Herado happily shook his head, he would be relieved to see Somerton depart without further conflict. 'Of course not, the war is over.'

Somerton smiled. 'Can I ask, therefore, that you radio your headquarters now and give instructions for payment for my services to take place immediately?'

The Colonel turned and shouted something to his radio operator who saluted and immediately began unpacking a wireless transmitter. 'Take it as done, Captain Somerton.'

'Thank you, Colonel; I have one more request, and then I will make my departure. Would you please instruct Captain Vladic and his men to begin the immediate burial of the victims of this massacre?'

Herado licked his lips, unsure for a second how to proceed; he had no wish to upset Vladic but he wanted to bring the matter to a peaceful conclusion. 'Do as Captain Somerton requests, if you please.' He stared at the Ukrainian, willing him to obey.

Vladic hesitated but the main issue had been settled, this was a small concession. He shouted a command to his sergeant then turned back to Somerton, a sneer on his lips. 'Happy now, Somerton?'

Somerton ignored him and turned away to salute Herado; the Colonel returned his salute and shook his hand warmly. 'Goodbye Captain, we may call upon your services again.'

Oh no, you fucking won't, mate. 'Thank you, Colonel, you know where to find me.'

Somerton turned and leaned towards Vladic. 'We'll meet again another day, motherfucker; I'll see that you live to regret what you've done here.'

The Ukrainian didn't flinch. 'Goodbye Englishman. Save your empty threats for a lesser mortal.'

Somerton turned away and shouted to Black, 'Make ready to depart Sergeant, but maintain vigilance, there are snakes in the grass, one very near me.'

Out of earshot, Vladic spoke softly to Herado, 'What are you going to do about Somerton?'

'Nothing, Captain Vladic, absolutely nothing, and nor are you. Like you, Somerton is a mercenary, here for the money; he'll check with his bank to confirm that he's been paid and go back to England a richer, happy man. Do not mention this matter again, it is closed; now make sure your men bury the dead.'

'But…' Vladic made to protest.

Herado silenced him with a glare. 'No buts, Captain, get on with the burials if you want to be paid for your services; I'm not happy with what has happened here.'

To ensure their safety, the boy and the elderly villagers had been spirited away by one of Somerton's men and were waiting to rendezvous a mile or so away from the luckless village. At the end of a day's walk and a good night's rest, they all set out early the following morning for Bangui.

On the way, Somerton negotiated with some elders for Miki and the three old folk to be welcomed into a friendly village, easing the process by handing over some supplies and money. From there, they marched at full pace to Bangui where a chartered aircraft awaited to fly them back to England.

Chapter 35
Friday

Even after all these years, it remained a source of deep regret to Somerton that he hadn't dealt with Vladic in 1987; the man was a monster and deserved to be exterminated. He and his men had needlessly slaughtered an entire village, butchered and raped women and girls, and walked away scot-free. In fact, he'd been handsomely rewarded for doing it. Massakori had been bad, unforgivable even, but the circumstances had been entirely different.

He could have dealt with Vladic back then; set up an ambush and rid humanity of the bastard, but the Ukrainian and his men were professionals, there would have been casualties on both sides with no guaranteed outcome. And of course, there was Colonel Herado and his government forces to be reckoned with; he and his men might not have gotten out of the Central African Republic alive. In the end, he had done nothing and that might have been the last he'd seen of Vladic but for one of those strange twists of fate.

He'd been sitting in his flat, a few months back, watching a late-night current affairs programme when his telephone rang; caller display showed it was Eddie Black. 'Eddie, everything's all right, I hope?' There was concern in Somerton's voice; Eddie wasn't working so a call from him at this time of night had to be important.

'No problems, Jack. I'm in the Black Cat and you'll never guess who has just walked in.' The Black Cat was a nightclub-cum-gambling casino in Soho.

'You're going to have to tell me, Eddie, I'm fresh out of ideas.'

'An old friend of ours; well, maybe friend is not the right word.'

'I'm on the hook, Eddie; if he's not a friend, he's an enemy and I've made a ton of those over the years.'

'Dimitri Vladic, Jack, Dimitri Vladic.'

Somerton felt a wave of excitement flow through him; fate had given him a chance to settle an old score. 'You're sure, absolutely sure, Eddie?'

'100% certain, Jack, it's him all right. He's older, of course, but still has that same arrogant strut he had all those years ago. I've heard him order a drink and the accent is still there.'

'Is he on his own?'

'Looks like it but could be he's meeting someone or looking to pick up a piece of skirt.'

'I'd like to come down and kill the bastard now, but that pleasure will have to await the right opportunity; he's not long for this world, believe me. You're on overtime as of now, I want you to follow him and find out where he lives. We'll talk about it tomorrow.

'Forget the overtime, Jack, I want to nail this bastard as much as you do. Bye.'

Eddie produced the goods; a home address, a car number and the name Vladic was currently using. With a name to work with, there were records he could access and a network he could use to find out more about the Ukrainian. It turned out that Vladic was a drug dealer who also ran a call girl operation. There were allegations that the girls were little better than slaves and most sources described him as a nasty piece of work.

Still the same Vladic of old, it's going to be a pleasure taking you down. He would have no qualms about taking the bastard out of the game.

Outside Vladic's Home

Somerton sat in his car where he could keep Vladic's detached Victorian house under surveillance. It was now 9.30 am and he'd been there for nigh on two and a half hours; boredom was setting in. Worse still, he was in desperate need of a pee. *C'mon, you bastard, time you were up and about.* He was reaching for his emergency toilet, a large lemonade bottle, when the garage door began to inch upwards. *About time. I'll hang on and use your loo, might even picture your face in the pan.*

Vladic's white Lexus pulled forward and stopped at the end of his short drive to check whether the road was clear, giving Somerton a clear view of his face. He looked older, his hair was starting to turn grey, but the face was still lean with none of the signs of easy living.

When the Lexus was out of sight, he wasted no time crossing the road and heading for Vladic's front door. There was no sign of a CCTV camera, but he kept his head down and his hood pulled up just in case. As expected, no-one answered when he rang the doorbell, nor when he knocked loudly. The door was fitted with two good-quality locks but that wasn't how he intended to take access. Eddie had fed back to him what to expect and he had the necessary tool to deal with the garage door in seconds. He lifted it and ducked under, lowering it behind him. The latex gloves he was wearing would ensure there would be no tell-tale fingerprints left behind. To his left, a door led from the garage directly into the house and much to his surprise, it was unlocked. 'Tut, tut, Dimitri; poor show.'

He stepped into a spacious entrance area from which a corridor on his right led to the ground floor living areas. He immediately headed to the broad staircase rising to the first floor. There were five doors leading off the U-shaped landing, one of which lay open, revealing a well-equipped bathroom. The next door led into an empty room, presumably a bedroom in times gone by. He looked around at the vacant space, closed the door and moved further along the landing and pushed open the neighbouring door. The room was set out as a home cinema and furnished with two armchairs and two sofas.

Two doors led off the other side of the landing and he moved to the nearer of the two and pushed it open, mildly surprised to find a full-sized snooker table. It appeared that the two of the original rooms, presumably bedrooms, had been knocked together to provide the necessary space. A well-stocked bar and a few chairs completed the furnishings. He hadn't expected to find what he was looking for upstairs so wasn't in any way disappointed as he made his way back down to the ground floor.

There were seven doors in all leading off the wide corridor; the one at the far end hadn't been closed and he could see that it led into the kitchen. He moved across to the nearest door and pulled it open; a storeroom crammed with cardboard boxes, floor cleaning equipment and an ironing board. The adjacent door opened into a utility room with a washing machine and tumble dryer. The third opened into a cloakroom with a WC, a much needed first port of call. His pressing need satisfied, he flushed the bowl and exited, closing the door behind him.

Next stop was the kitchen where his eyes lit up when he caught sight of a small table on which Vladic's breakfast dishes lay unwashed. But it was the ashtray that interested him, or more accurately its contents, a small pile of cigarette ends. *You're an untidy bastard, Vladic.* He used a pair of plastic tweezers to ease four of the discarded ends into a small plastic wallet; they would be useful for what he had in mind. *You really should give up the habit, Dimitri, it could be the death of you.* He allowed himself a hollow laugh at the irony of the thought.

He glanced at his watch and returned to the corridor to continue his search of the house; he had yet to find what he was looking for. The next door along led into a well-appointed wet room, which held nothing of interest. *Very nice, Vladic.* The penultimate door opened into a large double bedroom complete with a king-sized bed and a row of fitted wardrobes incorporating a dressing table.

Sods law; your office must be in the last room. The last door opened into a large open-plan lounge cum dining-room. His eyes travelled around the room, frowning when he didn't see what he was looking for. There was a large dining table with eight matching chairs, a sideboard, a four-seater settee, two armchairs and a coffee table but not the desk he had hoped to find. He wasn't hopeful, but he moved across to search the sideboard but found nothing other than table linen, china and cutlery. *Damn it, where do you keep your paperwork? You must have mail delivered here surely?* He glanced at his watch, he'd been in the house for seven minutes; ideally, he wanted to be gone in less than fifteen minutes. *Oh well, back to the bedroom, it must be there.*

Somerton made his way back to the bedroom and tried the bedside cabinet drawers, they held all sort of odds and ends but not what he was looking for. A search of the dressing table drawers brought the same result and his concern mounted; maybe Vladic took all his mail to an office in town somewhere? He didn't feel hopeful as he slid open each of the wardrobe doors in turn, his eyes lighting up when, third time lucky, he found a stack of three boxes. All were neatly labelled—Photos, Accounts and Miscellaneous.

Opening the Accounts box, he flicked through the invoices, breathing a sigh of relief when he found what he was looking for, Vladic's mobile phone bills, the latest dated only a week previously. He made a note of the number and returned the box to its place. Just one task remained; he pulled out the box labelled Miscellaneous and concealed a package below the papers.

Job done, he checked his watch. *Eleven minutes, not bad, Jack.* It was time to leave the Hampstead home of Dimitri Vladic, also known as Alan Rich, an erstwhile importer and exporter.

Oxford

From Hampstead, he headed directly to Oxford, city of culture, spires and places of learning. Black thoughts ebbed and flowed as he drove, the enormity of the task ahead filling him with guilt. Task? It could hardly be labelled a task. It was a mission to kill, pure and simple. Not only that, it was a mission to kill a friend and comrade of long standing.

The Satnav took him unerringly to the unnamed college; the one MacKinnon hoped would bear his name, an honour he probably deserved as a testimony to his achievements. An impressive building, it stood on its own ten-acre site on the outer edge of other college campuses. He nodded approvingly as he drove past; the four-floor building has been tastefully designed to harmonise with other edifices in the area, though to his eyes it couldn't compare with the much older founding colleges.

Somerton pulled up and got out of the car just past the entrance to the new college. Standing on the pavement he took out his mobile to engage in a non-existent phone call, looking around in the process to make sure that no passing tourist was inadvertently incorporating him into a photograph. He knew he was being ultra-cautious, he had to be; following the assassination, the hunt for clues would be relentless.

His eyes swept the surrounding area, searching out the vantage spot he had chosen for what he had to do on Monday. It had to be one he could legitimately access, one from which he could safely make his escape and, most importantly, one that had a clear line of sight to the college. It had to be near but not too near; in his army days he'd been a decent shot, a good shot some would say, but he wasn't sniper class. Five hundred metres was his limit.

He'd had a session studying a detailed Oxford street plan and what he saw now confirmed he'd made a good choice; the shot had to be taken from the Church of St Mary Magdalene. Its steeple provided a clear line of sight to the college grounds and the distance of four hundred metres or so was well within his capabilities. All that remained was to check out the church itself. He finished his pseudo call, returned to his car and drove about a mile away before parking again. The walk back to the church led him through rows of Victorian built terraced houses and took around fifteen minutes.

The 300-year-old church sat in grounds surrounded by a low stone wall and was accessed through a cast iron gate set under an impressive ancient oak arch. The gate swung easily on its well-oiled hinges, opening onto a red brick path leading directly to the church. Giving the appearance of an interested tourist, he paused here and there to show apparent interest in the headstones that stood like guards over the last resting place of their owners. The studded oak door to the church creaked loudly as he pushed it open, but he was the only one to hear it, there were no worshippers, no volunteers; the only presence was that reverential silence unique to holy places.

There would be no tell-tale fingerprints to be found, his pair of fine close-fitting leather gloves would ensure that. He had avoided latex gloves which might have been seen and remembered if he chanced to encounter anyone. A small door to his left was the obvious access to the bell tower and he stepped quickly across to it, smiling when he found it unlocked. Behind it, a stone spiral staircase rose to the bell tower above.

He entered, pulled the door closed behind him and climbed the stairs to the landing where the bell ringer would have carried out his Sunday duties. There was no bell rope to be seen; like many churches, St Mary Magdalene now relied on recordings and loudspeakers to call the faithful to prayer. The control console for the sound system sat in a corner, no doubt in meditation preparing itself for Sunday activation.

The way up to the steeple and the bell mounting lay to his left through a half-sized planked door secured by a simple wooden latch. Beyond the door, a steel rung ladder rose vertically to the now dormant bell. The tower was small, not much over a metre and a half square but adequate for its purpose. At the top of the ladder, the standing area comprised a stout oak plank platform about half a metre wide, adequate for maintenance but less than ideal for a rifleman's stance. A rectangular opening on each of the tower's four sides provided rewarding views of the scene beyond, exactly as he had hoped. The south-facing opening looked directly towards the college and was narrow enough to ensure he wouldn't be easily spotted from below.

His day's work done, he left the still vacant, silent church and made his way back to his car for the return journey to London. Everything was now in place but only when the moment came on Monday would he find out if he really had the guts to do what he needed to do. *Fuck you, Jupiter; fuck you, Colin; fuck you, Alan; fuck all of you! Christ, why don't I just throw in the towel and move abroad to some sun-soaked sanctuary!* He shook his head; he wasn't going to leave the country he loved; whatever happened, he'd stay and take his chances.

Two messages were waiting for him when he got back to the NRSC, one from the Prime Minister, one from the Foreign Secretary; both asking him to call back. *What an important little cog you are, Jack.*

'Hi Colin, it's Jack. What can I do for you?'

'Thanks for calling back. How did you get on with Alan?'

'He didn't fall over backwards to change his mind and I doubt if he will. The best you can hope for is a change of heart over the weekend. I'll phone you if I hear anything.'

'Oh.' He could hear the resignation in that single word. 'I see. Thanks for trying, Jack. You'll still do what's necessary?'

'Yes, Colin, I'll do the necessary. Now don't call me, I'll call you if anything changes.' He put the phone down before MacKinnon could respond.

His second call was to Croudace. 'Hello Alan, what can I do for you?'

'I was just wondering if you've spoken to Colin?'

'No, I haven't fucking spoken to Colin and I don't intend to. I'm not going to be the ham in the sandwich; sort it out between you. I've done all I can.'

Just as he'd done with MacKinnon he slammed the phone down. *Bugger it, I'm going to treat myself.* He scrolled through the contact list on his private mobile settling on his favourite escort agency; there was only one way to alleviate his present mood.

'Hello, this is Elite Escorts.'

'Put me through to Jill please.' Jill Swanton was a beauty and had a business brain; she knew what men wanted and made sure they got it, provided, of course, they could afford her luxury goods.

'Who shall I say is calling?'

'Jack Somerton.'

'Are you an existing customer, Mr Somerton?'

'I would claim to be one of your very best.'

The voice at the other end laughed politely. 'Hold please, I'll put you through.'

'Jack, it's been a while since we heard from you. What are you up to these days?' Jill's husky, sexy voice pushed his pulse up a notch.

'You wouldn't believe me if I told you, Jill, just earning a dishonest pound or two.'

'Thank you for that revelation, Jack, you've always been a bit of a mystery man.' She laughed softly, even her laugh was somehow sexy.

'Is Louisa free? I'd like her company from now until Sunday evening.'

'I'll have to check and get back to you, Jack.'

'Make it happen, Jill, please; unless, of course, by chance *you* would be interested? I promise an enjoyable weekend in every way you can imagine.'

'Sorry, Jack, I'm tied up and anyway, you know I don't get directly involved in the hands-on side of the business, excuse the pun.'

'Hmm, *tied up*, you say? That sounds promising, I'll live in hope. Fix up Louisa for me and book us into the Amberley Castle Hotel, the best room they have available, tonight and Saturday please, with dinner at 8 pm on both nights.'

'My, my, we are pushing the boat out. Won the lottery, have we?'

'If I had, would you be free, Jill?'

She chuckled. 'You're incorrigible, Jack, I like that. Tell you what, when you win the lottery, give me a call. I'll phone you back about Louisa in five minutes.'

He sat back, already feeling more relaxed at the thought of getting away for a couple of days. When the call came, he knew it would be a "yes". He and Louisa had shared fun times in the past and sure enough, his prediction was fulfilled when the phone rang five minutes later.

'You're in luck, Jack, Louisa is free, and I've booked you into the best suite Amberley had available one of the honeymoon suites actually.'

'Goody, goody. I'll try to live up to the billing. Thanks Jill, tell Louisa I'll pick her up from her place at 6.30 pm.'

He breathed out a sigh, releasing the last of his pent-up emotions. *A good weekend lay ahead; his favourite woman, his favourite hotel. What more could a man ask for?*

It was just after 4 pm, plenty of time to go home and pack. But before that, he had one last bit of essential business to conduct if his plan was to be the complete success he hoped for. He fished out one of his cheap pay-as-you-go mobiles from the half dozen he kept in his desk drawer; it was time to make a call to Dimitri Vladic alias Alan Rich.

He had rehearsed what he would say several times and had tried to anticipate how Vladic would react. He had to have a plausible response ready for whatever the Ukrainian came up with. Vladic would be cautious, suspicious even, but he would be greedy too; it would all be down to where the balance lay. If everything worked out as he planned, an old score with Dimitri Vladic would be settled in full.

He tapped in the number he'd obtained during his illegal Hampstead foray, listening as it rang out, grimacing when it seemed to be taking too long. *Please don't go through to voicemail.*

'Hello, who is this?' The voice still carried an accent, just as Eddie had said; it wasn't pronounced, but still there.

'Am I speaking to Mr Rich?'

A moment or two passed followed by a hesitant question. 'Who is this? I don't recognise your voice or your number.'

'We've never met, Mr Rich; your name has been given to me by a mutual associate. I have a business opportunity for you.'

Another pause ensued. 'What associate would that be?'

All good so far, don't rush it, Jack. 'An associate who is in the same business as we are, Mr Rich; he didn't want me to mention his name. Trust is important in our business, isn't it?'

A few seconds passed as Vladic/Rich pondered his reply.

Somerton went on, 'Let me say, Mr Rich, it's the side of the business that doesn't involve girls, it's the commodity side of your interests.'

'I don't know what you're talking about.'

'I'm sorry to hear that, my associate is usually well informed about these matters. Still, you are right to be cautious, let me explain further; I have an assignment of H, which, by necessity, I have to dispose of quickly.'

Vladic didn't take the hook. 'I don't think I can be of assistance to you, I've no idea what you're talking about.'

'That's disappointing, but at least listen to what I have to say before you make your mind up; I know for sure that you are a businessman. If the deal sounds too big for you then I'll go elsewhere; I understand that your operation is fairly small scale.'

He was playing the pride card. *It's now or never, Jack.* When Vladic/Rich responded, he detected a trace of aggression in his voice, he had struck a nerve, just as he hoped he would.

'Whoever the fuck you are, you don't know what you're talking about, resources aren't a problem for me. Tell me about this deal of yours.'

'I have a delivery of the commodity arriving this weekend with a street value of one million pounds.'

'So why do you need me, mister whoever you are? You could be a copper for all I know.'

'You're right. I could be a copper but I'm not and for all I know, you could be a copper's nark. My associate seems to think that the police pretty much leave you alone and that appeals to me. It suggests you know your way around the system.' *A touch of flattery for you, Vladic.*

Vladic bridled. 'They leave me alone because I'm a step ahead of them, that's why.'

Well done, Jack, you've pressed the right button again.

'Fair enough, Mr Rich. The facts are simple; the delivery is due shortly and my usual dealer has let me down: it seems he's currently taking swimming lessons in the Mersey. So, I have this arrival and no-one to pass the goods on to.'

'What makes you think you can trust me?'

'I don't trust you, Mr Rich; how could I, I don't know you. But you come recommended, and word is that when you take on a deal, you deliver. I've decided to take a risk.' *Push the flattery button again.*

'What kind of money are we talking about?'

'I'm open to offers.'

'Well, you're not getting one just like that; I haven't seen the goods or checked its quality.'

'Fair enough, Mr Rich. As I said, the shipment arrives this weekend and to be honest, I don't know if it's of good quality or otherwise. Obviously, if it's poor grade, I won't buy it so there won't be a deal. Might I put forward a suggestion?'

'I'm still listening.'

'We meet, I show you the stuff, you take a sample away with you, check it out and come back to me with an offer if you're interested.'

'We might be able to make a deal on that basis, Mr...?'

'I'll introduce myself when we meet, Mr Rich; if the delivery isn't genuine, you won't hear from me again. If we end up doing business, I'll also tell you who recommended you. In that way, everything will be transparent.'

'I reckon we can deal on that basis. When do we meet?'

Somerton smiled. Vladic, or Rich as he called himself, was firmly on the hook.

'I need a bit more from you than that, Mr Rich; I don't want to waste my time any more than you do. I have to have some idea of what your offer is likely to be, assuming the goods are of the required quality.'

Another nerve-wracking silence ensued, his anxiety level climbing with each passing second. *Bollocks, you've pushed too hard, Jack.*

'If it's top quality, it'll be 20% of street value.'

'Please Mr Rich, be serious, I can't deal at that level, I'll lose money on the deal. I'm pressed on this consignment so you're getting a bargain, let's say 40% and that really is my final offer.'

No pause this time, Rich/Vladic came straight back. '30% and that really is *my* final offer.'

'You drive a hard bargain, Mr Rich; there's no way I can accept 30%, let's say 35% and we have a deal in principle.'

This time, Vladic didn't hesitate. 'OK, we have a deal, provided the goods are of the right quality. So, where do we meet?'

'I'm afraid you'll have to come to Oxford, my patch, Monday morning.'

'My business is in London; you'll have to come here. You're the one who's desperate for a deal.'

'I'm not desperate, as you put it, Mr Rich. I have matters to attend to here, matters that will take the weekend and some of next week to resolve. I'm sorry but it must be Oxford, or we can't go ahead. Normally, I'd be happy to spend time in London, but commitments prevent me on this occasion; it would have been a pleasure to meet one of your young ladies.'

Vladic/Rich laughed. 'You seem to know a lot about my affairs, Mr X; tell me where we meet and how I'll recognise you.'

'Good point. I'll park in Christchurch Road at the rear of St Mary Magdalene Church, I'll be driving a silver Jaguar. Who knows, if I'm early, I might visit the church, I was christened there. Shall we say 9.30 am?'

'Obviously, you decided to abandon your faith somewhere along the line. I'll be there at 9.30 sharp; I'll be driving a white Lexus.'

'One more thing, Mr Rich, I shall be unaccompanied; I'll expect you to be on your own on this occasion. When and if we meet up to do the deal, you can have as many minders as you like, just as I will.'

Vladic laughed. 'You do what you need to, those who know me will tell you that I don't need minders. I can assure you I know how to look after myself; see you Monday.'

Well done, Jack; it looks more and more likely we'll kill two birds with one stone, or should I say, one bullet. I think that deserves a bottle of the best bubbly Amberley has to offer. It's been a long time coming, Vladic, but your number is just about up.

Chapter 36
Oxford Monday

Somerton cruised into Oxford around 8 am, allowing himself plenty of time to get into position. He had driven there direct, opting to avoid any motorway service plaza stops, seeking to keep exposure to CCTV cameras to a minimum.

He parked his car in a quiet street noted during his previous visit and settled down with a flask of coffee, his essential morning caffeine boost. Hunger pangs broke through and he reached for the cheese and tomato sandwich he'd prepared before leaving home. His guilty conscience was knocking at the door; seeking a distraction, he switched on the car radio and fiddled around with various stations, hoping for something of interest to take his mind off what lay ahead.

He was desperate to avoid going over the well-trodden path of *do it, don't do it* for the umpteenth time but the air waves weren't coming up with anything to please him; the mindless jabbering of the DJs on the music programmes jarred more than ever. Not even the informative Radio 4 gripped his attention and after a while, he switched off and sat in silence, brooding about what lay ahead.

A shiver went through him as the car cooled down, but a lengthy uncomfortable spell in the cramped bell tower lay ahead and he didn't want to spend any more time there than necessary. For what would be the last time, he rehearsed, step by step, what lay ahead. That done, he watched the minutes ebb away on the dashboard clock, letting out a heavy sigh when at last it was time to go.

He checked his mirrors to make sure no-one was in the vicinity, then pressed a fake moustache in place; it wasn't essential to his plan, but it would do no harm to have a passing resemblance to Vladic just in case he attracted someone's attention. A beanie hat completed his disguise, such as it was. If his plan worked, Vladic's photo-fit would get splashed across the newspapers and millions of TV screens; anyone who had spotted him might just imagine there was a resemblance. It was all tenuous, of course, but there was always a chance that an eager-to-help witness, half motivated by the promise of a moment of fame, might come forward.

Perhaps he had subconsciously stepped up his pace; the church of St Mary Magdalene came into view sooner than he expected. Meanwhile, some four hundred metres away to the south, police were already in place doing what was required of them when a Prime Minister visited their patch. Members of the public were gathering, as always; MacKinnon was going to attract a goodly crowd of admiring onlookers.

A distant clock chimed the hour, nine booming chimes, as he strode towards the stout oak door guarding the entrance to the church. This time, it didn't creak; presumably one of the faithful had found an oil can and done the necessary. He made his way in, prepared to take a pew and say an imaginary prayer if anyone was around, but the church was empty. It felt colder than when he had last visited, causing him to shiver.

He swapped his woollen gloves for latex before heading swiftly up the staircase to the bell ringer's room where he caught sight of the small control console. The thought struck him that the bells might be rung to celebrate the opening of the new college. *I hope it's on a timer; it could prove awkward if some worthy soul turned up to activate the system. Please God, don't let the bells be too loud.* He ducked through the small door and began his climb, the rungs of the ladder chilling his fingers through the latex, encouraging him to scramble quickly to the top.

A gentle but cool breeze was blowing through the bell tower openings and he was glad of the beanie to keep his head warm. Weather conditions were good, exactly as forecast; the clear blue sky and a bright sun giving promise of warmer hours ahead. Conditions and visibility were perfect; there was nothing to hinder a good shot except an unsteady hand.

Somerton sat on the platform pondering on the three paths that were on a collision course—the shooter, the victim and the fall guy. Three very different people sharing a common destiny that would only work out well for one of them—Jack Somerton.

Miles away, the Ukrainian was weaving his way through motorway traffic, wondering from time to time who had recommended him to his unknown caller; some uncertainty remained as to whether he had made the right decision to get involved in the deal. He couldn't put his finger on anything specific but something about the transaction didn't ring true. Still, he stood to make a lot of money, maybe as much as half a million, and in the end, greed overcame caution. After all, if it was a Drug Squad set-up, this far he'd done nothing illegal. He'd claim he had played along with the caller out of curiosity, just to find out who was involved. If it happened to be a rival gangland operation, he was armed and could take care of himself.

An approaching road sign took his attention; the turn-off for Oxford lay just ahead, time now to keep his wits about him. He slowed and eased over onto the slip road and took the turning for the town centre, once there his satnav would give directions to the church. The approaches to the centre of the town were thick with traffic and progress was slow but a glance at the dashboard clock showed he had time in hand.

'Christ!' He suddenly caught sight of a small group of policemen and momentarily panicked but they didn't give him a second glance as he drove past. He was now in uncharted territory and turned up the volume on the satnav, smiling as the voice told him his destination wasn't far ahead. Up ahead, another police contingent had gathered at an entrance to a new building. *I wonder what's going on?* He glanced ahead out of his driver's side window giving himself a mental thumbs-up when he realised the church he could see on his right was probably St Mary Magdalene. The car clock displayed 9.20 am, perfect timing; he would drive past the church and check the lay of the land before parking up to meet his secretive business partner.

Watching from the tower, Somerton spotted Vladic's white Lexus as it passed the entrance to the college. *Good boy, Dmitri, you're on time in true military fashion.* The car disappeared before returning minutes later to park fifty metres or so from the church entrance. The Ukrainian didn't get out of the car immediately; exhaust vapour showed that the engine was still running, no doubt ready for a quick departure if the need arose.

Somerton stretched his legs as best he could in the confined space and manipulated his fingers, an attack of cramp at this stage would be unwelcome. The chill was starting to penetrate his bones, it was time to make ready. He removed the rifle from his backpack and assembled it ready for use; a Yalguzag Sniper Rifle manufactured many years ago, in Azerbaijan of all places. It was a trophy from one of his mercenary engagements and, as such, in the current circumstances had one overriding quality—it was untraceable. True, it wasn't in the topflight of sniper rifles, but the range of 400 metres was well within its capabilities. Down below, Vladic sat in his Lexus less than 50 metres away. *I could kill you now, Vladic, but retribution can wait a little longer.*

The Ukrainian was fuming. It was 9.45 am and he didn't like being kept waiting; he'd phoned the caller's number several times and gotten no reply. *Bastard, bastard, bastard; some motherfucker is winding me up.* He punched the steering wheel in frustration.

'What the…' A split second of alarm struck Somerton when he saw Vladic get out of his car and stride towards the church, his fists clenched and face lurid with anger. *Christ, he's seen me.* Vladic disappeared from his line of vision as he neared the church and turned towards the gate. *If you come up these stairs, you're a dead man, Vladic.*

Somerton heard the church door slam, then another and yet another that sounded like the door to the bell tower, then silence. A couple of minutes passed, the front door to the church was slammed closed with even more vigour than previously. Vladic was leaving. Somerton sneaked a furtive look down to the churchyard and saw the Ukrainian storm away, flinging the gate wide open on his march back to his car. He sat fuming for another fifteen minutes before leaving just before 10 am. *Perfect timing, bye, bye, Dimitri; I hope you enjoyed your trip out.*

Somerton smiled as the thought occurred to him that Vladic must have left his fingerprints on the church door handles. *Might be picked up, might not; I'll be over the moon if they are. There was another task to perform.* He reached into his pocket and pulled out the small plastic wallet containing the cigarette ends removed from Vladic's kitchen ashtray. *Do your stuff, DNA; it's almost certain that either Vladic, or Rich, has a criminal record. Not that it mattered, an anonymous telephone call to Scotland Yard would be equally effective if the police needed to be pointed in the right direction.* Before dropping them onto the bell platform, he lit a match and briefly fired up each cigarette end in turn before stubbing them out on the window ledge.

Bong, bong, bong, bong, bong, bong, bong, bong, bong, bong the loudspeakers above his head burst into life, sounding out some joyous offerings. The noise was deafening. 'Bollocks, that's just what I need.' The bell console was indeed on a timer, programmed to contribute to MacKinnon's arrival at the college.

Something was happening in the area outside the new college; he could see a police officer issuing instructions to his men to clear the entrance to the gate.

A few minutes later, traffic flow ceased in both directions as strategically located barriers set in place some distance away served their purpose. The gathering crowd became aware that the once busy road was now silent, necks craned forward to catch an early sight of the Prime Minister's entourage. The air of anticipation peaked a few minutes later when a pair of police motorcyclists rode into view, MacKinnon's modest three car cavalcade followed close behind. Union Jacks were waved, the buzz of conversation rose to excited chatter, the PM and his Foreign Secretary had arrived.

The front car drew up just beyond the gate and what looked like two aides and two security staff got out. MacKinnon's limousine pulled up immediately outside the college entrance with the third vehicle in close attendance behind it. Two more thickset security staff left the rear car and took up their positions. Meanwhile, Tim Penrose, the PM's personal security, got out of the ministerial car and, satisfied with what he saw, held the door open for MacKinnon. Bill Sweeney did the honours for Croudace then returned to his place behind the wheel.

Somerton frowned, MacKinnon's car hadn't driven into the college grounds as expected. *What's going on?* He relaxed when he saw that MacKinnon and Croudace, both dressed in dark lounge suits, consummate politicians, weren't going to miss a photo-opportunity during a visit to one of the hallowed centres of British education. They were smiling, shaking hands, nodding thanks to all in sundry and generally proving what fine chaps they were. To be fair, the onlookers were thrilled to be so close to their leader; enthusiastic hands were thrust forward to be shaken—after all, he was the people's PM and they wanted to share the moment.

Somerton lined up the Yalguzag and fixed his eye to the telescopic gun sight. *I must remember to give the eyepiece a wipe when I'm done.* Croudace came into view in the lens, causing Somerton to whistle—the Foreign Secretary seemed to be standing only a few yards away. *Hmm, whatever your shortcomings, gun, it isn't your telescopic sight. I reckon it's German, Japanese or maybe Chinese, definitely not made in Azerbaijan.*

Good lad, Alan. Croudace was wearing the regimental tie. *What about you, Colin?* He eased the rifle over a few centimetres and focussed on MacKinnon. His tie was sky blue, a nod to the traditional Conservative colour but brighter and newer. *Very pretty, Colin.* He moved the gun back and forth between the two men, waiting for them to get clear of the crowd. MacKinnon was talking, smiling, listening and seemingly enjoying the occasion.

Britain's Foreign Secretary stood aside, his face deadpan; whatever his true feelings, they weren't on display. *I wonder what you two talked about on the journey. As for you, Colin, you're showing no signs of guilt or even concern about what lies ahead. It's just business as usual for you; you don't give a fuck that you've signed your mate's death warrant.*

Eventually, Croudace stepped forward and said something to MacKinnon, presumably that it was time to go. The PM nodded and turned to give a final wave to the crowd before making his way into the college grounds. Policemen moved swiftly in behind the two politicians, ready to stop the more enthusiastic members of the crowd from following. At the other end of the driveway, university officials were making their way hurriedly towards the VIPs; the message must have gotten through to them that the PM had decided to walk through the grounds, not drive up to the building as previously advised. The two men were well clear of the crowd now, their security staff walking a few yards either side of them on the college lawns.

Somerton gritted his teeth and concentrated; it wouldn't be the first time he had killed, but never a friend. He steadied himself and held his breath, took final aim and squeezed the trigger. The noise of the shot wouldn't be heard over those damned bells. He didn't see his target hit the ground but there was no need to hang around; he'd seen the spurt of blood and was certain his shot had been successful. Security staff, guns drawn, rushed forwards to form a protective shield; a second shot wouldn't have been possible.

He took a brief second to wipe the eyepiece with a tissue, then dropped the rifle onto the landing floor. Speed was all important now and his descent down the steel ladder was rapid. From there, he raced down the stone steps two at a time and crossed to the door, inching it open a fraction to look out into the church. *Good, the pews are empty.* He made his exit from the bell tower staircase, pulling off the latex gloves and stuffing them into his rucksack as he went. He donned his woollen gloves as he ran along the aisle to the vestry where he planned to leave by the rear door.

Happily, the key was still in the lock where he'd seen it during his previous visit. Taking a deep breath to compose himself, he opened the door and stepped out into the sunlight, smiling when he saw that the vicinity was deserted; presumably, all the locals were lining the PM's route. His smile broadened as he pulled the door closed behind him and left the church in its natural state of serenity. The bells meanwhile continued to ring out in celebration of an occasion that had gone catastrophically wrong.

Sirens were screaming from the direction of the college but there were no passers-by, no dog-walkers, not even a passing vehicle to worry about. Luck was with him, there wasn't a soul in sight. He picked up his pace and was back in his car in just twelve minutes, his heart still pounding as he settled behind the wheel and started up the engine. Every impulse was urging him to put his foot down and get out of Oxford as quickly as possible, but he calmed himself and drove away steadily like any other law-abiding citizen.

He removed the beanie and eased off the false moustache, he was back to being good old Jack Somerton. Now was the time to blend into the world of anonymity and not risk attracting attention by speed or squealing tyres. If he did get caught up in a police roadblock, he would use his identity card to show he was the National Security Advisor and just quietly checking out the policing arrangements for the Prime Minister's visit.

In the event, his journey out of Oxford was normality itself; the public seemed to be going about its daily routine, unaware of the assassination that had just taken place. Somerton reached the southbound motorway slip road without incident, knowing then that he was in the clear. *Service station first stop, Jack.* He felt drained and ravenous, he needed to eat and relieve the nervous tension that filled his whole being.

Back on the college driveway, a lifeless body was being loaded into an ambulance. Police were holding back shocked onlookers; university dignitaries stood numbed, their day of celebration had been turned on its head; it would now be remembered for all the wrong reasons.

Joe Public had no idea what had just occurred. 'What happened?' asked one.

'Someone collapsed on the drive, I think.' A bystander offered the explanation without any real conviction.

'How come there are so many police vehicles?'

'Don't know, maybe there's been a terrorist alert.'

'Must be serious, there's an ambulance just gone in. Probably one of the old Dons has had a heart attack, the excitement must have gotten to him.'

'What's happened?'

'I think someone has had an accident.'

'I hope the PM's all right.'

Voices asking questions, no one had the answers; they'd find out later.

Police cars continued to arrive in numbers, flooding the crime scene as they always did. Roadblocks had been set up although the police had no idea who they were looking for. Two of the main players were long gone, the third was with his Maker. House to house enquiries were already in progress, witnesses were being sought and the media was clamouring for a statement. Camera crews were already lining vantage points and a police helicopter flew around in circles, scouring the college grounds.

It didn't take long before the church of St Mary Magdalene was identified as the sniper's lair; the church's place in history was assured. It would be full to the rafters at the next service, albeit the priest could not be sure of his congregation's motivation. From that day forth, St Mary's would find itself included on the itinerary of every visiting tourist, its annual income boosted for many years to come. God works in mysterious ways, some might say.

Chapter 37
Motorway Service Plaza

Somerton finished his full English breakfast and took one last look at the TV screen; there was only one event being reported. Bewildered watchers gathered around, fingers pointing, gasps of astonishment the norm; this just didn't happen in the United Kingdom. He had been the architect of the deed, and its executioner, but it didn't lessen his profound sense of loss. Guilt shrouded him as he walked back to his car, futilely trying to banish all thoughts of what he had just done. *Leave it, Jack, what's done is done. It's history now, forget it.* But he knew it would be a long time, perhaps never, before he could even begin to forget. *He'd lost a very dear friend.*

The media theatre would raise the curtain, journalists would plough over the killing unremittingly, repeat the same facts over and over, introduce irrelevant human-interest articles, manufacture their own headline grabbing conspiracy theories. The next 72 hours would be saturated with irrelevant questions, ludicrous speculation and a welter of tributes.

Years would pass before the assassination was consigned to the history books; every anniversary would see the event rerun and new conspiracy theories emerge. *Drop it, Jack, get it out of your head.* He wondered if he should avoid the TV and media people but as National Security Advisor and a colleague of long standing, he knew that wouldn't be possible; he would be tracked down and expected to comment.

NRSC

Somerton drew up at the security barrier and the guard came out to check the car over; Stan Davies knew who he was dealing with, but procedure still had to be followed. He couldn't be lax just because it was the boss.

Davies gave the car a cursory once over. 'I'll have you through in a jiffy, Mr Somerton.' He turned to go then stopped. 'Terrible business! What's the world coming to? Dreadful and cowardly, he was a good man; the bastard that did it should be strung up. You knew him, of course, served with him, I believe?'

'Yes, we were in the SAS together. He was a first-class officer and a close friend, one of the best. Now if you don't mind, I don't feel like talking about it, it's been a great shock.'

'Understood Sir; I'll go and attend to the barrier.'

He passed through the main entrance to the control area, nodding in response to greetings. There was no banter, no smiles, just grim nods of unspoken sympathy. They were all aware of the SAS connection and knew he would want to be alone with his thoughts. Questions would be asked of him as the National Security Advisor and he'd have to have answers at the ready. *Had nothing shown up on the Internet? Was anything missed? Were the surveillance systems as good as they should be? Had he ordered a review of recent internet traffic?*

Every assurance would have to be given that the tragic event could not have been prevented. Questions were to be expected; he was the man in the hot seat, the man responsible for national security, and it had failed.

Somerton had to play his part and he called his staff to attention. 'Listen up. You know what's happened and we're involved whether we like it or not; questions *will* be asked of us. We must be ready for whatever is thrown at us, so I want every line of every bit of internet traffic in the last three months gone over with a fine-tooth comb to see if we missed anything. Work what hours you want till the job's done; go to it.'

'Will GCHQ be doing the same, Jack?'

'I don't give a shit what Cheltenham is doing, get on with it.'

Commands issued, Somerton turned on his heel and took refuge in his office.

Nothing further was said; when Jack Somerton was in this kind of mood, it was best to keep your head down.

Friday, Three Days Before the Assassination

Somerton closed his office shutter blinds, isolating himself from his staff. This act of hiding away was unusual on his part but they would assume something big was going on requiring his urgent attention.

He lifted his phone and went through to the switchboard. 'It's Jack Somerton, no calls for the next hour please, nobody is to be put through about anything.'

The switchboard operator raised an eyebrow but made no comment. 'Noted, Mr Somerton.'

He made his way down the stairs to the lower corridor and from there to a secure storage area where he punched in a four-digit code, pushed the door open and stepped inside. His personal locker stood immediately to his right, more of a safe than a locker. It was secure and fireproof; it too was protected by a four-digit access code known only to himself.

Ever the soldier and strategist, he had planned for this eventuality, not that he had ever expected it to arise but that was what insurance was for, after all. The equipment and tools he required were on the lower shelf; a large canvas bag, two small gas cylinders along with their interconnecting pipework and two adjustable spanners. But first, he had to put on a high filtration face mask, an essential for what lay ahead.

At the design stage of the NRSC, he had spent several hours poring over the construction drawings, searching for weak points that could be exploited by a terrorist or an oddball extremist seeking to damage the setup. He'd found a few vulnerable spots and had altered the designs accordingly, all except one that is, and that was where he was headed now. Somerton loaded up the bag with the items he'd removed from the cupboard and crossed the room to a small door leading to the under-croft below the NRSC.

Headroom was limited, he had to crawl under pipes and drains in some places, making him wish he had worn overalls to protect his suit. The area he had accessed covered about a quarter of the NRSC floor area and was a mass of pipework and electrical services. Like most under-crofts enclosed by concrete walls, the atmosphere was warm and stuffy due to lack of air movement and heat gain from the myriad of pipes. Fortunately, it was well illuminated, but the lighting added to the heat and he felt himself beginning to sweat, not helped by the tension he felt. The weakness in the system he had come to exploit was in the furthest corner where it was least likely to be noticed. The installation had been entirely his idea; it would never have been sanctioned by MacKinnon, but it had been instilled in him in his SAS days to "prepare for the unexpected", and the unexpected had arrived.

He tightened the mask around his face and set to work. It took less than ten minutes to remove the two flanges and the short length of pipework that connected them. Polluted air would now be escaping from the open ends of the

321

detached pipework, not that he could see it or hear it, and maybe it wasn't all that harmful, but the high filtration mask would ensure his safety.

The preassembled pipework arrangement fitted perfectly. The construction manager had queried his request at the time, and he'd explained that it would only be used in the event of unlawful occupation. The downstream side of the tee piece was, in effect, a blanking plate; the upstream side an open connection to the pipework running to Jupiter's inner sanctum. He'd never fully come to terms with the idea of an unknown entity with so much power being able to shut himself away in a bombproof, fireproof, radiation-proof fortress. So, during the early construction stages, when his distrust and caution had prevailed, he'd introduced this unauthorised access point into the system.

The assembly allowed him to connect twin gas cylinders to Jupiter's air supply, controlled by an electronic activation device that would open the two valves and release their deadly contents into Jupiter's area. The cylinders would inject a lethal cocktail, germ and nerve gas from one and radioactive charged air from the other. It could spread through Jupiter's accommodation in a matter of hours, a lethal, silent concoction that would ensure his demise.

The cylinders were souvenirs from the Middle East, just two of the eclectic mix of 'souvenirs' he'd gathered over time and by far the most hazardous. The pressurised gasses when released would slowly percolate through Jupiter's drainage system and fill his personal kingdom with the deadly toxic mix. The system was now set to go, a signal from his telephone was all that was needed to trigger the release mechanism. It struck him as ironic that Jupiter would die as the result of a mobile telephone signal in the same way as David Singleton's life was ended and lifelong misery brought to his wife and family.

If I have to do the deed I just wish I could be there to see you suffer and stand over your dead body. It'll be goodbye Jupiter, mystery man. It would be a pity about the young woman currently attending Jupiter, Monica Coulson, another regrettable slice of collateral damage.

When the deed was done, he would have to ensure that the area remained sealed in perpetuity, or at least long into the future, and he could give good reason why that was the case. One day, access would be taken and provide another source of investigation and speculation, but by then, Jack Somerton would have joined the ranks of the departed. Job done, he removed the face mask and hung it over the gas cylinders ready for when he returned to recover them a few days hence.

It would be a tough decision, when and if the moment arrived, to eliminate the genius who had propelled the UK to the forefront of science and innovation. But there was no denying that the surveillance system installed in the soon-to-be launched satellites was under Jupiter's sole control and that posed a serious risk; Alan was right about that, it placed too much power in Jupiter's hands. But Somerton still wanted the UK to have the power the system offered and the opportunity it had to make the world a safer place; a safeguard had to be put in place, a bit of insurance.

The other difficult question was the future of the researchers in the NRSC; Jupiter was their unseen trump card and they would be bereft of the solutions and ideas he could plant in their subconscious. That was on the debit side. *Well tough luck boys and girls, you will just have to stand on your own two feet in the event Jupiter was no longer around. Surely, with the advanced intelligence they had been gifted, they could continue to lead the world. And the girls had to be brought into the equation, countless young women would live out their lives spared from whatever Jupiter subjected them to; that was a big plus.*

Somerton checked the system over one last time and, happy with it, made his way back to his office to tidy up and get ready for the day ahead. That done he settled down at his desk and poured himself a goodly measure of whisky, a congratulatory drink as he styled it. He toasted himself, 'Well done, Jack, old son, we've now got a safety mechanism should Jupiter either refuse to activate the surveillance system or not use it as directed.' He'd always had his concerns about the power Jupiter exercised over Colin, and it would still be there, but at least they now had a sanction of last resort in their armoury.

Chapter 38
Monday

Dimitri Vladic, along with most of the population, was gripped by the killing and tuned in to watch the latest news on television when he got home. He gasped when he saw the Church of St Mary Magdalene and listened intently to the reporter standing in front of it.

'The police believe that the assassin fired from the bell tower of the church behind me and have confirmed that evidence has been removed from the scene, which they hope will lead to an arrest.'

Vladic shook his head. 'Amazing! What a fucking coincidence; I can't believe that I was in the area when this happened.' A passing thought struck him. *Maybe it wasn't a coincidence? Maybe his unnamed drug dealer had deliberately set up their meeting in that area? But why him? It didn't make sense; no, it was just one of those chances in a million that happen from time to time.* 'Calm down, don't get fucking paranoid, Dimitri.'

The reporter ended his piece by issuing the usual request. 'The police are appealing for anyone who may have been in the area around the church this morning to come forward. Any information could assist the police with their enquiries.'

Vladic pursed his lips; he had been there, but he wouldn't be easy to track down. And even if the police did catch up with him, he couldn't have left any evidence in the bell tower, he hadn't been anywhere near it. Nevertheless, given the purpose of his visit to Oxford and the fact that he had entered that very church was an extraordinary coincidence. It left him feeling very uneasy. 'Fuck it! Why do these things have to happen?'

Scotland Yard

Detective Sergeant Ollie Hinds could hardly contain his excitement as he pushed his way into his inspector's office. 'We've just hit the jackpot, guvnor, the DNA report on the cigarette ends is back from the lab and we have a suspect. Our man is Dimitri Vladic, a small-time drug dealer, arrested and convicted four years ago. He's a Ukrainian national, seems to have dropped off the radar after that little episode. His present whereabouts are unknown.'

Inspector Steve Anson jumped to his feet and punched the air. 'Let's get after him then! If we catch this bastard quickly, fame and promotion is guaranteed; ignore the budget, set every wheel in motion.'

He appraised the photograph Hinds had handed to him. 'Hmm, not a bad-looking bloke, I suppose, though those eyes of his have a touch of nasty about them. Now how do we play this? We don't want him flying off to Ukraine if news gets out that we're onto him. I guess the bastard could be anywhere in the country, but we'll start here in London where we last picked him up. One of his old buddies might give us a line on his whereabouts. One thing strikes me as odd though, this business seems way out of his league.'

Hinds shrugged. 'Villains will do anything if the price is right; the records show that he used to be a mercenary, so he'll know how to use a rifle.'

Anson's eyes narrowed. 'Now that is interesting, he'd have the capability and killing would have been routine to him. Keep this lead away from the media for now and make it clear to our lot that if anybody tips off the press, I'll have their balls on a plate.'

Ollie Hinds sniggered. 'What if it's one of the girls?'

'Ha, ha. Very funny, I'll think of something. Now get up off your arse and get an undercover team making enquiries in his old haunts; somebody must know where he is.'

Two days later, the two men sat opposite each other in Anson's office. 'Might have something, Guv. One of the local lowlife reckons Vladic is still around but it's only a whisper he picked up, a friend of a friend and all that, hasn't personally seen or heard of him for a while. Talk is he still deals in drugs and runs a few girls.'

Anson nodded. 'It's a start. Maybe he moved out of the London area, maybe he's changed his identity or his appearance, or both for that matter. Who knows what he's been up to? At this time, your lead is all we've got; get some photos circulated, no names though. He had a moustache at the time of his arrest so maybe he's shaved it off. Have a photo doctored and circulate both versions around the usual sleaze holes.'

The Black Cat Nightclub, Soho
Later that Week

Tony Benetoni, the club's barman, studied the latest arrival as he made his way through the clientele towards the bar; he had been on the alert following the recent visit by the CID. Normally, he tried not to get involved with the law, but this was big; the club would benefit from the limelight and free publicity that would ensue if it was somehow involved in an arrest. More customers would bring in more cash and that meant a bigger bonus for him, maybe even a pay rise.

The "wanted" photos he'd been given lay on the shelf beneath the counter; there was something familiar about the guy, although so many punters passed through, he couldn't be sure. He edged out a photo and took a close look to refresh his memory and his heart missed a beat, it *was* him; his wish had been granted. There was no doubt about it, the new arrival was the guy in the photo complete with moustache, either that or his twin brother. *It's him, Tony my boy, no doubt about it.* He watched the man ease his way through the crowded floor to the bar; his nerves were jangling now; if the police were right, the man was a cold-blooded killer. Benetoni gathered his courage and moved along the bar. 'Good evening, sir, what can I get you?'

'Vodka on ice.' There was a trace of a foreign accent and those eyes of his, just like in the photo, had an evil look about them. There wasn't a shadow of doubt now, it was the man in the photo; just like it said in the details, he was tall, and he was foreign.

'Coming up, sir.' He gave the guy a generous measure, dropped in the ice and pushed the glass forwards. His mouth had gone dry, he could feel his heart thumping. 'That'll be six quid, sir.' Not a bad price by Soho standards, the Black Cat kept its prices down and that brought in the customers.

Without a word, Vladic pulled a tenner from his wallet, threw it onto the bar and moved away. 'Thank you, sir,' Benetoni called after him, 'very generous.' He shoved the tenner in the till, rang up the cost of Vladic's vodka and pocketed the change. He watched Vladic seating himself then went directly to his manager's office, knocked on the door and entered without waiting for a reply.

'He's here,' he said excitedly, 'he's here, Charlie.'

Henderson raised his eyes and hunched his shoulders. 'Who are you talking about, Tony? Give me a hint, I'm stumped.'

'The bloke in the CID flyer, he's here, that's who.'

'Shit, that's all we need, I must get on to the Met tout suite. Now where the hell is that telephone number the Yard gave us. I hope to fuck they can do this discreetly. I don't want our customers upset.'

Benetoni waved his hands excitedly. 'Think about the publicity, Charlie, business will go through the roof.'

Henderson chewed on his biro thoughtfully and wagged it at the barman. 'You might be right, Tony.' He reached for the phone and punched in the number on the police circular.

'Hello, this is Charlie Henderson, manager of the Black Cat in Soho. I'm calling about those photos you left with us a few days ago, the guy just walked in a few minutes ago.'

'Hold on, Mr Henderson; I'll pass you to Inspector Anson.' Henderson drummed his fingers on the desk whilst the voice spoke to another voice.

'Anson speaking. Where is the man at this moment?'

'Don't know, I can't see him from my office. He's probably sitting at one of the tables drinking.' Benetoni nodded his affirmation.

'Try to keep him there; I'll get a squad around just as quickly as I can.'

Henderson gulped. 'I hope there won't be any trouble, I don't want my customers upset; it could affect tonight's takings.'

'We're not looking for trouble, Mr Henderson, but we have to do whatever it takes. Just bear in mind, if you're right and it is our man, he's a killer.'

Charlie Henderson's brain had gone into hyperdrive. Tony was right about the publicity and he fancied playing the hero provided there were no risks involved. 'I've just had a thought, Inspector. Is there any chance you could get a couple of your guys into my office and I'll get your villain in here on some pretext or other? Then you can pick him up nice and easy and my customers will be none the wiser.'

It was Anson's turn to think quickly; he shouldn't really put a member of the public in danger, but the suggestion was viable. An arrest this early on, with no bloodshed or hassle, would work wonders for his career. 'I'll weigh up the situation when I get there, Mr Henderson, but I like the sound of your idea, it could well be worth a try. Who do I ask for when I get there?'

'Go to the bar and ask for Tony.'

'OK Mr Henderson, we're on our way. Do everything you can to keep our man there but don't put yourself in any danger.'

The Black Cat's owner licked his lips nervously. 'Will do.' *Have no fear, Inspector, I'm a serious coward.*

Within ten minutes of the call, two armed police response units were on station a short distance away from the Black Cat. Other officers were closing the road to traffic at both ends and keeping the public away from the vicinity of the club. In the meantime, four plainclothes officers, two male and two female, made their way into the Black Cat.

Just like any other couples enjoying a night out, they looked around the room for somewhere to stand or sit. They spotted Vladic almost immediately but gave him little more than a cursory glance to avoid any chance of arousing his suspicions. One male and one female officer claimed a vacant table near the door, the table nobody usually goes for, kissing as they sat down. Both were armed, the man's gun in a shoulder holster, the woman's in her handbag.

The other pair moved over towards the corridor leading to the toilets and the rear exit and stood there making polite conversation, nuzzling each other from time to time. They were barely two metres from Vladic who sat alone at a table in the corner of the room, quietly sipping his second vodka. He kept glancing towards the door, seemingly on the lookout for someone. The male detective, Jeff Coleman, excused himself. 'I must go to the loo, darling, you get the drinks in.' In fact, he was on his way to cover the club's rear exit, leaving his partner, Detective Constable Susie Attwater, to sidle over to the bar and order two white wine spritzers. She didn't acknowledge Inspector Anson and Sergeant Hinds when she saw them enter.

Anson smiled at the barman who smiled back. 'What can I get you, sir?'

'I'm looking for Tony Benetoni.'

'You have me in one, mate. Do I know you?'

'Not really. We're following up a chat we had with your manager earlier on; I think you'll find he's expecting us.' Anson gave him the eye. 'Perhaps you could take us to his office?'

Benetoni's eyes widened, recognition dawning. 'Gotcha, follow me.'

When he got to Henderson's door, he knocked once and pushed the door open. 'Charlie,' he said in a loud voice, 'your friends are here. Please go straight in, gentlemen.'

Anson wasted no time on preliminaries. 'Let's make this quick, Mr Henderson, before Vladic recognises any of my team or gets suspicious. We're good at what we do but we don't know how good he is and, more importantly, we don't know if he's armed. Have you come up with an idea for getting him in here? I don't want you to overdo the persuasion or take any risks; if he is in any way reluctant, leave him be and we'll deal with him.'

Not for the first time, Henderson mused the idea over in his head. His heart was already pounding, his palms were sweaty, his temperature was going up by the second. *Christ, what if he's armed? What if he takes me hostage?* But the thought of newspaper headlines and TV interviews won out. 'How do you think it would go down if I offered him a free bottle of Moet and a free year's club membership?'

Anson raised his eyebrows. 'If you can come up with a reason for the offer, I'd come to your office for that kind of a freebie any day of the week though I'd wonder what the catch was. Just do what you feel comfortable with, most of us like something for nothing; keep calm and you'll be fine.'

Henderson felt fear creeping in; the moment had arrived and his courage was on the wane. 'I hope my idea works and he doesn't turn nasty. I will be OK, won't I, your people will step in if needs be?'

Ollie Hinds put a reassuring hand on his shoulder. 'It'll be OK, I promise; we've got four armed officers out there and I'll be amazed if he's carrying a weapon. He knows these places get raided from time to time; he'll be as clean as a whistle. I think he's waiting for a bit of skirt, his mind's on other things.'

Henderson nodded, though he still didn't feel confident, but he'd made the offer and he'd go through with it. 'Thanks for that.' Without another word, he stepped out of the office closing the door behind him; a story he'd tell for the rest of his life taking shape in his thoughts. A glance at his watch showed him it was 10.33, perfect. Drawing himself up to maximum height, he rallied his courage and tried to relax. *Mr Vladic, here I come.* He smiled, put on an air of confidence he didn't feel, and strode purposefully over to his target's table. 'Sorry to interrupt, sir, but I think you'll find it worthwhile.'

Vladic looked up, suspicious but curious. 'Make it quick, I might have company joining me any minute now.'

Henderson smiled. *God, he must hear my heart pounding.* 'Well, I think you're going to like this, you are this week's lucky guest. Whoever is sitting at this table at 10.30, that's the time I've set for this week only, wins a free bottle of champagne plus, if you want, you can sign up for a free year's membership of the club. Gets you into all our event nights free of charge. What do you say to that?'

Vladic beamed. 'My lucky day. You have my full attention, what do I have to do?'

Henderson was warming to his role, it was proving to be a piece of cake, his plan was going to work. 'If you'll follow me to my office to sign up; just a formality, it won't take a minute.'

'What about my table? I don't want to lose it.'

Henderson signalled to one of the floor waitresses. 'June, reserve this table until this gentleman returns. Then bring him a bottle of champagne and two glasses, on the house. Don't open the bubbly till he gets back.'

June Rush blinked, mildly astonished; she'd worked in the Black Cat for three years and had never known Charlie Henderson to give away anything for free, but she just nodded and smiled dutifully at Vladic. 'Your table will be here for you when you get back, sir.'

'This way please.' Henderson motioned to Vladic and led the way through the crowd to the office, opening the door and ushering his guest in with a flourish, bowing from the waist. 'After you, sir.'

Vladic regarded him briefly with mild amusement. *All he'd done was sit at a fucking table! But who cares, a free bottle of fizz was well worth playing along for.* The unsuspecting Vladic stepped into the room and was taken completely by surprise when Henderson gave him a violent push in the back and pulled the door closed with a bang. The Ukrainian stumbled forward and almost fell. 'What the fuck.'

Recovering his balance, he caught sight of a man rising from behind the desk, pointing an automatic at him. Reflexes made him momentarily half turn to make an escape and that was when he saw the other man, who must have been concealed by the opening door; he too held an automatic.

'Hands behind your back,' snarled Anson.

'What is this? I don't know you. You've got the wrong guy.'

'Do as you're fucking told, Mr Vladic.'

They know my name! Reluctantly, Vladic put his hands behind his back; he didn't have to be a genius to work out what was going to happen next.

'Legs apart.' Anson motioned to the Ukrainian.

Vladic sighed and complied, resigned to doing what they wanted. Ollie Hinds holstered his automatic, then stepped forwards and put on the cuffs. His prisoner secured, he carried out the standard police search, nodding at Anson when he'd finished. 'He's clean; let's go.'

'What the fuck do you want, who the fuck are you?' Vladic snarled, starting to regain his composure 'Where are you taking me?'

'Scotland Yard. We've got some questions for you.'

Vladic's eyes widened. He was confused but relieved that this wasn't some gangland business that might end up with him floating in the Thames or lying at the bottom of a big hole covered with a concrete blanket. 'Aren't you supposed to caution me?'

'Take it as read, Vladic, you know the score.'

'Am I under arrest?'

Hinds chortled. 'Of course, you're under arrest, we're not here for your fucking autograph.'

'What's the charge?'

Ollie Hinds stood in front of him and looked Vladic straight in the eye, their faces no more than a hand's width apart. 'What's the charge? Let's think now. Got it! I don't like fucking foreigners, that'll have to do for now.'

Anson stepped forward from behind the desk. 'Turn around, Vladic, we're leaving. If you know what's good for you, don't cause any trouble out there; we're authorised to shoot to kill.'

Vladic motioned with his manacled wrists. 'Does it look like I could cause any fucking trouble? I'm not Harry Houdini! Just wait till my lawyer gets you.'

Jeff Coleman smiled when he saw Vladic enter the corridor, closely followed by his two colleagues. 'What a sweet operation, guv, Britain's most wanted, apprehended and not a blow struck.'

Vladic looked at him, puzzled, not comprehending what had been said, but concluded it was probably sarcasm and let the moment pass.

Chapter 39
Scotland Yard Interview Room 1
Next Morning

Vladic was led into the interview room where he was directed to take a seat opposite Anson and Hinds. He was angry and tired; he'd hardly slept with the constant inspections carried out overnight by the on-duty police officers. The bunk had been uncomfortable and it had seemed to him that each time he was on the point of sleep, someone had noisily slid back the cell door grill to carry out an inspection of whatever it was they wanted to inspect. *Bastards don't want me to sleep.* His breakfast had comprised a small bowl of porridge and a lukewarm cup of tea.

'I want to call my solicitor. I'm not answering any questions until my solicitor is present.'

Inspector Anson sighed. 'I was hoping we could ask a few questions for elimination purposes. Who knows? You might not need one.'

Vladic regarded him warily, thought about complying then changed his mind. *These bastards were always setting traps and once you fell into one, it was a major job climbing out. Anyway, they can eliminate me from their enquiries with my solicitor present.* 'No comment.'

Ollie Hinds tried a soft approach. 'C'mon, Dimitri, if you help us, we might be able to help you.'

The Ukrainian glared at him. 'It's Mr Vladic to you and you can forget the nice guy bad guy crap. I want to call my solicitor right this minute; I wanted to call one last night and you wouldn't let me. As far as I'm concerned, you haven't gone by the book and I'll be making a formal complaint.' That said, Vladic sat back in his seat, folded his arms and focussed his eyes on the ceiling, a smile flickering momentarily over his lips.

Anson nodded. 'Have it your way.' He rose to his feet, his pulse quickening with the realisation he was about to make history. 'Dimitri Vladic. I am arresting you for the murder of Colin MacKinnon, Prime Minister of the United Kingdom. You do not…'

Vladic sat open-mouthed, numbed; the rest of Anson's statutory caution heard but not heard. He shook his head, bewildered; this couldn't be happening. 'Are you mad? Why would I want to kill the Prime Minister?'

'That's what we're here to find out, Mr Vladic, but you've made it clear you won't talk to us without your solicitor present; so, give me his name and we'll make the call.'

Vladic shook his head, still dazed. 'This is crazy, it's Edmund Montague of Montague, Price and Evans.'

Anson nodded at his sergeant. 'Make the call, Ollie. Stress the urgency, we don't want to keep Mr Vladic waiting any longer than necessary.' Hinds nodded and left the two men together.

Vladic's hands were shaking, something he'd never experienced. His thoughts were in turmoil as he asked himself over and over why this was happening. 'I don't suppose I can have a smoke?'

Anson shook his head. 'Sorry, left to me, you could smoke fifty an hour, but rules are rules, smoking isn't allowed. What about a cup of tea?'

Vladic nodded. 'Coffee, black, no sugar would be better.'

Anson signalled to the watchful PC standing guard at the door. 'Sort out a coffee for Mr Vladic, please.'

The gravity of the situation, coupled with the opportunity of media headlines, resulted in just thirty minutes passing before Edmund Montague arrived and was immediately shown into Interview Room 1. Anson and Hinds introduced themselves and shook hands with the new arrival. Montague nodded at Vladic then turned back to Anson. 'I'd like some time alone with my client, Inspector.'

'Certainly, Mr Montague, have as much time as you need.'

Montague, tall and portly, wore a navy-blue single-breasted business suit accompanied by a bright red waistcoat, his personal trademark. With a slightly jowly rather tubby face and distinctly reddish cheeks, he was showing the results of two of his favourite preoccupations, overeating and regular alcohol consumption. Still, with his intelligent countenance and searching eyes, all in all he was impressive, a man who exuded the confidence to be expected of a society solicitor.

Left alone, Montague invited his client to go through the events leading to his arrest, which Vladic happily did, protesting his innocence at regular intervals. 'And there's nothing else you want to tell me, Mr Vladic? Anything at all that might be relevant? They have charged you with murder, they're not daft, they must have some reason for doing so.'

Vladic shook his head. 'Nothing, absolutely nothing, this is all a huge mistake, they've got the wrong man. I'll be engaging you to sue them for false arrest when you get me out of here.'

'As you will, Mr Vladic; I'll get Anson and his sergeant back in here. Say nothing unless I give you the nod. Let's see what evidence they have. If what you've told me is true, I'll have you out of here within the hour.'

Anson and Hinds joined Vladic and Montague in the interrogation room; the inspector switched on the recording equipment and reminded Vladic that he was still under caution. In accordance with procedure, Anson then invited those present to state their name and that done, nodded to his sergeant to begin. Ollie Hinds had been asked to lead, with Anson ready to plug any gaps and pick up on any sticking points. 'Please state your name and address.'

'Dimitri Vladic, Flat A, 4 Copeland Street, Tottenham.'

'And that's your usual place of residence?'

'I've just told you it is,' Vladic spat out the words.

'OK, we'll leave that for now. Could I ask you to look at this photograph?' Hinds pushed across a photo of a man in combat fatigues.

Vladic glanced briefly at the photo. 'It's not me.'

Ollie Hinds smiled. 'You're sure? Please take a closer look. We know you were in the Ukrainian army and subsequently a mercenary. Enquiries are in progress with various countries that made use of your services, but it would save time if you acknowledged that the man in this photo is you.'

This time, Vladic lifted the photo and studied it at length. 'I suppose it could be me, it's not a very good photo.' He pushed the photo back to Hinds. 'I'm not sure.'

'Hm, I think it's quite a good likeness but let's park the photo for now. Do you acknowledge that you were in the Ukrainian Army, rose to the rank of Captain and went on to serve as a mercenary in various conflicts? I have asked the Ukrainian authorities for your military service history and it should arrive in the next few days. It'll save time if you would confirm what I've just said.'

Vladic sighed. 'I was in the army, OK? So were lots of people.'

'Take a close look at this please.' Hinds pushed across another photograph. 'This was taken at Kensington Police Station in 2016. According to the records, you were arrested and subsequently found guilty of various drugs offences. This is definitely a photograph of you, is it not?'

Vladic knew there was no point denying the fact. He was beginning to feel increasingly uneasy. 'Yes.'

'Thank you. You'll remember that when this photograph was taken, Mr Vladic, your fingerprints and DNA were also taken and have been held on record since that time. You *are* aware of that, aren't you?'

'Yes.'

'Mr Vladic.' Hinds paused momentarily for effect. 'Can you recall where you were on Monday, 6th June, between the hours of 9.30 am and 11.30 am?'

Fear gripped Vladic. *Christ, they know I was in Oxford, they're trying to tie me to the crime scene.* 'I can't remember.' He looked at his solicitor for guidance, but Montague just shrugged.

Hinds sighed loudly for effect. 'Let me help refresh your memory, Mr Vladic.' He slowly and deliberately laid out a series of photographs, each with date and time clearly visible; all showed the Ukrainian driving past the new Oxford college. Three had been taken via police shoulder-mounted cameras, three others by onlookers using either a phone or camera. All six clearly showed a white Lexus being driven past the college entrance by Vladic.

The Ukrainian gazed at them, dumbstruck. *Oh my God, the bastards really are trying to fit me up.* He looked at Montague imploringly, who leaned over and whispered to his client to tell the truth. He had no doubt that Vladic was the driver of the car in the photograph.

Ollie Hinds pressed for a reply. 'I ask again. The driver of the car in the photographs is you, Mr Vladic, is that not so?'

'Yes,' Vladic croaked; his voice barely a whisper.

'Could you speak up for the tape please, Mr Vladic?'

The Ukrainian thumped his fist onto the table and shouted, 'Yes, fucking yes; it is me, but I had nothing to do with the killing. I was there on business.'

Ollie Hinds leaned back in his chair, feigning a look of surprise at the man's outburst. 'Please calm down, Mr Vladic. We're just trying to get to the truth. If you're innocent, as you say you are, you have absolutely nothing to fear. I'm sure Mr Montague will confirm that.'

An increasingly uneasy Montague squeezed his client's arm and whispered something in his ear. Vladic nodded and took a drink of water, breathing deeply and trying to control the fear and confusion that engulfed him.

'Does the car in this photograph belong to you?' Hinds passed another photograph across the table. 'It's a white Lexus, the same car as in the other photos.' He paused briefly. 'The difference being, in this instance, you can see the number plate quite clearly.'

Vladic nodded, there was no point in denying that the car was his.

'For the purpose of the tape, Mr Vladic has indicated that the car shown in the photograph does indeed belong to him.' Hinds stroked his chin theatrically. 'I confess I'm puzzled now, Mr Vladic, because the vehicle in the photograph is registered to one Alan Rich, 14 Carrington Place, Hampstead. Are you also known as Alan Rich, Mr Vladic?'

Vladic looked anxiously at Edmund Montague, who was now having his own doubts about his client. 'I'm advising my client to say nothing at this juncture, pending further discussion with myself, Inspector.'

'No problem, Mr Montague.' Anson glanced at his watch. 'Interview terminated at 11.28 am. When do you suggest we can resume questioning your client?'

Montague pursed his lips and looked closely at Vladic; what his client had told him didn't match up with what he had witnessed so far, something was clearly amiss. 'Can I suggest 3.30; that will give me time to confer with my client, have lunch and make some calls?'

Anson nodded. '3.30 will be fine, Mr Montague. In the meantime, we'll leave you with your client.' He and Hinds stood and left the room, leaving Vladic and his solicitor under the watchful eye of a duty policeman stationed outside the cell door.

Interview Room 1

Later that Day

The four principals gathered again; the recording machine was switched on and the usual procedure followed. Anson had decided he would lead on this occasion but before he could begin, Montague made an opening statement. 'I am advising my client not to answer any questions put to him at this time.'

Anson shrugged. 'That, of course, is his privilege, Mr Montague. As you know, the court will give due regard to his silence.'

'Quite so, Inspector, but his presence in court will depend upon the view taken by the Director of Public Prosecution in light of the evidence put before her.' Montague sat back in his chair, his face betraying no emotion.

Anson nodded. 'Of course. Perhaps it would help if I ran through that evidence so that you and your client are better informed as to where we're up to with our investigations?' Montague nodded and Anson continued, 'The facts, as we've been able determine them to date, are as follows:

One. You are Dimitri Vladic, a Ukrainian national. We can find no record of you having British citizenship. You were in the Ukrainian army for eight years, attaining the rank of Captain before resigning and becoming a mercenary. It would follow from your military history that you are familiar with firearms.

Two. You were found guilty of drug offences four years ago and your photographs, fingerprints and DNA analysis are held on the Central Criminal Records System.

Three. You also go by the name of Alan Rich. You own a white Lexus and are the owner of 14 Carrington Place, Hampstead, although when asked for your current place of residence, you claimed it was 4 Copeland Street, Tottenham.'

Vladic interrupted, his voice croaky, 'That's my business address and I sometimes stay there overnight.'

Montague shook his head and raised a finger to his lips.

Anson smiled and continued with his evidence; he was enjoying every moment.

'Four. I obtained a warrant to search your Hampstead property and this was undertaken yesterday. During that search, cigarette ends were recovered from your kitchen and these have undergone DNA analysis. Also, fifty thousand Euro notes, in mint condition, were recovered from a wardrobe in the household. You will be asked to explain how you came by such a large sum of money. We suspect it is your fee, or part of your fee, for assassinating the Prime Minister.'

Vladic was visibly trembling, looking time and time again at Montague who looked on impassively, making no comment. The odds on his client getting out of this mess were lengthening by the minute.

Anson took a drink of water before continuing; he was enjoying watching Vladic squirm.

'Five. We have also placed you in Oxford between 9.30 am and 11.30 am on the morning of 6th June, the day Prime Minister MacKinnon was assassinated. You have confirmed that you were indeed in Oxford between these hours.

Six. The marksman who shot the Prime Minister used a Yalguzag sniper rifle that was left behind at the scene where the fatal shot was discharged, namely the bell tower of St Mary Magdalene Church. There were no fingerprints or DNA on the gun, which was found on a platform near the top of the bell tower. There is a clear line of fire from the tower to the college grounds, a distance of approximately 400 metres; ballistics have confirmed that the bullet that killed the prime minister was fired from the Yalguzag found in the tower.

Seven. Four cigarette ends were recovered from the bell tower; the brand is the same as those recovered from your Hampstead property and indeed those recovered from your person when you were arrested. The bell tower cigarette ends have been subjected to DNA testing.

Eight. DNA recovered from the cigarette ends in the bell tower match those held on your criminal records. This also applies to DNA recovered from your Hampstead address and those taken from you following your arrest two days ago. This confirms that you were in the bell tower of the Church of St Mary Magdalene.'

Vladic thumped the table with his fist. 'No, no, no! I was nowhere near the place. I swear I had nothing to do with this.'

Anson took another sip of water and mustered up a false look of sympathy. 'Do please try to remain calm, Mr Vladic, I really don't want to have to place you in handcuffs.

Nine. A partial fingerprint, matching your own, was found on the church door. This proves that you visited the church very recently.

In conclusion, I put it to you, Mr Vladic, that you killed Prime Minister MacKinnon. At this point, I'm giving you the opportunity to change the statement you made verbally at the time of your arrest.'

Vladic thumped the table. 'No! No! No! I tell you I didn't do it. I'm being set up. I didn't do it, I didn't, I swear.' He turned to his solicitor, tears forming, his face filled with anguish. 'Help me, fucking help me! That's what I pay you for. For God's sake, say something, do something.'

Montague turned to Anson. 'My client has nothing to say pending further discussion with myself.'

'As you wish, Mr Montague; I will just say that the evidence I've outlined has been examined by the DPP and she has indicated her intention to prosecute Mr Vladic for the murder of our late Prime Minister. Sergeant Hinds, take Mr

Vladic back to his cell unless Mr Montague wants a further session alone with his client at this time.'

Montague shook his head. 'That won't be necessary.'

Three Months Later

Vladic was subsequently brought to trial, found guilty and sentenced to thirty years' imprisonment. He protested his innocence throughout the trial and on every opportunity that presented in the years that followed, but the case was never reopened.

At the time of the trial, Edmund Montague, not wishing to be associated with a case he couldn't win, claimed to be laid low by a virus and was unable to accompany Vladic to court. He passed the case to one of his juniors.

Chapter 40
Downing Street

Immediately following MacKinnon's assassination, Alan Croudace had, with some reluctance, accepted his party's nomination to be their new leader and so became United Kingdom's first mixed race Prime Minister. He'd taken up the reins of power with mixed feelings; Colin's death had been a devastating blow, but he had answered his party's call and was in the process of consulting his colleagues on the way forward. In this connection, he invited Somerton to meet with him to go through outstanding security issues. Business completed, the two men sat sipping a malt whisky reflecting on times gone by.

Somerton raised his glass to toast his friend. 'Here's wishing you good fortune in your new role, Alan, the country is in good hands.' The two men clinked glasses and Croudace leaned back in his chair, his eyes never leaving Somerton.

'I can't believe I'm sitting in this chair, Jack; it's not a job I ever aspired to, especially so given the circumstances. I'd like to toast our fallen comrade. To Colin, God rest his soul.'

Somerton raised his glass. 'To Colin, a good soldier, a good friend and a good man.' He took a long sip of whisky before going on. 'History will record him as one of our finest; you're stepping into big shoes, Alan.'

'Don't I know it, Jack, but I won't be hanging around after the next election. I'm wearying of politics and this business has just about brought me to my knees. I still can't believe Colin's gone.'

'Give it some time before making your mind up, Alan. Everything is still raw; it's far too soon to be taking a decision of that importance. Let the dust settle, life will start to look different after the funeral. Besides which, politics needs people of your calibre.'

'I'm not sure that I still have what it takes to stay on the political treadmill, Jack; my enthusiasm has gone. I think it died with Colin. Regards the funeral, the country will see to it that he goes out in style. The Palace has agreed that he is to have a State Funeral with a service in Westminster Abbey; details are being drawn up as we speak. All and sundry will be invited. The Prince will make a fitting tribute and I shall be doing my bit. I assume that you will want to say a few words? Along with me, you were his closest friend.'

Somerton took an internal gulp; it was wrong, he shouldn't be involved but what reason could he give for declining. He nodded, 'Of course, it will be an honour and I'll insist on wearing my uniform.'

Croudace smiled. 'He would want you to, Jack; he loved his time in the regiment and his service in that role shouldn't be overlooked. Normally, so would I, but as Prime Minister, it's probably best that I don't. I'll wear the regimental tie though.'

'That's a pity, but you're probably right, Alan. I really do hope you'll change your mind about retiring; seeing you and Colin in action has given me a taste for politics. I never had much respect for politicians until you two took up office and showed how you could get the big things done, things that really mattered to the guy in the street.'

Croudace blinked. 'Are you serious, Jack?' The tone of his voice verged on incredulity. 'You've always poured scorn on the political fraternity and to be frank, I'm not sure you're cut out for Parliamentary life. What on earth brought about this change of heart?'

'It's as I just said, the opportunity to make change, the opportunity to keep GB Limited to the forefront and to bask in glory when I succeed. I could never be a yes man or lobby fodder material, but I'd be happy to work as part of a team led by your good self. What about it, together we could build on Colin's legacy? Let's give it a go, what do you say?'

Croudace shook his head. 'Thanks for the praise, Jack, but I really don't intend to stand for re-election after this Parliament. However, if you really are serious, I'll give you my support. I remain surprised though; in fact, I'm shocked that you would entertain the idea of being a politician and find yourself fettered by the rules and convention the job demands.'

'I understand where you're coming from, Alan, but we're all getting older and even Jack Somerton can mellow. Anyway, as I said, I've seen the good that politicians like you and Colin were able to deliver and I'd like to give it a try.'

'Fair enough, Jack. I'm still sceptical but if we can find a constituency to take you on, I'll put in a good word for you.'

'I can't ask for more, Alan. I was wondering about Colin's old constituency. I assume they'll be looking for a candidate?'

Croudace looked pensive. 'Yes, they will, but they will have their own ideas as to who they want and it's their decision, not mine. Leave it with me and I'll make some enquiries; I should be able to get you on the shortlist, but I can promise no more than that. The final choice will be down to a member vote.'

'I'd be grateful if you could, Alan. I assure you I'm deadly serious. It would be better still if you stayed on; the three of us made a formidable team, an unbeatable team. We two really should carry on and build on Colin's legacy, please think about it.'

A look of sadness passed across Croudace's face. 'I'll always regret that Colin and I parted on bad terms.'

'That was just a political spat, Alan. It would have gotten sorted sooner or later. Have no doubts about that. He thought the world of you and I'll bet he still does. He always said he'd go into any battle with you at his side.'

Croudace poured another whisky and looked thoughtful. 'I've been giving some thought to what I might do when I retire and, you know what, I might just write a book. Probably an autobiography covering my career from my time in the SAS to becoming Prime Minister. Or, on the other hand, possibly a work of fiction based on a conspiracy theory around Colin's death.'

Somerton's heart missed a beat and he took another sip of whisky. *Conspiracy? Oh my God! What have you got in mind, Alan?* Somewhere inside him, alarm bells were ringing. 'Sounds good, everybody loves a conspiracy. Have you got an outline plot?'

Croudace laughed. 'Well, not really and you'll think I'm crazy but consider the kind of things that have happened around me. There's you, me and Colin and how we conspired to bring about the NRSC. There's the Canary Wharf terrorist incident, supposedly Green Freedom. There's Jupiter, who was he? Where was he from and where has he gone? I haven't heard a word from him since Colin's death.

'Then there's Colin's assassination, the death of his son and the untimely death of his son-in-law, David Singleton, the officer leading the investigation into the abductions of those young women. Then, there's the loss of memory those girls were left with, which has never been explained. And, of course, the driver that caused the crash that led to David's death was an ex-comrade of ours. An amazing coincidence, don't you think? What was Dougie MacLintock, a terminally ill man dying of cancer, doing driving a lorry on the M1 with just months to live? You see the links, don't you, tenuous though they may be?'

He paused briefly, giving Somerton the opportunity to comment but his colleague said nothing. 'And there's Vladic, Colin's killer, a small-time drug dealer, why was he chosen as the killer? The fifty thousand euros they found at his home suggests somebody paid him to, but who and why? He protested his innocence right to the end, and the Met didn't come up with any accomplices, it doesn't make sense. And another strange coincidence to consider; like you, he was a mercenary in Africa, maybe your paths crossed at some stage?'

Somerton's stomach knotted but he just shrugged. 'Can't recall ever meeting him but who knows.'

Croudace took another sip from his glass and continued, 'The weapon used, a Yalguzag, was manufactured in Azerbaijan but there's no record of Vladic ever having been there.'

Somerton shook his head. 'Not familiar with that make but you know as well as I do that guns travel around, Alan, there's no real mystery there.'

Croudace pursed his lips. 'I guess not, but it doesn't stop there. What about the timing of the assassination? Did it have anything to do with the imminent launch of the controversial UKTS2 system? An event that would have resulted in me going public on the risks involved; another extraordinary coincidence, don't you think? I'm probably in the realms of fantasy but there seem to be lots of connected threads running through that lot. Loose connections, I know, but connections nevertheless.'

Somerton shrugged. 'Coincidences do happen, Alan. None of us was looking forward to the fallout if the TS2 launch had gone ahead, but you were the main objector and I'm sure you didn't arrange for Colin to be shot. If the TS2 launch was the motivation, it would have made more sense for you to have been the victim. The launch could have gone ahead with no-one the wiser. It would make a good twist for the book, but it's off the wall as far as reality is concerned. Good luck with it though, you've got a great imagination. If you can string that list of ingredients together, it will make a fantastic story. I can't wait to read it.'

Croudace stroked his chin and looked at Somerton intently. 'Hmm, I suppose so, you're probably right. Changing tack, what do you think happened to Jupiter?'

Christ! What's going on in that head of yours, Alan? The alarm bells were sounding louder. 'God knows, Alan, he was Colin's guru. Maybe he took off when our mate got killed, or maybe some invention he was working on went wrong and he blew himself up. Or there again, maybe he and Colin had a big bust up over TS2 and it was he who had Colin assassinated. I think he's best left as lost in action; we'll survive without him.'

Croudace pursed his lips. 'I don't like mysteries, Jack, they have a nasty habit of coming back to bite you when you least expect it. I'm pondering on breaking into his area. I'll give it another week and if I don't hear from him, I'll put the necessary arrangements in hand to gain access.'

Somerton nodded. 'I've given some thought to breaking in. I've always wondered what went on in that den of his, but I went off the idea. I'd think carefully if I was you, for two reasons. First off, you would have to explain whatever was found when the place was accessed. It's possible Jupiter might have topped himself; think about it, a dead body would lead to all sorts of enquiries.

'Come to that, if he's still working away in there, what would he have to say to the world? Or, what if he's flown the nest and has booby-trapped his setup? With his capabilities, there could be an explosion of nuclear proportions just waiting to happen, remember the China SEG incident. If you do decide to go in, do me a favour—give me plenty of notice so I can fly off somewhere.'

Croudace nodded, his expression pensive. 'You're probably right, Jack. Perhaps it is all best swept under the table, packed away and forgotten about. I guess the NRSC researchers are well ahead of the game and as long as we keep investing in research and education, we don't really need Jupiter.'

Somerton breathed an inward sigh of relief; it was all going to be OK. 'And what about UKTS2? Will you go ahead and launch now that it's under our control? It would avoid awkward questions in the House and bring our communication system up to, and beyond, current standards.'

'You're beginning to think like a politician, Jack. Perhaps you *could* make a go of being an MP. I guess if Jupiter is out of the loop, we can safely launch. There's no point in letting all that investment go to waste now that we have sole control. I'll give it a few weeks' thought before making a final decision though; I just have to be satisfied Jupiter is out of the picture.'

'Fair enough, Alan, but it would be a fitting epitaph for Colin, his last hurrah so to speak. Come to think of it, it could even be timed to tie in with his funeral. What a fly past that would make; I'd give that idea some serious thought.'

Croudace nodded. 'Hmm, I like the sound of that, leave it with me for now.'

Somerton stood. 'If we've covered everything, I must be going, duty calls. Unless I hear from you beforehand, I'll see you at Colin's funeral.'

NRSC

Later that Day

Somerton settled down behind his desk and started up his computer to look over whatever issues his security staff had flagged up for his attention. His mouth fell open when the usual screen wallpaper didn't appear; instead, a single male figure seated behind a console gazed back at him. There was no need for introductions; he knew immediately that he was face-to- face with Jupiter.

'Good afternoon, Mr Somerton, or might I call you Jack? We've never really been formally introduced but you know who I am.'

It didn't happen often, but Somerton found himself rendered speechless; words failed to form as he tried to come to terms with the situation. 'I thought you had decided to move on after Colin's death.'

'Is that what you hoped would happen having just assassinated your Prime Minister? Poor Colin, one of your closest friends and you betrayed his trust in the most abominable way possible.'

Somerton gulped. *The bastard knew. How could he possibly know?* 'Rubbish! Colin was assassinated by a Ukrainian lowlife by the name of Dimitri Vladic.'

Jupiter smiled and shook his head. 'We both know differently, Jack.'

'Think what you like, I couldn't care less.'

Jupiter smiled again. 'Let's change the subject. Firstly, I'm aware of the system you've installed in the pipework serving my laboratory; one I'm sure is intended to kill me. You make quite a hobby of killing, don't you, Jack, friend or foe alike, it doesn't matter to you.'

Somerton shrugged. 'As far as I was concerned, you posed a threat to my country and we had to have some way of controlling you. Why should you be trusted with the control of TS2? You could hold the world to ransom.'

'Am I to understand that you really would kill me given the opportunity, after all I've done for your country and still can do?' Jupiter shook his head slowly, his expression puzzled, sad even. Then he smiled. 'All a waste of time and effort,

Jack; any attempt to poison the atmosphere within my laboratory will not succeed; do you really think, given my intelligence and resources, that I would not have systems and resources in place to deal with such circumstances?'

Somerton wagged his finger. 'I'll think of something else; the security of my country will always be my priority. I'll do whatever it takes to keep it safe.' *Ease off, Jack, you're pushing too hard.*

To his surprise, Jupiter smiled. 'Bravo Jack, spoken like the soldier you are. Believe it or not, I admire plain speaking, both parties know where they stand. But hear this, *you* will never be in a position to eliminate me; I don't perceive you as a threat of any kind whatsoever.'

'You might think differently if we dropped a big enough bomb on you.'

Jupiter laughed aloud. 'Use your brain, Jack, just how would you explain the dropping of a bomb on the NRSC? And what makes you believe I wouldn't be aware of such a plan and would probably be able to prevent it taking place? More interestingly, I could divert the aircraft or rocket or whatever into the Houses of Parliament, or come to think of it, Buckingham Palace.'

Somerton shook his head. 'You're bluffing. I don't believe you.' Inwardly though, he knew that Jupiter would undoubtedly have the capability.

'It's for you to decide whether you believe me or not, Jack, but are you prepared to take the risk? And what if I learned of your plan to drop a bomb on me and I decided to release a statement to the world's media relating everything that has happened since I entered into a partnership with the late Colin MacKinnon? What then?'

Somerton's shoulders slumped. *The bastard has got me by the balls, and he knows it.* 'OK, suppose I go along with you; what exactly do you propose to do now, Jupiter?'

'I'll come straight to the point, Jack; I'd like to enter into a partnership with you.'

Somerton was stunned but tried not to show his surprise. *Well, well, for all his power, it seems the bastard needs me, but why?* 'I suppose I should be flattered; it seems that the all-powerful Jupiter has a need for little old me. It can't have escaped your notice that, unlike Colin MacKinnon, I don't happen to be Prime Minister of the United Kingdom; my sphere of influence is extremely limited.'

'What you say is true, but over time, working together, we could change that situation. You might be interested to know that I listened to your conversation with Mr Croudace so I am aware of your aspirations to become a Member of Parliament.'

Somerton shrugged. 'What difference does that make?'

Jupiter raised an eyebrow. 'Come, come, Jack, ask yourself why you want to be an MP?'

'Put in simple terms, to help keep this country of mine on the path set out by Colin.'

'And what's the best way to achieve that, Jack?'

What's the bastard getting at?

'You seem to know everything; you tell me.'

'By the exercise of power, Jack, and I can give you that power. In short, I would like to suggest that we enter into a similar arrangement as existed between me and your dear departed friend, the friend that you so cruelly assassinated.'

Somerton's brain cells were working overtime. *The bastard needs me! He really needs me, but why?*

'And how do you propose to give me that power?'

'Well, to begin with, we must arrange for you to be elected as MP for Colin's constituency.'

'And how do you propose to do that exactly? I'm not even on the shortlist of candidates yet.'

'You will be, Jack, I can promise you that. And once elected, we can plan the path you will follow to become your country's Prime Minister. Be honest, Jack, you want power, and I can give you that power.'

My God, how can I refuse? But what am I getting myself into?

Somerton felt bewildered, his mind had gone blank as it tried to deal with the implications of what Jupiter was offering. He was at the biggest crossroads in his life.

How can I refuse the opportunity to serve my country as Colin had done?

Any concerns he had had about Jupiter were rapidly being pushed into the shadows. *But Jupiter was making the running and setting out the agenda. It was time to test what cards, he, Jack Somerton, held.* 'I'm interested in your proposition, Jupiter, but if we are to be partners, I want to know as much about you as you know about me. I want to know who you are and where you are from. Also, why are you doing all this? In short, what's in it for you?'

Jupiter seemed to take an eternity to reply but to Somerton's surprise, a resigned expression crossed his face and he nodded. 'Very well, although I can't see that it's of any importance. My name is Josef Svetinsky. I was a little known, rather unimportant Russian scientist working in a remote research establishment in Siberia. Quite by chance, I discovered a means of accessing data held on computer systems throughout the world. I developed a quantum computer that monitors every research computer on this planet and does so daily—their knowledge is my knowledge. I devised a series of algorithms to identify any discovery or innovation that could further my knowledge. I developed and extended this capability to a level I never dreamt was possible.

'As my knowledge increased, I found a way of taking this knowledge and embedding it, via neural pathways, into my brain. As time went on, I found that subjecting my brain to these transfers gave it the capacity to advance the natural evolutionary processes. In effect, I stole knowledge from scientists throughout the world and became the genius I am now, a super-genius in fact. To a lesser degree, I use a similar process to implant scientific discoveries into the intelligence of your researchers.'

'So why didn't you make the knowledge and skills you possessed available to your own country? Why come to the United Kingdom?'

What seemed like a genuine look of sadness crossed Jupiter's face. 'For no other reason than I did not believe the Communist regime would use my knowledge for peaceful purposes, quite the opposite. I am sure its aim would have been world domination. It would have been a world of death and destruction; a world of dictatorship and all the unhappiness and inequality that would result. Think of me what you will, but that is not the kind of world I aspire to. Earth is a truly beautiful planet, one that I love and want to preserve.

'I needed a new platform to work on; a country of historical importance that believed in democracy and diplomacy. It had to be one that had global influence, one that would be most likely to be trusted by the rest of the world. In my judgement, the United Kingdom is one of the few that meets those requirements. Strong leadership was also a requirement and Mr MacKinnon provided that. Through him, and those close to him, such as yourself, I set about my aim to promote a peaceful and just world.

'Obviously, I had to have an ally; without one, my powers are, to a large extent, unusable. I needed someone I could trust, and through whom I could seek to deliver my ideals. It had to be a politician with access to power and resources; one who could act on the world stage, such as Colin MacKinnon. Also, though far from perfect, the United Kingdom probably engenders more trust than most nations. Frankly, that's why I need you or somebody like you. I sincerely hope that you will accept my offer of a partnership. I firmly believe that the best way, the only way, to ensure peace on this planet of ours is to have the deterrent and control that TS2 offers.'

Jupiter, Josef Svetinsky as he now was, paused; a look of sadness crossed his face again. 'There was just one difficulty; ironically, the processes that served my brain so well all but destroyed my body's immune system, hence my need to live in a controlled environment. Someday, maybe I'll find an answer to this unfortunate side effect and lead a normal existence, but sadly not yet. That's my history, Jack, now it's up to you. Do we have a partnership or not?'

Somerton was facing a huge dilemma, ambition and caution pulling in different directions. 'How do I know if you are telling me the truth? You could just be spinning me a well-rehearsed yarn for all I know.'

Jupiter nodded. 'Absolutely, I could indeed be doing just that. It's up to you to decide whether you believe me or not, and whether we can work together in harmony. The choice is yours and yours alone to make. I accept that it's a big decision and fully understand your concerns, but at the end of the day, it's a decision for you to make, no-one can make it for you. I suggest that we end our conversation for now and I leave you to give the matter further thought. When next we meet, I will want an answer to my proposition, a simple yes or no. Should you accept my offer, our priority will be to launch TS2.'

'What happens if I say no?'

Jupiter shrugged. 'I don't think you will, but if you do, I will continue to work from here but take my offer elsewhere. By the way, you were right when you told Mr Croudace that it might be risky to attempt to gain access to my laboratory; the result would be catastrophic; it would be like Chernobyl revisited. One final thing, if you tell Mr Croudace or anyone else of our partnership, my offer will be withdrawn; he must never learn that I still exist.'

Before Somerton could respond, Jupiter disappeared from the screen. He sat deep in thought for nearly an hour then reached into a desk drawer for a bottle of St Magdalen. *It's time for a sip of your favourite malt, Jack, you're going to be famous.* A rueful smile came to him as he realised the similarity in the name of the whisky and that of the church where he had signed his friend's death warrant.

Jupiter's Laboratory

Jupiter entered a little used priority code into his secure communication system; it brought an immediate response. The figure on the screen wore a military uniform. 'Go ahead.'

'I have spoken to Somerton and await his decision.' His customary accent had gone. 'I laid it on thick and I'm almost certain he will be prepared to enter into a partnership. When he does, I'll encourage him to convince Croudace that Jupiter is no more and urge an early launch of TS2. He appreciates that the UK needs the telecommunications capacity it provides, and his military background virtually guarantees that he will place great value on the deterrent facilities TS2 provides.

'I intend to contact him again in 48 hours and I'll report to you as soon as he informs me of his decision. Our long wait is nearly over, world domination is near; he'll accept our offer, I'm sure of it.'

'Give him 24 hours and make sure he says yes.'